THE SUN DOG

BOOK TWO IN THE NATIVE AMERICAN SAGA

Blank Slate Press
Harrisonville, MO 64701

Publisher's Note: This book is a work of the imagination. Names, characters, places and incidents either are products of the author's imagination or are used fictitiously. While some of the characters and incidents portrayed here can be found in historical or contemporary accounts, they have been altered and rearranged by the author to suit the strict purposes of storytelling. The book should be read solely as a work of fiction.

For information, contact:
Blank Slate Press
Blank Slate Press is an imprint of
Amphorae Publishing Group, LLC
www.amphoraepublishing.com

Manufactured in the United States of America
Cover Design by Asya Blue Design

Set in Bitstream Century Schoolbook

Library of Congress Control Number: 2025937590
ISBN: 9781966103042 (paperback)
ISBN: 9781966103059 (ebook)

Praise for *The Wolf and The Willow*

"A quest of Homeric dimensions. If you're in the mood for a historic saga that gets into the details of wilderness survival and indigenous cultures of centuries ago, *The Wolf and The Willow* is a riveting reading experience."

— *Marquette Monthly*

Praise for *Windigo Moon*

"A simply brilliant work of historical fiction"

— *Midwest Book Review*

"Intricately researched, tightly woven, and vividly imagined, *Windigo Moon* should be on every must-read list."

— *Petoskey News-Review*

Also by Robert Downes

The Native American Saga:

- *The Wolf and The Willow*
- *The Sun Dog*
- *Windigo Moon*

Nonfiction:

- *Raw Deal - The Indians of the Midwest and the Theft of Native Lands*
- *Biking Northern Michigan*
- *I Promised You Adventure*
- *Planet Backpacker*

Mysteries:

- *Bicycle Hobo*
- *Sandy Bottom*

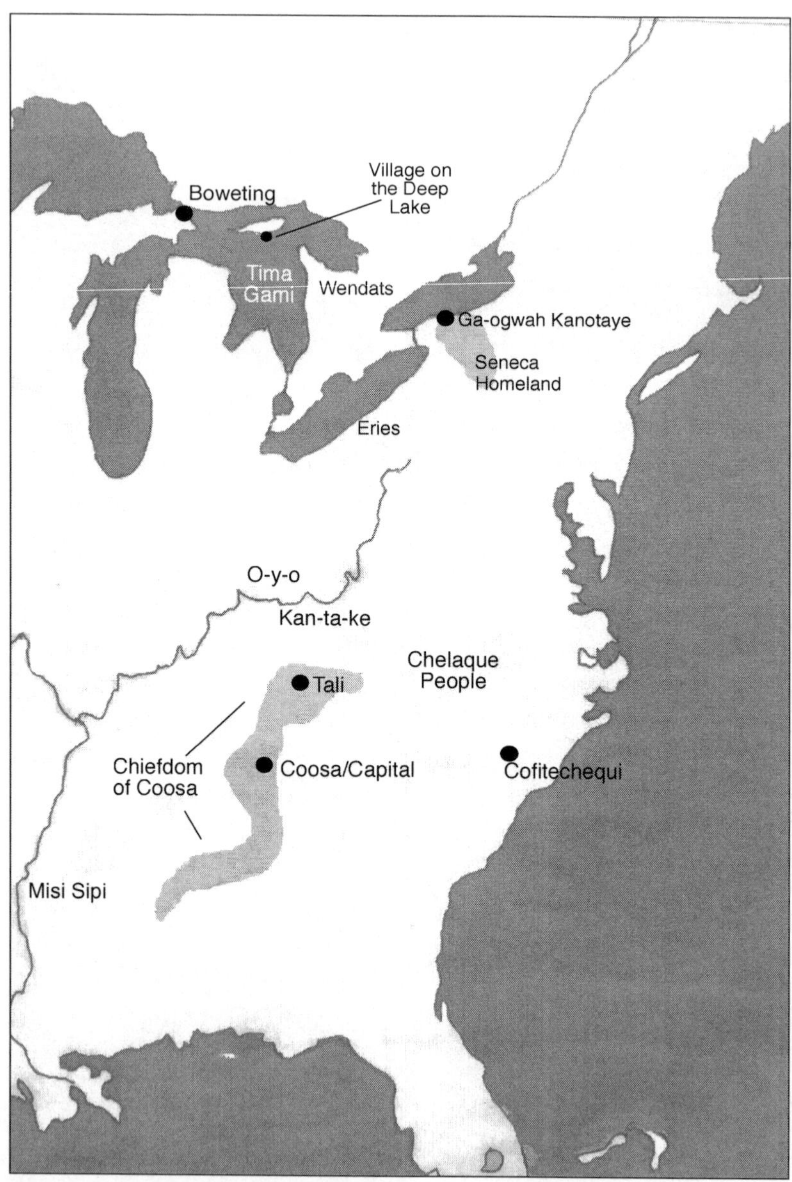

The Chiefdom of Coosa spanned 400 miles and had a population of 50,000-100,000. After its destruction by diseases spread by Spanish conquistadors, its refugees established remnant tribes, notably the Musgokee-Creek people.

THE SUN DOG

BOOK TWO IN THE NATIVE AMERICAN SAGA

ROBERT DOWNES

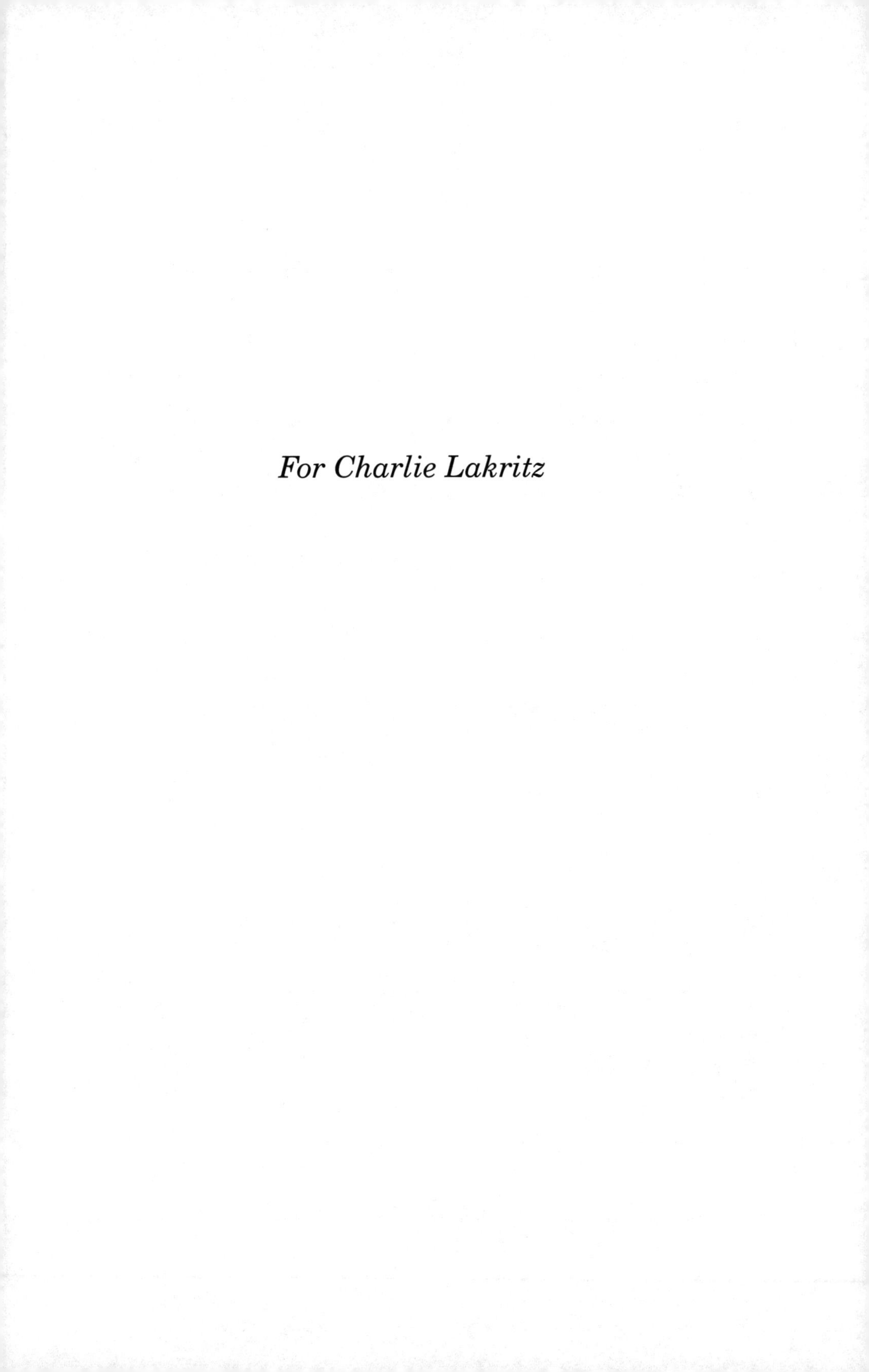

For Charlie Lakritz

A FEW WORDS

The names of the characters in *The Sun Dog* are drawn from the dictionaries of the Ojibwe, Seneca, Muskogee/Creek, and Cheyenne peoples.

The following are some other words that readers may find useful:

Anishinaabek: The alliance of the Ojibwe, Odawa, and Potawatomi, meaning "The People"

Chaiena: the ancestors of the Cheyenne

Chelaque: the ancestors of the Cherokee

Haudenosaunee: The "People of the Longhouse," including the Seneca, Cayuga, Onondaga, Oneida, and Mohawks—known today as the Iroquois

Wendats: the original name of the Hurons

Ga-ogwah Kanotaye: Native peoples often had prosaic place names for communities and geographical features (i.e. Tima Gami, "The Deep Lake"), thus, this simply means "The Big Town"

Sachem: chieftain

Hanishé: Devil, demon

Orenda: spiritual power

Mide-wi-win: the council of the Ojibwe shamans

Otgo: witch

Giimaabi: a spy

Kitchi Gami: the Great Lake, Lake Superior

Tima Gami: the Deep Lake, Lake Huron

Maize: interchangeable with corn

Lake of the Mohawks: Lake Ontario

Ehn: yes

Gaawiin: no

Eya: a feminine particle of speech that indicates the speaker's frame of mind as in, "well then," "now then," "and so," "truly," and, also, simply "yes"

BOOK ONE

SOUTH SHORE OF LAKE ONTARIO – SPRING, 1541

CHAPTER 1

THE NIGHTMARE

The old woman never saw what took place that night, but she heard it well enough. There had been a rustling in the rafters and then a crash and a heavy thud by the fire pit in the Great Lodge of the Seneca. Then the thing was among them, slashing in the darkness lit only by the red coals of the council fire. Screams and cries of shock filled the air. The beast roared as it whirled among the dying elders.

Only she, sitting at the head of the clan mothers of the town, had been spared as seven leaders of Ga-ogwah Kanotaye died that night during a meeting to discuss a shortfall in seed corn that spring. She had sat there as still as a stone amid the carnage, whispering a spell of protection that she had learned from her long-dead grandfather.

No one made it to the safety of the entry; in truth, many were so aged that they could not even rise to their feet in time to flee. Murmuring her spell by the winking coals, the old woman recoiled in horror as the thing crept up behind her, panting its hot breath to the side of her face. It seemed forever that it crouched behind her, huffing and slobbering as she sat, quivering like a rabbit. She sensed that it was staring at her in the darkness, cradling her fate in its claws before huffing a grunt and creeping away.

By then the town was in an uproar with warriors hammering at the entrance, which the thing had barred with a tangle of rafters ripped from the ceiling. When at last they entered, they found nothing—the thing had vanished. Only the old woman remained. Every corner of the Great Lodge had been searched by torchlight, from the spaces beneath the pallets lining its wall to the blackened rafters where haunches of meat dangled from cords of hemp. Nothing.

Her own good, true man had been among the seven killed. He had been the sachem of the town, yet soon he would rest in the cold ground with the worms taking their pleasure.

She lay in a torpor of shock and disbelief that night, frozen as if she were dead. There was no place to grieve in private in a town where everyone lived in a longhouse. On the morning after his death, she had fled to the cornfields, heedless of the lurking monster. She had nestled among the tender shoots of young maize, crying until it felt as if her eyes were bleeding. Her mind snapped, and she gaped like a beached fish, clutching at her head and screaming until her throat was burned raw; it was unendurable. Not until dusk did her torment ease, and, slowly, she stumbled back to the palisade gate, feeling her way through the cornfield where half the town waited with coiled stillness. The women of the town huddled forth to surround her, stroking her hair, back, and shoulders as they ushered her to bed.

In a year's time, she would see her husband again at the Feast of the Dead. His body would be disinterred, and the bones scraped of any remnant flesh and viscera, then buried along with treasures of jewelry, weapons, and tools in a mass grave with all the others who had died over the past ten years or so. But that was no comfort as she lay alone on her pallet that night with no one to speak to of her heartache and loss. *Ah, my heart is slashed in two and torn from its roots,* she thought as she lay unable to sleep. *Ah, husband, good loving soul, sunlight of my life, soon I pray I will join you in the burial pit, very soon, but not yet, not yet…*

Days later, a boy tasked with watching the crops at night was snatched from his watchtower in the field. Kicking and twisting, he had wriggled free of the demon's grasp and ran screaming for the palisade, swearing that the thing had flown behind him with its hot breath on his neck the entire way. Tracks were found in the soil below the tower with claws as long as a man's fingers.

"They are only the tracks of a bear," the old woman grunted to her frightened sister-cousins when the news reached her ears. Yet she knew that no bear could reach such a size.

There were five towers in the fields used to safeguard the crops from deer and other foraging animals. A decision was made to send warriors to replace the boys who usually manned them. But the men ran for the safety of the palisade on the same night of their placement, quaking with fear at the sound of the bellowing creature. It was spring, and the maize was only ankle-high, but at times the creature could be seen at the furthest edge of the field, wandering by the light of the moon. From all appearances, it looked to be twice the height of a tall man.

She had heard of such a thing from a shaman who knew many secrets of the world beyond. It was *Hanishé*, an evil creature of immense power whose thirst for human blood was unquenchable.

But that was not to be shared for now. In the days ahead, she maintained a steady calm when the panicked people of the Big Town, Ga-ogwah Kanotaye, approached her—always reassuring, always firm, exhibiting strength and resolve. But her heart was collapsing under the weight of fear and grief.

She was expected to fill her husband's footsteps until a new sachem was appointed by the clan mothers of the town, but she quailed at the thought of it. All that her people had fought for was at stake, and she had never considered herself a leader of anyone but children.

Ga-ogwah Kanotaye held more than eight hundred souls, perched on a low hill above the vast Lake of the Mohawks. By the standards of the Haudenosaunee, it was not a particularly large town—some of their cousins lived in communities of nearly three thousand. But the Big Town was newly built, and its people were justifiably proud of their home. An entire forest had been leveled by fire and stone axes to build the town and its palisade in a gargantuan feat of construction. Vast fields of maize, beans, sunflower, squash, pumpkin, and tobacco circled the town amid the stumps of trees. The timber had been used to fashion its walls and scores of longhouses. This, after the long battle with the savage Erie people to the west, who had been vanquished eleven summers before.

The heart of Ga-ogwah Kanotaye was the Great Square, which was large enough to accommodate all eight hundred of the townsfolk, with room enough besides for sporting events, festivals, and executions. Around its perimeter sprawled a market filled with traders, and barely a week went by without a dance, a parade, a play, or a proclamation filling the square's well-packed earth. At the center of the square stood a post rising to the height of ten men, the shadow of which was used to mark the passing of the seasons.

Fronting the square and towering over it like a long, sleek panther was the Great Lodge, the size of which filled visitors with awe. Sheathed in elm bark with a stout framework of oak, the longhouse was only two years old and the pride of the town. One hundred steps long and twenty wide, it was a place of ceremony, town meetings, the councils of shamans, and the greeting place for emissaries of other tribes. Yet now all felt that it was haunted and the lair of a thing not of this world. What was she to do? What could she do? The town's *orenda* had been weakened, its magic severed, and all knew it. In desperation she searched her thoughts: *why had this thing come? What had they done to bring it, and from what pit did it spring?*

Then came strange cries echoing from the cornfields, sometimes sounding just outside the palisade, only an arm's length beyond the tall pine timbers as the people of Ga-ogwah Kanotaye lay shivering in their pallets. The monster was close enough to reach between the chinks of the palisade and clutch a passerby, but no one dared approach those dark walls where a shadow could be seen moving between its seams amid the quarter moon. Warriors scrambled to the walkways along the palisade and rained down arrows at the shape they saw retreating through the cornfield. At times there were grunts as an arrow hit its mark. Yet nothing stopped it. On several nights, it was back again torturing the ears of every listener. The cries were a mix of screams and mournful howls, along with a strange honking sound like that of geese. The cries were anything but human.

"It is only the loons," the old woman told the terrified children, who clutched at her tunic in the safety of daylight. "They can't harm you. They are only loons."

"But grandmother, we know the three calls of the loons and they are not among them."

"Then it is only the wind whistling through a hollow tree," she replied. "Don't you see? The loons and an old tree, that is what you hear. There is nothing to be afraid of. And always know this," she smiled, caressing them, "I am with you always. We are together and we are strong and brave. We are Seneca."

The children gazed back at her with somber eyes. She knew they did not believe, and yet, what else could she say?

For she knew it was not so, nor did she believe it was their enemies among the Erie people living far down the lakeshore, as some claimed, or their neighbors, the Tionontati, who kept to themselves and rarely took sides. A delegation of warriors petitioned her to strike the Attignawatan, the nearest tribe of the Wendat people living to the north. More than a few felt that their age-old enemies were behind the attack and were eager to strike a blow. Perhaps it was a giant living among them who had somehow crept over the tall palisade. Perhaps the Wendat had a sorcerer who had summoned the thing. Seven men confronted her, radiating anger. The war chief Blackbird, Dzago-gih, cradled a pipe draped in a sash of black beads, motioning for her to sit.

"It is not them," she said, denying the war pipe as it passed around. "The Wendat are no more to us than the loons, no more than muskrats or deer."

"What then?"

"You searched the lodge and found nothing," she replied. "You have seen its tracks. It is not human nor an animal. What else can it be but a thing of the underworld, deyoedzotga-weh? Only those who walk the same land can help us."

“It is a witch then,” Blackbird spoke. “A sorcerer.”

She uttered a bitter laugh. “No brother. This thing is no simple witch banished to a lodge of corn stalks; it is *Hanishé*, and it has fastened upon us like a leech. Can your arrows kill it? We do not know, and who dares track it by night? It is a creature of the night, full of rage, and I fear it will come again. I fear it is a thing that cannot rest.”

“*Hanishé*? Sister, we know of it, but no one has ever seen such a thing,” Blackbird said. “It is only a story that mothers use to frighten their children when they wish them to be silent. Old men and women speak of it around the lodge fires in the winter, but only to pass the time. There is no such thing.”

The old woman spread her hands and bowed. “Yes, not in the world, and yet here it is, and it has taken seven of our people, including my old man,” she said. “If it was only a story, it would have no claws.”

“Then what would you have us do?” Blackbird asked in exasperation. “We can’t hide like rabbits in their holes. Now that the watchtowers are empty, the deer are eating the shoots with nothing to stop them. We‘ll be eating bark this winter if we don’t kill it.”

Behind him, the warriors nodded assent, though none seemed to have any more idea of how to proceed than did Blackbird.

“We can swarm it!” a young warrior named Long Tongue spoke at last. The son of Blackbird, Eeyos Oa-nohsa hoped to fill his father’s foot prints one day and had begged to attend the council. Now, his father frowned at his impudence, speaking out of turn, but allowed it.

“Go on,” he said.

Encouraged, Long Tongue hurried on. “Brothers, a caterpillar cannot stand against a swarm of ants, even though it is many times greater! Even if this *Hanishé* is as tall as the Great Lodge, it could not stand against all of us. When the thing comes howling at the walls, we will pour through the gate like a river while bowmen fire down from the walkways.”

“But how many men?” another spoke.

“All of us, and the women too!”

"Women? Young brother, would you also have us sending children with sticks?"

"Hah! Many of our women are stronger than men from hoeing weeds and digging roots all spring," Long Tongue sneered, "and they have as much to lose as any of us."

The men murmured amongst themselves as they considered Long Tongue's plan. It was unseemly that such a youngling would make such a proposal, and some of his talk had been insulting. And yet...

"I think we'll beat each other's skulls in if we're all swinging clubs and throwing stones, but I like it," Blackbird said at last. "The thing will be no match for all of us."

Despite himself, he was encouraged by his son's rashness. Long Tongue had always had a prickling way about him, but perhaps he would be smoothed by time, and his plan was a good start.

A chorus of excited words of approval fleshed out the plan, with each man imagining his role in striking the fatal blow or driving a spear into the *Hanishé*'s heart. The old woman brightened, nodding her approval; she knew that the men needed a way forward, and what could it hurt? Perhaps they would prevail.

But she did not think so.

Two nights later, the plan was sprung as the hooting of the creature sounded in the distance beyond the corn. Every able-bodied man and many stout women gathered at the single gate of the town, all bearing clubs, axes and spears. Many held nothing more than farm tools and digging sticks. The huge maze of branches and thorns that guarded the gate to stymie attackers had been removed to make it easier for the host to pour through its narrow passage. Blackbird and his under-chieftains would lead the charge while more than thirty bowmen stood on the walkway atop the palisade.

For a long time, nothing stirred in the corn field as the people of town fretted in suspense. The stars crept through the sky as the crowd swayed and murmured, heavy with fear and anticipation. Above, the newly-hatched moon was a sliver amid the stars, and when a silver-tinged cloud swept past its thin crescent, the people of Ga-ogwah Kanotaye were plunged into darkness.

Blackbird had done well in the war against the Eries, but in his haste to protect the town, he had not thought of the flaws in his son's plan to swarm the creature. The town's gate was only the width of three men, and the walkways along the palisade were meant more for peering over the ramparts at an approaching enemy than for firing arrows toward the ground below.

Thus, deep into the night, when many were yawning and exhausted from the long vigil, there came a tremendous racket just below the waiting archers.

"*Hadree! Hadree!*" Blackbird cried, with a full-throated cry echoing from his warriors and the people of Ga-ogwah Kanotaye. The mob surged through the gate in a trickle that soon turned into a stampede with many crushed against the pine timbers of the wall or trampled underfoot in the darkness. Boiling in a chaotic mass outside, those who made it beyond the palisade quickly found themselves enfiladed with arrows scattering through the chinks from above. Their screams and cries of alarm were all but lost to the bowmen, whose ears were filled with the war cries of hundreds seeking to push their way outside the walls.

But worse, those beyond the walls found themselves scrambling blind in the darkness under the thinnest slice of moon imaginable, for no torches had been lit in order to preserve the element of surprise. And then, the thing was among them, slashing and leaping from place to place in a frenzy.

Oh, brothers, sisters, that night and its slaughter was told around the lodge fires for many generations, and the next Feast of the Dead was overflowing with tears and the bodies of loved ones. Many felt the bite of its claws as the thing moved among them. Yet many more were struck down by their own people, flailing in the darkness at a thing that vanished in the starlight. But that was not all, for as the townsfolk ran for their lives in the tangle of the cornfields or at the bloody gate, a light appeared at last in the town. The Great Lodge was burning.

CHAPTER 2

THE WITCH

Far to the north, He Who Outruns the Wolves faced a difficult choice. He did not believe in witches, but with this woman he was not so sure.

Animi-Ma'liingan, known more often as Wolf, had been pestered by the people of a small Odawa village to do something about a thin girl with a drawn face whose shaking fits had thrown the band into an uproar.

Now, to his irritation, her life or death was in his hands.

The people of the Village on the Deep Lake, Oodena Tima Gami, were in a sour mood that spring. It had been a colder winter than usual, and the spring rains had lashed the village without end. Driven by the cruel north wind, the rains had buried the sun under a chill gray drizzle, darkening the land and spirits alike. It was a village of complainers in the best of times, occupied by fewer than forty Odawa drawn from the Turtle, Moose, and Sturgeon clans who often seemed to be at odds with one another.

The village sat on a stubby peninsula at the north end of the Deep Lake, Tima Gami, with only a chest-high fence of weathered pines adorned with skulls and crude wooden masks for protection from raiders and harmful *manitos* alike that ran along its inland side. The fence was laughable in Wolf's eyes; any raider could simply step around it or kick it down, and as for bad spirits, they had no fear of skulls. As for the masks, they would not frighten a child, much less a demon.

There were only four lodges in the village that could be called longhouses, and these could house only four families. A collection of huts sheathed in soggy elm bark made up the rest of the village, the limit of which was cut short by a grassy step-down at the water's edge; there was not even a proper beach unless one walked a distance down the shore. All that, and the dense pine forest which backed Oodena Tima Gami offered little in the way of game, other than squirrels.

The fog that lingered all spring had soaked everyone's lodgings, furs, and skins through and through, with little in the way of dry firewood for comfort. So, it was no surprise that the villagers were in a foul mood, looking for someone to torment.

Yet Found by the River, Mikigaazo Ziibi, was an in-between woman of fourteen winters, and the only taint of witchcraft that Wolf could sense about her was the spell she seemed to have woven on his mate, Willow.

When the last crusts of snow still lay in rinds beneath the spruce trees beyond the village, a delegation had come to him led by the old busy-body, One Toe, and his querulous wife, Crow's Meat, demanding that Found by the River be banished at the very least. Unspoken was their wish that she be sent to the Spirit Land with a hard knock to her head in the night. Such was often the fate of witches who, owing to decorum, could not be killed outright. One Toe, Bezhigwan Niisiigizidaan, and Crow's Meat, Andeg Wiiyaas, were hoping for a nod from Wolf to approve the deed. It could be done with discretion while the girl was off foraging in the forest. One Toe himself would deliver the blow and claim that she had fallen and hit her head on a rock. What could be simpler?

One Toe was the self-professed shaman of the village, and Wolf suspected that his talk of witchcraft was rooted in something deeper. He had been away fishing when the old man had tangled with Willow, yet word of their disgust for one another had reached his ears. Willow had little patience with fools, and that is how the trouble had started.

As was sometimes the case with bad men who claimed to have shamanic powers, One Toe had forced himself upon several women in the village under the threat of casting evil spells upon them if they resisted.

He was attempting to have his way with Found by the River when Willow came upon them far down the lakeshore.

One Toe had followed the girl one morning when she had set off to go fishing. He was backing her against a boulder when Willow came upon them with her own fishing net. Willow saw the leer on his face and fear in the eyes of the girl who trembled against the rock. She herself had been taken by bad men when she was only a little older than Found by the River, and now the memory filled her with rage.

"Get away from her, snake," she said, picking up a rock twice the size of her fist, "or I'll feed you to the fish."

As all know, to be called a snake is the greatest of insults, reserved only for one's enemies. One Toe prided himself as the big man of the village, and his shock at being called such a thing turned to outrage. Now, to his anger, he was shamed as well, with the delectable girl snatched from his grasp.

He and Willow had taken an instant dislike to one another when she and her man, Wolf, had arrived at the village only a few days before. "She is a sassy woman and needs to be chastised," he had said to his own woman, Crow's Meat, who was quick to agree.

But now, she was standing before him with her eyes blazing and a large stone in her hand. One Toe made as if to strike her, but Willow hefted the stone and chided him in a low voice, "Come on snake, and I'll crack your skull."

"Bad words! Threats! How dare you woman?" he cried, before slinking away muttering threats and excuses. "Spells, woman, I will lay spells upon you for this! You will cry bitter tears! Think on it!"

Willow had called out something in an unknown language that sounded insulting and tossed her stone at his retreating form, striking him in the leg. "Slither away snake," she cried as he let out a howl. "Tonight, all the women in the village will hear of your disgrace!"

She had spent the rest of the day fishing with Found by the River. By nightfall, they were chosen friends, and Willow took to calling her simply River.

That alone would have made One Toe hate Willow, but what came next set him on fire with vengeance.

One Toe had been called to the lodge of an old woman who had a burning in her stomach. She had been going down for several moons, yet he had tried to save her through the casting of spells. Each one had failed as she continued to grow paler, twisting in pain.

At last, One Toe determined to use the bone-sucking medicine upon her. After shrieking loud and long to chase the bad spirit from her body, he had placed the hollow hip bone of a dog on the tender spot over her abdomen to suck out the poison within her as a wide-eyed crowd of villagers looked on.

The old woman cried out in agony, and One Toe pulled a squirrel's claw from his mouth with a triumphant shout. "Here! Here is the bad thing that afflicts her!"

But pushing her way through the crowd, Willow had scoffed at his medicine, saying that it was only a claw that he had concealed in his mouth to fool the villagers. Her mate, Wolf, had told her that this was a trick that was often used to no avail by the shamans of the Ojibwe. Sometimes the ill ones got better on their own; other times it was claimed that the right spell had not yet been found.

Willow had knelt by the ailing woman, caressing the warm flesh on her abdomen. "I'm sorry, sister, but you have a tumor and will soon be gone," she said, looking into her eyes. "Make your peace with your family and lay comfortable in your lodge."

She had placed a cooling poultice on the woman's abdomen and gave her a swallow of a medicine that was made with fermented berries, telling her family to swaddle her with furs and say their goodbyes. As she predicted, the woman passed away that night.

The power of Willow's medicine over his own had embarrassed One Toe before the entire village, and now, many looked upon him with amusement and smirks. Women he hoped to lay with ignored his threats, and some who had succumbed under pressure threw dog shit at him and called him bad names. Even snake.

Now, he planned to wreak vengeance on Willow and restore his good name by denouncing River as a witch. Then he would start on Willow. He would claim that it was she who had killed the old woman, casting a spell on his own good medicine that would surely have saved her.

So it was that One Toe and his wife came to Wolf on the beach on the morning after River had suffered another one of her shaking fits.

One Toe had a large nose and beetling eyebrows that tended to rise in a permanent expression of incredulity, as if he could not believe his ears. Now, he wore that look with the air of a man who was simply being reasonable.

"We want her gone," he said, recounting the times that River had fallen among them in a fit. "All wish to drown her in the river from which she came! There's a snake within her, a water serpent itching to be free. We have all seen it!"

"It was two," Wolf replied, unbothered.

"What?"

"Her fits. It was twice. Perhaps she ate a bad fish."

One Toe and Crow's Meat exchanged glances.

"What does it matter?" Crow's Meat groused. "Once was enough!"

"And have you seen this snake?"

The old woman made a face. "The snake inside her?"

Wolf rubbed his chin and gave a grave nod. His gray eyes were rimmed with flecks of gold, and now, he gazed full upon her.

"*Gaawiin,* no," she said, flustered. "But there is something. It's a bad thing, and everyone knows it." Behind her, four elders nodded in agreement, but Wolf noted that they were among the most impressionable in the village.

Wolf cleared his throat and grunted, thinking of the girl's plight. He too was damaged and considered a cripple due to the club foot that made him walk with a lilting bob. He too had been threatened with death, not when he was nearly grown, but when he was a helpless newborn. To this day, some who did not know him turned aside and spat when he passed by, thinking that his bad foot might bring them evil. He had learned not to care, but it had not been easy. His affliction was not as bad as some who suffered from a twisted foot, but still, it placed great obstacles in his path, and now he surveyed the carping villagers with a storm of anger brewing behind his eyes.

He and Willow had been sent to this wretched village on the frontier of the lands of the Anishinaabek as the representative of Wabeno-iniini, the Man of the Dawn Sky. A sorcerer, Wabeno was leader of the Ojibwe shamans, and every villager knew that crossing Wolf would incur his wrath. That could include disfiguring spells and visits from the creatures of the underworld.

Thus, Wolf's judgment of witches was law. Only he could give the word that might send River to her death.

Wolf swallowed his anger and held his tongue long enough for One Toe and his clutch of elders to grow restive, rocking back and forth on their feet. Casually, he noted a length of driftwood at his feet that was as gnarled and twisted as an old vine. It recalled a trick played by a shaman he knew from years ago who loved a good laugh.

Wolf pointed behind the waiting elders. "Is that the snake?" he asked.

As they turned, he stooped to lift the branch, twirling it before them as they turned to face him. "Ah, here!"

Crow's Meat gave a shriek and blundered back, while One Toe stumbled, nearly falling in his haste to avoid the twisting branch.

Wolf tossed it at their feet with a contemptuous wave. "You see? You saw a viper when it was only a branch. It is the same with the girl; you are told that she is a witch, and you wish to believe."

"But what if it is so?" One Toe sputtered. "She is more than your trick with a branch. You know what a witch can do. Murder! Evil spells! Only last winter, an infant was turned into a muskrat by a witch at a village down the lakeshore, so it is said. All have heard of it. She is..."

Wolf gave him a cold glare. "Leave her be," he said. "She's done no harm to anyone but herself. And brother, know this—some say there is more than one snake in this village. Watch yourself."

One Toe began to protest but caught the look in Wolf's unearthly eyes and the golden glint circling his pupils; the man wasn't named Animi-Ma'liingan for nothing. He choked on his words as Wolf raised a hand in dismissal and turned away. "Muskrat." Wolf muttered under his breath, thinking he would ask Wabeno to turn One Toe into the same.

Yet even Wolf had been rattled later that spring when an ancient woman had breathed her last at the same moment that River had succumbed to a fit. Even worse, Woman Walks Tall was River's adoptive mother. Some claimed they had heard the death rattle of Woman Walks Tall echoing through the trees even as River lay quaking on the ground, writhing like a serpent with her eyes rolled back into her skull and her mouth awash with spittle.

All suspected that Woman Walks Tall had been a witch, albeit one who was allowed to live by dint of the healing deeds she performed from time to time. Some claimed that she was a mere healer who deserved to be cherished, but people being what they are, others said they had seen her flying through the trees on nights when the moon was half full and peering through the door flap of the lodges by the darkling moon. Healer, witch. Who knew?

Yes, who knew ... Except that it was well known that witches and certain among the shamans of the Ojibwe could lay spells on supplicants and the unsuspecting alike. Love spells, of course, and healing spells and mutterings meant to bring about the birth of a child to a barren couple. Spells to make a warrior invincible or put life in an old man's stones. *But dark spells too*, Wolf thought. Certainly, dark spells that could settle on the breast of a victim at night like a hulking bat and breathe malevolence into the sleeper's face—or worse, suck the life from one's body and fly off into the darkness.

"But few can do such a thing," Wolf said to himself. "Very few." In fact, he reflected, he had never met such a creature, save perhaps for old Wabeno, who had labored mostly in vain to teach him the path of the shamans long ago. But Wabeno wasn't inclined to cast evil spells, and certainly old Woman Walks Tall had been no Wabeno.

Woman Walks Tall had always been something of a mystery to the villagers. She was no beauty, but her face had a handsome quality that could verge on seeming haughty. She had never taken a husband, which deepened her mystery, and although she sprang from the large and lively Turtle Clan she had always maintained a distance from her sister-cousins. In time, her aloofness marked her as an "other," giving rise to gossip and speculation fostered by her preoccupation with healing roots and herbs. For who would care for such things unless they were also interested in what lay in the realm of the underworld? Only a witch, perhaps, or so it was said.

She had never borne children, yet had taken Mikigaazo Ziibi into her lodge, raising the strange child as if she were her own. Some felt that this was just one witch helping another, given Found by the River's unknown origin.

But long ago, Woman Walks Tall had saved the chief's youngest son by extracting a porcupine bone from his throat following an evening meal, breathing life back into his prostrate form. Thus, the villagers had reluctantly fed her in the slim hope that she was a simple healer, along with the request that she dwell at a distance, for who knew what guise a witch might take and what she might do under the influence of some passing spirit? Woman Walks Tall had been only too happy to dwell beyond the village and seemed to take no hurt from being shunned by all but a small circle of friends.

It seemed no coincidence that Woman Walks Tall had died at the same moment that Found by the Rivers's head reared back during the day's meal, and she fell flapping like a beached fish among the gaping villagers as the sun crept towards its slumber in the west. Only the dogs dared approach the writhing girl, whining and nosing at her cheeks.

Only the dogs and Willow, Wolf thought with a snort. His wife had cradled River's head in her lap as the villagers circled and gawked. She stroked her hair as the fit subsided while cooing a lullaby in the strange language that only Wolf understood.

"Star shine, long shine,
Light our way in darkest time.
Winter, spring, summer, fall,

Cast your light to guide us all."

"She is only ill," Willow said to the crowd once River faded to slumber. "Help me carry her to our lodge."

But everyone in the circle seized a final handful of whitefish from the wooden tray and fled.

Thus, it was only Wolf with his bad foot who helped carry the sleeping girl to their lodge, laying her in the folds of a bearskin. She slept on through the evening and into the next afternoon.

That night, the village had seethed in torment. Few slept, for who knew what might come creeping through the entry flap of a lodge in the dark of night when a witch was aroused? Their village was poorly situated on a chilly peninsula swept by endless winds, and so it was an unhappy place. It sat at the northern end of Tima Gami, the vast lake of the Wendat people that ran all the way to the lands of the Haudenosaunee. It had been many years since there had been a raid, yet still the Village on the Deep Lake was considered an unlucky place, and Wolf did not care for it. He had been sent here that spring by Wabeno for some inscrutable purpose he could not divine. But who could say what that old fox would come up with?

As was their custom, he and Willow had spent the winter among the Tionontati, the Tobacco People, who lived half a moon's paddle to the south. It was there that Wolf gathered news of the neighboring Haudenosaunee for the shamans and chieftains of the Ojibwe. It was his fate to serve as the eyes and ears of the shamans as a *giimaabi,* a spy. For years now he had posed as a simple trader at Wabeno's request, and owing to the club foot that left him too lame to run, no one among the neighboring tribes ever suspected him of being a warrior. At best, they thought of him as a bumbling trader and a fool who was often on the losing end of bargains, trading his canoe full of furs, fish nets, and copper in exchange for maize and tobacco from the tribes of the south. That, and a gifted storyteller who listened intently to the words of others in return. Those tales of the Ojibwe's enemies to the south, east, and west were shared with Wabeno and the council of the Mide-wi-win when Wolf returned each spring.

It was only on their way canoeing north along the shores of Tima Gami that spring that a messenger from Wabeno had intercepted them with a request that they spend two moons at the village. Wolf had groaned at the thought of it, but he had never denied his teacher, and so, here they landed.

For a change, however, Wolf and Willow were alone. Their daughter, Cherry Heart Flower, had taken one look at the dismal village and had begged to spend the summer with Wolf's mother, Cornflower, who lived in a much larger village, only a day's paddle to the west. Born twelve summers before, their daughter had friends in the village, and her grandmother was overjoyed at the thought of her visit. Willow had allowed it, knowing that her daughter would be miserable if she remained with them.

The village was shrouded in a chill fog on the morning after Found by the River's fit and the old woman's death, adding to the sense of malaise as gray faces peered from the entries of their lodges. By midday, there were knots of villagers muttering among themselves with many neglecting the day's fishing.

Soon, the village was in a fever, and even Willow could not explain how it happened that old Woman Walks Tall had died at the same moment that River had convulsed before everyone's eyes. Willow was no fool—she too had come from a land where witches, ghosts, jinns, and demons were common, but she had never felt any sense of that from River, only innocence and anguish.

That afternoon, when stomachs were rumbling in anticipation of the day's only meal, the temper of the crowd boiled over.

"There is proof now! She has become the witch!" Crow's Meat exclaimed. "I saw the old one's spirit enter this snake as she lay twisting! She will have us all shaking with spirits too if we let her!"

Willow was inclined to scream back at her but had sense enough to know that cooling words were called for.

"She is only ill," she said, swallowing the urge to shout. "In my childhood, I had a friend who had the same illness, and the healers of my land said it was a passing thing best healed with kindness. You will not touch her—she is my sister and has my protection."

"Kindness? Protection! Does a snake deserve kindness? We know you visited the witch. Everyone knows!"

"Yes, I spoke with Woman Walks Tall. What of it? She was a healer with much to share," Willow replied. "The woman you call a witch had nothing bad in her. You are cruel—you shame yourselves! She would have died of loneliness long ago if it had not been for her daughter."

"Hah" Crow's Meat persisted. "You are not one of us! You and your crippled man. Why are you here? You…"

"Enough!" Willow cried. "No more talk of witches!"

"And why not?" a strident young woman shouted from the crowd, which was now swaying like a panther waiting to pounce. "You are only one, and we are many. We will decide!"

Willow glared back. The villagers had always seemed an ignorant lot to her. If it had not been for the protection of old man Wabeno, she would have been suspected as a witch herself for her startling jade eyes, as deep as the green waters of Kitchi Gami. But no one dared cross Wabeno. She knew it, and they knew it.

"I have the will of Wabeno," she said with her eyes flaring, "and that is all I need. He will curse you and turn you into toads to be eaten by the snakes you are so fond of. Even now he sees you. Look about! His eyes are on you!"

But everyone in the village knew that old man Wabeno was a two days' paddle to the west, in his comfortable lodge on the rapids in Boweting, and not likely peering down from the clouds as Willow claimed.

The crowd surged toward Willow's lodge just as Wolf returned with a string of lake trout.

"You men, are you afraid of a sick girl?" he scowled. "There is a moose wandering down the lakeshore, and you would be better served to fetch it. And sisters, gather your skinning knives. Perhaps Woman Walks Tall has left you a final gift."

The crowd wavered, but it was their stomachs that ruled the day, for a moose would provide many fine meals. There were only four men in the village who could rightfully be called warriors, and, abashed, they turned away, seeking their bows. The women hesitated a moment and then followed them with their children trailing behind.

"This isn't over," Crow's Meat huffed. She and One Toe were the last to leave.

"Only Wabeno can decide her fate," Willow called back to them. "Only Wabeno. Remember that."

Crow's Meat waved a hand in dismissal as she walked away. "We'll see."

Willow and Wolf watched the villagers as they trailed down the beach toward the moose. "Thank you," she murmured.

"Thank our brother, the moose," Wolf replied.

"I hate this place. Why did Wabeno send us here?"

Wolf thought about it for a moment. "I doubt that even he knows," he said. "Maybe he knew of the girl."

Yes, perhaps it was so, Willow thought. *Perhaps Wabeno could heal the girl.* The old man surely worked in mysterious ways. He had sent Wolf on a mission down the great Misi Sipi river thirteen years ago in search of an unknown beast that turned out to be nothing more than a horse of the Spaniards. But it was on that journey that Wolf had rescued her from a band of conquistadors, and now here she was, half a world away from the land of her birth. It was as if Wabeno had known that Wolf would find her and that their vivid eyes marked them as lovers on the same path, mated forever.

Willow was so far from her homeland that now it seemed little more than a dream. As a girl, she had been nothing more than an *abn*, a slave, in the household of a rich old man, far across the ocean. Her mother's velvet skin had been as dark as the night sky of Timbuktu, while her father wore the golden tan of an Arab trader. Old Abu bin Nisar had called her a blackamoor, entranced by the jade green of her eyes, her umber skin, and her raven hair, which tumbled in curls down her back. It was Willow's skill as an animal trainer that had prompted the Spaniards to sweep her away to this land on a mission that was doomed from start to finish. Was it all just a dream? Sometimes she mused that Wolf's story seemed just as strange.

As it happened, Wolf was well aware of how a people could be so easily swayed by talk of witches and evil spirits, for he himself had been taken as a demon at his birth, with his strange gold-flecked eyes shining like those of a toothy beast. That, and his gimp leg that would not heal no matter how the shamans twisted it as he lay gurgling with delight. It was an old story, told only to a few through the years, but he had been left on a refuse pile of bones and rags outside the village of his birth for the wolves to devour, yet rescued by a woman who was also suspected as a witch. He had been dubbed Animi-Ma'liingan, He Who Outruns the Wolves. It had been a clever name for a babe with a bad leg who had somehow escaped his fate.

Now, Wolf's thoughts turned to his mother, Cornflower, who was caring for their daughter for the summer. There was warmth in the thought. A crazy woman by all accounts, and yet the spirit of mercy. What would she think of Found by the River? What would she do?

Witches, bad spirits, demons, faugh*!* Wolf thought.

It was only a quarter moon later that a young girl gathering reeds along the shore looked up to see six dugouts of the Haudenosaunee approaching from the southeast in the morning mist. Tossing her bundle, she ran screaming back to the village.

Only two warriors were on hand—the other two had gone hunting—but they, along with six boys and the band's simpleton, gathered their bows and spears, trailed by some of the stouter women who bore tree limbs to serve as clubs. Wolf strolled down behind them, thinking it a farce, since the age-old enemies of the Ojibwe were unlikely to attack in full daylight, even at such a wretched place as this.

Yet from a distance, Wolf counted thirty-six heads in the dugouts; more than enough to overwhelm the Village on the Deep Lake, and for a moment, the defenders considered running for their lives as cries of alarm filled the air.

But as the dugouts drew closer, there came a cry across the water in the language of the Anishinaabek: "Brothers! Sisters! We have returned!"

And peering into the sunlit mist, Wolf could see that a lone Seneca warrior sat at the prow of each dugout with his forehead painted white and his hands raised high, bound at the wrists with cords of leather. In the lead canoe sat a young warrior holding aloft a long belt of wampum.

CHAPTER 3

THE MISSION

"He says his name is Eeyos Oa-nohsa," said Wolf as their party gathered by the river in Boweting. "In the words of the Seneca it means Long Tongue."

It had been a two-days' paddle to Boweting from where the Senecas had landed. Long Tongue had been the warrior in the lead canoe, bearing a message written in the shells of the wampum belt. Now, all sat cross-legged in a circle outside the Lodge of the Shamans as the council pipe was passed around.

Wabeno-iniini cradled the long belt in his lap, admiring its artistry. As sleek as a snake, the belt was beaded with a mix of purple and white shells that could only have come from Zhewitaganibi, the far distant ocean. The shells wove a pattern of parallel lines signifying unity, if not friendship.

"It is a fine thing," Wabeno murmured. "Your women made this?"

Wolf translated, and Long Tongue nodded. "It is one of seven belts, sent to seven winds," he replied.

"Mmm, a fine thing," Wabeno said, laying the belt to the side as the pipe came his way.

Wabeno-iniini was a wizened old man with a thin chest and a straggle of gray locks that fell, unkempt and unadorned, to his shoulders. Legend had it that he was as aged as the red cliffs lining the great lake Kitchi-Gami. Even so, his hands were nimble and quick, and his face could be as changeable as the weather; black as a thunderstorm when he wished it, yet for now as quiet as dusk upon the water. He was held to be a sorcerer, and who could say otherwise? No one would dare.

The river flowed past down from where the council sat and all held their tongues in anticipation of what Wabeno might say next, but the old man sat silently as the pipe passed around again. Four shamans of the Ojibwe had joined Wabeno, Wolf, and the six Seneca warriors who had arrived three days ago amid wild jubilation at the village on Tima Gami. The joyful homecoming was due to the return of thirty-two Ojibwe and Odawa who had been adopted into the Seneca's town located many days to the south. That, and the warriors of their age-old enemy had brought a dugout filled with maize and fine tobacco as a peace offering.

Although it was not a hot day a sheen of sweat covered Long Tongue's forehead, creeping white paint into his eyes. A man of eighteen winters, Long Tongue's mission to the Anishinaabek was not a punishment for proposing the disastrous attack on the *Hanishé*, but neither was it a reward. As his father had explained, Long Tongue was learning the pathway to leadership among the warriors of the Seneca, and though the mass attack had been a failure, it had also been a lesson. Such would be the mission to the north, which might very well end in his death.

Now, as Wabeno held silent with his eyes shut as the pipe was passed around twice again, Long Tongue struggled to remain calm, fearing that the old man might give the nod at any moment to the score of warriors backing the circle. Unlike the six young Seneca, the Ojibwe guards were seasoned warriors bearing war clubs tipped with balls of granite and flint.

Sitting alongside the Senecas, the shamans of the Ojibwe had donned their most frightening apparel, including a mask of fish skin splayed with turkey feathers, crowns of horn and antlers, and a tassel of porcupine quills with a bugged-eyed squirrel gazing from its crown. One of them gazed at them from the eye sockets of a fractured human skull. But most frightening of all were the eyes of Wabeno and Wolf who sat facing the Seneca. The old man had flickers of lightning amid his smoky pupils, while He Who Outruns the Wolves had been aptly named for the fierce animal cunning in his eyes that came and went at will. Long Tongue found their eyes almost unbearable to gaze upon.

But when Wabeno finally spoke, his eyes were as placid as the morning sky and his voice had the music of a quiet brook.

"Grandson, your tobacco is a fine thing, and we see that you come in peace bearing gifts and the return of our people. But where are the others?"

Wolf was well-versed in the language of the Haudenosaunee, having spent many winters in the guise of a trader with their neighbors among the Tobacco People of the Tionontati. Although Wabeno also knew the language of their enemies, it had been agreed in advance that the old man would feign ignorance to eavesdrop on the Seneca when Wolf took his leave.

"Others?" Long Tongue asked, not understanding.

"Others of our people, captured by yours. Slaves."

"Yes ... there are others," he replied after a pause, "but they chose to remain with their bellies full of our maize. They are not slaves. Those who chose to stay became one with our families. They are honored members of our people now and much-loved; but should you choose, they will be asked to return."

Wabeno grunted, knowing that those among the Anishinaabek taken in a raid were often adopted by the Seneca to replace a missing loved-one—a father, son, mother, or daughter. There was little chance of starvation among the Seneca, given their great stores of maize, and the people of many tribes had accepted life among them. But more often, it was only women and children who were adopted: men were not so lucky. Wabeno noted that no men had accompanied the Seneca to the Ojibwe homeland, only youths and a few women.

But he was also well aware that such was the way of things, now and ever, and there was no point in dwelling on it, given the misdeeds of his own people from time to time.

He fiddled with the pipe, dumping its spent ashes into his hand and blowing them into the circle. “So, what do you wish of us?” he asked mildly.

The warriors standing behind the Senecas relaxed, and Long Tongue eased as well. His father had said that the peaceful mission would land, “like a dove on a branch.” Although he had scoffed at his father’s words then, he felt emboldened now.

The words tumbled from his lips. “Our sachem seeks the aid of seven shamans from seven peoples to help rid us of a demon,” he said in a rush. “It is *Hanishé,* a thing from the underworld. It picks at us without mercy, yet we cannot kill it. Even now, it feasts on the souls of the elders who led us, yet our shamans have been powerless against it. They tell us only that we must cast our net elsewhere. To you, wise one! To you!”

Long Tongue hurried on, describing the nighttime attack on the Great Lodge, the death of the seven elders, and the haunting of the town with the strange cries ululating from the fields. He told of the mass attack, omitting his own role in suggesting it, and how the Great Lodge had been set afire that night. It was preserved only by hundreds of townsfolk rushing to douse the flames with bark buckets of water, some burning their hands to tear down the flaming timbers. “The entrance was destroyed but has been rebuilt,” he said, finishing his tale. “But no one dares enter the lodge at night for fear that the *Hanishé* will return.”

Wabeno rocked on his haunches and nodded as the story wove on. “This *Hanishé,* are you sure it is not simply a man?” he said at last. “A big man of your enemies?”

Long Tongue shook his head, “*He-eh,* no, it can be seen at night, far across our fields. It is twice as tall as any man.”

“A bear then.”

“No. It has a strange cry and claws that are much longer than any bear. Its footprints are more like that of a bird the size of an elk! Some have seen it peering over the walls of our palisade at night.”

Wabeno thought it more likely that the Seneca had simply seen an owl perching on their pine fence, but this he kept to himself.

“There are bears much larger than our own far to the west,” he mused, “but let us suppose this *Hanishé* is what you say. Let us suppose that we may be of use to you. What do your people offer us in return?"

"We … we would offer peace and trade," Long Tongue stumbled, his eyes widening at the unlikelihood of such an offer being accepted. "Peace between our peoples after many lifetimes of bloodshed."

"Hmm…." Wabeno grunted, rocking on. "It does not seem likely."

This, Wolf did not translate, but the young Seneca understood it well enough. For many years there had been raids by the Seneca and their allies among the Haudenosaunee, who were as numerous as the leaves of the forest. The Onondaga, Oneida, Cayuga, and even the far-off Mohawks had been as ferocious as the black flies of summer, and the Seneca were the closest of them all. Many times, the Odawa and Ojibwe had repelled attacks on their villages, yet sometimes they had been cut down to the last man while their women and children hid in the forest. Many women and children had been spirited away, never to be seen again unless expeditions of warriors were mounted to retrieve them.

"Blood is always repaid with blood," Wabeno mused. "Are we to forget those who cry out to us from their graves?"

This, Wolf passed on and Long Tongue blanched. "It is what we have to offer," he said lamely. "But more than that, our sachem does you honor by seeking your aid. All know that you are the greatest of your kind among the people of the lakes. It is no small thing that we have come to you in our darkest time. It is no small thing that we have returned your people, and … uh…" Despite himself, Long Tongue gulped as his fellow warriors sat stone-faced, "we have been told to offer our own lives if you wish as a bond of our word."

Wabeno raised a hand. "Enough."

Again, came an agonizing pause that seemed to go on and on amid the murmur of the river. The warriors of the Ojibwe had stiffened again, the muscles of their arms flexing at their clubs as Wabeno pondered on. Long Tongue wiped his eyes with his backhand, cursing himself for the band of white paint he had drawn across his forehead. Across the way, the old man remained inscrutable with his eyes closed, and for a time Long Tongue thought that he had gone to sleep.

The shamans adjacent to Wabeno and Wolf grew restive, some feeling the stiffening of their old spines, yet none dared to speak. Wolf suppressed a grin, knowing that a tonsure of porcupine quills and a mask trimmed with feathers were likely to itch after such a long council. His grandfathers among the shamans were surely regretting their choices this day. Wolf wore a simple amulet of silver shaped like a fish on a leather thong around his neck while Wabeno's thin chest was adorned with a heavy necklace of bones and claws.

Then quietly, Wabeno began to hum, as if he were in communion with the spirits, and a soft drumbeat answered from the tree line up the hill. He motioned for the pipe to be refilled and lit with a coal. It was passed around as the circle relaxed and Wolf noted with some satisfaction that his grandfathers among the shamans took leave to doff their feathers and quills amid a chorus of grunts.

"A good smoke," Wabeno said with a smile, taking a draw on the pipe. "You and I will go," he motioned to Wolf. "I would like to see this bad thing, this *Hanishé*."

Wolf closed his eyes, holding back a groan. He wondered what Willow would say to this, another one of the old man's mad quests, of which he was often tasked. "We will need hostages," he said, indicating the Senecas. "Their lives held ransom for ours."

"No, I think not," Wabeno replied. "They will be our guard on the way south, showing us the way."

"Grandfather, would you give our enemies the gift of our lives?" Wolf protested. "We know their ways. Do you wish to end your life in their bonfire as they stand laughing? We cannot trust them."

Wabeno gave a slight smile and picked up the belt of wampum that the Seneca had presented, stroking it like the back of a favorite dog. "Wolf, you are wise in your counsel, and I hear your words. But harming us would bring dishonor to their people, intolerable dishonor, harming their magic at least as much as the wrath of their *Hanishé*. No harm will come to us, and it is my way to learn more of the world and what lies beyond. Come and learn with me."

Wolf nodded, thinking that the old fox had gone mad, yet grudgingly, he was willing to believe.

"Old one, I will follow you to the underworld if you ask me, but my woman will not be happy."

Wabeno grimaced, "Nor will mine, and she could make a panther shit itself."

Long Tongue gazed on as uncomprehending as a dog, sensing only that the old man seemed to have reached agreement and that for now, at least, his skin was saved.

Wabeno spent the next few days consulting the spirits on the intentions of the Senecas and what might be known of the *Hanishé*. Yet as was often their way, the spirits remained silent, giving Wabeno a measure of disquiet. Still, he had given his word to the Senecas in council that he would attend, and he could hardly break it now.

As for Wolf, he was tasked with provisioning the long trip to the Seneca's homeland and securing canoes to take them there. With a memory as sharp as an obsidian blade, Wolf had shown great promise as a shaman in his youth and had been inducted by acclaim into the lodge of the Mide-wi-win. But his teachers had soon raised their hands in dismay, for their young pupil was always given to sneaking away from his lessons in order to go fishing on the waters of the great lake, Kitchi Gami. The shamans had grown fat on the fish he provided, but other than learning a bit of herb lore, he was judged too poor a student to serve as a shaman. So it was that he had been enlisted as a *giimaabi* to serve as their eyes and ears across the Great Turtle Island in the guise of a simple trader. Wolf had survived several dangerous missions, and Wabeno knew there was no one better to accompany him on the way south. Wolf was no warrior, but he more than made up for this with his wits.

So it was that Wabeno, Wolf, and the six warriors of the Seneca took their leave, traveling down the wide river of Boweting to the big lake

Tima Gami on their way south. Yet this time the party traveled in the sleek canoes of the master builders of the Ojibwe, ensuring a speedy journey and greater stability amid the waves of the sweet-water sea.

As Wabeno predicted, his old woman screamed and wailed all the way down the hill from her lodge, raining curses and threats at his back amid tearful pleas to stay. Truthfully, no one in all the bands of the Ojibwe had ever known Wabeno to stir from his lodge, so it was a wonder to all that the old man was leaving. Twelve shamans of the Ojibwe stood agape as Wabeno left; they vowed to keep their peoples' medicine strong while looking uncertain at the prospect. The old man was more than just a shaman, and all knew it.

Nor was Willow happy when the party stopped at the village on Tima Gami for Wolf's parting words. "Another of this old man's crazy schemes," she hissed out of earshot of Wabeno as they stood with their toes curling the sands by the shore. "I'm going with you."

And then there were more screams, angry words, and wailing as Wolf demanded, then pleaded that she stay behind.

"You say it's not dangerous, but you won't let me go!" she raged, her jade eyes flaring.

Willow was no longer the petite beauty that Wolf had met at a dismal village on the far-off Red River when she was seventeen summers of age and he nineteen. Her hands had been hardened by the toil of dressing skins and fetching firewood, and her face had been scoured by the sun and the endless wind. But her hair was still jet black, sleek, and as silvered in the sunlight as a raven's wing, and if anything, she was more beautiful in Wolf's eyes now that they had been one for thirteen years; their love had only grown keener with each passing season. Gazing into her eyes, Wolf felt a stabbing in his breast at the thought of leaving her behind.

"I would take you with me in the beat of a robin's wing," he said, "but though Wabeno says that no harm will come to us, how can I know that the Senecas will keep their word? How can I know that they will not take you to replace a dead sister or a wife? It is their way of things, and

I will be one man among many with no one to help us."

"Hah! We will help ourselves!" she replied, "You know as well as me that we have slipped the noose before."

"Ah, but you forget. Who will care for our daughter if we're gone? My mother is as old as the stones. And who will watch over Found by the River?"

These last words found the tender spot in Willow's heart, dashing her hope of leaving.

"If you leave, the villagers will find some way to kill your sister-cousin," Wolf went on. "They will say it was an accident, but still, the deed will be done."

"*Faugh*! I would just as soon they were all dead in their robes tomorrow morning," Willow shot back spitefully. "Some, at least. That old man with the big nose and his wretched wife."

But she agreed that Found by the River's fate would be sealed by her leaving and knew that Wabeno would never agree to both of them coming along.

"We can make your meals and patch your canoes," she said weakly.

"I will not be gone long," Wolf replied, raising a hand. "I will see you before the geese fly south. This I promise."

"Oh, *ayreh feek* you men!" Willow said tearfully, using a bad word uttered by the coarse traders of her native land. Her life among the dusky people of that far-off land was almost forgotten now, kept alive only by her skill as a storyteller, rivaling that of Wolf himself.

Willow fumed and stamped, kicking up a spray of sand on the beach as Wabeno conversed with the villagers up the way. The Senecas waited in their canoes, which had been laden with furs, dried meat, and fish nets as gifts in a gesture of the trade to come.

"Go, then, but tell Wabeno he'd better lay a curse on this village that will send them all to hell if anyone touches a hair on our heads!"

Wolf managed a grave nod, suppressing a smile. Willow had told him of this place called hell, and though he and his people did not believe in it, he knew it was his wife's strongest condemnation. "I will tell Wabeno to send them to hell and make them understand that it is a place that will sear them forever like a goose on a spit."

Willow glared back, her dark face flushing even darker. "Tell them they'll face worse than that if they toy with me."

"It is done."

CHAPTER 4

WABENO'S FOOL

It was a long way to the land of the Senecas, nearly a full cycle of the moon, but the canoes of the Anishinaabek were light and fast, and the waves of the big lake Tima Gami were gentle beneath the summer sun as the party made their way south.

Long Tongue and the Seneca warriors marveled at the speed of their canoes, and for once, they had no fear of being overtaken by their ancestral enemies, the Wendats, who lived further south along these shores. The Wendats were farmers, not mariners, and their clumsy dugouts could hardly be expected to keep pace. "Besides, grandfather, we have your magic to protect us," Long Tongue said earnestly as they camped at night on a tiny island.

To this, Wabeno sniffed. He had kept to himself, sitting at the prow of a canoe paddled by Wolf, who was the equal to two of the young Senecas when it came to prowess on the water. He Who Outruns the Wolves had been born a club foot and had difficulty keeping up on long trails afoot but had compensated with the strength of his arms, chest, and back when it came to paddling. Many compared him to an otter for his skill at fishing and comfort in the water.

The day after leaving Willow's village, the party passed the mouth of a river that emptied into the sparkling waves of the big lake.

"This is where we came from," Wabeno said, casting a hand to the river's mouth.

"Here? It is the way to the Nipissing," Wolf replied from the back of the canoe. "They live along the big lake upstream. You sent me there on my first mission. Do you remember?"

"I suppose so," Wabeno mused, "but I meant far beyond. Our people came this way many lifetimes ago from the big salt water, Zhewitaganibi."

"Ah."

Wabeno motioned for Wolf to pull ashore, telling the Senecas that they would meet them at camp. "I would have a smoke here and remember," he said.

Wolf pulled in, and they sat smoking on the ruin of a haggard tree that had washed up on the shore. "Though you would not believe it, I was a young man when I last saw this river," Wabeno said. "I sat right here as we looked upon this lake and our new home."

It was an old story and Wolf knew it well, but he was happy to hear it again from Wabeno's lips and see it from the old shaman's eyes. It was why Wabeno-iniini was called the Man of the Dawn Sky.

"We were not always a scattered people, living here and there on islands and in the forests, scrambling for fish and game," Wabeno began. "Once we were one people—there were no Ojibwe, Odawa, or Potawatomi—there were only the Anishinaabek. We lived in a village larger than any that our people can imagine now—a place the size of many large villages. It was a happy place by the shores of Zhewitaganibi."

Wabeno said that the town was so big that one standing on a hill at its center could not see the end of it. Its people relied on crops, shellfish, and fish from the sea.

"I forget why we left. Disease, perhaps, or there was not enough food for our numbers, but I remember the spirits of the sea who came among us."

"The Guardians."

"Yes, the Guardians. One day, six of them rose from the ocean and entered the town. They shone as bright as the sun! We shielded our eyes, and gazed at them through screens of pine needles, yet no one could make them out. They glimmered as if they had been fashioned from the stars."

Wabeno took a draw on the pipe and coughed up a lungful of smoke. "Ah, this tobacco is strong!" He took another draw and coughed again.

"But know this," he went on, "One of the spirits was so terrible that its gaze was death. Our greatest healer set out to meet it and was struck dead as if by lightning. He must have seen its eyes. He must..."

"It is said that he was your father," Wolf said of the healer. "It is said that only you could meet the spirit's gaze."

Wabeno's face went somber as he looked out over the waves, lost in memory.

"Yes," he said. "I was only a child, but I was chosen, and the spirit who killed my father returned to the sea to keep us from further harm. The five who remained gave us the first clans of the Anishinaabek."

Wolf pondered this for a time and then asked what he had always feared to know.

"Tell me then grandfather, how is this so? For this was many lifetimes ago, beyond the days of our grandfathers' grandfathers. How is it that you are here?"

It was a rude question, but Wabeno did not take offense. "I am old," he said, spreading his hands, "and you too will be old."

"As old as you? I would not have that."

"Older than the stars, perhaps." Wabeno paused a moment. "That is why you are called Old Man."

Wolf frowned as darkness clouded his brow. Wabeno had bestowed the name Old Man upon him as an honorific for the cunning and wisdom he had shown on his mission down the Misi Sipi years ago. He had always considered it a trifle, yet now he realized the name had a deeper meaning.

"Old Man," he scowled.

"Yes, long will you live," Wabeno nodded in satisfaction.

For the first time Wolf understood why he had aged very little since reaching his manhood. Something in his substance had rubbed off on his adoptive mother, Cornflower, who was still living beyond a hundred summers. Wolf could only hope that the same would be true of Willow.

"Then I am cursed. I do not want this! Old as the stones ... who would desire such a thing?"

"Complainer! Many would call it a gift!" Wabeno snapped.

"A gift? To watch those you love grow old and die while you live on? That is no gift."

Wabeno smiled and shook his knee. "If you do not care for the gift of Kitchi Manito, then you can jump off a cliff. You will live only until your body hits the rocks below."

"That is a comfort," Wolf said, brightening.

"*Ehn*, but don't give up your gift so freely," Wabeno went on. "Do you know what my years have meant to me? I led our people to the west over many lifetimes when bad times overtook us. Four times we settled on our way to this land, building our villages and raising our children. Hah! We were uprooted each time and driven like leaves before the wind."

"Yes, but..."

"We were guided by the spirits," Wabeno went on. "Their lights rose among the stars, shining like cowrie shells, the *megiis*. Each time, they shone the way as we settled first on the Lake of the Mohawks and then in the shadow of the great waterfall that is the lapping tongue of these lakes. Whenever we failed or were stricken with disease or raiders, the *megiis* would appear again, leading us west."

Wolf threaded the fronds from a sprig of grass, thinking that he was unlikely to ever lead his people anywhere.

"I could not fill your footsteps," he said, "nor could any man. But grandfather, our people must have met the Haudenosaunee on their way to the west."

"Yes, they were our enemies, then and now."

"And now we go to help them."

Wabeno shrugged. "Perhaps some good will come of it, and it will be good to meet the Seneca in their own land. That and a chance to defeat their *Hanishé* has made me young again!

"You see grandson," he confided, leaning in close. "I have envied you many times through the years. As our *giimaabi,* you have traveled among many peoples in far-off lands, while I have sat like an old toad in a hole, listening to the babble of the river and the complaints of our shamans. I wish to be you, if only for the summer."

"You're crazy, old man, and you have dragged me into a trap," Wolf growled, yet with a touch of mirth in his eyes.

"Yes, but who is stronger and wiser than you?" Wabeno slapped Wolf's back. "Together we will show them the power of the Anishinaabek. Together we will hang their *Hanishé* from a tree and spank it with our clubs."

Wiser? Wolf did not think so. As was so often the case, he felt more like Wabeno's fool.

CHAPTER 5

WALKING TURTLE

There was no easy way to reach the land of the Senecas. Traveling up the river where Wolf and Wabeno had rested was a long paddle upstream through a swift current and many rapids. The river was also the northern boundary of the Wendats' homeland, which the Seneca were eager to avoid.

They took the longer southern route to the end of Tima Gami, then two rivers and another lake to the big Lake of the Eries. This, too, required some caution for the Seneca had long been at war with their neighbors and there were several days that the party paddled by night along the southern shore.

There were also days filled with rain and chill winds, and though all had been careful to grease their jerkins and leggings with bear fat, that did little to keep the watery breath of the lakes from soaking them to their bones. Sometimes they camped on a tiny island or defensible peninsula with no hope of a fire to dry out and warm themselves. And always, their canoes needed patching with their stores of pitch and spruce roots after a day's rough handling in the waves.

But most days were sunny with the lake sparkling beneath them, and the Seneca's spirits rose at the promise of home with each dip of their paddles.

Wolf and Wabeno spent their time talking amiably with the Senecas around their campfires, gathering their stories and learning more of their language. Long Tongue let it be known that he was a big man among his people, even though he was only eighteen winters of age. He embellished many tales of his hunting and trapping exploits and hinted that he had proved his valor as a warrior while tagging along as a helpmate on one of his father's raids.

"One night, during a raid on the Eries, three raccoons came to pillage our supplies when the warriors were gone, and I drove them off with my club," he insisted. "They were very large."

"Mmm," Wolf replied.

"There is still blood on my club. Would you like to see it, brother?"

"*Ehn*, that would be a fine thing," Wolf said, feigning interest. He eyed the club as if it were that of the demi-god *Manobozho* himself. Across the way, two of Long Tongue's companions hid their faces in their hands and giggled.

The young warrior did indeed have a long tongue, which he was quick to demonstrate when asked; it curdled down to the tip of his chin, as long as that of a deer. But Wolf noted that his fellow Senecas sniggered at times when Long Tongue boasted of his feats, which were often of slight import or imaginary. He quickly deduced that there was a double meaning to Long Tongue's name, even though the young braggart had no idea of the derision behind his back.

"He chatters like a jay," Wolf muttered to Wabeno in their own language after Long Tongue had given them a long and boring tale of his deeds as a child.

"He is young," Wabeno replied. "A few knocks will bring him wisdom."

"Someday."

"But for now, I would rather not have his tongue in my ears," Wolf replied, spitting off to the side.

"Those who chatter are often of the most use to us, remember that." Wabeno said.

"*Ehn*, I know it well. But he says bad things about his father. He has no shame."

"Perhaps his father is a bad man."

"Perhaps, but I think he would use his father as a step-stone to raise himself up."

"That is the way of braggarts," Wabeno replied. "But they are little men and all know it."

"Even so, his father would be wise to guard his back."

"So should we all," Wabeno said. "So should we all."

Then one day, a quarter-moon on, as Long Tongue filled their ears from a neighboring canoe, they heard a low rumble in the distance as they made their way along a river beyond the Lake of the Eries. It grew louder in a ceaseless rumble.

"A thunderstorm," Wolf said, "and yet there are no clouds."

"Hah! You are a prophet, brother, but the storm is in the water itself," Long Tongue called over the din. "It is the passage between the lakes, Onguiaahra, where the water turns to thunder."

And so it was, for soon a great mist rose up higher than three pine trees stacked end-to-end, and the party pulled to shore. "That way lies death!" Long Tongue laughed as he pointed ahead, barely heard above the roar. "We must carry our canoes around it."

Brothers, sisters, it was the torrent of all the lakes to the west, thundering for eternity over cliffs that made the smallest ant out of any traveler. The river widened as it tumbled over the falls, and the rocks at its sides looked as if they had been cloven by the hand of a giant. Wolf had heard of the great falls but never thought that he would see them. He watched as the wreck of a huge tree swept over the edge and went crashing down through the torrent, disappearing into the mist and plunging into the base of the falls far below. It was as if the ancient oak was nothing more than a twig.

They made their way by a well-worn pathway down the north side of the falls with two men carrying each canoe, then scrambling back uphill to fetch their supplies. It was half a day before they had completed the portage, collapsing in exhaustion at an early campsite.

"From here it is only a day's paddle," Long Tongue said that night. "Even now, they will be preparing a feast in your honor."

"I could eat," Wolf said, weary of the pemmican and dried fish that they had brought along. "But how will they know of us?"

"Ah, they know. We have watchers throughout this land, from the mouth of Onguiaahra to the land of the Cayugas, our neighbors to the east. There will be runners; look to the far shore!"

As he said, the silhouette of a distant man waved from the opposite shore and took off running to the east along the riverbank.

They noticed more people wandering along the shore; a family fishing with nets looked up in silence as they passed by. Then, a growing number of men who gaped at them as the Senecas hallooed greetings and chattered from their canoes. Home! Many of the onlookers were heavily tattooed, with their scalps plucked clean, save for a strip of hair three fingers wide ribboning the top of their skulls. Soon, corn fields appeared along with crops of beans, squash, pumpkin, tobacco, and vegetables, all tended mostly by women.

"There are many of them," Wabeno said.

"Grandfather, far more than you know," Wolf replied as he paddled from the rear. "As many as the pebbles in the river. They live dull lives scratching at the dirt for their crops, but they are never hungry."

"Until the winds blow dry, and the rain fails to come."

"Oh, it rains enough to please a duck along this lake," Wolf said, recalling the many soggy days he'd spent with the neighboring Tionontati.

Wabeno thought of their own time drenched in their canoe as it rained for three days in a row. "I believe it," he said. "But if there are so many living here and so well fed, it seems strange that they would seek our help. There must be many medicine-makers among them."

"Perhaps it is simply a ruse to hang our stones from their lodge poles," Wolf muttered, eyes narrowed. "I know them only as tricksters."

"They would have little use with mine," Wabeno replied with a frown. "They've gone dry as dust."

To this Wolf had no reply, for he had employed his own parts a great deal while nestled with Willow, and now he felt a twinge at the thought of her, stuck in the dismal village of the Odawa, so far to the north.

The crops seemed to go on and on, and in the distance, they spied a low hill topped by a forest of bare trees. Yet as they drew closer, they saw that the trees were in fact a vast palisade of thin pines sharpened to points with tendrils of smoke rising from beyond them. The fields ran all the way to the top of the hill and far out of sight on either side beyond it. Hundreds of Seneca farmers were working the fields, cultivating the soil and pulling weeds.

Ahead, they saw a landing on a wide beach covered with dugouts, and just beyond stood an assembly of two hundred warriors bearing clubs, spears, and pennants festooned with feathers and the tails of animals. Their Seneca canoe-mates gave an excited shout that was answered by a roar from the multitude ashore.

The warriors on the beach began jigging, ululating war cries and raising their weapons. Gazing upon their scowling, snarling faces, Wolf considered whipping his canoe around and bearing Wabeno away as fast as his arms could paddle.

But anticipating him, Wabeno called, "Land us," from the front of the canoe, and they grounded on the shore just as the entire body of warriors ran screaming toward them with every intention of lifting their hair.

But of course, it was all for show, and the storm of warriors broke only a long step from Wolf and Wabeno's canoe, laughing and cheering as they helped them to shore. Then came much slapping of backs, good-natured jostling, and words of welcome.

Yet that was the least of it. From the rear of the crowd came the long tones of a conch shell and the music of rattles and cane flutes. The warriors parted, falling silent as two figures appeared at their flank. Leading the way was a tall man with a sharp face painted black around his eyes, splendidly dressed in doeskin leathers dyed indigo. Three strings of purple and white quahog shells draped around his neck, and a headdress of a dozen long swan feathers bobbed behind him as he strode forward. Wolf thought he'd never seen such a noble looking man.

But hanging on his arm was his opposite: an old woman whose face was painted black in mourning. Her own clothes were as tattered as castoffs and her hair was unkempt—half of it had been hacked off at the rear of her skull, as was the custom when a loved-one died. She stepped along with a staff on her other arm, and what remained of her gray tresses ran past her shoulders much the same as the locks of old Wabeno. To Wolf's eyes they could have been brother and sister.

But this he did not say, and as the tall man approached, he prepared to greet the chieftain of the Seneca, appraising his eyes for signs of treachery.

Yet, to his surprise, the man paused and handed a stalk of young corn to the old woman, who stepped forward with the aid of her staff. He breathed a word in the woman's ear, sidling her gently before Wabeno.

"Brothers," she said, handing the tasseled stalk to Wabeno. "Welcome to Ga-ogwah Kanotaye. I am Yota-ine Ha'no-wah, Walking Turtle, *sachem* of this town."

The old woman's eyes were as silvered as moonlight on the water, and Wabeno nodded, knowing that the old woman could not see. Walking Turtle, chieftain and priestess of Ga-ogwah Kanotaye, was completely blind.

CHAPTER 6

WITCHES – BOTH OF YOU

Far to the north, Willow felt that her world was spinning. This was the third time since their union that Wolf had been sent on a mission by old man Wabeno, and each time had filled her with dread that he would never return. She knew that He Who Outruns the Wolves was given the most dangerous tasks by the shamans of the Ojibwe, who never seemed to have a care for his safety, sitting in their council circles like a ring of croaking frogs. Once, he had returned to her badly wounded, and the scars were still drawn in red across his chest and back.

She had scoffed at Wabeno's claim that her man would be protected in his guise as a simple trader with a gift for storytelling. "The people of every land need stories, and all love a taleteller," Wabeno had told her in his know-everything way. "Even if they suspect, still they are willing to forgive if their ears are filled with another legend."

Eya, Willow knew this well enough, since she herself had become a great storyteller among the Anishinaabek, offering tales of her own journey from far across the ocean with the devilish Spaniards and their ill-fated quest.

But the girl who had toiled as a house slave in the casa of Abu bin Nisar had never quite settled as a woman in the forests and lakes of this new land. It was a trade with no clear satisfaction. There had been more comforts in the land from which she had been stolen, yet far more freedom in her life among the Anishinaabek, where she could come and go as she chose with no man to order her about. For that she was grateful, yet in her heart she would always be a child of the desert and its dusty trails, following in the tracks of her father. And though she loved a good story told around the lodge fire as much as any, she doubted that this alone would protect her man, Wolf.

Father, Mother, if you could see me now, she thought as she cast a net on the waters of Tima Gami. She looked to the south, wondering where Wolf was now, hoping that Wabeno was right about their safety among the Seneca. It was no solace that the old shaman would be lying in his grave with her husband if he was wrong.

Stories, she thought bitterly as her gill net drifted at the end of its float. There are good ones and bad, and she was powerless to stop the one being told around the village. One Toe and his wicked wife, Crow's Meat, had spread the tale of Wolf turning a branch into a snake and then back again; they had seen it with their own eyes, as had the elders seeking to be rid of Found by the River.

"It was longer than my arm with the fangs of a rattler," One Toe claimed to all who would listen. "He flung it at us, twisting and snapping! I nearly shit myself."

"I saw it too," Crow's Meat had nodded. "Only a witch could do such a thing. Only a witch."

The tongue-waggers of the village were convinced that her man was likely a witch, as was Found by the River, and it was no stretch for them to believe that Willow was also a creature of the underworld. She knew that her own stories were of no protection since her tales of white men, lions, and monsters of the sea only confirmed that she was of the Other, more easily feared than cherished. It would take only one mishap in the village—a broken leg or a stillborn baby—for the band to descend on her with clubs and stones no matter what curse Wabeno had promised them as a warning. This, because the other story being spread by One Toe was that Wabeno and Wolf were dead and walking with the spirits. He had dreamed that they had been killed by the Senecas, and so it must be true.

Willow felt the yank of her net and glimpsed the golden green of a perch lodged in its cords. “Oh, you are a fat one!” she sang out, giving thanks in the same breath. She pulled it to the shore and clubbed it, gathering up the walleye that she had caught earlier. It was enough.

Willow called out to Found by the River who was fishing down the shore. She too had taken a perch in her net and now the two chattered happily as they made their way to Willow’s lodge. Willow had invited the in-between woman to stay with her shortly after Wolf had departed, reasoning that they would be safer together.

That afternoon she told Found by the River of the stories being spread around the village and presented her with a war club that Wolf had fetched on one of his missions. “At least we will have the pleasure of mashing the brains of One Toe and Crow’s Meat if they come for us,” she said, hefting her own club.

“I can barely lift it,” the girl replied with a wan smile. It was a club of the Dakota people with a large round stone at the end of its shaft.

“Then you will have to practice on the beach until you are strong enough to brain a panther,” Willow replied.

“I will do it, sister-cousin, and if they come for us, I will strike the first blow.”

This, Willow doubted, but she held her tongue. Found by the River had always seemed more tender than tough in a way that was not meant to survive the harsh winters of the big lakes. Thin and frail with watery eyes, she seemed as sylph as a mink, as shy as a possum. Her face was as peaceful and trusting as that of a baby, and there was no strength in her that Willow could detect, no more than a placid brook.

They had taken to fishing each day since Wolf’s departure, then walking the shoreline and along the pathways of the island. Always there was a need to collect firewood along with the plants, nuts and mushrooms that kept hunger at bay when there were no fish, and the two often gathered enough to share with the aged of the village. This alone, perhaps, kept the hostile members of the band at bay, for the most elderly of the villagers were Willow’s friends and protectors, sassing back at those who spread evil tales.

One day, as they walked the trails collecting mushrooms, Willow asked Found by the River about her mother.

"Woman Walks Tall was my mother, though not of my birth," the girl replied. "A hunter and his wife found me lying beside a river far to the north. I was just a babe, but by the favor of the spirits the woman had milk in her breasts."

"How did you come here?"

"They were passing through, bartering meat and furs. My mother traded a string of elk teeth for me."

"And they knew nothing of where you came from? There were no others living nearby who might have known?"

"No, Mother said that they were of the Cree tribe, a shy people who are very clannish. They knew everyone for many days' walk to the four directions. Woman Walks Tall told me that I had been born a tadpole."

"A tadpole? The spawn of a frog?"

"Yes, one that became a member of the True People. Who knows?"

"Little frog, you did not question this?" Willow said with a snort, stooping to pluck a morel. "Look, a ring of them!"

Found by the River laughed in delight, gathering her share. "Sister-cousin, you are a magician!" she said. "Ah, no, my mother's story was only in jest, something to amuse a child."

"What then?"

"I have often thought of this," the girl frowned as they rested on a fallen tree with their baskets between their feet. A shaft of sunlight split the trees ahead, but otherwise the forest was as cool and dark as a cave of green. "Perhaps the woman who birthed me did not want me or was starving and did not have enough milk in her breasts, which is often the fate of the poor Cree."

"That is likely enough."

But Found by the River seemed not to hear. "Perhaps I was stolen from my crib by a wolf who found my taste not to his liking," she said in almost a whisper. "Or perhaps it is true that I was born a tadpole as Woman Walks Tall told me. Truly, she did not know, but she loved me as deeply as any mother could and nursed me whenever the shaking sickness came over me."

"Did you ever know her to be a witch?" It was ill to ask, and Willow regretted it as soon as the words left her lips.

"*Gaawiin,* no, she was only a healer; she knew many mysteries of the forest and its herbs. But...," she hesitated, "there were times when I woke at night to find her missing, and times when our lodge shook like the breath of the north wind, Biboon, even though no wind was stirring. Did that make her a witch? I do not know. I only know that she was my mother."

Willow had never known a witch, even though there were many stories of them told in the land of her birth. Often, accusations of witchcraft were nothing more than a greedy man seeking the treasures of a defenseless widow. In her youth, she had rallied with other women in defense of one who had been accused. She knew that Wolf didn't believe in witches, but she was not so sure herself, having been told of a prophecy once long ago that had come to pass.

"On my way to this land, I heard the tale of a witch that came true," she said. "We were on a ship—a thing you would know as a big canoe. It was filled with men whose skin was as white as a fish's belly, and the witch said that no man who entered the forests of this land would come out alive."

"And did they?"

"Not a single one, as far as I know," Willow said.

"Ah, but you are no man," Found by the River mused. "Perhaps your womanhood saved you."

"Perhaps. But more likely it was greed that killed them. Their chieftain told me they had a sickness that could only be cured by a thing called *oro*."

"I do not know this thing."

"It is a metal like our copper but softer. It shines like the setting sun, and the white men were mad for it."

"Then we are lucky to have none of it."

That evening, as they passed Crow's Meat lodge, they heard a hissing from its darkened entryway as the gnawed leg bone of a turkey was tossed at them. "Witches, both of you!" came a voice from the darkness within.

Willow pulled down her lower eyelid, giving back the evil eye. "You'll wish there was a witch to save you if you keep wagging your tongue, snake!"

She picked up the bone and whipped it back into the darkness, cheered to hear a yelp as it struck home.

CHAPTER 7

TALES OF WALKING TURTLE

There had been an embarrassing moment on the beach when Wolf and Wabeno met the sachem of Ga-ogwah Kanotaye. Wolf had been presented as Wabeno's translator, yet before he could speak with a lie in his mouth, Walking Turtle had raised a hand.

"I know who you are, Old Man," she said.

Old Man. Wolf flinched, wondering how the woman could possibly know the name that he himself did not care for.

"You are He Who Outruns the Wolves," she went on. "For many years you have tricked us, living among the childlike Tionontati. But I heard of you and know that you are your peoples' spy, gathering stories of the Seneca and our brothers among the Haudenosaunee."

Wolf stiffened and was about to speak when Wabeno spoke for him. "Grandmother, you are wiser than us," the old man said smoothly. "But do not blame my young brother, for it was the Mide-wi-win of our people who sent him here with my blessing. And truly, he did not collect much more than the Tionontati's tobacco and corn."

Walking Turtle sniffed at this but replied, "Old Man, you are welcome among us if you can rid us of the *Hanishé*. I trust that you are more than a taleteller and a crow."

If he had been among friends Wolf would have cawed at this, but now he wisely kept his silence.

Turning, Walking Turtle said, "You are the last to arrive."

The first thing Wolf and Wabeno saw upon entering the town was two young bears being chased by a mob of excited children and their dogs. The yearling bears gamboled happily down a long course of the palisade and then back again with one pausing to lick Walking Turtle's hand.

"Ugh, not now little one," Walking Turtle said, giving the scruff of the bear's neck a shake. "Run and play."

The entrance to Ga-ogwah Kanotaye was a corridor of pine logs that divided the palisade. Any war party that attempted to enter would be hemmed in, and beyond the corridor was a maze of thorns and spiked branches meant to further confuse an enemy. Yet this narrow passageway had proved a death trap for those who jammed its walls on what was called the "Night of the *Hanishé*."

Wolf had seen much bigger towns on his mission down the Misi Sipi. Some had been dominated by earthen mounds and pyramids arrayed along broad pathways and squares jammed with markets and thousands of dwellers. Still, he found the town of the Senecas impressive. There were rows upon rows of longhouses, sheathed in bark that were much bigger than those of the Odawa. Most were the height of four tall men and more than fifty steps long.

"How many live here?" Wabeno asked, beckoning to the nearest lodge.

"It is ten families to each lodge, but sometimes as many as twenty," said Blackbird, who had accompanied Walking Turtle back up the hill.

By now, Wolf and Wabeno knew that Blackbird was war chief of the Senecas while Walking Turtle led the affairs of the town with a council of clan mothers known for their wisdom. Or, at least, they had before the *Hanishé* took four of them in its rampage. It was no surprise that Walking Turtle was sachem of the town, since the Odawa also had women chieftains who tended village affairs. Wolf and Wabeno were only taken aback by Walking Turtle's lack of sight.

She said that her place as sachem was expected to last only a short time.

“My mate was the leader of this town, and I fill his place only until the clan mothers pick a new man,” she explained. “But it will be a while…” her words trailed off.

“Why is this?” Wolf asked.

“Because the clans have not yet selected the grandmothers who will lead them!” she replied in exasperation, as if this was obvious. “Like your own people, we spend a long time in council before anything is decided. If it was possible, I would go to my grave tomorrow to be with my husband. But for now, I lead the clan mothers of the town. I am leader of the Deer Clan.”

They made their way down a pathway through the longhouses, surrounded by children and the elderly. All the others were working in the fields or out hunting and fishing. Walking Turtle hummed a song as they walked along, and Wolf divined that it was her way of measuring her steps from place to place.

Ahead, they saw the Great Lodge, which rose far above the neighboring longhouses. The front of the lodge was badly scorched and tattered with several blackened timbers still laid bare where repairs had not yet begun.

Five old men and a woman sat in a line before the lodge, raising their hands in greeting. It was clear that they were all shamans of great power, bedecked in cunning arrays of feathers, antlers, beads, bones, skulls, and other raiment that might tempt the spirits or frighten evil *manitos*.

Wabeno bowed respectfully. “Wise ones, I look forward to learning more of your ways,” he said, receiving much the same in reply.

“You see? You are not alone,” Walking Turtle said. “We have cried out to the medicine-makers of many tribes, and the best of their shamans have come forth. Some have come out of curiosity and some to prove their worth.”

“Grandmother, I am humbled to be in such company,” Wabeno replied, “but I fear I will be as thin as the milk of a doe compared to those you have gathered.”

“You flirt with me, Wabeno,” she replied with a smile. “You know we desired you above all others. The earth told you, the birds whispered in your ear.”

"I will do what I can."

"Do you fear to stay in the lodge where the demon fell upon us?"

Wabeno eyed the lodge and recalled the tale of Long Tongue and the slaughter of the elders.

"Oh yes, grandmother, I do fear to stay here if your demon is still lurking about, but so be it," he replied. He placed his hand on Wolf's shoulder. "I have a wolf here to protect me, and he will sleep with one eye open, howling when your *Hanishé* comes creeping in the night."

"Then I have chosen wisely," she said with a secretive smile. "But if you have your meal here, be careful not to eat any food that remains the next day. What is left in the night is meant for the spirits, and they will be angry if you eat their food."

"Not a kernel will pass my lips."

Wabeno wondered what other dangers might lie ahead. How was he to know that every other shaman had refused to stay in the haunted lodge? They were all sleeping with twelve families in a crowded longhouse down the way.

Wolf spent the afternoon painting Wabeno's face and arms with designs meant to enhance his presence in the ceremonies to come. He seldom wore paint himself, but like all men he paid close attention to his hair, which was shaved close toward the front of his scalp with a neat plait trailing past the back of his neck. He had every intention of impressing the Seneca and had brought along the cowl of a wolf's head, the snout of which jutted over his forehead. That, and he wore a wolfskin breechclout adorned with lines of white shells. Willow had made it for him.

"We must look our best," he said to Wabeno as he daubed the old one's face with red paint.

Yet unlike the other shamans, Wabeno was not eager to stand out, and his own hair was a ragged bird's nest that fell to his shoulders in a snarl of unkempt locks.

"You are a disgrace, grandfather," Wolf jibed. "Let me fix you." Wabeno waved him away until Wolf's nagging grew too much to bear, finally allowing him to comb his hanks until they were halfway presentable. But that was all that Wabeno would allow beyond his paint. He wore a simple headpiece of a young buck's short antlers with a skirt of mink tails tied around his waist and a necklace of bear teeth and bones dangling across his scrawny chest.

"Ah, you look the part of a great sorcerer now," Wolf said as he straightened Wabeno's antlers.

"I am glad of it," Wabeno replied, pursing his lips and nodding.

"Here, let me…"

"Enough!"

That night there was a parade through town with all eight hundred of the townsfolk lining the lanes that led to a dusty square outside the Great Lodge. Walking Turtle led the way, carried on a litter by eight strong men. Behind them danced the seven shamans drawn from seven winds, all dressed in their finest.

Leading the shamans was a medicine-maker from the Illini people to the west. He wore a mask carved in the semblance of a bear along with a long wooden phallus that dangled between his legs by a cord attached to his waist. Wabeno thought him a fool and brought up the rear of the troupe, bobbing half-heartedly as the shamans made their entry dance.

As for Wolf, he swayed along on his bad foot in the company of warriors who were in the next rank. With his club foot he would have preferred a place among the crowd, but Blackbird had insisted that he accompany the warriors, and such an honor could not be refused. Fortunately, Wolf had brought his staff on the journey south; it was a length of hickory that also served to give an opponent a knock on the head when called for. Aided by his walking stick, he had no trouble keeping up.

The air thundered with drums and a choir of maidens raised their voices in song as the parade wound its way around the square. Behind the choir came more than one hundred women performing an eagle dance, soaring with their outstretched arms swooping high and wide. It was a dazzling scene and Wolf stumbled and nearly fell as he gazed back over his shoulder, trying to take it all in.

Dancing in step, the women of the Seneca wore their hair far down their backs, carefully combed and oiled with the essence of sunflowers. Many also wore tufts of their hair tied with strips of eel skin at the crown of their heads; others wore flat bonnets of shells. Their doeskin skirts ran from waist to knee, and their breasts were heavily draped with necklaces of shells traded from the far-off sea.

Next came the pick of the Seneca warriors, presenting a riot of hair styles as they danced into the square. Some had half their heads plucked with long locks down the far side of their skulls. Others had tonsures, with the top of their skulls plucked clean, or with a protruding topknot. But most had their scalps plucked bare except for a strip of hair three fingers wide down the middle of their heads that was dyed red and roached higher than a man's upraised hand.

"They look like woodpeckers," Wolf said to himself, meaning no disrespect. He noted that like the men of his own people, the Seneca took great care with their paint. Many also wore elaborate tattoos with designs in black and red. A few wore leggings, but being summer, most dressed in simple breechclouts. Here and there, some men danced naked except for their paint.

Both the men and women of the Seneca wore earrings and ear spacers, some of which were fashioned from the fine purple and white wampum that was prized among all peoples. Wolf resolved to trade for some as a gift for Willow, and his heart rose at the thought of her.

A hush fell as the parade and its dancers settled into the square. With all eyes upon them, Wabeno and the shamans were given a place of honor before the Great Lodge, sitting silently as Walking Turtle welcomed them in a loud voice.

"Wise ones, you have come in our time of need, and we embrace you now as members of our own families!" she called out, though it was the rumbling of bellies that spoke even louder, for it was past the time of the daily meal, and a long line of steaming food troughs were being carried into the square even as Walking Turtle spoke.

Then came a feast of deer, beaver, turkey, turtle, and fish, along with a porridge of corn meal that had been carefully sealed in clay jars since the prior year to fend off the starving time of early summer.

But as is often the way of things, there were far more mouths to feed than there was food for such a multitude, and most ate nothing but stale maize while the shamans stuffed themselves to groaning.

We will have more of this than we could desire, Wolf thought glumly as a wooden shingle of corn mush was passed his way along with a sliver of venison. He had eaten more maize than he cared to remember during his time with the Tionontati and knew there was often little meat to go with it.

After the feast came the spectacle of acrobats leaping and somersaulting in the plaza, and a circle dance of women who sang and pounded hand drums as they stepped high in time. This was followed by another dance of the town's warriors, who looked quite capable of taking down a score of *Hanishés* to Wolf's eyes. They were fierce men, hard-muscled, and heavily tattooed: the terror of all the peoples of the big lakes. It was clear that it was only fear and the *Hanishé*'s guile that had allowed it to escape their clutches. That, or it truly was a demon of the underworld and could not be grasped by human hands or harmed by human weapons.

That evening, as the sun was setting, Wolf and Wabeno entered the Great Lodge and made their bedding along pallets close to its entrance. The interior of the lodge loomed like a cave with the faint light of dusk filtering through its three smoke holes.

"It stinks of charred wood here, and I fear we will have ghosts for company," Wabeno said, fidgeting.

"Don't worry old man, these ghosts are our friends," Wolf replied. "Let us smoke and think on it. Spare them some words of comfort. We are here to avenge them."

"Yes, but even so," Wabeno replied with his eyes darting in the dusk.

For the first time in all their years together, Wolf realized that the elderly shaman was afraid. And why shouldn't he be? He was far from the home where he and his old wife had lived for many years with never a reason to travel beyond his lodge.

"Now you have gotten your wish," Wolf said, lighting his pipe with a coal he had cradled in a seashell. "Now you walk in *my* footsteps and will see what *I* have seen."

"Yes, but I fear I have been a fool." Wabeno said, feeling himself shrivel. He had envied Wolf for the travels that he had forced upon him, and yet now he wished only to be with his old woman, snug in his lodge above the river at Boweting.

"Courage, grandfather," Wolf said in an easy way, hoping to put the old man's fear to rest. "I will sleep with one eye open as you wish and remember that we are wiser and stronger in the ways of the spirits and the world than all of the other shamans together."

"I suppose," Wabeno said, though he did not sound convinced.

"And know this," Wolf added. "It is well that we are lodged here instead with the others. If there are ghosts, then they are surely our friends, while the shamans will find themselves sleeping with their faces against the buttocks of others and plagued with the mice and fleas that come from being crowded together. Ah, and lapping dogs too, always sniffing at your face when you're trying to sleep! We have this place alone and will have no fear of vermin or crying babies."

"I do not fear crying babies," Wabeno said.

"That is because you have never slept among them."

Wabeno seemed to brighten a bit, and they enjoyed their pipes in silence. As darkness fell, the old man nodded with his chin reaching his chest, and Wolf laid him gently down on his pallet, covering him with his own bearskin robe.

He sat smoking his pipe at the entrance of the Great Lodge, feeling a shiver down his spine as the ghosts of the murdered elders gathered behind him. He could almost make out their voices as they murmured in the darkness.

But Wolf had encountered ghosts before, and though he feared them, it was not enough to keep him from yawning and wishing them away. “Go in peace old ones, and let me rest,” he spoke to the darkness, from which came no reply. The stillness was unsettling, but he brushed it aside.

He settled on his own pallet, listening to the gentle snores of Wabeno across the way. Moonlight crept into the entryway and with it came a distant sound that was neither ghost nor man. Faintly, he heard a long wavering cry and a honking like a wounded beast far across the cornfields, far beyond the walls of Ga-ogwah Kanotaye.

CHAPTER 8

THE TREE OF PEACE

Wabeno was unsettled by his night in the Great Lodge and arose the next morning feeling ashamed of his fear. He had fallen into a dreamless sleep, unmolested by the ghosts of the lodge, yet still he felt disturbed and out of place. He missed the comfort of home where he could sit outside his *wigi-wam* on the hill overlooking the river and answer the pleas of his people, healing when he could or consulting friendly spirits on their behalf when he couldn't. Here in the land of the Senecas he felt as uncertain as a grounded bird or a fish pulled from the water. The *orenda* of the Senecas was strong and he felt the lightning in his own eyes diminished in its glow. And the *Haniəhé*! He knew nothing of it. How was he to grapple with a demon that was beyond his knowledge? He had undertaken the quest in the spirit of a child who had no idea of the dangers ahead.

But a stone lifted from his chest as he looked at the sleeping form across the way. He Who Outruns the Wolves was by his side and that gave him courage, for the younger man seemed as easy with the Seneca as if they were old friends back in Boweting.

Wabeno knew that only knowledge could cure his unease, and so after washing the prior evening's paint from his face and running his fingers through his hair, he made his way to Walking Turtle's lodge where he found her sitting outside, enjoying the morning sun.

"Grandmother, can I join you?"

Walking Turtle nodded. "I was waiting for you, grandfather."

"How shall we know each other?"

"Let us be sister and brother."

"Thank you, sister. It is a good thing that we talk."

Her hair was as gray as her sightless eyes and fell past her shoulders to a tunic of doeskin dyed a light green. She sat cross-legged on a leather pad and bid Wabeno to sit beside her. "Let us feel the sun together," she said. "Tell me your thoughts."

"Ah, I would rather you tell me yours," Wabeno replied. "I have much to learn before I can be of any use to your people. Your town has humbled me."

"Well spoken."

They talked in an easy way; Wabeno had learned something of the Haudenosaunee's language in his youth and had picked up more on the journey south with Long Tongue. Now, although he stumbled at times, he understood Walking Turtle well enough. They spoke of small things at first, and to the surprise of both, their words came easy.

"How came you to be the leader of your people?" he asked.

"My man was leader of this town, and when he died, I was asked to take his place until our women pick a new sachem," she said with a sigh. "It is a burden beyond what I can bear."

"It is the women who choose?"

"Ah, it is a long story, but I will tell you some of it," she replied. "Women hold a far greater place among the Haudenosaunee than your people because we owe everything to a great spirit named Sky Woman. Do you know of her?"

"No, sister, but I am willing."

"Then listen. We are taught that long ago, a great spirit named Sky Woman fell from the stars and landed on the back of a turtle that became the earth. She brought all things to life, every plant, flower, bird, and animal. But finding herself alone, she gave birth to a daughter who became the mother of our people."

"Ah, but who was the father?"

"Who can say? But just as all men are born of women, so too did Sky Woman's daughter give birth to the Haudenosaunee. So, although our sachems are men, it is women who choose the man who will lead us. He must be a man of wisdom, caution, and bravery with strong ties to the best people. Soon the clan mothers will choose a man, and I will be set free."

"I see the sense of it, but what became of Sky Woman's daughter?" Wabeno asked.

"Ah, she gave birth again, this time to two sons, a Good Twin and an Evil Twin. She died upon giving birth to the evil one, but four plants sprang from her grave—maize grew from her heart, beans from her fingers, tobacco from her head, and squash from her belly. It was the Good Twin who taught us how to grow the plants."

"Are these twins still with you?" Wabeno asked.

"Yes," she said, smiling, "they are standing right behind you. Can't you see?"

Wabeno snorted. "You could use their help now," he said.

"Yes, but there is only me and I am afraid, brother," she said. "I pretend to be strong for my people, but I am weak. I am nothing. I'm just an old blind woman, chosen by my people because I survived the demon's attack. They think I have some power to protect them, but I know it is not so."

Wabeno took her hand in a caress. "I too am afraid," he said. "As afraid as a rabbit in the teeth of a fox or a mouse in an eagle's beak. We are both weak, sister, but together we might be strong."

"Against the *Hanishé*?"

"It has no chance against us."

"Then you are a foolish man."

"Yes, but that is why I am here."

Wabeno learned that although the towns of the Haudenosaunee seemed mighty in appearance, they were abandoned after a single generation.

"After a time, the fields grow barren, and the game is hunted out for many days around," Walking Turtle said. "And as the years pass, the insects chew our longhouses and pickets to ruin with the help of the rain and snow. There is no stopping them. The old town grows shabby and tumbles down, while our people begin to starve. But long before this our grandmothers find a new place, guided by our hunters, and our men set out to prepare the way."

So it was that the Big Town, Ga-ogwah Kanotaye, had risen above the Lake of the Mohawks within the last ten summers. Fires had been set to clear the land for the crops, and gangs of men had been sent to the hills to topple pines for the palisade.

"It took many hands to build this place, but also the captives of many peoples who were welcomed into our families," Walking Turtle said.

"You took our people," Wabeno said dryly.

"Yes." She spread her hands. "It is the way of things. That is why we returned them when we sought your help, though many chose to stay."

"Mmm." They sat in silence for a time, listening as a loon flew overhead.

Wabeno had marveled at the palisade, which took thousands of trees. "Why is your wall needed?" he asked, at last. "There are so many of you; who would dare to attack?"

"Oh, brother, we have enemies, including your own people," she replied. "The Eries to the west, the Wendats to the north and the Susquehanna to the south among them. But long ago our greatest enemy was ourselves as we fought each other. The hills and rivers ran red with our blood for many lifetimes, with revenge laid upon revenge in feuds that never ended. It was only when the Great Law of Peace came among us that we learned to live together."

Wabeno knew that there were five tribes of the Haudenosaunee—the Seneca, Cayuga, Onondaga, Oneida, and Mohawk. These same peoples had warred against the Anishinaabek as they made their Long Walk to the west.

But as Walking Turtle told it, the five tribes had once been locked in furious warfare and blood feuds for as long as their grandfathers' grandfathers could remember, with nothing but more blood and tears to come.

"In time, we were utterly broken, yet we found a way out of the hatred that made us its slaves," she said. "It was the Great Law of Peace, brought to us by a prophet of the Wendat named Deganawidah."

"I have heard of him. But why did he come to you?"

"Oh, just like you, out of curiosity," she replied. "There are many stories of Deganawidah, but I will tell you one. It is said that he came to us in a white canoe made of stone. How this is possible, I do not know; perhaps it was only made of white birch that we took to be stone. But although Deganawidah brought a message of one-ness and peace, he had great trouble with his tongue and could barely speak."

"A crow had his tongue," Wabeno said, thinking of those who stuttered among his own people.

"Yes. But as he wandered, Deganawidah came upon Ayenwatha, an orator of the Onondaga people whose words were as sweet as songs. People loved his voice and clamored to hear his stories. Together, they traveled through the lands of our warring peoples, bringing us together. Some say that the spirit-woman, Jigonsaseh, also took a hand, telling our women to stop feeding the warriors until they gave up fighting their cousins, though I suppose she told our women to deny them more than that."

"And was the peace so easily won?"

"Ah, no, there were holdouts. The last branch in the Tree of Peace was that of the Onondagas, who live to the east. A powerful shaman held them in his hand. He was Tododaho, a sorcerer who wove snakes into his hair and terrified all who dared to look upon him."

Walking Turtle took a draw on her pipe and blew a long plume of smoke as the story came to her.

"Tododaho was jealous of Ayenwatha, and he killed his three daughters," she went on. "He was a *Hanishé*, like our own terror, but Ayenwatha believed so deeply in Deganawidah's message that he never sought revenge. He vowed that no man should ever feel the pain of such a loss, not even Tododaho."

"That seems unlikely," Wabeno said. "Who would not avenge his own children? Perhaps he was simply afraid."

"Perhaps," she agreed.

"Perhaps this Tododaho has returned," Wabeno mused. "Perhaps he is the *Hanishé*."

"*He-eh,* no, he was only a man."

"Yet somehow he was tamed."

"Not tamed but shown his error. Deganawidah came to him with a single arrow and challenged him to break it. This was easily done, but then Deganawidah gave Tododaho a bundle of five arrows and challenged him again. Though he tried with all his strength, he could not break them, and his eyes were opened to the strength of five tribes of the Haudenosaunee bound as one. He joined our tree of peace on the condition that our councils meet at the great town of the Onondagas whenever there are decisions to be made. And brother, know this," she concluded. "Every sachem from the five tribes must agree before the Haudenosaunee will act. It was the council at Onondaga that allowed me to summon you and the shamans of other lands."

"But surely the Haudenosaunee have many shamans of their own."

"They have come, and they have gone, and the *Hanishé* remains."

Wabeno felt a chill in the air as he thought of the might of the Haudenosaunee with their countless warriors and the many shamans that they surely had at their beck.

"I don't know if we can help you if your own medicine is not strong enough," he said. "What can we do?"

Walking Turtle cleared her throat and sat a little taller. "This *Hanishé* is an outside thing," she said. "That is all that our shamans could tell us. They said it would take those from outside our lands to bury it."

Wabeno scoffed at this, thinking it was all too often the excuse of a false medicine-maker, but he held his tongue. Instead, he asked, "Sister, forgive me, but I would know. What took your eyes?"

Walking Turtle turned to him with her sightless eyes reflecting silver as they caught the sun. "A demon took them when I was only a child."

CHAPTER 9

THE SEVEN SHAMANS

Then began the Rite of the Seven Shamans as it came to be known in the stories told thereafter. Each of the shamans who'd been summoned was challenged to weave the magic that would rid Ga-ogwah Kanotaye of the *Hanishé*.

Wolf watched their efforts through skeptical eyes. Although he had neglected his lessons in the five years he had spent with the shamans of the Ojibwe, he knew enough of magic to sort trickery from truth. And though most of the shamans gathered at Ga-ogwah Kanotaye conducted themselves with dignity and had the appearance of sorcerers of great power, there were times when Wolf thought their strivings were little more than comedy.

As for Wabeno, for the most part he found his companions among the shamans to be wearisome. "Most are old men who mumble and brag without end," he complained to Wolf, "yet I doubt they could heal a wart."

"Perhaps they say the same of you," Wolf replied.

"They are too busy pissing in my ears with their deeds to give a thought to me," Wabeno scoffed.

Things did not go well from the outset.

The first attempt was by the phallus-dangler of the Illini, who had a leering face and the look of a man with addled wits. He appeared in the square before the Great Lodge wearing a headband that was festooned with corn tassels. Rather than a breechclout, he wore a skirt of long corn leaves and between his legs was a young corn stalk that raised trills of laughter from the women in the crowd. It stuck out the length of his arm at both his front and behind as he gripped it below his groin.

"What foolishness is this?" Wolf asked as he and Wabeno stood off to the side.

"He means to do a fertility dance," Wabeno replied.

"How would this frighten the demon?"

Wabeno only chuckled in reply.

Freeing a hand, the shaman of the Illini pulled a flute fashioned from a heron's leg bone from the cord around his waist and gripped it between his teeth. He blew a tuneless strain as he shambled toward one knot of women after another, bobbling his corn stalk tassel at the delta of their legs. Some squealed with laughter but others wrinkled their faces in disgust and waved him away. Word passed around the square that perhaps his own man-thing could not rise as well as the cornstalk cock which dipped up and down in the manner of a dousing stick.

As he danced on, the shaman of the Illini looked increasingly lecherous, and this was his undoing. A beautiful young woman waved him away with a look of contempt, but he persisted to the point of sweeping his corn tassel across her groin. It was too much; her lover stepped from the crowd with a face that was black with anger and slapped the shaman hard in the face, knocking his flute from his lips. Gaping like a beached fish, the shaman dropped his corn stalk and hurried from the square, looking over his shoulder.

A roar of laughter and groans rolled over the square as the remaining shamans looked on in chagrin.

"He is a clown," Wolf said.

"Yes, a clown, but it is a bad beginning for us," Wabeno replied. "Already the people scorn us."

"You are too quick to judge," Wolf reproached him. "What have you planned?"

"Planned?"

"Your ceremony. How will you defeat their demon?"

Wabeno grimaced, took a deep breath, and sighed heavily. "Young one, you know as well as I," he said. "I am waiting for a sign."

Barely had the shaman of the Illini left the square when the call of the *Hanishé* came wafting from far off in the distance, as if mocking his dance.

Wolf listened to its call intently. It was no animal, of that he was sure, yet neither did it sound quite human. There was something akin to bird-song in its call, like the honking of a goose or the trumpeting of a swan.

The next day brought forth a spirit-dancer of the Wendat. Although the Wendats were avowed enemies of the Senecas, there were often times of peace and even trade, and now the people of their southernmost tribe, the Attignawantan, had been invited to send their best. Their shaman and his helpmates had been escorted into town with an honor guard of Seneca warriors, who made him feel as welcome as they would one of the Haudenosaunee's own sachems. There was a great feeling of fellowship and friendship in his visit, but of course, such is the way of things that it did not last.

The spirit-dancer did wonders, juggling a baton high in the air with only his feet and catching it with the same as he flipped on his back. Then came a series of tricks as he bobbled the wand with his feet, performing somersaults and other feats of agility, each more ingenuous than the last. The crowd in the plaza uttered many *oohs!* and *aahs!* as the juggler worked himself into a gleaming sweat. As darkness fell, each end of the baton was set afire with a burning pitch. The dancer whirled the flaming baton in the darkness until it grew into a fiery disc, outshining the moon as he chanted a spell known only to the Wendats.

"He means to draw the *Hanishé* into his whirlwind and consume it with fire," Wabeno said as he and Wolf stood watching in the deepening gloom. "This is powerful medicine. I think he has a chance."

"But grandfather, you scoffed at this thing being of the spirits," Wolf said, remembering their talk on the way south.

"Do you think that I know everything?" Wabeno snapped in irritation. "I have never seen a demon walking the earth."

"But you would like to."

"Of course," the old man nodded.

"If this is true then we will see the *Hanishé*'s shade drawn through the air as it is summoned," Wolf said, though he did not think so.

Time passed and the flames at each end of the baton began to die. With a final flourish, the spirit-dancer tossed the baton high in the air, fell on his back, and caught it with his feet. It was a rich entertainment for the bored farmers of the town, and howls of acclaim rained down upon him from around the square.

The Wendat spirit-dancer was given high praise for his ceremony, with vows that his people and the Seneca would soon be united once again. Many young men tried to recreate his fire dance in times to come, getting burned for their foolishness. Many of these would war against the Wendat in the years to come, forgetting their promises of peace.

But as had been the case on the night before, an eerie cry came floating over the fields and just as suddenly, the flames of the whirling baton went dead.

A smoke-seer of the Mahicans came next, vowing that he would trace the *Hanishé* in the confines of a sweat lodge to divine its intentions. "I will see it walking in the smoke and from this we will know how to act," he said.

When all was ready, the Mahican stripped and entered the sweat lodge, which was already engulfed with more smoke than he wished, but it was too late to back out. As soon as he entered the darkness of the hut, he discerned patterns in the smoke revealed by the thin light coming in from the smoke hole above.

"I see it moving!" he called out, loud enough for all to hear outside.

"I think not," Wabeno said to Wolf as they waited outside. He had endured the smoke-seeing ceremony himself once, coming away with only a bad cough and burning eyes.

Inside the sweat lodge the Mahican could barely breathe, and only by fanning the dense smoke furiously could he keep from coughing himself raw.

Little did he know that the Seneca had brought him the wrong wood for the ceremony, not understanding his request. As any woman knows, there is wood that throws little smoke, which is used to heat a lodge at night. Then there is wood that throws a little more, which can be used for cooking the day's meal. But wood that throws much smoke is best used at the border of a village as smudge to keep insects at bay in the summer.

It was this last that the Seneca provided, and it proved too much. As the afternoon wore on, there came a few choking exclamations from the sweat lodge and then a long silence as his fellow shamans called out to the Mahican in vain. At last, Wolf brushed them aside and crawled into the lodge, holding his breath. He grabbed the Mahican by his feet and dragged him outside, as dead as a stone.

And again, came the call of the *Hanishé.*

Now the remaining shamans grew restive, with some claiming that it was the *Hanishé*'s evil spirit that had entered the sweat lodge to take the life of the Mahican and had likely eaten his shade as well. They began to fear for their own shades upon their deaths, imagining them caught in teeth of the *Hanishé* and devoured, leaving them with no way to pass on to the Spirit Land.

Of the four remaining shamans, only Wabeno showed no fear. "Ah, my shade will be too tough for the *Hanishé*," he said when asked his opinion. "It will break its teeth if it dares to bite."

Wolf was of the same mind.

"We have come on a fool's mission," he said to Wabeno at the Mahican's death ceremony. "Whatever the *Hanishé* is, it has nothing to do with the Anishinaabek."

He chafed at being away from Willow, who was likely having a rough time with the villagers and their ignorant talk of witchcraft. He also knew that even though the villagers had been given Wabeno's direst warning, they might well harm Willow and Found by the River anyway, claiming that there had been an accident.

"Patience," Wabeno counseled. "It is an honor to have been called here, and we will soon be gone."

"Gone? We should be away from here as soon as we can. I have a bad feeling about home."

"Home?"

"That wretched village that you sent me to. I don't trust those who live there."

"Ah, don't worry. Your wife is a wildcat when she wants to be. She will beat them bloody."

"Grandfather, two women cannot stand against many," Wolf said in exasperation. Couldn't the old man see?

"The villagers will have my curse on their heads," Wabeno said mildly.

"That will be no solace if they have no fear of it. If my wife is harmed, it will be you that is cursed."

"We will see, wild one, and we will leave soon, as you wish. But I have some thoughts on this *Hanishé* that honks like a goose yet howls like a wolf. I have a mission for you."

"I'll go beyond the fence and wrestle the *Hanishé* myself if it will get us out of here," Wolf growled.

"Not that, but this." Wabeno told him his thoughts. Wolf nodded and said, "As you wish. There will be wings on my feet."

The fourth shaman was a woman of the Mohawks, who lived far to the northeast. She was a shaggy woman in her mid-years who rustled forward in a cloak of turkey feathers with her face painted gray with ashes.

The woman was a finder, skilled in finding lost things. She was consulted when the Mohawks wished to know the movements of their enemies and where to find them. She could find the right man for any woman. She could also find a cheater when a man or woman had been cuckolded. For this last thing she had many beseechers.

She used the fire ceremony to find what she was looking for, ignoring the spirits, who could be whimsical, and even deceitful. Wabeno knew of the fire ceremony, of course, and had used it himself on occasion, but he was eager to see how it was practiced among the people who were called the "man eaters."

As darkness fell, the shaman drew a circle in the center of the plaza, and then, blindfolded, she placed a forest of pine splinters within its bounds. Then, lifting her blindfold, she took a torch and carefully lit each one. It took a long time before all were lit, and many were extinguished before she had finished.

But most blazed on as she sat before them, mesmerized by the fire. The watching crowd held its breath as one-by-one, the blazing splinters died, trailing smoke.

At last, all of the splinters were extinguished, and she called for torches and three fires to be lit outside the circle. When these were ablaze, she looked intently upon her work. Some of the splinters had barely burned, others had flamed nearly to the ground. She gave a satisfied grunt.

"The *Hanishé* comes from far away," she said solemnly. "It plans to stay with you forever."

Standing close to one of the fires outside the circle, Walking Turtle grimaced. "Yes, this we know already," she said. "But how will you rid us of this thing?"

The disheveled shaman of the Mohawks looked up at her with a mild look as if gazing upon a fool. "Grandmother," she said. "My purpose here is to find your demon. I have no power to sway it."

And again came the howl from afar, bellowing as if from the bowels of the earth.

Quaking with fear, the fifth shaman consumed a scallop shell of mushrooms the next day, hoping they would calm his senses as he journeyed to the spirit world. There, he hoped to speak with those unseen beings who might reveal the mystery of the *Hanishé* and how to kill it.

But, as Wolf knew, that was a fearsome journey. He had spoken with the spirits only once before and had been badly frightened, vowing never to visit them again. There were dark things beyond this life, clawing at the curtain that held them back, and all who risked entering their domain did so at their peril.

But the fifth shaman vouched that he had visited the spirits often, sometimes in the guise of an otter, which is what he called himself. The Otter, Dawe-do, was of the Susquehannock people to the southeast and had been more than eager to reveal his powers when he arrived at Ga-ogwah Kanotaye.

But that was before the smoke-seer met his doom, and now thoughts of the *Hanishé* lurking behind the curtain of life filled him with terror. *Only as an otter could he pass unnoticed among the spirits*, he thought as he choked down the last of the mushroom shreds with a tea made from elderberries.

Little did he know that there were many spirits that the shamans of the Haudenosaunee had already consulted, finding no word of the *Hanishé* among them.

Nor did he know that the spirits friendly to the Haudenosaunee were not always kind to the Susquehannocks.

Beyond the veil of life, he might well meet the skin-eating giant Stone Coat, *Ge-no*-sgwa, and other spirits that hungered for his shade.

Otter refused to enter the sweat lodge where the Mahican had died, choosing to begin his journey in the Great Lodge itself with Wolf and Wabeno to watch over him during his trance.

"He is a brave man," Wolf said. "Surely he knows that there are ghosts here."

"He thinks of ghosts as we think of shadows," Wabeno replied. "And that is just what they are—shadows of this life—but few men can endure them. Imagine if men leapt in fear at their own shadows! But that is our way with ghosts."

"Hah! Many men do leap at their shadows," Wolf replied. "Do you fear them old man?"

"Of course," Wabeno nodded, "but I also fear spiders and hornets. Ghosts? They are no different to me."

Sitting at the doorway of the Great Lodge as the sun dimmed, Wolf and Wabeno softly padded fingertips on the buckskin of flat drums as Otter slipped into his trance under the influence of the mushrooms. He did not meet the *Hanishé* on the other side, but neither did he return.

Otter heard Wolf and Wabeno's drumbeat as he made his way to the spirits and found the sound comforting. But ahead lay a great darkness, lit at times with lightning flickers of many colors and hues that he had never seen before. Moving in the darkness were odd things—big things!—shapeless to his vision and slowly taking form. He had become an otter moving among them, feeling sleek and swift, but an otter for all its guile is still a meek thing, and the mushrooms had done little to ease his fear. If anything, they made it grow stronger.

He found himself laughing as great forms reared up in the darkness. But it was laughter drenched in sobs. There was Stone Coat, with tatters of skin hanging from his maw! There was a snake with the head of a crow! Behind them was a spectral lynx with blazing eyes, creeping his way with gnashing fangs. Their eyes glittered as a skein of lightning flickered around them.

Otter scrambled back in his trance, hoping to swim away as swiftly as his spirit animal could allow, but his feet seemed mired in mud, and he could barely lift them. He struggled to awaken but could not find his way. The spirits of the Haudenosaunee engulfed him as he began to sink, and dimly he heard the drumbeat growing louder and louder, pounding at his chest as if it were his own heart—his terror rose to heights beyond his imagination, driven higher by his pounding heart as vine-like fingers reached out to clutch him. One circled his neck and too late he realized that his journey to the spirits of the fierce Haudenosaunee had been a terrible mistake.

At the mouth of the Great Lodge, Wolf and Wabeno heard Otter give a choking scream as he clutched at his chest with a look of stark terror on his face. Before they could catch him, he toppled over, dead at their knees.

That was all it took for the last shaman remaining, besides Wabeno. On the following day, he made his excuses and fled, shame-faced and showered with dog excrement by a jeering crowd as he hurried from the walls of Ga-ogwah Kanotaye.

"It is our path now, grandfather," Wolf said as they watched the disgraced shaman flee with no escort to guide him.

"Mmm … What have you found?"

"It was as you suspected."

Wolf had made a careful inspection of Ga-ogwah Kanotaye's palisade, hobbling along its entire length. Not all of the pickets were stout pines; many were no thicker than a man's leg and some as thin as an arm. It was these that Wolf sought out, and nearing a place along the wall where it came closest to the Great Lodge, he found what he was looking for. Two of the thinner pines had been severed at the height of his knees, then patched with a mixture of sap and sawdust to hide the disturbance. A hinge was created by a binding of hemp rope higher up. Giving the pines a shove, Wolf found that they eased open wide enough to allow a man to enter if he crawled in sideways. He returned the pines to their places and daubed them as best he could to hide the rupture.

That afternoon Wabeno was summoned by Walking Turtle.

"I suppose that you too will be fleeing," she said in a stiff way, facing straight ahead with a stone face.

"Sister, no."

"No?"

"No. I have a feeling about your *Hanishé* that will soon be revealed. But for now, I would give you this."

He reached into the medicine bag worn around his neck and pulled out a small stone, fastened with a leather cord.

"What is this?" she asked, confused. Its surface was unpolished, and by her touch it seemed nothing more than a pebble, pierced with a tiny hole through which a cord had been threaded. "A stone?"

"It is my gift to you, sister."

"But what has this to do with the *Hanishé*?"

"Nothing, but in time you will see why it has come to you."

"And what will you do now?" she went on, flustered. "What is your ceremony? What are your tricks? What…"

"Shh…" Wabeno replied, taking her hand. "No tricks, sister, and no ceremony. Tell your people to bring me to your dead."

"Our dead?"

"Yes, those who died in the Great Lodge. Bring them from their graves. I will meet with them."

CHAPTER 10

THE DEAD

Many protested disturbing the dead in their graves, but Wabeno was obeyed, and his standing among the Seneca rose nonetheless because who but the greatest of shamans would dare to speak with the dead?

"You will wake them, brother, and they will walk among us," Walking Turtle said.

"Sister, they murmur in your Great Lodge already," Wabeno replied. "They will not sleep until they are avenged."

Timidly, she asked, "My man … do you hear him?"

Wabeno had forgotten that Walking Turtle's husband was among those killed, and now, he regretted speaking of ghosts as she seemed to shrivel into herself.

"They are only dark forms without words, sister," he said in a low voice. "Forgive me for speaking of them."

"Tell him I will join him soon."

He nodded, "I will take care with his body."

The seven dead elders had been buried together on a hill outside of town. There were other signs of recent diggings, and Wolf realized that it was a graveyard as they trudged up the hill.

But scattered among the graves were a number of shattered platforms, and Wolf could see that they had stood on poles as tall as two men before their ruin.

"The *Hanishé* did this," Long Tongue said in a low voice. He had accompanied them to the burial ground. "We buried the seven elders in the sky, as is the custom with all of our dead, and the monster came in the night, tearing down the scaffolds and dishonoring the elders. It carved their bodies—they were mutilated! It is why they lie beneath the ground now in the hope that it will not dig them up to dishonor them again."

"Why didn't your warriors watch over the dead?" Wolf asked, knowing the answer as soon as the words left his lips.

"Who would dare to stand watch?" Long Tongue replied. "The dead are fearful enough, but the *Hanishé*..." His words trailed off as he looked over the field of graves.

"Our dead rest here until we move the town again," he continued. "Then we will have the Feast of the Dead, making us one again."

"All of them?"

"Yes. It is forbidden to include those who died by violence in the feast, for they are angry spirits, but Walking Turtle says she will allow it."

"I have heard of it," Wolf said. "This ceremony is practiced among the Nipissing and the Wendats."

"It is much the same," Long Tongue replied. "We are cousins of the Wendats and live in much the same way. Our fields are the same, and our lodges and towns. Though we are enemies we speak the same tongue. Some say that we were all one people long ago."

"Why are you enemies then?"

Long Tongue gave him a puzzled look, as if he had never considered such a thought. "Because we are."

Wolf scoffed at this, "It is the same everywhere with people fighting like two stags in rut when they could just as easily live in peace."

"Yes, older brother, it is true."

"Tell me of your feast then."

"You do not have this? No, for you are a simple people," Long Tongue said to Wolf's annoyance. "Whenever the Seneca move a town, we unearth our dead and mingle their bones in a single grave so that they may rejoin their families and friends. It is a great celebration that lasts for ten days or more with feasting, dancing, and feats of great strength and daring by our warriors. The spirits of the dead eat with us; we set out food for them. I saw the feast myself when I was a boy! It is the great wonder, and all look forward to the time when our own bones will be mingled."

"These bones, there must be many after so many years," Wolf mused, thinking that he would not care to have his own bones treated in such a manner.

"Oh yes, many bones and more skulls than any man can count," Long Tongue nodded. "As many as pebbles in a river. We scrape the dead down to their bones and bury them in a pit lined with beaver hides. The pit is deeper than a tall man, sometimes deeper than two men, and many steps long. Then we shower them with gifts—pots, tobacco, clothing, weapons—all to help them in the place of the spirits."

"But what of the newly dead?" Wolf said with a grimace. "They would stink."

"They are treated just the same, even those who are rotted and crawling with worms. Our women strip their flesh and scour the bones. And know this, grandfather, they are bound to do it with no sign of sickness or disgust."

"Uh," Wolf grunted. "Then I think that the women of the Seneca are the true warriors and their men are chipmunks."

Long Tongue laughed at this. "It is true that they have stronger stomachs!"

Indeed, it was a party of women trailing behind them who offered to unearth the slaughtered elders, but Wabeno waved them away when they came to the graves. "We will do it ourselves," he said to Wolf.

"You mean me, old man," Wolf said hinting at sarcasm.

"*Ehn*, thank you." Wabeno nodded. "My old bones are useless."

"I will dig joyfully."

"*Ehn.*"

Wolf took up a hoe tipped with the shoulder blade of an elk and scraped at the earth, striking a sheath of elm bark only a knee's length under the ground. This was weighed down with several large stones in the hope of keeping wolves, coyotes and other creatures from digging up the dead. With the help of Long Tongue, Wolf lifted the bark and reeled back at the smell of death. Trying not to gag, he peeled back a wrapping of beaver hide, and a woman's face looked up at them, or what was left of it. Soil filled her eyes, and the withered flesh of her face was a ghastly gray-green.

But it had been only two moons since the slaughter, and the wounds on her head were still apparent. Wabeno examined them carefully, measuring the spaces in between the slashing cuts with his fingers.

"Another one," he said. "We need another one."

A stink filled the air, and it was a hotter morning than usual, making their task all the more oppressive. But what man has not filled his nostrils with the smell of death? Wolf labored on next to the old woman's corpse, unearthing the body of a painfully thin man who seemed birdlike in his frailty.

"It is Walking Turtle's man. He looks as old as the moon," Wabeno said, reaching in to brush the soil from the corpse's head. "Pardon us, father. We come to avenge you, if we can. Let us dig around here a bit."

One of the women onlookers gave him a hand broom. "Use this," she said.

"Thank you, sister." Wabeno swept around the dead man's head. Unlike most of the Senecas his head was not plucked clean, and his long gray hair made his wounds harder to discern.

"His hair is matted with blood," Wabeno said, as he searched the dead man's scalp for cuts. "There ... and there," he said at last. "And there."

Once again Wabeno measured the space between the wounds with his fingers, grunting at what he found.

"A weapon did this," he said, looking up at Wolf who stood leaning against his hoe. "But not like any weapon we know."

"A weapon? Not claws?"

"No, and not of flint either."

"Then obsidian."

Wabeno pried at the dead woman's head wounds again. "Perhaps," he said.

Together, with what Wolf had discovered at the palisade, they made plans to share their findings with Walking Turtle. But starting down the hill from the cemetery, they heard a strange bugling sound along with drumming in the distance, and over the broad pathway leading south from Ga-ogwah Kanotaye, they saw a cloud of dust.

Up ahead, the people of the town were streaming from its entrance and rushing up from the fields. A handful of warriors started down the path at the head of the crowd but with little conviction that an attack was underway. War was always waged at dawn, not under the full sun with the blare of conch shells and the beat of drums.

The people of Ga-ogwah Kanotaye covered the hillside as the procession came on. There looked to be over one hundred men, women, and children coming in the distance, beating drums or clacking sticks together in time as their conch shells bugled and blared.

But a greater wonder was the figure striding at the head of the crowd, dressed in a white tunic embroidered with strange symbols. He was a tall, well-built man wearing a crown of multicolored feathers, each as long as a man's forearm, with two brilliant white egret wings attached to either side of the headdress above his ears. It gave him the look of a giant.

Huge copper earrings dangled from his ears, while copper bracelets circled his arms. This, and his staff was topped by a copper disc, wider than a man's outstretched hand and polished to a high sheen. All knew that it could only be a symbol of the sun.

But it was his dark and impassive face that sent a gasp through the crowd, for turning toward the hill under the full glare of the sun, his face lit up as if it had been struck by lightning—glittering, shining, radiating as bright as the sun itself. It was as if his face was made of crystal—the face of a god. He raised his arms, and his headdress fluttered like a rainbow drawn to earth.

"I am Sun Dog," he thundered in a deeply accented voice. His words rang over the multitude spilling down the hillside, awestruck at his dazzling face.

"Bring me to Walking Turtle. I have come to kill your demon!"

CHAPTER 11

NO MAN CAN KILL ME

Eya, the sensation that swept through Ga-ogwah Kanotaye at Sun Dog's coming was like that of a miracle as the people of the town roared a welcome. Performing a pirouette that sent his feathered headdress whirling, Sun Dog's crystalline face vanished, revealing the features of a man with a noble air. He called over his shoulder to one of his followers, who rushed forward with a small cedar box. Then, without seeking permission from the Seneca warriors lining the path to the town, he made his way past them up the hill just as Walking Turtle was being escorted down by two women.

They met halfway to the town's entrance with hundreds looking on, and although Walking Turtle could not see, she had been told of the newcomer's magical appearance and of his followers.

"He is before you," one of her sister-cousins whispered in her ear.

Sun Dog raised a hand, silencing the drums and conch shells behind him. Silence reigned for several long moments, and then slowly, he dropped to his knees.

"Grandmother, I have come with a gift," he said, extending the box.

Walking Turtle nodded, and one of her attendants retrieved the box, placing it in her hands. She turned it over and returned it to her sister-cousin unopened.

"Stranger, how should I know you?" she asked.

"Know me as your friend," he replied. He had a strange accent and spoke in a tongue similar to that of the Chelaque people living far to the southeast who shared the same language as the Seneca. Same, but different.

"A friend? How?"

"I have heard your peoples' tears. The birds have come calling to me, begging me to come. I have come to free you from the demon that haunts your fields."

"But what of these people?"

Sun Dog hesitated. He had hoped not to broach the subject so quickly.

"If you will have us, we hope to live among you," he said slowly. "We have heard the greatness of your people and have much to offer in return."

Walking Turtle gazed back at him through sightless eyes with her face showing no emotion. The Seneca were always hungry for more people to swell their families and increase their *orenda*, but these were times when one must be wary.

"How will you free us?" she asked at last.

"I bring the powers of the south," he said. "I bring mysteries that are unknown to your people, indeed to all the peoples of the north."

"And you know of this *Hanishé*?"

Sun Dog rose to his feet with a rustle of feathers. "I do, and I have no fear of it," he said. "I have wrestled with a feathered serpent and have commanded a monster of the earth. My people know this! Ask them! Your demon will obey me."

A finger of ice ran down Walking Turtle's back as she weighed his words. If this sorcerer was powerful enough to defeat the *Hanishé*, then it occurred to her that he might also be a threat to her people once the demon was gone. She brushed the thought aside and motioned for Sun Dog's gift.

Opening the box, she found a long string of beads similar to pearls and just as smooth. Each bead was shaped as perfectly as the next.

The women beside her gasped. "It is a thing of great beauty," one said. "The beads are of many colors, and you can see through them!"

"Thank you, sister," Walking Turtle said to her, "I imagine it is so." She closed the box and handed it back to her for safekeeping.

"You are welcome, Sun Dog, but first we must see some proof of your powers."

"Everyone will see," he promised. "Everyone."

Wolf and Wabeno had witnessed the meeting off to the side and followed Walking Turtle as she made her way back up the hill. Sun Dog had requested that a lodge be constructed outside the town's palisade to prove that he had no fear of the *Hanishé*. But he also asked that his own people be sheltered within the town, and there was a hubbub not unlike a bazaar that afternoon as those in need came forward to claim one of the newcomers.

Walking Turtle had given her assent after listening to one of her sister-cousins, who described the newcomers as a ragged people who looked as if they had been on a long, hard journey. She deduced that they were no threat and also that her people were eager to welcome them. A mother was needed here, a husband required there. Children were eagerly gathered, but always along with their mothers. The newcomers had learned something of the Seneca's language, thanks to a young man of the Chelaque people who had traveled with them. There was a feeling that the town's *orenda* had gained mightily by their arrival. The townsfolk gabbled happily over the cooking fires in their longhouses that evening, marveling at the people from the south and plaguing them with questions that they were hard-pressed to answer.

But Wabeno was skeptical of Sun Dog's claims and said as much when he met with Walking Turtle that evening.

"We don't need another magic-maker," he said, "We need a warrior."

He and Wolf shared their findings. The dead had the markings of a weapon, while two timbers of the palisade had been severed, making it possible for an intruder to enter the town unseen. "Your monster dwells in the forest," Wabeno said. "It is not of the spirits. It can be killed, but not by a shaman."

"Sun Dog says he will kill it," she said.

"*Ehn,* and so did the shamans gathered from the winds," Wabeno replied. "He will have his tail up and running in his own time."

"How then do you explain his glittering face?" she asked. "My people say it beamed like the sun."

"A magician's trick."

"I suspect you are jealous, brother," she said with a light smile on her lips.

"I only know what I know, sister. Call your greatest warriors, and I will call mine. Let Sun Dog weave his spells in the meantime, but be ready when he fails."

"As you wish, brother," she said mildly. "As you wish."

As had been the case with the call to seven shamans, runners were sent out the next morning, calling for the mightiest warriors from any tribe that would listen. All who heard the summons knew it would be a great honor to do battle with the *Hanishé,* a boast upon which a warrior could claim his place as a star in the night sky.

Yet what came two days later gave Wabeno second thoughts, just as it took the hearts of the townsfolk prisoner. Sun Dog vowed that he would escape death itself to prove his powers.

His people had built a shabby hut of bark, brush, and old corn stalks at the center of Ga-ogwah Kanotaye's square. It appeared little more than the burrow of an animal. Clay pots filled with coals were placed on either side of the hut, and alongside these were torches of pitch and flax.

That evening, while the summer sun was still high above the horizon, Sun Dog had conch shells blown after the day's meal, drawing a host of onlookers to the square. Callers were sent running through the lanes, telling of a great deed to be witnessed by all. Soon, the square was seething with townsfolk gathered in a circle fifty steps from the hut.

There was a pounding of drums, and then Sun Dog stepped from the hut wearing his white sheath embroidered with mystic signs. His arms and face were painted red with vermilion, and there was a handprint of red paint on his tunic above his heart.

"Bring me your best bowman!" he cried.

A murmur ran through the crowd and someone shouted, "Stone Eagle!"

Yes, Stone Eagle, Ga'sgwa-a Do-nyodah, the best of the best, proven in many competitions. It wasn't long before he emerged from the crowd with his bow and a quiver of arrows.

"What is this?" he asked.

"Sun Dog asks that you kill him," one of the newcomers said in halting words. "You must place an arrow in his heart."

Stone Eagle replied with a low chuckle. "Your sachem is a mad man!"

"Yes, but that is what he begs of you." The newcomer's face was grim, and his eyes were steady. He had a long scar riven along his right cheek. "You must do it," he said. "We cannot."

Stone Eagle looked around the square with all eyes upon him, then at the crazed shaman of the newcomers. *This cannot be,* he thought.

Stone Eagle counted out thirty steps from where Sun Dog stood with upraised arms. It would have been a long shot for most men hoping to hit the mark, but Stone Eagle's arm was as steady the rock for which he had been named. He raised his bow as Sun Dog began speaking a spell in an unknown tongue and then dropped it just as quickly.

"I cannot do this," he said. "This is murder."

Sun Dog ignored him, continuing with his incantation as the crowd held its breath. One of his helpmates ran forward, pointing at Stone Eagle's bow, and then at the sorcerer, gesticulating that it must be done.

"Do it!" the crowd commanded. *"Do it!"*

Whipping his bow up, Stone Eagle fired as if not even aiming. His arrow whipped only a hands-breadth from Sun Dog's right ear and buried itself in the pines of the palisade.

Sun Dog's eyes flickered, but he kept on murmuring his spell as Stone Eagle approached him.

"It was a warning shot," Wolf said as he and Wabeno looked on.

From a distance, they saw Sun Dog speaking in the Seneca's ear, who nodded in agreement.

Stone Eagle returned to his post and sighed as he lifted his bow. It was a handsome thing, carved of hickory and strong enough to bring down a moose with a single bolt. Now, he took extra care to aim at the red hand painted on Sun Dog's chest as the sorcerer's spell grew to a shout, heard throughout the plaza.

With a twang the arrow flew, and in an instant a gush of blood erupted from Sun Dog's chest. He clutched the arrow in surprise. "You have killed me!" he cried, falling to his knees and toppling over sideways.

Brothers, sisters, the funeral was to be right then. Sun Dog's people wailed in horror, with some dropping to their knees and clutching at their faces at the death of their leader. Screams filled the air with cries of "Sun Dog! Sun Dog! No!"

Then began a drumbeat in time to the rhythm of a human heart as two of Sun Dog's men rushed forward and dragged him into the hut, trailing blood down his fine white tunic. His eyes were rolled back, and his tongue lolled from his mouth in the agony of death for all to see as his body disappeared into the entryway. Emerging, his men dipped their torches in the coals and swept flames over the brush and dried corn stalks. In a thunderclap, the hut was a tower of flames with sparks flying into the air. Every eye turned skyward, wary of the cinders catching the longhouses of the town afire. Every onlooker held their breath as the roof of the hut crackled and roared with flame, claiming the arrogant boaster who thought he could survive a shaft of the Seneca. The arrow to his heart, the burial in flame—the great shaman of the south was destined to be only a tale of folly told round the lodge fires like all the others and then forgotten.

The wind was still that night, and the stream of sparks reached their apex and died as the hut burned on. Some of the townsfolk turned away, only to hear a murmur over their shoulders that grew to a roar and ululations of awe, for exploding from the walls of the flaming hut in a towering pillar of sparks was Sun Dog, completely naked except for his paint, untouched by Stone Eagle's arrow.

Gleaming red from head to toe, he strutted from the hut, raising an arm aloft with a conch shell. Turning in a circle, he blew a note from its chamber, which was echoed by a ring of others bugling from the crowd.

"You see," he cried in a loud voice over the roaring fire. "No man can kill me!"

"What do you make of that, grandfather?" Wolf muttered in Wabeno's ear. "First his face beams like the sun and now this."

For once, age-old Wabeno was confounded, with a stricken look on his face. "We'll see," he said.

That afternoon, Wolf walked among a group of Sun Dog's people who were talking amongst themselves in the square. It was obvious from their worn faces and tattered deer hides that they had made a long journey. But to Wolf's surprise, he noted that many of the newcomers had scars all over their bodies, including their faces. Some were heavily pitted, some even missing an eye. Had Sun Dog done this to them? They seemed cowed, nervous, though perhaps this was only because they were not yet accustomed to their Seneca families.

Later, he and Wabeno sifted through the ashes of the hut, searching for a flat stone which Sun Dog might have concealed under his tunic for protection. There was nothing.

Collapsing to the ground, Wabeno sighed. "Do you believe in magic?" he asked.

"Yes, grandfather, I have seen it," Wolf replied, "though only at your feet."

"*Eya,* I do what I can. Most who practice are tricksters and witches, but this man, he is something more than a witch."

"A sorcerer."

"Yes, truly, but how? He seems a brother to the sun. Last night I spoke with the spirits, and none could say where he came from or how he came by his powers. They only knew that once, he was a small bird, fallen from its nest."

BOOK TWO

NORTHERN GEORGIA – SUMMER, 1530

CHAPTER 12

WREN

Once there was a boy named Wren, Coleyhka, who longed to become a mica trader like his mother and father when he grew to manhood.

Wren's parents lived a carefree life, trading the silvery mineral that glimmered as bright as the sun on still waters. They had a secret source of mica that they jealously guarded against other traders. Those who looked close enough swore they could see their reflection mirrored in the crystalline surface of their wares, a miracle that Wren's parents often revealed to the peoples of Coosa, a great chiefdom of the South.

It was a walk of thirty days from one end of Coosa to the other, starting from the Gray Mountains of the north to the swamplands far to the southwest. It was a sun-blessed land of pine forests mingled with oak, walnut, cedar, sweetgum, and mulberry trees. Along every river lay fields rich with maize, beans, sunflower, tobacco, and pumpkins. No one ever went hungry, except in times of the direst drought, which was not often.

Eight great towns crowned by earthen mounds surrounded by palisades made up the trade centers of Coosa along with hundreds of outlying villages. Wren was proud to say that he had been to many of them on his parents' trading expeditions. But most of all, he was proud to live in the capital of the chiefdom, which was also called Coosa. Located on a bend of a great river, Coosa had the most pyramids and mounds of any in the realm and the highest as well. Its women were legendary for their beauty and the elegance of their apparel, while its men were held to be the noblest in all the world. That, and the Exalted One, Halw-i em Mekko, made his home there atop the highest pyramid to be closer to the sun from which he was descended. Though none of his playmates would ever believe it, Wren himself had been to the top of the Exalted One's pyramid and within a few paces of the demigod.

Coosa was little known to the tribes living far to the north, except for a few Odawa traders willing to risk their lives bartering copper, furs, red pipestone, and fish nets for the riches of the south. This meant paddling for many moons across the great lakes and down a skein of rivers, often hauling their goods and canoes over long portages. This was followed by trekking over a range of mountains that looked as if they were veiled in smoke.

The Odawa rarely traveled with fewer than seven men, for the way could be dangerous. Nor did they venture any further than Coosa's northern boundary, hoping to avoid the endless wars and raids of the chiefdom. They established a trading post within sight of the mountains, and it was here that Wren's mother and father met them each summer.

Coosa's people numbered far beyond count—as many as the leaves of the forest. Most were simple farmers, dressed in animal skins and worn down by ceaseless toil in the fields and the building of mounds and pyramids. But the higher-ups were richly adorned in jewelry and dressed in fine furs and robes of many colors, spun from the inner bark of mulberry trees. To the high ones of Coosa, the traders of the Odawa, in their worn leathers and crude necklaces of bone and teeth, looked as uncouth as animals. If it were not for the treasures they brought, they would have been scorned and sent home with insulting words of disdain.

But who could resist the copper that the Odawa brought? Coosa's rulers, priests, and warriors of note prized it above all else, for most of it came from the far-off mines of Minong on the north shore of the vast lake, Kitchi Gami, and thus was so rare among the peoples of the south that they assumed that it rang with supernatural power. The canny traders of the Odawa did nothing to dissuade them of this, returning from their journeys of half a year to the south with their canoes brimming with pearls, shells, mica, tobacco, and other trade goods. As for their copper, it was hammered into amulets, bracelets, crowns, knives, and many other things treasured by the highest of the high in Coosa.

Wren's mother and father did well for themselves, gathering shells, stingray spines, sharks' teeth, pearls, and tortoise shells from the tribes living along the great salt water to the south and trading for copper from the tribes to the faraway north. Once, they even fetched the long, brilliantly colored feathers of macaws that came from the far-off jungles of the south. But it was in the silver-shining mica that they excelled. Mined in the mountain chain to the east of Coosa, it was valued by medicine-makers and as an adornment by women and men alike.

Each fall, they returned to the vast markets of Coosa. There, beneath its earthen mounds and pyramids and along its wide plazas, they bartered for the cornmeal, nuts, dried fish, and meats that sustained them through the winter months. Often, their slaves groaned beneath their loads as they settled into their winter home.

Wren loved the life, for his father was a big man among the traders of Coosa and was allowed to climb the highest pyramid in the vast town of the elites with his boy in tow. There, in the shade of a canopy of palm leaves, high above the plaza and the little people gazing up from below, Wren's father spread his multi-colored blanket, revealing his treasures to the rulers and priests who lived in the heights.

But they never saw the god-ruler, who remained hidden behind a screen. Even his name, Halw-i em Mekko, could not be spoken—the son of the Sun God was known to his people only as the Exalted One or the High One. Their goods were brought to him for examination by a priest named Black Serpent.

Black Serpent, Cetto-last-i, was on friendly terms with Wren's father, who was careful to oil his hand with a gift on every visit. These visits, it must be said, were few, because the Exalted One expected to receive gifts of copper and mica that had been worked into jewelry or fanciful implements. It was only when he had ingots or mica of singular purity that Wren's father was allowed to show them at the top of the pyramid.

But on those occasions, Black Serpent was playful with Wren, giving his head a tussle and telling him that someday he too might take his place as a helpmate of the god-ruler. This seemed almost like blasphemy, for Wren knew that the common people were required to bow low in the god-ruler's presence with their faces planted in the earth, not daring a single glance. The idea that Black Serpent would tease him with such an unlikely prospect gave him a chill.

"Would you trade for your boy?" the priest asked Wren's father. "He will walk with the high people, and I will teach him to speak with our gods."

Wren's father gave a companionable chuckle at this, as if they were two friends jesting with one another. Black Serpent had a greasy way about him and wore a necklace of rattlesnake heads with bared fangs. Wren's father had no need to even glance at the alarm on his son's face.

"You are too kind, high one," he said. "But my boy is learning the way of a trader, and his mother and I will need him to care for us when we reach the winter of our lives. Besides, who will carry our loads as we make our way through the land?"

"You have slaves," Black Serpent said.

"Yes, but they are not family and would pick at us like crows when we grow old. You know how it can be when a mouse takes the corn from a man's bowl." He nodded toward the screen where the god-ruler sat waiting.

This was a bit of a sting, but it passed over the priest's head. Black Serpent gave Wren a wistful glance but could not argue for his keeping. There was a cough from behind the curtain, and a look of irritation crossed his face as he gathered their copper ingots for the High One's review.

Wren was grateful to his father for not trading him away, even though he imagined it would have paid for ten slaves to replace him. He had no desire to serve Black Serpent, and there was much to fear in the company of the god-ruler who was known to be beyond human. Wren imagined himself tiptoeing around the heights of the step pyramid, as fettered as a bird with a broken wing.

But there was no need to grovel before the lesser elites who lived in the lodges below the pyramid, and seeing the eyes of a noble light up at the trade of a stingray's spike or a tattooed princess entranced by a tiara studded with mica filled Wren with delight, as did traveling throughout the realm of Coosa and beyond.

In his heart, Wren felt that he was a big man like his father, who had gifted him bracelets of copper. They were treasures beyond imagination to other children, and gazing upon them made him feel powerful and knowing in the ways of the world. His father was a shrewd trader and his mother a cunning helpmate, and thus, early on Wren learned how others might be twisted to one's will with praise and clever words. Bartering, he learned was a form of magic in which a tight-fisted man might be convinced to give something of great value in trade for something of little worth and leave convinced that he had come out on top of the bargain. Little did Wren know how much this skill would help him in his manhood.

As is often the way of things, it was greed that spelled doom for Wren's family. Seeing the riches that they acquired each year and the prestige they garnered from their trade with the elites of Coosa, other traders began creeping in their footsteps. Just as the portions grow smaller in a trough of corn mush when there are more mouths to feed, so it was with the mica trade.

One summer, Wren's father was enraged to discover four new traders dealing with the Odawa and hedging on his territory. And though there had been warnings from the war chiefs who defended Coosa's borders, he resolved to spend the following summer traveling north to the foothills of the Gray Mountains in the hope of meeting the Odawa before they reached their trading post.

"And why not?" he spoke to his wife. "The traders come from beyond the mountains groaning under packs filled with copper. We will meet them early on and exchange gifts long before they reach those who would eat from our bowl."

"But those are hard men who are used to living like animals while we are fat and married to our comforts," his wife protested. "And it is said that bad men roam the mountains. They'll feast on our bones."

To this Wren's father waved a dismissive hand. "We will bring two warriors with us to watch over us."

"Four. We must have four."

"No, only two. No more."

Wren's parents bartered back and forth over the number of warriors that would be required for their protection, and as is the way of things, his mother won with the toss of a dice when they decided to gamble on it. She had steadily bargained for more, and so it was that five warriors all told were enlisted with promises of copper and mica. As warriors, they were no better or worse than any of their ilk—two were barely out of their boyhood, while another was so aged that he had lost almost all of his teeth, but to Wren's eyes at least, they looked fearsome enough.

Wren's heart had pulsed at the news, for he longed to become a strong-armed warrior in defense of his parents' journey to the north, imagining himself driving off a band of thieves with the toy club his father had bartered for in the market at Coosa.

So, it was in the late spring that Wren marched at the head of his parents, five warriors and ten slaves bearing litters filled with mica, sea goods, jewelry, bolts of fine linen spun from mulberry bark, and the plumes of exotic birds. They hoped to find new trading partners or cross the paths of the copper traders heading south. For half a moon they journeyed steadily north past the last small villages of the realm, paying little heed to the warnings of the villagers or the scouts that patrolled the border. The wide path linking the villages of the north dwindled to a thin trail as they pushed along, but on either side the magnolias were at their peak, creating a tunnel of brilliant white blooms festooned among emerald-green trees, a bower that was almost blinding in the sun. Wren's mother said it was a good omen.

But not all agreed.

"There are no villages beyond the next river, only wild men and a meager people who shiver and starve in their huts when the north wind blows," the headman of the last outpost said of the mountains ahead. Beyond the village of Tali was the trading post of the Odawa, who were not expected until the coming moon. "There is still snow there, much snow, and wolves that feed on those who are foolish."

"Ah, but we have no need to cross the mountains," Wren's father said. "We only hope to meet the traders passing through and wish to know the way."

"The way?"

"Yes, the pass from the north."

At this the headman squinted and hemmed until his lips were loosened with the gift of a bracelet for his wife.

"You must go there," he pointed to a far-off notch in the mountains. "That is the way the traders come."

As an afterthought he said, "It is a place of good hunting, with many deer and bear. Our men often hunt in the hills beneath the mountains. If you set your post there, you will not go hungry."

"And do your hunters also meet the copper traders?"

"Sometimes, but there are also times when they run for their lives."

This, Wren's father did not tell his mother, but standing by his side, the boy took it in and resolved to sleep with his eyes open.

Two nights later with both eyes firmly shut, Wren was awakened by a wavering scream. But a boy of ten winters is not easily roused, and Wren huddled half dreaming beneath his blanket with feet pounding all around him along with hoarse shouts and screams filling the air long before he realized that the camp was under attack.

His father had named him Wren in the hope that he would one day fly far yet remain unnoticed by those who might do him harm, and so it was now.

Hidden beneath his blanket and nestled against a tree, he went unnoticed as the wild men of the mountains did their work, attacking from all sides at dawn. There were more than twenty of them, against whom the warriors of Coosa were no match. Only the toothless sentry died among them, brained as he sat dozing against a tree when the raiders came creeping from beneath the magnolias. All the rest were captured, the four bloodied warriors, ten slaves rounded up from their hiding places in the forest, and Wren's mother and father.

But not Wren. With a child's fancy he had plucked an armful of magnolia flowers the night before, scattering them over his blanket as the good omen that his mother had predicted. Now he lay as still as a fawn in its day bed, blending in, looking like a carpet of flowers that had fallen from the magnolia limbs as the raiders caroused only a few steps away. They knocked his parents' warriors about for a bit and kicked at the cowering slaves, but otherwise no harm came to them as they were tied one-by-one with stout cords of hemp. Wren flinched as he saw his father given a hard slap across the face when he protested their treatment. He offered all of the treasure they had packed along for trade, but this was met with sour laughs. The wild men of the mountains had come for slaves, and now they had trade goods to boot. Hurrying, with sharp blows and slaps, they commanded their captives to pick up their bundles, leading the way toward the gap in the mountains. Risking a backward glance, Wren's mother looked to where her son lay hidden beneath his wilting flowers. "Run," she mouthed silently. "Run!"

Wren followed the raiders at a distance that day, conceiving a plan to free his parents. That night, he would creep into their camp and release them from their bonds. Together they would flee to the safety of the woods.

But how? He had no knife and there would likely be a watcher, perhaps even two sentries listening for any rustle in the night. With a sick feeling he realized that even his club was useless against anything but a squirrel.

Still, he had to try, and his eyes were hard upon the faint trail down which the raiders and their captives had fled. He was only footsteps away from one of the raiders' scouts when he saw the tall man's legs.

He was a dirty man, thin as a weasel, heavily tattooed and scratched with brambles, with a long braid lopping to the side of his face. The other side of his head was plucked clean.

The raider murmured words in a language that Wren did not understand and crept toward him with outstretched arms, beckoning him forward. Wren's eyes grew as wide as the moon, and without thinking, he whipped his club at the wild man's face and ran.

Now a boy of ten winters can run like a deer, but he soon wearies and is no match for a grown man. Wren heard the tall man scrambling at his heels, growling and grunting as he drew closer. It was a chase between a rabbit and a fox that the fox was sure to win! But then, perhaps, Wren's guardian spirit intervened and whipped a thin vine of raspberry thorns across the pursuer's eyes. Wren heard a yelp and then cries of dismay as he pushed on into a thicket of shrubs. He zig-zagged deep into their concealing maze as the raider's cries grew fainter, collapsing at last with his chest heaving and the drumbeat of his heart thundering with fright.

All night he lay there, bitten by insects and chilled with no blanket to comfort him until he was sure that the scout was gone. At mid-morning he crept from the safety of the shrubs to find himself utterly lost. Climbing a tree, he looked for the notch in the mountains, but it had blended with the smoky peaks, and there was nothing to be found, nor the trail that the raiders had taken. Wren sat and wept, stifling his screams of lamentation; his mother, his father—*gone!*

What to do? What could a boy do? Wren thought of the nobles of Coosa—his father's mighty friends who lived among the clouds atop their proud pyramids. They could help! They could send a thousand warriors to fetch his parents with the wave of a hand.

Even a boy of ten knew his directions. The sun rose in the east and set in the west, and at midday it was reckoned to the south, shining down on the lush and happy land of Coosa. Snapping a stout branch between the cleft of two trees, Wren fashioned a staff that might serve as a weapon and began his journey south, marking one far-off tree and hilltop after another. He vowed that he would never rest until his mother and father were home again.

CHAPTER 13

THE MASTER

It was a full moon and a half before Wren found his way back to the capital of Coosa, starving and tattered in rags with his hair in a tangle and his thin cheeks painted gray with dust.

Wren had wandered south with few trails to guide him. Each night he shivered to his bones against the evening chill, only to awaken even colder in the morning dew, shaking like a willow in a thunderstorm. Sometimes, he followed an animal trail, only to find it disappearing into the brush. Once, he heard the growl of a cougar deep in the night and scrambled to the base of a broad oak, holding his staff before him and growling his own warning in return. Always, he was afraid, always lost, miserable, and hungry. He drank from brooks and clawed his way over and around rocky escarpments. Unable to find the notch in the mountains, he climbed them instead, spending precious days in starvation on the rocky slopes. Delirious with fear and hunger, it was five days before he found a wide trail leading south and the first of many villages. He was treated kindly by many as he passed by, but once, he felt uneasy and ran with the village dogs chasing him and peals of laughter ringing over his shoulders.

He came upon countless rivers and creeks, sometimes spending half a day in search of a ford. Twice, he came upon rivers so broad that his heart collapsed at the thought of trying to swim them; yet each time he was able to hail a passing canoe and beg for a crossing.

Some fed him as he made his way along, begging from a friendly villager or a forest-dweller who had food to spare. But at last, he was forced to trade his precious bracelets, and not at the bargain of which his father would have approved. Those who saw him reasoned that a boy in grievous need had no advantage, and thus, Wren surrendered his copper for what amounted to a few days of maize, some dried meat and a cast-off beaver robe that had been chewed full of holes by mice.

But by then, Wren had no care for copper, mica, or any of the fine things that his parents traded; his only thought was of reaching the big town of Coosa where help would surely be offered. At night, he wrapped himself as thickly as he could in the beaver robe and dreamed of revenge.

The capital lay on the bend of a river filled with dugouts bearing traders and emissaries from throughout the South. A flotilla of war canoes lined its bank, a testament to the endless wars of the chiefdom. Fed by spring floods that were heavy with silt, Coosa's outlying towns and fields of maize, sunflowers, tobacco, and other crops spread for half a day's walk in all directions, worked by countless hands. Those same hands had raised the capital's pyramids and mounds through one basket of earth at a time over many years of toil. Only an eagle flying high above could take it all in, and often, rustic visitors from the outlying lands found themselves lost amid the countless huts, avenues, temples, and markets that filled the town. Coosa was alive with long lines of farmers trudging to and from the fields, along with knots of finely dressed women and the well-off nobility strolling its avenues, stopping by its ponds, chatting in its plazas, and always, talking of the games and the athletes that gripped the passions of all who lived there.

Wren passed a long line of men and women bearing baskets of soil on their backs as he made his way into town. A new pyramid was rising in the distance, although as yet its base was only as high as a man's shoulders. Once their farm work was done, the people of Coosa often joined in raising new mounds and pyramids, knowing that their labor would be rewarded in the afterlife. It was a joyful task. Wren and his own parents had joined the line whenever they were in town, scraping soil from one of the pits beyond the palisade and piling it alongside the loads of others. Once, when he and his father were allowed to climb the Exalted One's pyramid to offer their gifts, he had looked down on the line of supplicants, thinking they looked much like a stream of ants.

It was no trouble finding Coosa's tallest pyramid where the god-ruler lived with his wives and their children. Black Serpent would surely receive him as a friend and speak to the High One on his behalf, of this he was certain. Gritting his teeth, he imagined the happy greeting and care he would receive, bathed by slaves and fitted with a tunic of fine doeskin as his tale spilled from his lips. Then he himself would lead the warriors of Coosa north to free his parents and wreak havoc on the wild men.

But the guards at the pyramid's base sniffed at the boy's tale, chuckled, and regarded him as a simpleton. Standing there filthy and in rags, Wren persisted, screaming and crying in desperation, trying to push his way past the warriors whose faces turned grim. They were heavily tattooed in bluish designs of the sun, moon, various animals, and depictions of death, making them seem even more forbidding.

"Black Serpent will see me!" he cried. "He knows me! He knows my father!"

"Black Serpent would make a feast of you, boy," a guard spoke in a gruff voice, "and he would be sure to diddle you first. Better you were ridden out of town on a lodgepole than fall into his hands."

But Wren would not be dissuaded, and he began calling Black Serpent's name up the side of the pyramid as the alarmed guards commanded him to be silent.

One of the guards had a round belly by dint of feasting on too much corn, along with the crude tattoo of an eagle on his chest, and by this Wren knew him.

"Look!" He pointed to the bracelet on the guard's wrist. "You were given this by my father! Even now he cries for your help! He..."

But gazing down from his platform, the pot-bellied guard gave him a quizzical look, lifted his sandaled heel to Wren's head and gave him a hard shove sending him flying to the paving stones.

"Away you go, young dog," he called out, laughing as Wren stared back in shock.

Bloody and bruised, Wren scrambled to his feet and stumbled to the side of the pyramid where he began climbing its steep bank.

Yet by now many passersby were watching, and one called out, "Assassin!" drawing the guards along with a mob of helpmates. Spears flew, barely missing the boy, and then a club found its mark on the back of his head, and he fell tumbling back down the pyramid's face, having gained only a few lengths of its height.

Wren would have been sent to the spirit land with a clubbing right then were it not for the guard who suddenly recalled him as the son of the trader who had gotten the best of him in the bargain for his copper bracelet. He had surrendered his prettiest daughter to Wren's father for a night of pleasure, along with a bolt of mulberry linen that she had woven with many exquisite designs, and ever since, the thin bracelet had felt as if it was cursed. It certainly was in his daughter's eyes. It was beyond reason that he would allow the trader's filthy wretch of a son to sully the gaze of the ruler above, who even now was looking down and frowning in the company of his family and nobles. Nor would he take the boy's life. It was clear that Wren was no assassin, and there would be inquiries if he was killed. He was still just a boy with no hair on his stones and with luck, he would be rounded up and fed to *Eh-noq-waa* in the Sacrifice of the Virgins.

"Long live your misery," the guard called out, clearing the way with his club and shoving Wren past the onlookers down a narrow lane. "The shitting pits need cleaning. Go and live among them."

The shitting pits—only the lowest of slaves toiled among them, dredging the filth that fed Coosa's corn fields. Yet now, Wren felt even lower than those as he stumbled down the lanes of the town with his head bleeding from where he'd been struck. Dogs and flies trailed in his footsteps, alerted to the smell of his blood. At last, he made his way to the main plaza and collapsed in agony at the foot of a tall pole that marked the end of a playing field. A fringe of scalps lined the pole along with a pendant of three skulls, threaded through with a rawhide cord. Gazing at the skulls, Wren could not have felt more dismal and alone.

Wren had been told of an uncle who lived in far-off Itaba, but he did not know his name. His father had been estranged from his brother and never spoke of him. That, however, was Wren's only family, and what is a man in this world without his family or clan? He was nothing now. His mother and father were surely dead. If only he had a knife, he would join them in the land of spirits where he would find them smiling and whole, welcoming him to a happier place beyond his wretched life. He would beg a knife, or steal one, or…

"I know you," a voice called from the side. "You are the trader's son."

Wren looked up to find an old man standing there, leaning on a staff. He was dressed in a filthy tunic of deer hide without a single adornment, tattoo, or feather. His long gray hair fell in greasy rivulets to either side of his face which was lined with crevices. His eyes were rheumy, searching. The man looked as old as the mountains.

"Where is your father? Where is your mother?" he asked, leaning down to peer at him as if he were a bug.

"Dead! All dead or taken!" Wren cried in response. The words spilled from his lips. The raiders, the killer on the trail, his long way home, his hunger, the treachery of the guard, his hopeless mission to the Exalted One…

"There, boy, have no worries," He reached down to stroke Wren's scalp as if he were a favored dog. "Come with me now. Come with me."

The old man handed him his sling of produce. "Carry this," he commanded as he turned and shuffled north through town.

A pang of hunger stabbed at Wren's belly as he considered the ancient one and his food. What else could a lost boy of ten do? He hesitated, but only for a moment. He shouldered the sling and followed along.

It was half a day's walk to the lodge, far beyond the cornfields, until they reached a low hill overlooking the valley.

"Welcome to the happy place," the old man said as they reached his tumble-down hut. "I will trade you a meal and a place to lay your bones tonight for your tale, but then you must go."

Weary almost beyond speech, Wren agreed, thinking that he would be on his way to Itaba on the morrow, hoping to find his uncle.

But as it happened, Wren was clever with his hands.

The next day he quickly mended the old man's roof, which had ushered in torrents of rain. He plucked the weeds from the garden and filled the hermit's pipe with tobacco. But mostly, he filled his ears with clever words and stories of his parents' wanderings.

"Ah, you are a fox, but I like you, youngling," the old man said as they sat smoking by the lodge fire on the second night. "You have no people. You have no family. You must stay! You can help me on the pathway to my death. In return I will teach you the secrets of the earth and of the spirits that dwell both above and below."

"But what should I call you?"

The old man pursed his wrinkled lips as he considered. "You will call me master for now, and I will call you boy until I find you fit to be called man."

And so, the bargain was struck.

CHAPTER 14

THE MONKEY AND THE SPIDER

Although the master called him his servant, Wren knew that he was little more than a slave. Still, what could be done? He was a beggar with no prospects and no hope of following in his father's footsteps as a trader. For now, at least.

The master had many curious things in his hut—a stuffed owl, along with the claws and feathers of many birds, a sheath of snake skins, various herbs hung up to dry along a wall of mud and wattle, a huge turtle shell from the far sea, and a string of animal skulls. The largest bat that Wren had ever seen was spiked to a lodgepole with its wings outstretched, and its desiccated head reared back in a fanged snarl. There was also a fox curled up in a corner, which Wren thought was dead until it raised its nose and sniffed at him. "He is the lord of this place," the master said, throwing the fox a twist of dried meat.

Most curious of all was a hideous little man, only three hands tall with large green eyes. The creature was extremely ugly, and thinking it was a demon, Wren stepped back in alarm. The little man's eyes seemed to follow him, though he realized that it was dead and stuffed like the owl. Its eyes were stones that the master had dotted with pupils.

The master gave a low chuckle and said, "It is only a monkey, traded from the same lands where we obtain macaws."

Wren had seen a monkey before, though the ghastly creature before him seemed almost unrecognizable.

"You have shaved him."

"Yes, with a blade of the black stone. And I plucked him where the blade would not suffice. It took a long time. It was very difficult."

"You cut off his tail."

"Yes," the master nodded with satisfaction.

"But why?"

"Why? To make him fearful!" he chuckled. "He looks more like a man now than a monkey, does he not? He is horrible, a terror, so much like a demon! Watch."

The master picked up the bladder of a large animal lying on a shelf and blew into it. Then, tucking the bladder into his armpit, he lifted two sticks alongside the monkey and made it dance with the help of two thin strings.

Wren was mesmerized at the monkey's dance as its long arms and legs fluttered and swayed in a crazed pantomime, yet suddenly, the old man gave the bladder under his arm a squeeze, and it gave out a piercing howl that made him jump and cry out in alarm.

The old man convulsed in laughter. "Ah, you see how easy it is to make people dance like the monkey?" he choked out the words between guffaws. "A woman fainted once at seeing him. She pissed herself! And children run screaming, though they always return for more."

Wren allowed himself a nervous laugh. "What is his name?"

"Little Demon. He is worth more than a grown man for all the gifts that are showered on me when we do a ceremony. But look here, this is his companion."

The old man pulled a box made of bark from the shelf alongside the monkey and opened it, revealing a huge spider, bigger than a man's outstretched hand and bristling with hair.

Again, Wren drew back, shivering. "This cannot be!"

"Oh yes, he comes from the same place as the monkey, far to the south in a place beyond the knowledge of most men," the master said with a satisfied nod. "You are not the only one who has done some trading."

Wren's skin crawled as he gazed at the spider and the monkey, wondering what kind of madman would toy with such things.

"You are a sorcerer, grandfather."

"Master."

"Yes."

"A sorcerer, boy," he nodded. "But more than that, just a simple magician, and sometimes a healer. I saved your father's life. That is how I know you. He was bitten by a snake when you were still a babe and was brought to me on a litter with his leg swollen as big as the pole that holds up this roof. Oh, his leg was purple and red and horribly swollen, and all thought that he would lose it. Even your mother thought so. She even brought a knife of the finest obsidian to make the cut!"

"He limped a bit," Wren said, recalling his father's gimpy way of walking.

"Yes, but he lived! The gods smiled on him, for I had just finished making a healing poultice when he was brought to me."

The old man explained that by using a sucking tube taken from the hip bone of a deer he had drawn the venom from the wound. "I stuffed the tube with milkweed down to keep the poison from reaching my lips, for that would have meant instant death. To me!"

Then the master had applied a poultice of ground walnut shells and beneficial herbs that leached the remainder of the poison from his father's wound. "Ah, your father was in agony, and your mother screamed and cried, but within a half-moon he was up and walking again, wearing the snake's skin as a belt."

"I know it well," Wren said. He had long admired his father's belt but never thought to ask of its origin. "But he must have gifted you something of great value in return."

"Ah yes, boy, he did, he did," the master nodded. He turned and lifted a box of elm bark from a shelf, lifting its lid. On the far side of the hut the fox lifted his head with a steady gaze.

"This was meant for the big man who rules us, Halw-i em Mekko, the Exalted One," he said with a sneer, "but your father gave it to me."

It was a mask, perfectly formed to a grown man's face and covered with countless bits of glittering mica. It sparkled as silvery as a mirror even in the thin light coming through the hut's door.

"Ah! I have never seen anything like it!" Wren cried, overcome by its beauty. "It is the face of a god! There are men who would kill for this!"

"Yes, many," the old man pursed his lips. "But it's of no use to anyone but a god. If the Exalted One knew I had it, his men would come for my head, but this will be our secret, yes, boy?"

"Yes."

"Yes, what?"

"Master."

Wren held the mask gently, turning it to and fro as the light sparkled across its surface. It caught the light of the entryway and flared as bright as the sun, blinding him with its brilliance. Chuckling, the master let him place it to his face.

"Ah, you have become the Exalted One!" he cried with a mocking bow. "Command me for anything you might wish!"

But Wren neither spoke, nor removed the mask. He stared back for many long moments until the old man was unnerved.

"Give it," the master snapped.

Carefully, Wren handed the mask back for wrapping, vowing that someday the mask would be his alone.

Wren soon learned that the master was more of a magician than a healer. He could disappear before a gaping crowd and reappear behind them. He could pull flowers from his mouth or pluck feathers from a man's ears. He could breathe fire and make his eyes turn blood red. He could make a man seem irresistible to a beautiful woman. "But that is the most difficult trick of all," he said with a nod.

Magic, he said, did not require the aid of spirits, ghosts, or demons. "You tell people what they will see and then you show them," the master said. "Though Little Demon and his spider are dead and can do no harm to anyone, all that is needed is a word in a man's ear to make them come to life and send him into fits of terror. It is within his own thoughts that the magic appears. The monkey and the spider just lead the way."

"But what of the spirits?" Wren asked. "Our priests say that..."

"They are useless!" the master cried. "They are without form and can do nothing! All of magic—*all of it*—is nothing more than a host of simple tricks performed by a cunning man. Remember that, boy. Remember it!"

It was a lesson that Wren never forgot. As the seasons passed, he learned all the master's magical tricks and even devised some of his own. He also learned how to kill.

As the pampered son of a trader, Wren had never killed anything, not even a frog or a fish. His father's slaves had done the killing for their dinner. But early on the master bid him to carry home a duck from the market that had been bound by its legs.

It happened that priests were scouring the market in search of a vagabond boy for the Sacrifice of the Virgins, but when they went to seize Wren the master hissed and turned himself into something quite frightening to gaze upon. Something with the appearance of a fanged snake.

"Leave him!" he commanded, as the priests slunk away in terror.

Returning home, the master told Wren to wring the duck's neck and prepare his meal.

"I ... um ... I have never done such a thing," Wren protested, looking into the duck's beady eyes.

"Don't tempt me, boy," the old man snarled. His eyes grew dark, malignant.

Stricken and without thinking, Wren seized the duck's head and gave it a twist, hearing the snap of its spine. He felt a twinge in his own backbone as a warm feeling flooded his limbs. To his wonder, it was a good feeling, even enjoyable.

"You see? You have no trouble killing," the old man said, chewing on his lower lip. "I *see* the killer in you, boy."

Thereafter, Wren killed many things, not just for their daily meal, but also for the old man's collection of stuffed animals, which soon included a bobcat, a young bear, a grouse, a porcupine, and more, all staring balefully from a wall along the hut through eyes fashioned from pearls, gems, and mica.

Wren made himself useful in the years ahead, expanding the old man's hut to make a room for himself, tending the garden, and foraging for herbs, mushrooms, roots, and firewood. He was attentive to his lessons and soon accounted himself a magician. In his secret thoughts he even considered himself a sorcerer. Taken with what he had learned in the mica trade, Wren grew to be far more clever than most during his in-between years. He also learned to be cruel.

The old man had a habit of knocking him about when he least expected. Sometimes there were blows with a cane, other times a hard shove. Once he had been toppled into the cooking fire.

"Why?!" he protested one day under a savage blow. The old man had cuffed him in the ear as they sat smoking, knocking Wren's pipe from his hands and scattering the flaming tobacco.

"It is part of your learning," the master replied with a grunt. "There is no such thing as a man who is alone with himself. Every man has two men within him—a good man, and a bad man. When times are at peace, the good man rules over his happiness. In hard times, the bad man must step forth, for he knows that the good man is weak. I strike you to make the bad man within you stronger. It is a blessing."

Wren did not think it a blessing, but he learned to be wary, expecting a blow or a kick at any moment. Yet the old man never failed to deliver, for such was his magic that he could turn Wren's thoughts elsewhere when it came time for a sharp rap with a stick or a hammer blow to his head. Someday, Wren vowed, he would be the one to do the beating.

Early on, he had noticed something disturbing about the master, who was already far more disturbing than most. He was a strange man, who had never taken a wife or produced a family beyond his collection of stuffed animals. But that was the least of it.

On many nights, the master seemed to be wrestling with something evil in his dreams. Often, he cried out and wept in his sleep, and if Wren dared to wake him, he responded with a cold glare and snapped that it was nothing. At other times the master fell into a trance, muttering to himself in an unknown language as if in conversation with some unseen being. For this reason, Wren had built his own hut alongside the lodge, hoping to avoid whatever it was that lived beyond the master's eyes.

The old man grew older, and Wren grew wiser in the ways of magic until they were almost equals. By his twentieth year there was no man in all the realm of Coosa who was cleverer than Wren. The boy who had cried and struggled thin and weak in the forests far to the north of Coosa had been blessed by the spirits to grow into a man who was tall, strong, and handsome.

His dark hair fell as long and sleek as a woman's, in loose twin braids down either side of his back, bound together by an exquisite copper brooch, that gleamed as bright as the discs threading his ears and the necklace spangling his chest.

In the markets of the town, he melted the hearts of maidens, made hard men step back in alarm, and delighted crowds with feats of magic that rained gifts at his feet.

Soon there were gatherings of hundreds, awestruck by the magic shows offered by Wren and the master as they performed feats riven with fire, juggling, and sleight of hand. Wren and the master could vanish or suffer mutilations in turn, only to appear whole again, sometimes within the crowd itself. When the crowd grew to more than a thousand, they were granted a man-high mound from which to perform so that all could see. The master had a willow screen constructed atop the mound to help with their vanishing act.

Standing atop the mound, Wren was dizzy with the cries of adulation from the onlookers below. At times the light of a blinding ecstasy flashed through his mind like lightning. Magic! It seemed there was nothing he could not achieve, and the joy of it washed through him like a drug. In time, the rulers of Coosa took notice, and he was invited to display his powers in the temples atop their mounds. He was even offered a lodge among them, but Wren declined. He preferred to live outside of town, staying at the lodge of the master.

But in his ecstasy, Wren failed to notice that the master often gave him an appraising look through cunning eyes as he charmed the crowd below. There was a wolf in the master's eyes—a predator—but Wren was too smitten with himself to see it.

The master had long since stopped striking him after Wren had struck back, knocking him across the length of his hut. "You are a man now, boy," the old man said, rubbing his jaw. This, though Wren had been only sixteen winters at the time.

"Then call me man," Wren growled in return.

"Someday," the master replied in a quiet voice. "Someday."

Wren was happy, and the good man within him ruled. But as is the way of things, soon the good man was stood on his head.

One day, Wren was walking through the market, bartering for mushrooms to provide the evening's meal, when he heard a voice at his feet.

"Wren?"

He looked down. It was an old woman dressed in rags, sitting in the dust with a begging bowl. Her thin face was lined with worry and the look of a kicked dog.

"Wren, is it truly you?"

For a moment the earth swirled, and the blood rushed through his ears as Wren struggled not to faint. There in the dirt of the plaza sat his mother.

CHAPTER 15

SHINES LIKE THE SUN

Shines Like the Sun had been a slave of the Timucuan people of the far south when Wren's father bartered for her with a gourd full of mica and a cotton shawl. She did not come cheap, but Wren's father had no intention of keeping her as a slave. He made her his wife, though some would say that was much the same as slavery.

What she had been called before, Wren did not know, but his father had renamed her Shines Like the Sun, just like the mica for which she had been traded.

Aside from her beauty, Wren's mother was gifted with her hands, and soon turned the simple materials of mica, pearls, shells, and obsidian into trade goods that were sought by all who saw them. As has been told, they had a happy life together, and a son; but all that was swept away in the clap of their hands when the wild men of the mountains took them far to the north.

After their capture, Wren's mother and father shuffled north at the point of the wild men's spears for more than a cycle of the moon. They were barely fed and treated with no more respect than their slaves. Both thought they would die on the journey as they waded knee-deep through snow-covered trails. Descending from the mountains, they endured the chill rains of spring as they made their way through a fertile land criss-crossed by rivers and creeks. Once, they were tasked with building rafts to cross a river that was terrifying in its width—so wide that a man standing on the far shore looked like the smallest of ants. After crossing the big O-y-o, they knew they would never see Coosa or Wren again.

One day, when they were fainting from exhaustion and sure to be killed and tossed by the wayside for lack of pushing on, they encountered a band of strong-armed warriors whose scalps were plucked, save for a strip of hair running down the center of their skulls.

The warriors outnumbered the wild men by twice and looked just as fierce. Harsh words were spoken in an unknown language, yet Wren's mother and father were savvy enough to know that the wild men intended to trade them to the newcomers. That was just so, for seeing their weakness, and yet their promise, the newcomers fashioned slings and carried them north with the slavers trailing along behind.

Two days later, they spied a low hill and, beyond it, the sea. The hill was topped by a palisade that was less than half built, and they soon learned that the sea was a wonder of fresh water. Yet their new captors were not of the Odawa like the traders they had met in the past. Soon, Wren's parents learned that they had been taken by a people known as the Seneca.

"One of our slaves perished in a fire as a sacrifice to their evil god," Shines Like the Sun said as she sat in a place of honor outside the master's hut. "He had only one arm and was no use to them. We thought the caress of fire would also be our fate, but instead they put us to work."

It was the Big Town, Ga-ogwah Kanotaye, located four days' walk from a ruined place that the Seneca called the Old Town. The site had been chosen by the Seneca's clan mothers after a long search, but the women who chose it knew there would be far more work than their people could bear, and so the call went out for slaves. Thus, would the *orenda* of Ga-ogwah Kanotaye increase as the fields were cleared of timber, the huge lodges were constructed, and the palisade rose on the hill overlooking the lake.

"Ah, perhaps we would have been better off dead," Wren's mother continued, as she helped herself to another gourd of stewed turtle. "The work was never-ending. From the moment we rose in the morning to when we collapsed on our pallets at night. Your father and I would have been as skeletons if not for the Seneca's maize."

Shines Like the Sun had been given the task of stripping bark from the mighty elms that had stood on the shore. These had been girdled by men of the Seneca well before their people's arrival and were half dead by the time huge bonfires were lit at their base. Men pulling ropes had brought them crashing down with the aid of the fire, and then Wren's mother was put to work, hacking and peeling at the remaining bark until her fingers were as horned as claws. Yet even then, the work was not done. The elms were hollowed out with coals to produce dugouts that could carry thirty men or more, and the bark was collected to sheath the longhouses.

But it was Wren's father, known simply as Big Trader, who was given the fatal task of hauling timber. The Seneca had set fire to the forest by the lake to clear it for farmland, but there was still the palisade to be constructed, and this required tall pines beyond count.

Wren's father had married late and was by then a man of forty-four winters. Many years of trekking along the trails of Coosa had not been kind to his joints and now they ached with a breaking pain as he struggled under the eyes of hard men who showed no pity.

Far out in the forest, he was charged with stripping the limbs from fallen pines with a stone axe. The work was a torment that left him scratched and bleeding from his face to his toes. But that was a pleasure compared to what came next. Once a pine was stripped of its branches, he became one leg of a human centipede, hoisting the tree upon his shoulders with a host of other men and then hauling the timber for long stretches back to the town and up the hill to its crest. To say that it was backbreaking work was just so.

"We had been adopted by one of the leaders of the town, who was kind to us, far kinder than most," Wren's mother said. "She put in words on your father's behalf, begging that he join me among the bark-strippers. Ah, but that was the work of women, she was told and would never do.

The man who commanded the pine-bearers was cruel. He had no heart. Only she, an old blind woman tried to help us."

"Blind?" the master asked. "A blind woman was among their chieftains?"

"Yes, the clan mothers hold great power among the Seneca. To her, the world was as dark as the new moon, but perhaps that made her feel more deeply for others."

"But what of my father?" Wren asked.

"Your father did not last long," she said, facing him with tears in her eyes. "His shoulders fell to ruin. He could barely lift his arms, and then his backbone was crushed beneath the weight of the pines. Every step was agony! But still, his master made him carry on, telling him that he would be fed to the Seneca's cruel god, *Aireskoi,* in a fire ceremony if he did not keep on. Ah! I think that was just what his master wanted, and if only I had a knife and came upon him sleeping, I would have buried it in his eye!

"But," she continued in a quiet voice, "your father's pain did not last. One day he did not return to our longhouse, and I learned that a man walking in front of him had stumbled as they carried a big tree back to the town. It was too much. Your father's back would not hold, and he fell, crushed beneath the tree. It was a blessing."

CHAPTER 16

THE WAY BACK

Years went by as Ga-ogwah Kanotaye slowly took shape, as did its fields of maize, tobacco, sunflower, and more. When at last the town was habitable, the elders and those with small children were sent from the far-off Old Town, which by then was rotted away by the rain, wind, and snow, along with the ceaseless chewing of ants and beetles.

Wren's mother was given easier tasks once the town had been built. The old woman who adopted her was a noted healer who instructed her to forage for certain roots and herbs in the forest, well beyond the town walls.

"You will know them by their smell," Walking Turtle said, handing her a bundle of herbs. "That is how I know them."

So it was that Shines Like the Sun was granted more freedom than most with no fear that she would ever leave. She was an honored member of Walking Turtle's family now, and who would wish to leave its comforting bonds? Sometimes she took a boy along to watch over her, as there were known to be panthers in the forest and raiders from enemy tribes, eager to spirit away a captive for their own clans. But just as often, she roamed the forest by herself. The long trading journeys with her husband had filled her with far more courage than those who resided behind the walls of a town.

One day, she wandered further than usual, seeking an herb that was of particular interest to Walking Turtle. She had not forgotten how the old woman had spoken up for her husband and was always eager to please her with what she found in the forest.

On this day, she came to a towering hill that rose as a lone pillar of limestone rising far above the treetops. The heights of the karst were carved with sheer cliffs, and she could see that there was no way to the top. But she stumbled across an animal path, winding through the brush that meandered up its base. Climbing halfway to the crest, she could see Ga-ogwah Kanotaye in the distance, standing on its hill by the shore.

Something in that vision reminded her of Coosa, and a pang stabbed at her heart as she thought of Wren. *Run!* She had told him, *Run!* Did he still live? Was he even now in the great town of the god-ruler, crying for his mother and father? Ah, she would never know. Never, ever know.

Scrambling down the escarpment she came to a ledge in the rock that made a platform from which Ga-ogwah Kanotaye could still be seen, but just barely. Peering over the ledge she saw a hollow hidden behind a large bush; and then, although she risked falling, she inched her way around the slope until she found herself at the entrance of a cave. There were old bones lying there as if it had once been the den of wolves or a panther, but the bones were dry as dust, and there was no scent to belie anything living there. It was early spring, and the sun was low enough on the horizon to permit a shaft of light into the cave's recess. On an impulse, she took a few steps inside.

It was a cool place, but dry, and Shines Like the Sun was brave enough to attempt a few steps more until she was almost engulfed in darkness. What a hiding place this would be, she thought.

In the fading light, she saw a glimmer that she took to be a pool of water. But dipping a finger, she recoiled at the touch and scrambled up and out to the sunlight. Looking down, she found her finger painted in a strange black ooze unlike anything she had ever seen before.

Unknown to Shines Like the Sun, the pillar of stone was known as the Tower of the Dead to the Seneca. Only a few years before, there had been a great battle with hundreds of Erie warriors at its base, and now, it was haunted by many vengeful ghosts. Young men and women who might normally have swarmed over the stone peak, hoping to savor the view from its top, now shunned the tower and the ghosts that dwelled in the meadow below. No one had climbed it in all the years of Ga-ogwah Kanotaye's rising—no one but the enslaved woman of Coosa.

Walking back to town, the thought of escaping took root. She had felt as empty as an open grave since her husband's death, and each night, her face was washed with tears at his memory as she lay on her pallet of straw. Just as often she thought of Wren. Surely, he would have found his way back to Coosa if he lived. Perhaps even now he was a trader, following in his father's footsteps. If she could only find him, she could begin her life anew, she and Wren, trading mica. She would care for his children, love his wife, and help them with the cleverness of her hands.

For the first time in years, Shines Like the Sun found herself smiling, engulfed by the happy dream. And why not? The Odawa came from an even greater distance. And what of it if she died on the journey? She had nothing to live for among the Seneca. Without her husband and son, she might as well be dead. She was already dead in her heart.

The cave would make it possible, she thought. It was hidden behind a wall of brush, and the way there was a rocky slope where no signifying footprints might lead.

The next day, she hid a gourd of parched corn beneath her tunic and set out for the forest. Her plan was not in earnest. It was more of a dare to see what might be done. With trembling hands, she placed the corn in a rocky depression in the cave and covered it with a flat stone.

For a long time, she sat there, looking at the stone and thinking of the corn below. If one gourd of corn could be stored, then so could twenty, along with nuts and twists of dried meat. Walking Turtle would not know. She was blind! Besides, the people of the town were constantly showering the old woman with food. She would not notice anything missing.

She tried again the next day and the day after that, and with each addition to her stores, her dream of escape grew stronger, seeming more possible. She simply had to head south to where the mountains rose, and beyond them lay the safety of Coosa. It was a long hike, but she would blend in with the forest, wary of any bad man or spirit she might meet on the way.

She also gathered supplies. A chill day gave her a chance to sneak a rabbit-fur blanket, explaining that she needed it as a wrap against the cold. Then she snatched a leather sack from an adjoining lodge and found a worn knife in another. What more could she need?

When at last she had enough food to fill her sack, Shines Like the Sun rose for her final day in Ga-ogwah Kanotaye, vowing never to return.

Yet as she crept toward the lodge door, she heard a voice from over her shoulder.

"Where do you go each day, daughter?" It was Walking Turtle, sitting on the pallet across from hers, gazing at her through sightless eyes.

"I go in search of herbs for you, mother," she replied, knowing it sounded like a lie.

"And why are you taking food?"

Shines Like the Sun choked. Was she so easily seen by a blind woman? "It is a long way to the herbs," she said. "Almost half a day. I take something to eat."

The words fell lame from her lips, sounding like a lie even to herself.

Sitting in the half-light of the longhouse, Walking Turtle gave a skeptical grunt. "You can't fool me, shining one," she said. "I know what you're doing. The spirits told me."

"I..."

"Don't lie to me. There is nowhere you can go. Nowhere but to me."

"Yes, mother, I am grateful. You have been kind, far more than anyone else would have been."

"And?"

"I only wish to bring you more herbs," she said, simpering. "I will see you at the evening meal..."

Walking Turtle snorted and gave her a gruff wave. "Bring a kiss to my cheek and go. But remember, we are still family, you and I. Always family, and if your hair turns white with fear in a day or two, you can still return. But if you are gone any longer and our men find you, I warn you, our people will have you punished."

Shines Like the Sun stood for a moment at the open door of the lodge and then crept away with Walking Turtle's words hanging in the air behind her. "Blessings on you, daughter! Stay safe!"

That night she slept in the cave, listening to the earth murmuring from the throat in its depths. She stayed there all the next day and night, listening to the cries of searchers who had been alerted to her absence by those living in Walking Turtle's lodge. Within two days, all believed that the woman from the south had been taken by a cougar, or perhaps by a skulking raider of the Erie. Such things often happen, even within a few bow shots of Ga-ogwah Kanotaye.

It is one thing to dream of escaping into the forest and quite another to surrender to its dark embrace. Shines Like the Sun was far braver than most. As the wife of a wandering trader, she had traveled down more faint trails than ten men would follow in a lifetime. She had nestled in her sleeping robe with the grunt of bears in her ears and, once, even the growl of a jaguar when she lived in the far-distant southern land of the Timucuas. But she had never been alone—she had always felt the comforting presence of her husband, a fire, and the rough camaraderie of their slaves. Yet now, she crept south with her heart awash with terror, even though the morning was not half gone.

It was the hunters of the Seneca that she feared. They would be up before dawn, hoping to take a deer or a bear in that misty time between darkness and daybreak. She had stayed up all night, leaving well before dawn under the light of a half-moon in the hope of outpacing any leaving the town that morning, but still, there could be small camps ahead. It would be days before she'd be clear of them.

Shines Like the Sun knew that stumbling across a hunting party would mean her return to the Big Town and punishment of the sort that could leave her deformed at the least. Others had tried to escape their adoptive families and were punished with flaming brands or the loss of fingers for their treachery. She had rehearsed a story of getting lost in the forest, but that would not explain her leather sack of food. She knew that she would be instantly judged with harsh eyes by any who came upon her.

She crept along, down the path to the south, keeping to the shelter of the trees as much as possible and stopping often to listen for any sign of hunters. Most, she thought, would be watching faint game trails deep in the forest, or hiding amid the glades of saplings and other forage that had been cleared by fire. Still, anyone returning to Ga-ogwah Kanotaye would likely be heading her way down the trail.

By the third day, her heart was in her throat and her nerves in shreds as the trail grew thinner, yet still there were signs of hunters. A muddy footprint here, and further on, the gut pile of a butchered deer, swarming with flies. She imagined dark eyes peering at her from the brush as she made her way along, with strong arms reaching to seize her from behind at any moment. Once, she heard the murmur of voices just ahead and scrambled into the brush just as two hunters rounded a bend in the trail. She buried her head in her hands, convinced that they would see her only a long step off the trail; perhaps they would step on her! But they were young men, full of mirth, and passed by chattering without a glance at their feet.

It was five days before she felt that she was finally free of the Seneca, yet now, the trail had dwindled to nothing, and she wandered through a trackless forest, knowing only to push south. The spirits of the forest pressed in close upon her, filling her with dread as she imagined their faces in the boles of trees or the patterns of clouds. Once, she climbed a tall hill, searching in vain for the mountains that she must cross. There was nothing to be seen but an endless carpet of trees and meadows spread in every direction over rolling hills to the horizon. At night she risked a fire, hoping that the flame would keep whatever evil might chance upon her at bay. Feeling utterly alone, her sleep was plagued by a tangle of frightening dreams. Once she woke deep in the night with the feeling that something was lurking just above her face in the darkness, sucking the breath from her lungs.

She rationed her maize, soaking it in a gourd each day and swallowing only a handful of it along with a few nuts and a chew of dried venison. Mostly, she gathered mushrooms, leeks, and whatever plants were known to nourish as she made her way south. To her satisfaction, she was not hungry, and in time, her fear began melting away as she left the Seneca far behind.

But fear is a tide that ebbs and flows, and after half a moon of wandering, Shines Like the Sun began to despair of ever finding the mountains, much less the notch that signified the pass to Coosa. One night, a raccoon crept into her bag of food while she was sleeping, and in the morning, she found nothing within its folds but a few kernels of maize.

Twice, she came upon villages unexpectedly and crept past them, gleaning what food she could from their fields. On another day, she passed by a lone hut, nodding at the man and woman who sat at its entrance, watching in silence as she passed by.

So it was that at last she reached the Beautiful River, O-y-o, with her tunic in shreds from being torn by the brush and her belly empty for three days with nothing to eat but a few mushrooms and the bark of a tree that she thought might be edible. She had vomited soon after choking it down, leaving her weaker than ever.

Her heart fell as her eyes swept the current. The immensely wide O-y-o was the same river where a man standing on the opposite bank could barely be seen, if at all.

"Oh, I am a dead woman!" she groaned as she collapsed on the river's muddy bank. In her despair she hungered for death, calling out, "Father of Fathers, Mother of Mothers, bring me home to you and my husband! No more of this torment. No more! I cannot bear it."

Choking with tears, she tore at her hair and buried her face in her hands. Looking at the sun shining bright on the broad expanse, she sobbed again. The Beautiful River was aptly named by the Haudenosaunee, but its beauty was cruel to anyone hoping to cross without a canoe.

Still, she had to try, and her spirits rose a bit after finding a pool of crayfish that she roasted on a slab of stone as the sun lay low on the horizon. That night, she banished the thought of any more crying—she was a trader after all used to hard bargains, and she would bargain with this river. The Gray Mountains couldn't be more than half a moon to the south. And then, Wren! Coosa! And her life again.

That morning, she found two half-rotted fallen trees, and after a great deal of effort, she managed to snap away their branches and drag them to the riverside, panting with exhaustion, soaked with sweat and pestered by flies. But what then? There were many vines tangling the trees along the river, and though her knife was old and dull, it served well enough. She twisted the vines around the trees, tying them as stoutly as she could. Glumly, she considered that three trees would do better, but she had scoured the area for a distance, and there was no other log to be found. Her raft of two trees would have to do.

She stripped off her tunic and wedged it along with her empty sack, her knife, and her staff in the tangle of vines and pushed off into the current, paddling with her feet.

The current was gentle by the shore, but as she made her way deeper into the river it grew faster, and her wretched raft no longer obeyed the commands of her flailing legs. To her horror, the vines holding the logs together began to separate and snap, and then the raft itself rolled over, dumping her tunic and her scant possessions to the depths of the O-y-o. Naked and clutching the stoutest log, she screamed, choking on a torrent of river-wash that poured down her throat and up her nose. She gagged, screamed again as the current sped faster, and then what was left of the vines severed as she clutched at the slimy log, bobbing under and fighting for her life. Blinded by the river washing over her face and swallowing more water, she choked helplessly as the Fish Man of the depths reached up to clutch at her feet.

That would have been the end of Wren's mother, whose shade would have walked the mud at the bottom of the O-y-o forever were it not for hoarse shouts and the silhouettes of men paddling hard in her direction.

They were the Odawa—the very men that she and her husband had dealt with for many years. They pulled her choking and vomiting from the brown current and laid her naked body glistening in the sunlight atop a pile of furs in the middle of their canoe. Never in all her years had life seemed so sweet as that moment when Shines Like the Sun knew that she would live to see Coosa again. And beyond all her dreams, she was among friends! For glancing up with a string of drool edging down the side of her face, she recognized Long Time Trader, her husband's favorite among the Odawa.

It is said that Long Time Trader had lived ten times the lives of ordinary men in his many travels. He had even met Animi-Ma'liingan, the man known as Wolf, on the islands of Minong and had pointed the way to the Misi Sipi on the mission that brought him to Willow. He also knew the river pathways to the South, gaining the trust of those he met along the way. That included Wren's father; the two had conducted an easy trade at the Odawa's trading post beneath the mountains.

Now he clothed Shines Like the Sun in a deer pelt, promising to trade for a more suitable tunic at the next village. That night, she filled his ears with her abduction, slavery, and escape as they camped on the riverbank.

"The spirits smiled on you then because we met a party of Seneca traders not far downstream," Long Time Trader said. "We shared a meal with them and news of their people."

"Did they say anything of me?" she asked.

"No. They have many villages in their land, and the people you spoke of would not come this far to trade."

"But you have come much further."

"*Ehn,* but we are men who have no roots. We blow in the wind."

Long Time Trader told her that she had wandered far to the southwest and that the land of Coosa was still a distance of half a moon or more. She was welcome to join them if she would prepare the day's meal, to which she was happy to agree.

The Odawa in turn were happy to have her, for though the current was not swift, it was still a struggle making headway and by late afternoon, they were thankful that she took charge of making camp.

Two days later, they reached the stopping spot and hid their canoes beneath the low-hanging limbs of a tree under a blanket of wet leaves to keep them supple upon their return. There were seven Odawa, including Long Time Trader, and hefting their packs, they made their way down a game trail through the forest until they came to a well-trammeled pathway. This led to a village where they bartered a lump of pipestone for a tunic for Shines Like the Sun. It was of a soft doeskin, running to her knees.

"Lucky man thinks he got the best of the gifting," Long Time Trader said with a knowing smile after the trade. "He will be a big man in his village once he carves his pipe."

"But what of you?" she asked. "What can I give you?"

"It was only a stone," he said, casting a hand to the sun. "It is my gift to you."

That night, she lifted his bearskin blanket and nestled against his body, feeling his warmth as he twisted with desire. It had been a long time since she had known a man, and then only her husband for a long time before that. But she was more than happy to reward him for his kindness. She was considered an old woman by then, yes, but still comely, and all know that a woman of many years knows how to please a man far better than does a maiden.

At last, they came to the big village at the northernmost territory of Coosa where her husband had been warned of the wild men ten years before. This time there had been no nighttime ambush, for the Odawa were wise enough to set their camp well out of sight from the main trail each evening and did not fear attack by day.

Shines Like the Sun walked through the gate of Tali as if in a dream, feeling as if she might faint.

"Here is where we leave you, unless you wish to follow us," Long Time Trader said.

She searched his eyes for some hint of promise but found none. He would never settle down, and though she loved the trading life, the wilderness ranged by the Odawa was a far cry from the comforts of trading in the land of Coosa.

"Ah, brother, I owe you my life, but this is where I belong," she said. "If I can find my son, perhaps we will meet again at this place. He will likely be a trader if he lived."

The leader of the Odawa nodded and granted her a final gift. It was a box crafted of birch bark, filled with dyed porcupine quills. "It is something for you to trade as you make your way home," he said.

Shines Like the Sun was hollow-eyed and gaunt as a cadaver by the time she reached the capital of Coosa. It had been the trudge of another cycle of the moon to reach sight of its pyramids, and by then she had traded away all her quills for food. When this ran out, she begged. Villagers viewed her with suspicion as she walked among them. No one had ever seen a lone woman walking the pathways alone. Yet even though there were times when she was showered with cornmeal mush, meat, and fish, still her body consumed her meals as if it were on fire. When at last she staggered down the lanes of Coosa, she felt blue-lipped and faint, barely able to lift her legs. Reaching the main plaza, she collapsed beneath the goal post on the ball field and lay there for a day and a night before Wren found her.

"You are a spirit—a ghost," she breathed to him in her delirium.

"Yes, mother," he said, bending down to cradle her in his arms. "We are spirits together."

CHAPTER 17

THE WHITE MEN

Wren felt a wave of ecstasy unlike anything he had ever known at his mother's return. A sun rose in his heart and exploded in his thoughts with a happiness he had not known since his days as a small child.

The master took to Shines Like the Sun as well and was eager to know every detail of her time with the Seneca, including a few words of their language. But he expressed doubt at her wish to resume the trading life.

"You are an old woman now," he said as she frowned with downcast eyes. "Your son may travel the world groaning under a pack of copper and mica, but you will remain here with me to cook my meals."

And do whatever else he might desire, she thought.

Looking up in defiance, Wren's mother said, "Old man, I have wandered two moons in the forest, braving spirits, bad men, and wildcats. I will keep to the trading path as long as I can hobble and crawl if I must."

The master gazed back at her through rheumy eyes, and to Wren's surprise, gave a throaty laugh. "Perhaps you are a wildcat too," he said. "Perhaps I will stir my bones to go with you, a short way at least."

With that Wren and his mother made joyful plans to take up trading anew, and the master granted them a small store of mica that he had kept in a clay pot for many years. "It is just dust to me," he said.

But though it was only two handfuls, Wren looked upon it as a treasure. A wily trader could exchange it for shells, pearls, and other gifts from the sea and then make a good trade with the copper bearers from the north, with one trade piled upon another until a larger share of mica could be obtained, repeating the cycle again.

And Wren, of course, considered himself a wily trader.

But his mother had doubts about bringing the master with them. Though he had treated her well enough and had allowed her to stay in Wren's hut, she felt uneasy around the old man. One day, when he had left the lodge, she had questions.

"Has he treated you kindly?" she asked.

Wren thought of the slaps and blows he had suffered at the master's hands until he was old enough to fight back.

"Sometimes," he said, hesitating, "but even when he was cruel, he taught me things of great value. Magic."

"Magic?"

"Yes, simple things … like this," he said, pulling a flower from his mother's hair.

Wren pulled Little Demon from its shelf and told her of the times they had mesmerized crowds with the shaved monkey and other tricks.

She looked back, stupefied, hardly knowing what to say.

"It is a good thing to know," he said, telling her of the magic shows they had staged in town and the many gifts they had received in return. "We have even performed for the Exalted One, though we were not allowed to gaze upon him."

"And has he told you his name?"

"It is Master. Only Master. He seems to have no other name, nor any family."

She scoffed at this but fell silent at the master's return. "A man with no name has a secret," she whispered. "And it can only be a bad one."

As everyone knows, there were eight large towns in the land of Coosa, with villages beyond count spread between them. Wren, his mother, and the master planned to travel south to several middling villages and a town of lesser note where trade goods such as mica were not as common as the riches of the sea. There, Wren hoped their small store of mica would be planted as a seed fulfilling their dreams.

Had they not been held up by a thunderstorm they would have missed what came next by a single day. Runners from the north streamed through the town, bearing incredible news—an army of demons was making its way to the capital down the wide trail with hundreds of slaves and strange creatures trailing in their wake.

Even the master did not know what to make of it as every tongue in town loosened in wild speculation. Were they demons, gods, or men stained white with some unknown pigment? No one could explain the large deer upon which some of the ghostly men rode; some thought they might be female elk, but that did not explain their flowing manes and tails, nor their gnashing teeth. Nor could anyone account for the carapaces of a shining metal that some of the newcomers wore as if they were beetles. There was so much more that could not be accounted for; the only certainty was that the white men were coming to Coosa.

The chieftains of Coosa had known of the intruders for nearly a year as tales of their progress circulated from the south. Beyond the eastern mountains in Cofitechequi, it was said that the beautiful niece of the land's ruler had crossed a river to meet them, gliding to shore in her canopied galley, dressed in her finest gown with her handmaids and servants gathered behind her. By signs, she had bid them welcome, though surely, she was filled with terror. The leader of the demons had accepted her gift of pearls but had taken her hostage in order to bargain with her aunt. Only good fortune allowed her to escape as she cut her way through the wall of one of their cloth lodges and fled to the forest.

It was reported that the white men had weapons against which no warrior could prevail and that they possessed a magic that could utter a thunderclap of lightning and fire, mowing down men by the score. The

Exalted One and his shamans puzzled over what to do for many moons, deciding at last to welcome the invaders in the hope that they might be enlisted against Coosa's enemies to the four directions. Quite possibly, the leader of the white men was a god, and though the wise men of Coosa did not dare to say it, it was possible that he was even more godlike in his power than the Exalted One, Halw-i em Mekko.

A quarter-moon later, Wren, his mother, and the master joined thousands lining the fields outside town as a cloud of dust rose in the north. Long before they saw the army of the white men, they heard the pounding of their drums and a bugling sound that was quite unlike the tones of a conch shell. Then, as the vanguard of the army appeared under the banner of long streamers of many colors, the air was split with a thunderclap, even though there was not a cloud in the blue sky. A great cry arose from the crowd, with many fleeing in terror.

But the power of Coosa was no small thing, and many were heartened to see the litter of the Exalted One borne on the shoulders of the highest nobles of the town in their finest robes and feathers. Behind him came sixty other nobles among Coosa's people, including its priests, who danced and sang in their wake. Then came an orchestra of drummers and musicians playing flutes and the trumpets of conch shells. And behind them all was an escort of hundreds of Coosa's warriors, painted for battle with their clubs slung over their shoulders and pennants of feathers flying from their spears.

Wren, his mother, and the master were standing at the very spot where the two processions met. In advance of the white men's party were a number of savage dogs, three times as large as the dogs of Coosa, who were girdled in leather and metal plates. Baring their fangs and snarling at the crowd on either side, the dogs were pulled back on their leashes by their tenders, with shouts to clear the way as the riders came forward.

The spectacle was far beyond the dreams of all who saw it. First came a shuffling man with a shaved head, clad in a brown robe, who emerged from the cloud of dust bearing a tall wooden cross, which Wren took to be a symbol. Behind him came the thunder of drums and the blare of horns. And then Wren and his party gaped as a huge creature strode forth with a being dressed in shining metal astride its torso. Even the rider's head was covered in metal, and only when it had cleared the crowd with a long lance bobbing before it did the creature lift its visor to reveal a human face.

Satisfied that there was no treachery, the rider beckoned to his rear, and a man dressed in many colors rode forth. He too wore the strange metal covering but only as a sheath around his chest and abdomen. To Wren's surprise, his chin and cheeks were covered with hair, as if he had wrapped the pelt of a mink around his face.

He was thin with dark, close-cropped hair and a rakish air that commanded obedience. Nearly fifty of his warriors sat grim-faced on their beasts with their lances pointing skyward, while behind them were hundreds of men on foot, each armed with weapons that no one in Coosa had ever seen before.

Amid the pounding of drums and the blare of horns, their leader stepped forth with a guard of men bearing long knives of the same strange metal just as another thunderclap erupted from the rear, sending a plume of flame and smoke skyward. Again, the people of Coosa gasped and fell back in alarm, only to surge forward as they craned for a look.

The nobles bearing the Exalted One's litter halted and slowly lowered it to the ground. Then, for the first time in anyone's memory, the lesser people of Coosa saw their god-ruler up close under the full light of the sun.

As was commanded, all bowed to their knees, burying their faces in the ground, yet such was the temper of the day that many risked a glance, and then, emboldened, looked up to witness a meeting of the gods.

Unlike the thin farmers of Coosa, Halw-i em Mekko was a tall, big-bellied man, well-fed with maize pudding, fine meats, and delicacies of snails, shellfish, pigeons, and ducks. His face was obscured by a curtain of pearls hanging from his headdress of feathers, but even so, one could tell that he was heavily jowled and flabby with a sprinkling of hairs twisting on his upper lip. To Wren's eyes, his face had the look of a frog, and he wondered; how could such a frog be descended from the sun? Walker in the Sky, Master of the Underworld, Bringer of the Rain, Guardian of the Maize, Son of the Sun. These were the names by which the Exalted One was known, yet for the first time Wren understood why the god-ruler remained hidden behind a screen, high atop his pyramid. With a shock, he realized that if the frog-faced man could lay claim to such titles, then anyone could. Even himself.

The High One stepped forth, wearing a long white gown that trailed behind his feet, embroidered with symbols of the gods of Coosa. Atop his head was a headdress of multicolored macaw feathers that stood straight up in the hope of making him seem even taller. Two white egret wings were fastened on either side of the headdress, just above the god-ruler's ears. Draped across his chest was a necklace of copper beads fashioned to look like seashells, while his staff was topped by a large copper disc that was polished to a high sheen in order to resemble the sun. Cynics among the people said that he pissed himself at the meeting that day, but the only certainty was that his eyes were as wide as full moons with fright. In the many stories told of Coosa thereafter, no one ever remembered the High One's name, but all knew the name of the evildoer who became his master—"De Soto."

An interpreter stepped forward and offered the greetings of De Soto, which were answered in turn by the Exalted One. The two men stepped forward and the crowd gasped as the white man grasped the god-ruler's arm. Shock swept over the High One's face at the transgression, the touch of which would have meant certain death for anyone in Coosa, yet Wren could see that the gesture was meant as a greeting and, perhaps, a way to show who was master. The two looked at each other as if they were two dogs sniffing as the interpreter mumbled and bowed.

But then De Soto gestured to a man at his rear who came forward bearing a gift. Glancing down, the Exalted One's face was stricken with horror at the sight of it. It was a wooden cross, as long as a man's forearm, and upon it lay the figure of a man whose hands and feet were pierced with spikes and whose head was wrapped in thorns—obviously the victim of some hideous torture. He recognized it was a symbol of worship. All heard the High One gasp as he threw it to the ground and backed away in disgust as De Soto mocked him with a thin smile and glittering eyes.

Afterward, De Soto and his army followed the High One's entourage beyond the palisade gate and along Coosa's main avenue to the main plaza beneath the great pyramid. Trailing in their wake were hundreds of slaves and bearers, grim-faced beneath their loads. By their tattoos and clothing Wren knew that many of them came from far-off Chiaha, Chelaque, Hapi, and Cofitachequi—lands filled with as many warriors as the leaves of a forest. Had the white men conquered them so easily, or had they gained them through trade? Many were bound with chains of black metal.

Then came men tending hundreds of strange creatures the size of dogs, with curling tails and upraised ears that deafened those they passed with their grunts and squeals. An immense cloud of dust covered all—the warriors, their slaves, and their animals as they filed into the plaza, intending to make camp.

Thousands of painted warriors stood ringing the plaza as the white men made their way to its center. Not a word was spoken among them as they stood staring forward in an ominous silence. Behind them, their chieftains roamed up and down the line, keeping order. Wren scrambled up a small mound to witness the bloodbath that was sure to come.

But that was not to be, for the white men had yet another wonder. Eight huge beasts appeared, bound two-by-two and pulling what appeared at a distance to be logs of black oak mounted atop discs that rolled as they were pulled. The beasts were as large as buffalo but with widespread horns and a peaceful temperament. They dragged their loads into the center of the plaza facing four directions as the Exalted One and his train pushed on to the safety of his warriors.

Now will come the signal, Wren thought. There were easily five warriors for each of the strangers, and they would be engulfed like a swarm of bees upon a toad. The countless warriors of Coosa were battle-hardened veterans who held sway over as many as fifteen other chiefdoms and tribes, collecting tribute and slaves when they weren't busy murdering their enemies with their flint-edged swords and war clubs. Mighty Coosa! Surely the white men did not know that they were marching to their doom.

But then came the blare from a metal horn, and all fifty of the white men's horses dashed forward, racing around the perimeter of the plaza with pennants flying and their long knives flashing. The Coosa warriors recoiled. This might have been overcome but for what came next. The four monsters that Wren had taken for logs spat fire with an incredible clap of thunder, whipping flaming balls high into the sky over the palisade. One shot low, splintering the log stockade as if it were made of twigs. A mix of screams and roars of wonder filled the plaza as thousands ran for their lives or milled in anticipation of what might come next. Chaos was the ruler that day, and even the warriors were thrown into disarray by the milling crowd. Many turned and ran for their lives.

That night, the sky was lit with immense spheres and umbrellas of multi-colored lights exploding overhead as the white men did more to demonstrate their god-like powers. Wren could see flames snaking into the sky before each ball of fire erupted in dazzling colors of red, green, blue, and white, but this was magic far beyond his imagination. Not even the wisest men and magicians in all of Coosa could explain it.

Cowering atop his pyramid, the Exalted One along with his priests, nobles, and war chiefs, saw their own doom written in the sky. All agreed that the best plan was to appease the white devils and send them on their way with whatever they might desire.

CHAPTER 18

THE EXALTED ONE

The demons stayed in Coosa for a full cycle of the moon, throwing the capital into a panic. While their men, dogs of war, and strange animals were quartered in the main plaza, the nobles and priests of the town were evicted from their fine lodges at the base of the great pyramid. These were occupied by De Soto and his principal chieftains. Their lodges were guarded each night by men clad in metal, accompanied by their vicious dogs, who looked capable of eating a man alive.

So too did the beasts on which the white men rode. A man on an animal's back was a marvel in itself, but it was quickly spread that these animals had been taught to devour a man if their rider so chose. With their gnashing teeth and upward kicking heels, no one among the people of Coosa dared to stand near them.

De Soto made many demands of the Exalted One, whose anguished face was pale with sweat as he agreed to the demands one after another, no matter how outrageous. There was the demand for food, of course, and though it had been a lean summer with a harrowing drought that left the people little to spare for themselves and the coming winter, the god-ruler opened the granaries and stores of nuts and dried meats to the white men, who pillaged them with the avarice of hungry dogs. Ah, and even the dogs of Coosa ran for their lives as the white men fell upon them, hungry for their meat to the horror of all who bore witness. It was known that brute peoples living far beyond Coosa's borders ate dogs, but no one in the realm would ever dream of such a thing, except in the direst time of starvation.

Then came the demand for women, both as servants and for pleasure. This too was granted, with fifty women torn from their homes and sacrificed to the white demons. Many wept as they were handed over, terrified almost out of their minds. But just as many shrieked with delight as they were showered with presents of colored beads, the like of which no one had ever seen before. The beads were as clear as crystals, yet in a range of colors that would have satisfied a parrot. Soon, to the men of Coosa's dismay, many nubile young women were flocking to the white men's camp, flirting outrageously and opening their legs to claim their own share of treasure.

With a trader's eye, Wren appraised the beads' worth as a covey of bedecked women passed by. To his dismay he realized that fine shells and jewelry of copper and mica were as nothing compared to the rainbow of beads that had been crafted by some unknown art. He reasoned that if such a treasure could be obtained, he and his mother could reach even greater heights as traders than in the days of his father.

Then came a demand for slaves to replace those who were worn to their bones by De Soto's journey from the southern ocean. These too were meted out by the Exalted One, who grew ever more obsequious and accommodating. Unknown to his people, he had become a prisoner in his own temple, forbidden to leave or to meet with his underlings. De Soto called him his guest and allowed him to speak only to Black Serpent when relaying his orders. Black Serpent had turned to fawning at De Soto's heels, all but rolling over on his back like a cowering dog. The Exalted One promised himself that he would throw the man to the fires of *Eh-noq-waa* when the white demons left.

Early on, De Soto had come to him demanding a strange metal called *oro*. *Oro, oro, oro*, again and again where was it to be found? Where was it hidden?

It was as if the man had gone mad.

In his confusion, the god-ruler had opened his treasury, showing De Soto his riches of copper, mica, shells, and pearls. All were sacred, fashioned into animals, necklaces, arm bands, or symbols of the gods. They were works of art that no one had ever gazed upon but the Exalted One and his ancestors. He had even presented his own staff, topped by a copper disc that was as wide as a big man's outstretched hand. Burnished to a high sheen, it had been fashioned by the Sun God himself, handed down through the generations to those who ruled Coosa under his authority.

But DeSoto had swept the staff away as if it were nothing, ordering his men to seize the treasury's pearls. Once again, he brought forth the gift of the wooden stick bearing the likeness of a tortured man which the Exalted One had rejected upon their first meeting. Above the man's head was a small disc of metal that was the same color as the setting sun before it turned red.

"*Oro*," De Soto said, pointing at the disc with a strained face, as if he were speaking to an idiot. Again, the Exalted One presented his staff, topped by the copper disc with its mystic powers and authority of the sun. His disc was larger! There was no comparison! Yet the white demon could not see!

"*Ah! Idiota!*" De Soto steamed in reply.

It was soon thereafter that the Exalted One was treated to the sort of indignities that his officials reserved for blasphemers. First his fingernails were pulled out one at a time as his torturers bellowed "*Oro!*" in his ears. Then came the tickling of his feet with a metal knife heated red-hot, yet all in vain as he screamed, begged, and cried that there was no *oro* in his land; only there, far off to the southwest where Coosa's enemies dwelled. There, there, *there!*

Mercifully, the Son of the Sun was spared further torment, for it was clear that there was no gold in Coosa, save for a few trinkets that had come from a failed Spanish colony on the coast beyond the eastern mountains. But the Exalted One's trial was not over. Upon their departure, De Soto's men carried away all the food they could bear, along with even more slaves bound by chains all in a row. Among them was the Exalted One, trudging in misery along with his people, not daring to whisper his name for the shame of it all.

CHAPTER 19

THE FALL OF COOSA

No one knew what to do after De Soto's departure. Rumors flew that the god-ruler had been eaten by the white men in a farewell feast. Others said that he had risen to the sky to consult with the sun. It was even said that he had been enslaved by De Soto and was now as low as those who mucked the shitting pits, though this seemed unlikely.

Only the highest of the high nobles knew that the Exalted One was gone and would likely never return. None of the common people knew that Halw-i-em Mekko, their all-powerful ruler, was now nothing more than a slave, marching in chains to the south. The chaos gripping Coosa was so great that the normal rites of succession were tossed to the winds as men with gimlet eyes sought to claim the Sun God's staff.

The god-ruler's family fled for their lives after his eldest son was found murdered in his bed. Some said it was Black Serpent who thrust an obsidian dagger into the boy's ear, but who could prove it or would dare to say such a thing? In the company of a guard of thirty splendidly dressed warriors Black Serpent began speaking to the people each day from the lowest tier of the pyramid, claiming that the Exalted One had left him as their guide until his return. It was a powerful display that promised the return of order, and many were happy to acquiesce to the priest's reasoning. Those among the high nobles who demurred were soon found lying with their eyes open to the sky in the trash heaps of the town.

Wren had no such worries, however. At the master's hut far beyond the town walls, he and his mother had many long talks about her captivity and the customs of those who had enslaved her. And although Shines Like the Sun was now more than forty winters old, she professed to be strong enough to resume the trader's life. Long ago, she and Wren's father had buried a jar full of mica against the day that all of their fortunes were upended, and now to their joy, the jar was still there, nestled in the roots of a plum tree.

"Let us head north to Coste where the white men have already come and gone," she said. "If the town is as plundered as Coosa, then its people will be happy to see some traders."

It was a good plan, and in the distance, far beyond the hill where they lived, stood the flat-top pyramid where Black Serpent thought that he had made a good plan too.

But it was not to be.

It happened that De Soto had left behind a black slave who was suffering from a disfiguring illness. The sick man was as dark as midnight on a new moon, and the physicians of Coosa had offered to care for him, partly out of curiosity to determine if he was a demon and partly because De Soto had gifted them with strings of his dazzling beads. Through his interpreter, De Soto warned them that the slave's spirit would speak to him if he died at their hands, and so, he was given the best of care. Sacred words were spoken over him along with the wafting of smoke from sweet herbs that were dried and bound in bundles. He was given a healing tea each day, and when he was strong enough, he was bathed in the sweat lodge. All were pleased that he seemed to be recovering.

But though the slave's illness seemed slight, it was not so with that of his caregivers, who were engulfed with horrifying sores within days of his treatment

The sight of a black cloud over Coosa was the first that Wren, his mother, and the master learned of the calamity that befell the capital.

"What can it mean?" Wren's mother asked as they watched a storm of countless birds circling far off beyond the fields. The master squinted into the distance and muttered under his breath, shaking his head. "Prophecies," he said as his greasy locks dangled before his eyes. "The prophecies I've had ringing in my ears since my childhood! They tell of the sun giving way to a great beast of the underworld. Long have we waited, and long have our priests warned us of this day. If the prophecies are true, then perhaps the Great Death is upon us."

Wren glanced at the old man and back to the birds, all of them black, buzzards, ravens, crows, and vultures. The Great Death? The end of all life? All knew of the prophecy that someday the Sun God would be eaten by a demon of the underworld and would forsake his children to save his own life.

But Wren did not believe it.

"Look up, old man. The sun still shines on us," he said.

"Master."

"Look up, Master," Wren went on. "The old stories have no roots; they are meant to frighten half-wits. Did the prophecies ever speak of the white men? No! Perhaps they came back to slay our people and were slayed by our own warriors in turn. We are many, and they are few. Perhaps it is they who are meat for the buzzards and crows."

"Perhaps," the master said glumly. Turning, he retreated into the darkness of his lodge.

But that very afternoon, Wren found a dead man in the field below when he went down to gather some maize for their evening meal. The farmer was covered with sores, many of which had broken open in fissures across his body, and his face was contorted as if he had died in great pain. Elbowing his way through the corn stalks, Wren found a woman who was just the same and then the bodies of two men with their eyes open to the sky. Above him, he heard the cawing of crows.

"It is as you said," he told the master in a low voice upon his return. "The dead are planted everywhere in the fields."

That night, the three of them decided to wait and see. "We will remain here as quiet as mice," the master said. "Few people come here, and we will keep it so. The prophecies spoke of a great evil blocking the sun with its wings. I always imagined it would be as big as the hills, yet now I see it was birds that the prophecies spoke of. It is only birds."

The master was not known for his hospitality. Although he had accepted Wren as a son, most of his years on the hill had been spent scaring trespassers away with his magic. No one was likely to pass their way, and he forbade Wren and his mother from leaving the sanctuary of the hilltop.

But wandering over the far side of the hill, Wren was able to see the trail exiting Coosa to the north, and far off in between the trees lining the path he could make out a long line of people fleeing the town.

But as the days trudged on, he grew both anxious and bored as the cloud of birds over Coosa grew darker with their numbers. On the fourth day of their seclusion, he resolved to creep into the town to see for himself.

"Ah, that is a bad idea," the master said with a pinched face. "What if you don't come back?"

"I will keep to the corn instead of the pathways and peer through the palisade," Wren said. "No one will see me."

"You must run if you find evil there."

"I will outrun a rabbit."

Wren's mother was not happy with his decision, but it was true that they couldn't hide on their hilltop forever. Whatever was happening in Coosa had dashed their dream of taking up the trading life for now. She agreed that they had to know what was taking place in the town. She looked on sadly as he made his way down the hill to the field below.

The stench of death had risen from the corn field where many farmers had collapsed in agony. The higher-ups had told them to work or starve. Many, in fact, had starved as they lay unable to move, consumed with sores and pecked at by crows.

Gagging as he made his way through the field, Wren picked up the head scarf of a dead farmer and wrapped it around his face, hoping to block the stench. He passed more bodies—scores of them—and the wings and dark forms of crows, buzzards, and vultures exploded here and there as he drove them from their prey.

At last, he came to the palisade and found the place where one of the white men's thunder throwers had blown down a section of timbers. Fortunately, the deep, defensive ditch ringing the palisade was dry, and he was able to scramble up its side with little difficulty. Climbing through the gap in the palisade, he beheld a scene of horror that sent him reeling in disbelief.

There were bodies everywhere, lining the pathways and spilling from the lodges for as far as he could see. Moving among them were hundreds of animals of every type—coyotes, wolves, raccoons, foxes, and bears—all feeding on the dead in the company of the ravenous birds. Coosa had become the realm of scavengers and ghosts.

Wren had gone only a few steps into the town, nearly stumbling over a corpse. He looked down to find a richly dressed young woman, clearly one of the highest of the high, yet now her beautiful face was riven with scars and her eyes pecked by crows. On her wrist was a copper bracelet, studded with gems. Thinking of their desperate situation, Wren forced himself to pry it from her festered arm. They would need all the trade goods they could find if he and his mother hoped to start anew.

A raven sat only two steps away, fixing its golden eye on the dead woman. Wren gave it a savage kick, and it tumbled off, shrieking with a broken wing.

In his shock at the sight of the dead carpeting the town, he had not heard the moans of the dying. But now, they reached his ears with prayers to the sun and more in a chorus of the damned—"help *me, help, water, mercy…*" The cries rising over the dead and dying were like the sound of a river, unceasing in their murmur.

Wren was no coward. He had endured many trials as a wandering trader and during his time as a boy lost in the wilderness. As the master had told him, there was a good man and a bad man within everyone, stepping forth in their turn when called upon. Now the good man within him rose to his duty with the help of the bad. His stomach turned. Gagging, he found a gourd and filled it with water from one of the reservoirs. It was the same pit from which the great pyramid had been built.

Moving among the dead and scattering the scavengers, Wren knelt to wet the lips of the dying. Many offered their last words on earth; others begged for death.

Wren came upon a warrior who lay dying alongside his wife and child. The warrior had bludgeoned his family, sending them to the spirits to relieve their agony.

"Kill me, brother," he begged, writhing in pain. Like the others, his body was covered with bleeding sores. "Kill me so that I may join my woman and daughter … I have no hope."

"No, brother, be still," Wren said, stooping to offer a drink. "You are strong. You will recover."

"No!" the warrior cried. "There is nothing left for me. They are on the trail of the dead. Send me with them—we will journey on together. You are the warrior now, brother. Send me to them. You are strong, untouched; strike the side of my head at the temples, strike hard!"

The warrior's club lay beside him. Its hickory shaft was richly carved with twining vines that culminated in the gaping head of a frog with a large chunk of flint in its mouth. It was the warrior's most prized possession, yet it had never been used, until now.

Wren's throat went as dry as a stone and tears filled his eyes as he met those of the pleading warrior. It was plain there was no hope for him.

"Do it brother, the sun will bless you," the man gasped. He closed his eyes and began his prayer.

Wren closed his own eyes, hesitated a moment, and swung hard at the side of the warrior's head. He heard the skull crack, and his knees went liquid as he swooned, gulping for breath, trying not to faint. Looking down he saw the dying man gazing at the sky as the light faded from his eyes. Wren bent over, leaned on the club, and vomited. Moments later, as if walking in a nightmare, he pushed on, meting out water or death to all who begged for it.

By the end of the day, he was covered with blood, offering water to those who begged for it and showing mercy on those who craved death. How many, he did not know, but his arms were sore from the effort, and there were so many more calling out from far into the town—far too many. He tossed the club aside and bathed in the reservoir, scrubbing himself the best he could.

Down the way, he saw a black man shuffling toward him with a load of plunder in his arms. His eyes flared with fright. What demon was this? Turning, he ran for his life.

It was long after nightfall before Wren reached home where his mother and the master were waiting for him. Wren stood before the fire with his breech cloth stained pink with blood that had not washed away.

"Wren, what did you find?" his mother asked. Her face was stricken with fear, as was that of the master.

"They are dead, all dead. Most of them," he replied. "The dead lie unburied. Others lie waiting to die. The town is gone, all of it. It is a town of ghosts. We can never go there again—no one can go there."

He told them of the animals feasting on the dead and what he had done to offer water and comfort. "But there were too many," he said, shaking his head. "Far too many."

"Is that blood on you?" the master demanded.

Wren looked up and met the old man's eyes. "I did what I could. Many begged for death."

"You did well then."

A long silence followed as the three of them gazed into the fire, lost in their thoughts and wondering what to do next. Then Wren remembered the bejeweled bracelet he had taken from the dead woman. He pulled it from the thong of his breech clout and handed it to his mother.

"A gift from one who no longer needs it," he said.

His mother cradled the bracelet in her hand and then gently laid it on a rock by the fire. It glimmered in the firelight with its gems winking at the flames.

"Thank you, son," she said, "We are in your hands now."

CHAPTER 20

THE NAMING

They had made plans to head north on the trail that Wren had glimpsed from the hilltop, but first they gathered as much maize as they could from the fields below their lodge. The cobs were scraped clean, and the red, yellow, and purple kernels were parched and bagged. Wren was sure that it would be a long journey, and the corn would be useful for trading. Fashioning hammocks between two poles, he made a long dragger for himself and a shorter one for his mother. The master was too aged to drag anything and would have to follow along the best he could with the aid of his staff.

At night, the master's dreams and moaning grew worse, and Wren and his mother froze in their pallets as the old man cried out "No!" in his sleep and babbled in a strange tongue. Sometimes he did nothing but scream until he lurched upright, wide-eyed in terror.

And then Wren fell sick. The last thing he remembered was his mother bending over him and wiping his forehead with a cloth dipped in cool water. How many days he lay writhing in pain he did not know, but he dreamed that he was being chased by a monster which appeared as a black form and without any shape. He ran down tunnels, over hills and through the pathways of the town. Yet still the thing followed, sniffing only a step behind his heels.

Gradually, his fever ebbed, and the monster shrank to a whisper. He awoke one morning with the sun shining bright into the entry of the lodge and a gourd full of water lying alongside. With a gasp, he reached for the gourd and slaked his thirst.

Blinking into the sun, he noticed a storm of flies filling the lodge, and there beside him lay his mother, dead in a puddle of her own blood.

Shines Like the Sun had lost hope of ever seeing her son on this side of life and decided not to wait. The disease had crept over her with frightening speed, but before she endured its agony, she opened her wrists with the master's obsidian blade. Now she lay beside Wren with her eyes open and dried blood pooling at her waist.

Wren looked at his mother without a word, but something within him cracked in an explosion of white light from which there seemed to be no end. *Gone*. He spent the rest of the morning sobbing and rocking with his arms around his knees. His mind was shattered—there were only shards of light piercing his thoughts, along with a pain far greater than what he had endured in his illness. Gone! All gone! All hope was gone, all their dreams were gone. His mother had endured so much, and there was so much to live for, but now...

It was noon before Wren found his way back to his senses. He wiped away his tears and laid his hand on his mother's shoulder, praying for her safe journey onward. She had cheated the plague. She had been brave, undefeated. He shooed the flies from her blood and covered her with a blanket. As soon as strength allowed, he would bury her with ceremony, hoping to see her and his father again one day when the sun called for his own spirit.

Across the way, he heard a rustle, and sitting up, he saw the master lying against the far wall.

"Water," he croaked. "If you ever loved me, bring me water."

Wren crawled to where the master lay and lifted the gourd to his lips. "My mother is gone," he said.

"Soon I will follow her. Bury me alongside her. We will journey together."

As with many others, the old man was so disfigured with sores that Wren barely recognized him, yet he seemed calm, resigned.

"You have no pain?" Wren asked.

"There is a flower whose tincture lessens pain," the master said with a wan smile. "I have tasted it many times these past few days, but I will not be with you much longer."

He winced and motioned for a small gourd, grasping it in the darkness of the lodge. "I saved the last, hoping that you would return," he said. "The gods are kind—my prayers have been answered. Lift me up."

Wren propped him against the wall. The master looked around the lodge for a final time, eyeing his collection of strange and marvelous things. "We've had good days together, boy," he whispered. "Perhaps we will meet again."

"Soon."

"No, not soon," he said, waving a hand. "But there is one thing I would have you do for me before I go."

"Yes," Wren said, "anything. Say it."

"Take my name. Take my name, and I will live on through you. You will remember me and…"

The old man sipped at his gourd and then threw his head back and swallowed it whole. "Bitter," he mumbled as his eyes began to glaze. "So bitter … but so sweet…"

"Your name?" Wren said. "Master? You would have me call myself Master?"

"No, no, not that foolishness," the old man said waving a hand in a lazy way.

"What? How? You never told me your name. I do not know it."

The master gave him a wan smile as the light died in his eyes. "It is Sun Dog," he said. "Hasi Efa, say it! You are Sun Dog now. You are *Hasi Efa!*"

CHAPTER 21

THE KNIGHT OF GENOA

"*Hasi Efa,*" Wren said, turning the name over in his thoughts. "I will honor your wishes, great one. Take comfort in your journey. I will remember you."

He felt strange as soon as the words left his lips, as if something of the master had come along with the uttering of his name. Shaking the thought aside, the young man who was now Sun Dog rose to his feet and stumbled outside, collapsing in the mid-day sun.

He lay there for a long time, looking south to far-off Coosa. The birds still circled overhead, but not as many as before.

It had been days since he had eaten, and suddenly a ferocious hunger overtook him. The sacks of corn they had so carefully collected were still inside the lodge, though the mice had been busy with them. Taking two handfuls of the dry kernels, he doused them in a bowl of water, not waiting until they had fully absorbed the liquid. Looking up, he remembered the rabbit they had smoked, dangling by a cord from the ceiling of the lodge. The gods were kind … it was speckled with flies, but he wrestled it down and gnawed at the leathery flesh, not waiting to steep it. Nothing had ever tasted so good.

Afterward, he made a sacrifice of tobacco, offering it to whatever gods had saved him. He stripped and examined his body; there were no scars upon it except for three small pock marks on his right cheek. They were perfectly spaced in a line, much the same as the three stars that made the bracelet of the Nameless One who watched over the night from his place in the sky. It was a good sign.

That night, he lay on the dirt floor of the lodge alongside the body of his mother, vowing that he would not leave her. But the next morning he dragged her corpse outside along with that of the master and piled brush and dead branches upon them at a distance from the lodge. No animal would disturb their grave—he would bury them in the sky with the same honor given to warriors. He sat before the fire until it had burned down to cinders. A plume of smoke towered above the hillside, but he had no fear that it would attract visitors.

Nothing held him to the master's lodge, and there was nothing for him in Coosa, so on the next morning, Sun Dog hefted a sack of corn and set off over the hill to join the great pathway to the north where he had seen so many fleeing.

It was a long scramble through the forest, but at last he hit upon the trail and turned north. The trail was empty except for a corpse here and there that was riven with decay and the ravages of animals and insects. Everyone who could flee had long since left the town, and he trudged on, buried in his thoughts with no idea of where to go or what to do.

Sun Dog's concentration was so intense that he never heard the whinny of horses until they were upon him. Rounding a bend in the trail, he looked up to find a company of white men only steps away. One of them cried out, and he scrambled for the brush at the side of the trail, hoping to zigzag through the undergrowth like a rabbit.

But it was the men of his own people who chased him, not the white demons. Sun Dog was still blue-lipped and weak from starvation and disease, and they easily ran him down, fetching him back to the waiting soldiers.

The white men spoke among themselves from atop their mounts, and one lifted his hand to another who nodded. Behind him sat a smaller man on another animal that was like the tall deer of the white men, only much smaller and with long ears like that of a rabbit.

Shoved from behind, Sun Dog was led to his new master, Battista Giovanni de Noli, a knight of Genoa, accompanied by his squire, Pedro Lopez of Castile. Sun Dog did not know what they were called, only that the first spoke and the second obeyed, their roles etched as plainly as the dust on their boots. Held in place by his captors, Sun Dog was manacled with two rings of a black metal around his ankles, a length of chain as long as his arm linked the rings together, and he realized that his bonds gave him just enough freedom to walk but not run. *A slave,* he thought, *I am to be a slave of the white devils.*

And so, he was for many days as the party moved south. There were twenty-two of the white men, including fourteen that Sun Dog took to be warriors dressed in tunics of gray metal ringlets and eight servants in a light armor of padded cotton. This, and another thirty or so of his own people, some who were servants that walked freely and others who were slaves, bound like himself.

Sun Dog was given a bag of camp tools to carry along with his corn. That night, he slept on bare ground with no blanket to keep warm. His only meal for the day was a porridge made of parched corn. It was clear that the white men did not treat their slaves as well as did the people of Coosa, and as he trudged along day after day, Sun Dog realized that his life was worth nothing to his captors. They would wear him down to his bones and throw his corpse by the side of the trail.

There were many bodies alongside the trail as the procession moved south. The sick among those fleeing had fallen in their tracks as the plague crept over them. Many of the white men touched their foreheads, their stomachs, and each shoulder as they passed the dead. Sun Dog assumed that this was their way of honoring the spirits, but once, coming across the bodies of a woman and her daughter, one of them uttered what sounded like a crude jest, and then made an obscene gesture with his hands. The others looked at him in disgust and one called him a name.

It was obvious that the white men feared the dead, for some of them had fallen sick as well, but the plague seemed to have a lesser effect on them than on the people of Coosa.

But there were other things to fear besides the plague. From time to time an arrow would fly from the surrounding brush, with the sight of warriors running swiftly back and forth among the trees. The white men could not reach them on their horses, nor were they quick enough with their crossbows. Often, the attackers' arrows bounced harmlessly off the white men's armor, but not always. One day, Sun Dog saw the shaft of a cane arrow whip through one side of a soldier's neck and out the other. The white man lived for a day, moaning in agony before being buried by the trail. Again, the white men made their sign of reverence at the grave and moved on.

They passed a scattering of empty villages, some with bodies rotting within their palisades. At one, they found the heads of two Spaniards jutting from posts at the gates with their hacked-off arms and legs dangling from nearby trees and atop the palisade walls. These were retrieved and buried while the white men's shaman uttered words of ceremony as their dogs fretted and sniffed around the grave.

It was around this time that Sun Dog sensed that the master had journeyed on with him, living on with his name. One night, he awoke to find a dark form standing over him. He sat up in alarm only to find that the shape had disappeared. Other times, it was as if the master was whispering in his thoughts as he trudged along the line of slaves. Perhaps it was the master who whispered how he might go free.

Gradually, a plan took shape in his thoughts. The knight's squire used signs to teach him how to set up their camp each night before chaining him to a tree. Sun Dog feigned ignorance until the squire beat him in exasperation. He took on the guise of a simpleton, cowering and whining before managing to learn his chores, reasoning that the white men would be less likely to watch an imbecile. The men of his own people were doubtful of his charade, but the Spaniards had no trouble believing that he was simple-minded.

From one of his fellow captives, Sun Dog learned that the white men were a foraging party that had stayed behind to plunder outlying villages for food and slaves. De Soto and the others had gone to far-off Itaba, and it would be at least a cycle of the moon before the foragers joined them again.

So it was that Sun Dog offered to make his master's meal one evening when his servant was setting out a pot made of the same metal that bound his ankles. The man was happy to surrender this chore and set about chattering with others of his station and making moon eyes at one of the enslaved women.

It was unseemly for a man to prepare a meal, and Sun Dog ignored the jibes of his fellow captives, who called him woman-man and asked if he squatted when he pissed. He flashed a toothy grin in the direction of his mockers and bobbed his head as if he were an idiot. Making meals was no disgrace in his own eyes; the master had charged him with these duties from the first day of their meeting.

But it was the meals that were the undoing of Battista Giovanni de Noli and Pedro Lopez.

Battista had been born in the village of Noli, a sun-drenched port in Liguria, south of Genoa. He might have languished there forever as one of the minor nobility, had it not been for the ceaseless wars between Venice and Genoa over control of trade in the Mediterranean. Venice had the far greater fleet of warships and galleys, and so, troops were needed in Genoa to repel invaders from the sea. Thus, thanks to the crying need for the fortress garrison and some opportune family relations, Battista Giovanni de Noli was made a knight of Genoa. Yet after five years of service in which he saw no combat, Battista was charged with a scandal involving a duke's daughter, and as the saying goes, he packed his trunk by the light of the moon and fled.

It was far across the Great Ocean Sea to the island of *Hispaniola* that he landed, and from there he enlisted in the cause of Hernando de Soto with promises of gold and treasure to be shared to every freebooter once in *La Florida,* the Land of Flowers. All knew of the disaster of the conquistador Panfilo de Narvaez, whose men had disappeared almost without a trace twelve years before, yet De Soto planned to delve far deeper into the New World, and the brave men who accompanied him were assured of reward.

Yet in the seven months in which they had wandered, Battista had seen nothing but corn, pumpkins, and gaping natives who knew nothing of gold or treasure. Coosa was the largest town they had encountered so far; indeed, it was larger than many of the cities of Spain and Italy, but its treasures consisted mostly of feathers, shells, and slaves.

So it was that Battista and his squire soldiered on under a cloud of pessimism, fearing for their own skins under the dark-eyed glare of their captives and the constant threat of arrows, darts and javelins from the green tangle of the forest. Their only hope was that De Soto would have the sense to return to the sea where they might be swept back to the good life on Hispaniola. Yet so far, their leader had shown no sign of doing any such thing.

Sun Dog knew nothing of this but was well-versed in the herbs and medicines of the earth, having been the master's student for the past ten years. The master had taught him many things in addition to magic, including that certain potions, powders, and drugs were far more powerful than spells.

Early on, Sun Dog had also invented a game in his guise as a simpleton. One night in camp he had fashioned a short length of grapevine into a loop. Holding onto a shaft of hickory, he had tossed the loop high into the air and then attempted to catch it with his stick. This quickly drew attention as both the Spaniards and their captives turned out to watch the fool at play. For the most part, Sun Dog failed to catch the ring on his stick, but when he did there were loud huzzahs of approval. One of the white men asked if he could try it and then others came forward. For soldiers who were aching with boredom, it was a huge entertainment.

Sun Dog was allowed to keep the hoop and the stick tucked into his belt thereafter. No one took notice that the shaft of hickory was as long as his forearm and twice as thick as his thumb. Nor did anyone remark that he had filed it to a point during the night with the aid of a coarse rock. Then he had hardened the point in the cooking fire.

All of this escaped the attention of his captors as the simpleton and his stick walked along, bent under his heavy load each day. The game grew tiresome and then forgotten as the white men returned to their pastimes of dice and wooing the women.

Yet over the next few days, Sun Dog eyed the side of the trail with care, seeking out a plant whose berries could help set him free. Often, he was only able to grasp two or three of the small pink berries at a time, not wishing to draw attention to himself. He kept them hidden under his doeskin breech clout beneath his testicles, savoring the irony of what was to come.

Finally, he had a handful. That evening, he waved off the squire with a face full of cheer, as usual, and prepared the evening meal. It was corn again. What else could it be? But Sun Dog had seized a tortoise by the trail that day, and the white men licked their lips as the aroma of the stewed meat rose over the camp. Sun Dog felt a moment's alarm at the thought that his carefully prepared meal would be shared out by too many, but a young doe was also on a spit over a neighboring fire, and there was sure to be good eating for all that night, even the slaves.

Even so, Sun Dog was careful to see that a generous bowl of his meal was offered to Battista Giovanni de Noli and the squire, Pedro Lopez before the venison was ready. Sadly, there was none left to go around.

The next morning, Sun Dog prepared their breakfast, making their porridge a little soupier than usual and ignoring their complaints with a grin and a stupid expression.

Sir Battista was in a sour mood. The fine charger he'd paid a duke's ransom for in Cuba had been shot in the rump with a poisoned arrow shortly before they had arrived in Coosa, and he'd been compelled to put it out of his misery. Now he rode a sway-backed white mare petitioned from the baggage train that had thrown a shoe and was gimping along with a cracked and bleeding hoof. Soon, he would have to take his squire's donkey as a mount if he didn't want to walk, but the indignity of a knight astride an ass was too much to bear. Other knights had been forced to walk by now and so would he, unless he could beg for the use of pack mule, which seemed unlikely.

He cursed this wretched land and himself as a fool for enlisting in De Soto's mad dream of treasure when he could still be lording it up in Cuba with plenty of servants and women. And food! Not the horrid corn mush his Indian slave prepared morning and night without a thought for salt or spice. Twice he'd cuffed the man for playing his childish game of the hoop and the stick, receiving only the look of a craven dog in response along with a few confused giggles—no horse, no hope of return to civilization, and a simpleton for a servant—all that and mosquitoes in the millions. He was in hell.

With a sigh he thought of Angelique, the dusky woman with the plummy buttocks and soft belly who had warmed his bed back in Santiago. God's balls, what he'd give to lie in her arms again! But despite all the hints and grumbling by almost every knight and nobleman in the army, De Soto refused to return to the sweet succor of the ships waiting on the coast, insisting that they push on in his mad quest for gold and treasure. Gold? They'd found nothing but maize cakes and mush. By now, Sir Battista imagined there was no more gold in this horrid land than a barrel of bananas.

The morning's march had not progressed long before the knight of Genoa and his squire felt a powerful need to relieve their bowels. They dropped behind the procession and did the deed behind a clump of trees as Sun Dog waited patiently by their steeds.

But not long thereafter, the need arose again, and Pedro Lopez begged for his master to stop. This was all well with Battista, whose own bowels were once again in an uproar. Again, Sun Dog waited quietly, noting that the line of conquistadors and their slaves was now far out of sight.

Battista Giovanni de Noli strove mightily thereafter to contain himself but, to his dismay, found himself squirting at the rear and soiling his underwear, which was already badly in need of washing and repair.

Cursing, he dropped from his horse and made his way into the brush with his squire seeking the bushes on the opposite side of the trail.

Now Sun Dog's heart began to beat like a hundred drums, and a faintness crept into his head that he fought with all of his strength. He reminded himself of the master's words regarding the way that a magician must present himself—collected, stone-faced when needed, or beaming with good cheer to fit the situation. Now the stone face was called for, and though he felt like vomiting, he held himself firm, summoning the bad man within him with all his might.

He had asked one of the white man's long-time captives how to pronounce a certain word in their language, repeating it over and over to secure its memory. As the knight of Genoa returned from the brush, tugging at his breeches with a scowl on his face, Sun Dog pointed behind him.

"*Serpiente,*" he said quietly.

It was the way of magic taught by the master—tell what is to be seen and then show it.

Battista's face went wide with alarm as he turned to face the snake, finding nothing there. Turning back, he was surprised to see what appeared to be a snake in the Indian's hand just shy of his own face.

But that was the last thing he saw.

"*Serpiente,*" Sun Dog said again, driving the sharpened hickory bolt through the knight's left eye and deep into his brain. The knight gave a single convulsive twitch and fell heavily at his feet.

Battista had a strange club hanging from his saddle, with a heavy chunk of metal studded with blades at the end of a shaft. Sun Dog reached for it and hid it behind his back as Lopez emerged from the bushes.

"*Serpiente!*" Sun Dog cried, pointing at the prostrated knight. "*Serpiente!*"

Lopez ran to his master's side, turning the body over to see the long hickory shaft protruding from his eye. His mouth fell open, not comprehending, and looking up, he said, "What are you doing with the master's mace?"

But that was all he said.

Sun Dog had observed the small bit of metal dangling on the knight's belt that was used to bind his manacles. There was a magic to it that he didn't understand, but he had watched as others had been released. The trick was to insert the metal twig into a hole in the manacles and give it a twist. He plucked it from the belt and slid it home. To his surprise, his bonds instantly fell from his ankles.

Hurriedly, Sun Dog stripped the knight of his chain mail, thinking it would be a valuable trade item. Battista also had a mantle of chain mail covering his head, topped by his helmet. Sun Dog tried the mantle on, finding it ridiculously heavy. He tossed it and the helmet into the brush and considered the knight's weapons.

Besides the mace, Battista wore a long sword and a serrated dagger that was almost as long as his forearm. Although Sun Dog could not have known, this was a French *misericorde*—a dagger with a hand guard that was used to parry blows from an opponent's sword and to slip between the gaps in his armor. Sun Dog took the dagger and mace, ignoring the sword. Then he stripped the squire of his thick cotton jerkin, which he knew was a crude sort of armor that could blunt an arrow. It would keep him warm on the long walk back. Emptying his camp gear into the brush, he stuffed the chain mail and jerkin into his sack along with a store of corn.

But in his haste, he stumbled and fell headlong across a pack that the squire had carried on his back. It let out a loud squeal. He looked inside and pulled from the pack an oddly shaped bladder like the one the master had used to frighten people when he made Little Demon dance. This one had four tubes extending from it. Three of them appeared to be flutes, while the fourth was smaller, made for inflating. Despite his haste, Sun Dog smiled, thinking how enchanted the master would have been at such a marvel. It would make his burden heavier, but he decided to bring it along. Perhaps it would prove useful.

He dragged the bodies into the brush and shooed their beasts down the trail in the opposite direction of the company of soldiers, which was now far ahead. Then, hefting the knight's mace and securing the long dagger at his belt, he took to the woods, keeping a bowshot from the trail as he headed north.

It would be the evening meal before anyone knew that Battista Giovanni de Noli and his squire, Pedro Lopez, were missing. Four men were sent riding back up the trail the next day to find them, but their bodies were never found. Nor was the simpleton who served them.

CHAPTER 22

BLACK SERPENT

It was half a moon before Sun Dog made it back to Coosa. For three days, he kept to the woods alongside the trail, once crouching down behind a fallen tree as four riders loped past him on their beasts. He saw them riding back again in the late afternoon and reasoned that he was free of the white men. Even so, he kept off the trail until he was sure.

Coosa was in ruins by the time he reached home. Hundreds of huts were starting to sag for lack of care, and the town's crops lay rotting in the fields. Bones were scattered everywhere along its avenues, and the skulls of the dead gaped at him as he stepped past.

Sun Dog had had a great deal of time to think on the journey home, and little by little, had given up his dream of resuming the trading life. He had met refugees living in small camps in the forest, and they all told tales of desperation. The plague that had destroyed the capital had been spread to hundreds of villages throughout the chiefdom until all hope was lost.

Once, Sun Dog had come across a farmer and his family who had fled their village when they first heard of the plague.

"We only meant to hide our corn," the farmer said, "but soon there was no one to guard against."

"Have you met others?" Sun Dog asked.

"Not many. There are more dead than there is sand on a beach. Not one in ten survived, but this seems only the beginning of our troubles.

Coosa's enemies are attacking from all sides, taking slaves or revenge. Many of our people are even begging to be taken as slaves."

"But why?"

"Some feel it's better than starving in the forest," the farmer said, "or being sacrificed to their demon gods."

He thought for a moment longer, chewing on a sprig of grass. "Or for that matter, eaten."

No one knew the vastness of the chiefdom of Coosa better than Sun Dog, who had wandered its length and breadth with his parents. It took a full cycle of the moon for a swift man to walk the realm from the mountains in the north to the swamplands of the south. Every town and village had been struck, with many of their residents huddling together in the hope that strength in numbers would scare the demons of disease away. But this only made a feast of souls for the plague.

Coosa had many enemies among the neighboring chiefdoms and had warred with some for several lifetimes. Others were trading partners, but these, too, sniffed opportunity, like vultures eyeing a wounded animal. Sun Dog sensed that his homeland was mortally wounded and unlikely to rise again in his lifetime, if ever. He would need to seek a different path than trading.

But what?

At last, he reached the palisade of the town, which stood in a deathly silence. He came to the base of the great pyramid, and the town seemed all the eerier as he looked to its height. There were no guards now, yet the temple still stood at the top of the pyramid, forlorn and silent in its majesty.

Sun Dog couldn't help but smile as he took his first steps to the top. The gods of Coosa were dead, and surely the Exalted One had died with them. But he decided to take a final look over the town before leaving it forever. Perhaps the god-ruler still lived if he truly was the Son of the Sun.

Reaching the top, he looked out over the bend in the river far below, which was empty now of the many dugouts and barges that once swarmed at its banks. The plaza and avenues below were also empty—once they had been filled with thousands, hustling to the fields and markets. Now only a few wolves and coyotes moved among the rank dead, clutching at bones.

Entering the temple, he stood before the curtain where Black Serpent had welcomed him and his father many years ago. The pillars of the temple were crafted from mighty trees standing the height of four tall men and big enough around to require two men with arms outstretched to gird them. Here and there, sections of the palapa roof had been blown away in a windstorm with no one left to make repairs.

Sun Dog stood before the curtain for a long time, wondering if somehow the god-ruler still lived behind it by the grace of his father, the Sun. Beyond the screen was sacred ground, and though he had lost faith in the gods, still, a man can seldom shed his dread of such things.

But no sound came from behind the curtain, not even when Sun Dog called out, and moving the curtain off to the side, he dared to look beyond.

There lay Black Serpent with his necklace of rattlesnake heads splayed across his chest and the staff of the god-ruler lying alongside his corpse. His leathery face was drawn in an expression of horror, yet he was barely decayed and Sun Dog surmised that he had lived for many days atop the pyramid as the city died around him before his own death came stalking. Indeed, there was still a wisp of smoke coming from a bier across the way.

The High One's crown of macaw feathers and egret wings had tumbled to the side of the priest. On impulse, Sun Dog picked it up and placed it atop his own head. Then lifting the staff of authority, he looked down at Black Serpent and smiled.

"I am the Exalted One now." It was blasphemy, but who was to say otherwise? If Black Serpent objected, he did not speak.

He grabbed the priest's body by the ankles and dragged it from the temple, sending it tumbling down the side of the pyramid. Two dead servants followed, along with the body of a noble, heavily draped in necklaces and garbed in a fine cloak of badger fur.

But that was not all. Before the white men left, they had planted a large wooden cross atop the pyramid in homage to their tortured god. It stood as high as three tall men and could be seen to the far horizon. No one had thought to tear it down until the white men's army was well away. Now Sun Dog piled all of the clothing and furniture that he could find at its base, and fetching a coal from the bier, set it ablaze as the sun began to set.

It was the boy, Wren, who decided that he would test himself in his new role as Sun Dog that night. If he could sleep here among ten thousand ghosts, he could do anything. He wrapped himself in a robe made from the skins of mountain lions and slept like a contented baby by the light of the blazing cross, wakening at sunrise with the seed of an idea forming in his thoughts.

That morning, Sun Dog made the half-day walk back to the master's lodge on the hill. The wind and rain had done their work, but for the most part the lodge remained undisturbed. There on the shelf stood the hideous form of the shaved monkey, Little Demon, and in the bark box beside him was the hairy spider that was as large as man's hand.

But it took a long time before he found the treasure he sought the most. It was the glittering mask made of countless bits of mica that his father had given the master for saving his life. After searching every crack and crevice in the lodge, he finally found it concealed in a vault beneath a slab of limestone in the floor of the lodge.

Lifting the mask from its hiding place, Sun Dog carried it from the lodge and turned it toward the sun, recoiling as it blinded him with its reflected light. The mask shimmered with a crystalline light, almost too bright to bear. His father's legacy was the mask of a god.

He lined up his treasures outside the lodge, appraising which one he would bring along. There was the white man's chain mail, dagger, and mace. Then there was the squire's cotton armor and his odd noisemaker. The master's Little Demon, spider, and the mica mask were delicate and would require boxes made of wood or bark. Add to this the feathered crown, robe, and staff of the Exalted One. It was a lot to carry, but Sun Dog couldn't bear to part with anything.

He recalled that the slaves of the white men had carried large packs that were fashioned with straps around their shoulders. He had seen such a pack lying alongside a dead slave in Coosa. It had appeared to be well-made, and he decided to fetch it on the following day. A terrible loneliness fell upon him as he sat considering the things he planned to take along. What good were all of the riches in the world to a man who is all alone? All of the magic that he had learned from the old man and all of the skills he had acquired as a trader were worthless to a man without an audience. His skills were meant to command the will of men and bedazzle women, yet on his own he was nothing.

Nor could he bear the thought of slavery. Many of those he had met in the forest told him that slave-catchers from other lands were everywhere, taking advantage of Coosa's misfortune.

The life of a farmer was little different than that of a slave in Coosa, except when it came to the life beyond death. The high-born nobles and priests of Coosa could expect to be buried in a sacred mound of privilege with treasures that would aid them in the afterlife, while a farmer and his family were interred in a lesser mound with a few pots and tools. But slaves were buried in a pit with no ceremony and nothing to aid them in the spirit world. Who would choose such a path? That, and slaves were fed little better than the town's scavenging dogs. Many were captives from other lands and unless they were adopted, there was little reason to be kind to them. It was common to sever the nerve in one ankle of a slave so that he or she could hobble but not run. That would be the fate of many who had fled Coosa, only to be captured.

Hoping to quiet his mind, Sun Dog picked up the squire's bag-like instrument. He deduced that it was meant to play a kind of music, but how? When he pressed at its side it gave out a loud squawking sound like a parrot. To amuse himself, he gave out the howl of a wolf as he squeezed the bladder. The howl and the screech of the instrument blended in a hilarious roar that convulsed him with laughter. With a smile, he imagined onlookers marveling at its mad screech, perhaps leaping back in alarm.

The next day, he made his way back to Coosa to find the cast-aside pack. It was well-made of leather and big enough to hold all of his things. He resolved to take the path to the north where he had seen so many refugees fleeing. Perhaps someone would take him in.

CHAPTER 23

THE WAY NORTH

As he expected, the great pathway to the north was also lined with the dead, although by now their bodies were worn to bones and sinew. Sun Dog had breathed in the smell of death for so long that now he barely noticed it, yet gradually the air grew fresher, and his heart began to lift.

Here and there, he came upon knots of survivors, only to find that a lone man is often viewed with suspicion. Sun Dog was tall and well-built, and though he offered friendly intentions, such was the terror of the times that most of those he met were eager to have him move along. It didn't help that he had the conquistador's serrated dagger in his belt, the staff of the Exalted One in one hand, and the wicked looking mace slung over his shoulder. Few had ever seen the staff, except at a great distance at the top of Coosa's highest pyramid, but it was clearly a thing that could only belong to the highest of the high-born. It was carved all along its length with intertwining snakes clutching the copper disc of the sun at the top of the staff.

"Who are you that owns such a thing?" an old man asked, noting that Sun Dog was dressed in humble skins, unlike the nobles of the town. "You must have stolen it!'

"I took it from the hands of a priest, and it was freely given," he replied. In a way that was true, but it did him little good with the old man and his small group of survivors. Sun Dog moved on.

Once, three men emerged from the brush at the side of the trail as he rounded a bend. They wore the geometric tattoos of the warriors of Coosa, but now they were nothing but thugs, perhaps even slavers. They were dirty, shabbily dressed, and their hair was unkempt. He judged that they had been living in the forest like animals. All had clubs in their hands, but Sun Dog had the blade-studded mace.

"Give us your pack," one called out. He was the smallest of the three, possessed of a pinched face and a cocky manner. Sun Dog judged that he would be the fastest on his feet and the one to watch for.

"Why do you want it?" he replied.

"We just want to see," the weasel-faced leader replied. "Give us a look and we'll let you pass."

Sun Dog looked down and closed his eyes. "You would not find it pretty," he said in a low voice. "It is a bag of heads, and I need a few more for *Eh-noq-waa*."

He looked up, craned his head forward and leered, offering a ghastly smile as he stepped toward them.

Two of the three raised their clubs half-heartedly while their leader shifted back and forth on his feet as if he was aiming to attack. But by now Sun Dog was committed; he had come too far through too many troubles to submit, and during his captivity he had practiced summoning the bad man within himself. Sometimes, the master had told him, one's bad man turns coward and flees, but the ambush had arisen so quickly that Sun Dog steeled himself before fear had time to take him. He raised the mace and bared his teeth with a crazed look in his eyes. The three wavered, then turned and shuffled off, calling insults over their shoulders. They were crows, and he had been too much trouble to peck at. Weaker prey was sure to come along.

Even so, Sun Dog took time to don the chain mail he had taken from the white man and took to the woods, following alongside the path for half a day until he was sure that no arrows would be fired at him from the brush.

Thus, caution became the cousin of his loneliness. The few people that he came across spoke of raiders from all directions except that of the haunted capital. They also told of gangs of men who had turned to robbery and other outrages. The bond of civility that had ruled the chiefdom of Coosa through the strength of its priests, nobles, and warriors was broken, and its refugees were fleeing everywhere in desperation.

Sun Dog's anguish deepened as he headed north. If there were no settled villages, then there could be no trade; nor was there any place that he could find a home, even if he humbled himself to take up the life of a farmer. Like thousands of others, he was tormented with the question of what to do and where to go. His pack drew no comment—every man, woman, and child was also carrying every possession that they could manage.

Still, he went on, hoping that the furthest reaches of the chiefdom would have gone untouched by the plague. He recalled the village of his childhood, where the headman had pointed out the notch in the mountains. Where his father and mother had been captured and spirited away. The village of Tali was remote and off the main pathway to the north. Perhaps it had survived.

But Sun Dog had been a boy of ten when he and his parents had visited the village, and now he had no idea as to where it might lie. In the distance, he could see the mist-shrouded mountains but not the notch that might give a clue to Tali's location.

He came upon a narrow trail leading off the main pathway to the northwest and, on an impulse, decided to follow it. He walked for half a day before hearing voices up ahead late in the afternoon. Thinking that he must be near the village, he quickened his stride, anxious to be free of his heavy pack. But then—*no*—he heard weeping ahead and gruff voices. As he had done so many times before, he took to the brush.

Down the trail came a line of captives, tethered by their necks with a long rope of hemp. Herding them both ahead and behind were men with the markings that Sun Dog had seen long before. They were of the same wild men who had captured his mother and father.

Now, eight of the wild men came trooping along with ten women and children and three men. The children wandered untethered alongside their mothers, being shushed over and over again not to cry. The men had their hands tied behind their backs and one struggled along with his head covered in blood.

Sun Dog hugged the ground, burying his face in the earth as the line moved past, only a few steps away. If any had glanced to the side, they would have seen his pack lying there with a new slave lying beneath it.

He listened as they filed off into the distance, thinking that there might be a scout staying behind to watch for followers as had been their practice when he had escaped so many years ago. No one followed.

Sun Dog didn't spend any time thinking of the fate of those who had been captured. That was the way of the world for so many, especially in these times of trouble. But he had taken only a few steps down the trail in the opposite direction when it was as if a hand fell on his shoulder, holding him back.

These are my people, he thought. Their captors were of the same men who had led his parents into slavery. They were the same men who had led to his father's death. Now, he heard his father's voice calling from the grave. Now he heard the master's voice in his ear. He had no way to battle eight men who lived as animals in the forest, but the master whispered that he had a weapon that might defeat them all. He had magic.

The raiders had walked with an easy stride, meaning that they had no fear of being followed and would likely be making camp soon. Sun Dog crept through the woods for a long time, listening to the sounds up ahead. At last, he heard the sound of a child crying. As darkness fell, he glimpsed the light of a fire at a glade two bowshots ahead.

Lowering his pack in a thicket of brush, Sun Dog stretched his aching shoulders, thinking that he had been a fool to bring such a load along. But there was one thing now that might make all his suffering worthwhile. He pulled the squire's noisemaker from the pack and blew into its tube, capping it when the bladder was full.

Creeping a bit closer to the camp he saw that the women captives had been tied by their long rope to one of the wild men's ankles. The captive men sat with their backs to a tree, bound tightly by a rope around its trunk.

As for their captors, they were sitting before their fire, stuffing themselves with corn. After a bit, they took to casting the bones of a small animal before the fire in a game of chance. Sun Dog eased forward to the distance of a single bow shot, thinking it would allow him time to escape if they came running.

He found a young maple tree, no bigger than his wrist, and began shaking it slowly, hoping that it would sound like something big moving in the forest. The leaves of the tree rustled against those alongside it, and up by the fire he heard the murmur of low voices.

It was then that he gave the bladder a mighty squeeze, mingling it with a howl of his own. The night was shattered with the screech and squeal of a demon.

During his time with the master, Sun Dog had learned how to mimic the sound of many animals for their magic shows in town. Now he mimicked the grunts of a bear, the howl of a wolf, and the cackle of parrots accompanied by moans of the noisemaker, then scuttled away to a new location, only to repeat the charade again. The sound split the stillness of the night like the call of a fiend.

Shouts of alarm came from the camp as the raiders leapt to their feet, scanning the darkness and rearing back on hearing the demonic screams resounding from the forest. None dared to move beyond the firelight. The captive children screamed in terror, but those who were bound quivered in silence, not daring to make a sound.

At last, Sun Dog gave a few huffing grunts and squawks and then lay silent. The wild men stared into the darkness for a long time thereafter, talking amongst themselves. Gradually, they relaxed and settled by their fire.

Sun Dog had crept in dangerously close—close enough to have his skull split if someone threw a club. But he had a clear path behind him for his escape, and it was a gamble he was willing to take. Whatever gods that still lived were with him, or so he hoped. Hefting a rock, he chucked it at the fire, raising a shower of sparks at the same moment that he howled and squeezed the bladder with all his strength.

But then, his heart fell as one of the braver men seized a flaming branch from the fire and ran into the darkness directly toward where he stood hiding behind a tree! But a man waving a torch can see only a little way ahead, and now he was silhouetted by the fire. The last thing he saw was a dark shape swinging toward his face from behind a thick oak tree. He gave a howl as Sun Dog's mace crushed the side of his skull, gurgling with pain as he fell to the ground.

It was too much—the wild men almost did somersaults in their haste to flee just as they saw the shining face of a god reflected by the light of the fire.

Sun Dog crept down the trail behind them for a bit, howling along with the screeching bladder every so often to make it sound as if he were the demon on their trail. In the distance, he could hear thrashing and cries as the wild men ran for their lives. Sun Dog was sure that they were as frightened of ghosts and demons as any man—perhaps far more so.

But he would wait until dawn before daring to show himself back in the camp. For a long time, he sat by the trail, holding the mace in his hand for anyone foolish enough to return.

That morning, he made his way to the wild mens' camp. The captives had freed themselves and were gathered, tending the head of the wounded man when he stepped among them.

"Were you happy with my demon?" he asked.

CHAPTER 24

SURVIVORS

It took a full day for Sun Dog and the freed captives to make their way home to their village of Tali where they were greeted with cries of joy and disbelief.

"It is a good thing you have done," said the headman of Tali when he was told of Sun Dog's feat. To Sun Dog's surprise, the chieftain was the same man who had shown his father the way north ten years before. His name was Nere-hasi, Half Moon.

"I remember you," Half Moon said, "though you were only this high then. Your parents were taken by the warriors of Chelaque. They are the ones you call the wild men, though we call them snakes. Now that the gods have failed us, they come like crows to a sparrow's nest. They killed two of our men and seized the rest while they were working the fields. We will talk more about this tonight at the feast, so you will know our story as we celebrate you and the return of our people."

After preparing a feast for Sun Dog that night and celebrating the return of the captives, Half Moon shared the fate of his village.

Before the plague, Tali had been a town of five hundred, boasting a double palisade to protect against raiders, but for many years its people had been troubled by the wild men of Chelaque, who had grown more numerous even as Tali's own numbers waned.

"We were few before the plague. The plague nearly took the rest of us, but for the advice of my wife, who is a healer," he said.

"Our shamans said we should gather in a lodge to find strength against the demons of the plague. But my own good woman said it was the people fleeing Coosa who brought the sickness among us. She argued that we should hide in the forest instead, just as women and children do when raiders come. There was a great debate over what to do. What could I do but obey her?

"Those who had remained in the lodge, defended against the plague with prayers, chants, and frightening masks died, while Half Moon and many of those who fled the village lived. Yet now there were only a little more than one hundred survivors.

"Many of those who fled Coosa have gone over to Chelaquens, swelling their numbers while ours grow fewer. Some of our people have even become warriors among them, returning to seize us as slaves. We are betrayed by our own people!"

"It is the same everywhere," Sun Dog replied, turning his eyes away from Half Moon towards the fire.

"I have no wish to be their slave. I will open my veins before I submit."

"Ah, but you are an old man," Sun Dog said. "Those who are young might choose slavery over death."

"Not among the Chelaque," Half Moon scoffed.

Perhaps, Sun Dog thought. But perhaps there was another way.

He spent the next few days helping the people of Tali to strengthen their rotting palisade, felling pines, and digging holes for their placement. It was hard work, and Sun Dog ended each day covered with dirt and sweat. The labor made him think of his father, who had been carried off by the wild men and enslaved far to the north by the Senecas, only to be worked to death in the building of their town. The Senecas had also deprived him of his mother. For ten years, she was their captive, only to have her life snuffed out at their reunion. It was they who had heaped so much misery on his head.

That night, he heard the master's voice in a dream, speaking as loudly as if he were cupping his hands in Sun Dog's ear. *"Your father cries out from his grave. Avenge him. Avenge him..."*

He awakened in a chill sweat. The voice had seemed so real—he shivered beneath his blanket thinking that the master was lying beside him in the darkness. Trembling with his heart in his throat, he forced himself to turn over. There was nothing there, but outside the entrance to the lodge, he saw a shadow passing over the moonlight.

The double palisade of Tali was almost completed when the wild men attacked. They came creeping through the cornfield at dawn, with the youngest of them scaling the timbers of the palisade as easily as squirrels. But reaching the top, they were stymied by the double row of sharpened timbers. Several were knocked on their heads from the shelter of the palisade walkways, but three made it over the wall, engaging in a desperate fight below.

Tali had lost many of its men to the plague, and their war chief had been the man with the wounded head who Sun Dog had rescued. He was still recovering but roused himself from his pallet and climbed a ladder to the top of the palisade with his bow.

Now, Tali's women rushed from their lodges with stones and clubs to batter the invaders senseless while their men fired arrows from the palisade walkways above.

Yet just as it seemed that the battle was won, a line of hundreds of warriors emerged from the forest beyond the fields, shouting with hoarse voices and screaming their war cries as they rushed the entrance of the town, which had been piled high with branches, timber, and thorns.

That would have been the end of Tali, its women and children enslaved, and its men roasted, had they not had a sorcerer among them.

The charging wild men had come within a bow shot of the palisade when a ragged figure with a tall, plumed crown appeared atop the wall. Gradually, the figure grew taller until it was twice the height of an ordinary man. Then, to the unforgettable memory of all who saw it, the demon turned toward the rising sun, and its sparkling face lit up as if it were the sun itself.

It was then that the demon let out a hideous squeal, just as a lucky bow shot struck the leader of the wild men in his chest. Drums started thundering from behind the palisade wall, and the demon threw back its head, letting forth a screech that seemed to break the sky and bring all the spirits of the forest were flying to the rescue.

Below, a Chelaquen warrior stooped beside their fallen leader. Seizing his ankles, he dragged him away from the demon on the palisade. Those near him followed and then a stream of others, looking fearfully back over their shoulders as a barrage of arrows rained down from the battlement. Above them, the demon with the radiant face was slowly lowering and then springing back again, as if it meant to leap upon them.

For a long time after that, the people of Tali told of the day Sun Dog had defeated more warriors than there were leaves on a tall tree. But it was the lucky arrow fired by Little Fox, Col-oci, the wounded son of the headman Half Moon, that did as much to save the day. His arrow had gone clean through the breast of the war chief of the Chelaquens, and together with the apparition on the palisade, the wrath of the spirits had been more than the wild men could bear.

As for himself, Sun Dog breathed a prayer of thanks. It had been the simplest of magic—the trick of a child—and he had been far from certain that it would work.

He had borrowed a cloak of raven feathers from Half Moon, draping it over a cross piece he tied to the shaft of the Exalted One. The cloak was a splendid thing—its long feathers shimmered silver-black in the sun, giving it the appearance of a dark beast that fluttered in the passing breeze. Smiling at the spectacle to come, Sun Dog had placed his shimmering mask of mica atop the disc of the sun, securing it with a sinew cord. That, and the squire's squawking bag had transformed him into a demon that grew ever larger as he raised the shaft above the palisade wall. If the war party had taken only a few steps further, they would have seen through the charade.

But everyone among the wild men of Chelaque had heard of the demon in the forest and how a party of raiders had narrowly escaped with their lives, if not their souls. One had been killed and devoured by the thing! As the master would have said, they were told what to believe, and then they were shown. Sun Dog was sure that somewhere beyond this life the master was smiling at the deed. Perhaps he had even played a hand.

One of the Chelaquen raiders who'd made it inside had lived through his beating by the women, though just barely. That night, the people of Tali made plans to dispatch him in a way that would be long and painful, but it was Sun Dog who begged for his life.

"We may have need of him," he said, and to this there was much grumbling, for the townsfolk were eager for revenge and the sport that came with it.

But Sun Dog had become a big man among them now, and no one dared to cross him. He had the Chelaquen warrior carried to his own lodge where the same women who beat him senseless now took care to heal his wounds.

CHAPTER 25

TO THE NORTH

"They will come again," Little Fox said with a frown. He and Sun Dog had been honored at the celebration that night, but it had ended early, and now he lay propped up with a pillow, lying in his mother's lodge. His head was still bruised and blue from where he'd been struck days ago.

"But not for many moons. Perhaps not ever," Sun Dog said, drawing on the pipe he had been given by the villagers in thanks. "Fall is the time for hunting, and winter will bar them from coming over the mountains."

"Yes, but then comes summer."

Several elders and warriors were also crowded into the lodge, and now they sat in silence with each man considering what the following summer would mean. It was the season for raiding when the leaves were thick on the trees, hiding the movements of men.

"There are many more warriors among the Chelaque than those of us," Little Fox went on. Sitting beside him, his father, Half Moon, laid a hand on his knee and nodded. "Snakes," he murmured, "snakes waiting to devour us."

It was time for Sun Dog to offer his plan.

"Do you love your village so much that you would die here?" he asked. "Would you see your women taken by the men you call snakes? Your children?"

The circle raised their eyes to him but said nothing.

"I know a place we can go, far beyond the mountains where the Chelaquens dare not follow," he continued. "It is among a people called the Seneca."

Sun Dog recounted what his mother had told him, that there was a new town of the Seneca, who also farmed maize, beans, and other crops.

"They would make us slaves," Little Fox said.

"Yes, perhaps. But they have a custom of adopting others to swell their numbers. They believe it increases the power of a thing they call their *orenda*. It is a spiritual power that makes them whole."

"And was your mother adopted? Your father?" Half Moon demanded.

Sun Dog couldn't lie. "Both were adopted by a blind woman who was one of the chieftains of their town, but my father was worked to death as a slave by her cruel stepson. They sent him to work felling trees in the forest for their fence, and his body gave out. He was crushed beneath a tree that was too heavy to bear."

"You want revenge," Little Fox said.

"Yes."

"How?"

"I have a plan," Sun Dog waved in dismissal, "but that does not concern our people. For our people I would create a new home among them, far from your enemies."

"Revenge? A plan? Then why would we choose such a path?" Half Moon said in exasperation. "You tell us this is a walk of at least two moons, crossing the mountains and many rivers in the hope that these people might welcome us. Why? Why would they welcome us? They would take in our women and children, yes, but what of our elders? What of our men?"

Sun Dog smiled. "Because we will bring them magic," he said. "I will bring them a magic unlike anything they have ever seen before."

That, Sun Dog thought, and he would avenge his mother and father by becoming the Exalted One among those who had enslaved them.

Even so, there remained many long councils with the elders and warriors of Tali to weigh the good and bad of Sun Dog's plan. Among the doubters was Little Fox, the war chief of the town whose word was law.

Little Fox had been on only one raid three years before when he was twenty summers of age. He was considered handsome yet had an ugly knob of protruding bone on his shoulder where it had been dislocated by a blow from an enemy's war club. Back then, he had seen what happens to a man who is captured by the enemy; indeed, he had expected to receive the same from the Chelaquens before his rescue. The memory had made him more cautious than most.

Little Fox had killed two men on his lone raid, proving his worth, but it was his caution that made him war chief by acclaim. His father, Half Moon, had been the chief before him and had taught him that it is more important to bring one's warriors home without the loss of a single man than it is to heap woe upon an enemy.

Now, Sun Dog was asking him to believe that he had magic enough to safeguard the lives of everyone in Tali who would choose to make the long trek north to an unknown people. Yet from what Little Fox had seen, Sun Dog's magic was a series of tricks, and not what one might expect of a sorcerer. His opinion was soon to change.

One day, a quarter-moon after Sun Dog had presented his plan, the earth began shaking violently, just as another council of elders had gathered at the center of the village. The timbers of the palisade began to rattle and chatter while the earth below felt as if it was rolling.

Sun Dog had heard of this thing before. The master had told him it was a colossal snake of the underworld that strayed close to the surface of the earth, making the ground shake. The vast serpent had not come around for more than a lifetime, but the master had witnessed it as a child, and his own master had told him that it came for only a few moments and then gradually faded away, never breaking free of Grandmother Earth, whose power was far stronger.

Seizing the moment, Sun Dog leapt to his feet and cried out, "Leave us, Great Snake! By the power of the Sun, I tell you, return to your burrow!"

Raising the staff of the Exalted One skyward, he closed his eyes and muttered an obscure spell that was meant to drive fleas from a lodge, though none could know this but him. The ground shook a little more and then ceased.

"It was only a snake of the underworld," he said, waving a hand as if it were nothing while half the town gaped at him wide-eyed. "It has gone home to its mother. I have ordered it away."

Ordered it away? The council sat agog at this, and thereafter, Sun Dog was held to be far more than a simple magician. He had freed the captives, saved the village, and now he had driven off a great serpent of the earth that might have devoured them all if it had burst forth.

Thereafter, no one doubted that Sun Dog was a sorcerer with powers far beyond those of mere shamans and witches. It was said that he could walk easy with demons and converse with the dead. Some had even seen him flying through the trees by the light of the moon. Others said that he was clearly the Exalted One, who lived on in a direct line from his father, the Sun. "Does he not have the god-ruler's staff?"

Despite Sun Dog's smiles and comforting words, fear crept over the people of Tali. Such a man was not one to be denied, and no one had been more impressed by Sun Dog's power over the serpent of the underworld than the skeptic, Little Fox. Another council was held, and it was quickly decided that every man, woman, and child would leave the town that autumn on the way north before the wild men of Chelaque could fall upon them again. They would establish a winter camp in the hunting grounds beyond the Gray Mountains while Sun Dog and a few picked men made their way north to parley with the Seneca.

And so, they left piling their possessions on draggers and making their way through the gap in the mountains where the boy Wren and his family had wandered so many years before. Even the elders came with them, though there were only two left in the wake of the plague. Aided by a staff, Half Moon could still walk, while an old woman was carried on a litter by four in-between men. Alas, she died at the first river crossing when her raft overturned in the current. For the boys who carried her, it was a blessing.

It was a long march, but the people of Tali had packed along a great store of food, almost more than they could carry. They wept bitterly upon leaving their home and the graves of their ancestors, for none were used to traveling more than a day beyond Tali. Even so, their spirits were brightened by the dream of safety and a new life that the great Sun Dog had promised them.

The leaves of the aspens fluttered golden in the sun as they made their way north, and the maples and their sister trees were on fire with blazing hues of red and yellow that cheered everyone who walked beneath their limbs. The mountains were crossed just before the snow began falling; rivers were forded or plied with rafts; and Sun Dog led them ever north to the sacred hunting grounds of Kanta-ke.

As all know, the valleys and hills of Kanta-ke are the sacred hunting grounds shared by many tribes. All could hunt there with no fear of attack, with the only stipulation being that no one could establish a village amid the ancient preserve.

So it was that the people of Tali came upon a scattering of hunting parties, including the Chelaquens. But it was the season for hunting, not for war, and the wild men they met greeted them as if they were old friends as they busied themselves seeking game for the long winter ahead.

"Many of these were surely among those who attacked us," Little Fox said as the people of Tali pushed beyond a camp of somber-faced hunters.

"Yes, but they would rather hunt deer than trophies," Half Moon replied. "Our heads will be of no use to the Chelaque unless they wish to starve this winter."

At last, they came to a quiet valley with a spring creeping through the face of a rock wall nearby and broad meadows that were leaping with deer and the browse of buffalo, bear, elk, and turkeys. All agreed that it was a fine place to spend the winter, and soon the valley rang with the sound of stone axes as trees were felled to make camp.

It was on this journey that Sun Dog began feeling the masters' spirit growing stronger within him, as if by taking his name, the old magician had begun eating away at the innocence of the man who had been Wren, replacing his soul with something darker. Sometimes at night, he awakened shaking with fear as the master's voice muttered in his dreams. It was a voice that seemed to grow louder as winter fell, blanketing the valley in snow. Sometimes he found himself speaking words in a crude, unknown language, as if learned from the ancient people known as the Old Ones.

He spent the winter conversing with the Chelaquen warrior whose life he had saved. Scalded One, Akrofita, was a man of seventeen winters who took to Sun Dog as if he were a dog, grateful to having been spared the tortures of the vengeful Tali. As Sun Dog's mother had told him, the wild men of the Chelaque spoke much the same language as those of the Seneca, and now, little by little over their lodge fire that winter, Akrofita taught Sun Dog the tongue of his people… "I, me, you, tree, lodge, woman, man, bear, deer, fire…"

CHAPTER 26

THE CAVE

There was still snow on the ground and a skin of ice on the lakes when Sun Dog, Little Fox, Scalded One, and two other men set out that spring while the rest stayed behind.

Two babies had been born that winter, while two among the Tali people had died of a coughing sickness. It was an even trade. All agreed that the balance was a good omen. That, and there had been good hunting, with the game of *Kanta-ke* seeming to kneel before the arrows of the Tali hunters. A fine store of smoked meat had been packed away, along with many baskets of nuts, calming the fears of those who wondered how they would survive without their fields of maize.

Things had gone well, and many took heart with Sun Dog's plan to meet with the Seneca people far to the north in the hope of securing a new home among them. All except Sun Dog himself, who gradually came to doubt the wisdom of his plan. He had intended to dazzle the Seneca with his magic and earn their worship in the footsteps of the Exalted One. *What a foolish dream!* he thought now. Little by little, his plan splintered as he lay awake at night thinking on it, even though the master whispered in his dreams that it would work. There was still something of the boy, Wren, within him that was a frightened child, struggling against the will of the master's spirit and afraid that he was simply leading his people into slavery rather than safety.

But by now, the bones of fate had been cast, and Sun Dog had no choice but to put on a brave face, assuring all that he would prepare the way for them. He forced himself to appear confident and jolly as he said farewell to the hopeful faces of the Tali folk, but behind his eyes lay a storm of fear and uncertainty. He felt sick to his stomach as he met Half Moon's eyes at their parting and so roiled that he feared he'd vomit.

Be strong, the master whispered in his ear. *You will tell them what to believe and they will obey.*

But would they? Sun Dog wondered. *Or would the Seneca have their own magicians who would see through his tricks?* One night, he drew a circle in the earth and cast the frail bones of a baby that had died of the plague, hoping to find an answer in their tangle. The bones revealed nothing.

Half Moon had seen the fear in Sun Dog's eyes but was old enough to know that any man would be mad not to fear such an undertaking. He had never really believed in Sun Dog's plan, such was their plight, though, that it mattered little what his people did. They were like falling leaves, blowing in the wind wherever it might take them.

"Take care of my son," he said simply, "and may the spirits shine your path."

"I will care for him as if he were a suckling babe," Sun Dog said, half in jest, "I think it more likely that he will watch over me. It will take us a full moon to reach the Seneca and then another moon for Little Fox to return to you. If the gods are willing, he will bring your people north where I will be waiting."

That was the sum of Sun Dog's plan, all hanging on the vague directions passed down to him by his mother and the slim hope of parleying with the Seneca for his people's safety.

But that is not how it turned out.

For a full cycle of the moon, the five men made their way north, wading through snow at times and fording icy rivers as winter held onto the throat of spring. Sun Dog had no landmarks to guide them, but his mother had said that if he held his arm straight to the night sky, the Seneca lived in a place that was three outstretched hands to the right of the north star. But a woman's hand is smaller than that of a man, and his mother's arm was much shorter than that of her son.

"Follow the geese," she had said. Yet the only thing that Sun Dog was certain of was that the Seneca lived on a hill alongside a lake that was as vast as the sea, and that within sight of their town there was a tower of limestone that could be seen to the far horizon.

Perhaps it was the Sun God, the wayfaring of friendly birds, or even the master who blessed the travelers on their way because late one afternoon, as they reached the top of a hill, they spied a towering karst in the distance that seemed to touch the clouds.

"That's the place," Sun Dog said, pointing the way. "It is as my mother said—we are in the land of the Seneca."

"But they may not be happy to see us," Little Fox replied.

"No, not until I have met with them."

Little Fox sniffed at this, but said nothing, and the next day the five of them crept down from their camp, making their way through the forest until they found a well-trodden path leading north. From then on, they traveled only by the light of the moon and stars, for who knew what sort of reception they might have?

A day later, they made camp at the base of the pillar of rock, which towered the length of many tall pines laid end-to-end above them.

"There are bones here," Little Fox said in alarm as he collected an armful of leaves for his bed. "Many bones!"

Stooping, Sun Dog picked up the rotted shaft of an arrow that abruptly cracked and fell to earth. "A battle," he said. Nearby was a cracked skull grinning up through the disturbed leaves.

"We can't sleep here," Scalded One said, looking about with wild eyes. "There are ghosts here. They will feed on us!"

Sun Dog doubted this, but there was no point trying to soothe his companions or guile them into believing that he would keep the haunts at bay. "Let us go further up," he said. "These men died in the shadow of this hill and are bound by the underworld. They can't come to us if we go higher up."

Who could doubt such a thing? For all knew that ghosts were bound to their graves with unbreakable bonds except when they were allowed to creep by night. The way up the tower was steep, but at last they came to a level place, and there in the distance was Ga-ogwah Kanotaye, the town of the Seneca.

It was a disappointment to Sun Dog, compared to the splendors of Coosa. He had hoped for something better, but there was not a single pyramid rising above the palisade of the Seneca's town. Even the village of Tali had a respectable mound where ceremonies were conducted. But then he remembered that his mother and father had spent their time building the town's lodges and palisade instead of mounds—perhaps it was too new for its people to have raised the earth one basket at a time.

Few of them slept that night for fear that the ghosts of the dead warriors would come creeping up the hillside. Nor did they dare to light a fire. And weary though they were, Little Fox, Scalded One, and their two companions were eager to be on their way south the next morning as had been agreed upon. Sun Dog would remain behind to meet with the Seneca and smooth the way. Or so he hoped.

It was still early spring, and an icy breeze blew steadily from the broad silver lake in the distance, offering little comfort. Given this and their ghostly camp, Little Fox and the others were eager to be on their way. As agreed, they would make their way back to Kanta-ke and lead their people north to a fork in a river that lay three days to the south of the limestone tower. Sun Dog would meet them there in two moon's time with the decision of the Seneca.

"May your magic be strong," Little Fox said upon their parting. "As strong as your magic with the Great Snake. You would do well to summon it again."

Sun Dog gave him a quizzical look, wondering if he was needling him, but Little Fox had the look of a true believer.

"I will, brother," he said. "I will ride it into their town and dazzle them with tales of Coosa."

"Eh. I hope so, and know that we will meet again, if only on the path of the spirits. Go with the sun's protection."

"And you as well."

Sun Dog watched as his four companions melted into the forest on their way back south, feeling terribly alone even before they vanished from his sight. Would he ever see them again? He doubted it. They would stay in Kanta-ke until the Chelaquens fell upon them for violating their hunting grounds.

The master stirred within him like a slow-turning reptile, but that was no comfort—it only increased his despair. Shaking it off, he turned and pushed on farther up the hill, looking for the ledge and the cave that his mother had described.

It took him half a day to find it. By now the animal trail she had spoken of had vanished, but there was still a rough passage through the trees to a place where a shallow ledge appeared black against the sun. Dropping his pack and scrambling up, he burrowed under a thick hedge of brush and clutched at an overhanging rock. And there, just as his mother had described it, he found the entrance to the cave where she had hidden only a year ago. Creeping beneath its low eave, he was blinded by the transition from sunlight to darkness and sensed rather than saw that he had entered a high chamber. The cave had a rank smell, but was dry and warm—it would make a good camp while he determined how to approach the Seneca.

Gradually, his vision cleared as a dim light filtered into the cave. He took a few steps into its gloom, only to have his feet fly up, slamming him hard upon his back. He had landed in a sticky ooze seeping up through the limestone. Raising his hands, he saw in the half-light that they were both painted black.

CHAPTER 27

HUNGER

It was hunger and not vengeance that drove Sun Dog to the Great Lodge on the night that the seven elders died.

After Little Fox and his men left for the south, he spent half a moon scouting Ga-ogwah Kanotaye at night, feeding bits of frog, crayfish, and carrion through chinks in the palisade to the dogs that came sniffing around. In this way, he became friends with them as he eavesdropped in the darkness beneath the town's wall.

There was little to be gained from the dull chatter of the town's farmers as Sun Dog listened only a few footsteps away on the other side of the palisade, but still, it was good to hear human voices. Sun Dog was not made of stone—like anyone, he craved the company of others, and in his camp at the lonely cave, he heard only the drip of water in its recesses far below and the whispering of ghosts down the hill. He did not fear them—the master had told him that ghosts were powerless against the living, and to prove it he had made the boy, Wren, sleep in the graveyard of Coosa among thousands of the dead. It had been a cruel lesson, and he had seen and heard many horrifying things there—rotting specters, the spirits of wailing children, and the like, but as the master had said, they had done him no harm. But ghosts are not good company, and now Sun Dog avoided them on his nightly visits to Ga-ogwah Kanotaye by blazing a diagonal trail down the hill, bypassing the bones of the battlefield.

Other than the faint whispers of the ghosts below, his only company in the cave had been that of the master, whose voice seemed almost continuous in his dreams, chanting, scheming, advising, always in a sly way that was frightening in its tone. At times, he even heard it in his thoughts when he was fully awake as the master intruded on his revery.

"No!" he cried in his sleep. "Leave me!" Some nights, he woke shivering, longing for his past life when he was just a boy who yearned to become a simple trader. But who was that boy? What was his name? He writhed on his bed of straw, struggling to remember. Sometimes he caught the faintest thread of it before Wren flew away.

He began to feel as if he was going mad, sitting beneath the pitiless stars each night by a small fire at the mouth of his cave. Thus, it was the craving to be near the voices of others that drove him to the wall of the town and the hope that he might glean enough to be able to present himself as an emissary of those who had fled Tali.

He decided to scout within the walls of the town itself. Using the serrated dagger he had taken from the knight during his captivity, Sun Dog found a place in the palisade where there were only two thin pines neighboring one another. It was an easy task to saw through them; both were bound together with a hemp cord high up, creating a hinge. By this means, he was able to ease his way into Ga-ogwah Kanotaye on the darker nights, strolling the lanes between its longhouses and grunting when he met a passerby. In a town of more than eight hundred, he aroused no suspicion.

But by then, he was almost out of the parched maize that had sustained him on his journey to the north and was wretchedly sick of it as well. Only a few kernels remained in the sack he'd brought along, and these had been doled out as the thin rations of a starving man. Sun Dog had never been a hunter and did not even know how to snare a rabbit. Nor did he dare enter any of the crowded longhouses at night where he knew there was smoked meat hanging from the rafters.

But his mother had told him there was also meat hanging by leather cords from the rafters of the Great Lodge, with a fire kept perpetually burning below one of its smoke holes. The lodge was empty each night; it was a sacred place given over to meetings and ceremony, with no families allowed to sleep there. On one of his nightly visits, Sun Dog used his blade to free up a sheath of elm bark in a corner of the lodge, not far from the pines he had severed in the palisade. So it was that one night, Sun Dog risked the waning light of a quarter moon to ease through the passage in the palisade and creep into the Great Lodge.

The lodge was nearly one hundred steps long and twenty wide, and Sun Dog marveled that his mother had helped to build it. It seemed almost as vast as the lower chamber of his cave, and at its far end he saw the red embers of the fire that kept slabs of meat drying above. His mouth salivated at the sight of it—he planned to carry away an armload of venison, bear, and whatever else the Seneca had set dangling amid the smoke. But that was only if he could reach it.

As always, whenever he entered the town, he carried the knight's mace with him in case he was challenged, but now it was an encumbrance as he surveyed a way up. The shaft alone was as long as his arm, and its metal head, riven with blades, was bigger than a clenched fist. He shoved the club in his belt as he crept to the fire.

Even the Great Lodge was infested with mice, and so the Seneca had taken care not to string their drying meat from cords near the ground that could be easily reached. But in the darkness, Sun Dog gradually made out chinks in one of the lodge posts along a wall that served as a ladder. Quietly, he made his way up to a crossbeam. It stank of smoke and grease in the rafters, but midway across he saw that it would be an easy matter to seize the precious meat. He wriggled forward in the darkness on the slippery beam, straddling it with his legs as if he were riding the back of a snake. Reaching a haunch of deer, he gave it a tug, and the cord holding it broke free.

But just as he was about to drop the precious meat to the floor, he heard voices at the entryway.

Sun Dog froze on the beam, gripping it tightly with his legs as he struggled to hang onto the precious meat. One-by-one, eight elders made their way into the lodge as he looked down from above. The last of them was an elderly woman guided by a thin old man. She was clearly blind. Surely, this could only be Walking Turtle, the woman who had shown kindness to his mother during her captivity.

The elders gathered in a circle around the fire below, and one of them tossed two sticks of wood on the coals. It was the kind of wood that produces a great deal of smoke for curing meat, burning Sun Dog's eyes and filling his lungs. He stifled his breath as long as he could as the smoke engulfed him, coughing into his armpit when he could bear it no longer. But no one below took any notice; they were busy talking about the lack of maize to use for seed that year, and as is often the way of such things, one of them blathered at length, as if he were an actor in a play.

Do something, fool, a voice whispered in his thoughts. *They are your enemies—you are their master. Take your revenge—Do it!*

Sun Dog brushed the droning voice aside, but still it persisted. *Now, you are among them, fly to them like an eagle, tear at them. Feast on them. Suck their bones...*

The thoughts kept at him, itching and scratching, but Sun Dog had come to parley with the Seneca, not make enemies of them. He pushed the master's voice aside, yet still it nagged on. *Strike, bite! Now is your time. Blood and bone, blood and bone, drink it...*

Time dragged on, and still those below talked on as if such a trifling thing as maize was worthy of an epic. Another stick was tossed on the fire, and the windy elder sitting below began speaking of a grievance that involved his daughter and her lazy husband. Sun Dog squirmed above them, holding the haunch of venison with one hand, while trying to maintain his balance on the crossbeam with the other. It was impossible—it was agony lying prostrate on the beam, which was slippery with the grease of dripping meat and the film left by the smoke.

And then, just as the elders fell silent and looked as if they meant to make their way out, Sun Dog slipped and fell heavily among them.

It wasn't the master who pushed him from the beam, but it was his malignant spirit that overwhelmed Sun Dog as he crashed into those below. He landed square on one of the frailest of the elders, crushing the man with his fall. Another grasped his ankle, and something bubbled up within him in a rush, like gas exploding from the muck at the bottom of a river. Without thinking, Sun Dog roared and went berserk as he swept the mace from his belt and began swinging. Later, all he could remember were dark shades of black and red behind his eyes as he swung the club and hit bone with every blow. After the first death, he knew there was no going back. There could be no witnesses if he wished to present himself as an emissary of his people. The master's voice swept through him in a mixture of glee and exultation: *Swing, swing!* He roared like a beast, gulping and slobbering as his berserk dance claimed one life after another.

At last, there was only one left—the old woman, Walking Turtle. He stood panting behind her with his upraised mace as the master nagged him to send her to the spirit world. *Kill her! Kill her!* But no. *No!* Whatever was left of Wren stayed Sun Dog's hand. This was the woman who had been kind to his mother. She had kept her silence, allowing his mother to flee. She alone of all the Seneca deserved to live.

Wrenching himself away, he ran to the entrance of the lodge and pulled down the poles supporting the entryway just as shouts of alarm began ringing from outside. To his surprise, the doorposts gave easily and barred the way with a cascade of elm slabs and timbers. He snatched the leg of deer from its place among the dead and dying and ran for the secret entrance at the far end of the lodge.

That night was the tipping point between what was left of Wren and the master whose name he had taken. It was also the night that he decided to sway the Seneca with terror rather than peaceful words. Sun Dog would become a demon the likes of which would fill their dreams with dread.

So it was that he began his mournful honks and squeals with the white man's noisemaker, blending them with his own howls and screams. They echoed over the fields from the far-off cave, amplified by its chambers. Donning the chainmail he'd taken from the knight during his captivity, he started prowling the fields of maize at night, sometimes using his staff to raise his cloak to twice its height, appearing as a giant under the moonlight from the town's palisade. It was Sun Dog who terrified the boys in the watchtowers overlooking the fields, and then the warriors who replaced them. Twice he was struck by arrows from atop the palisade walls, but each time they were shattered by his vest of steel.

Then, one night when the moon had gone to sleep and there was only the dim blanket of stars to guide him, Sun Dog had crept to the walls of Ga-ogwah Kanotaye planning more mischief when suddenly he heard the rush of feet in the darkness and war cries of *"Hadree, Hadree!"* filling his ears. In an instant he was overwhelmed by a boiling mob wielding spears and clubs. It was only his mace, his chain mail, and the darkness that saved him as he whirled and struck out in a frenzy.

Oh, the people of Ga-ogwah Kanotaye would not admit it, but more of them died at their own hands that night than at the blows of Sun Dog, who scrambled to safety over the backs of those who'd been trampled by their brothers. He barely escaped with his life, yet in his rage, he managed to slip back into town by way of his secret entrance and set the Great Lodge afire before fleeing back to his cave.

There, bleeding from half a dozen cuts to his arms and legs, Sun Dog smiled as he applied a healing poultice to his wounds. His magic was complete. He had become the *Hanishé*—the terror of the Seneca.

The next day he began making a sort of rake, fastening it with four long claws that he carved of oak along with a huge talon for a heel. Sun Dog found himself giggling as he carved the finger-length claws. It was magic! At times, he stopped to wonder if he had gone insane, but then came the master's voice, *Keep going, keep going …* Venturing out late at night, he stamped at the earth, making footprints twice the size of a bear. The loose, cultivated soil of the Seneca's fields were soon covered with the footprints of his monster. Then came the desecration of the graves as terror reigned in the town.

He savored his plan as if it were a delicious meal. Reunited with the people of Tali, he would become the savior of the Seneca. The great Sun Dog, sorcerer from the far south, would do what no other shaman could possibly achieve. He would defeat the *Hanishé* and take his place as the Exalted One among the Seneca.

CHAPTER 28

REUNION

As had been planned, Sun Dog met up with the villagers of Tali at the forks of the river two moons after Little Fox and his men had left him. Sun Dog had warned them not to establish a village in the sacred hunting grounds of Kanta-ke where no tribe was allowed to settle but expected that they would not heed him. Yet to his surprise, he came upon their camp by the river with all waiting for his arrival.

"We feared the Chelaquens more than the way north," Little Fox said by way of explanation. "Twice we found them creeping around our camp and knew it would not be long before they gathered their men."

"Then you were wise because I have found a way for us," Sun Dog replied. That night he shared what he had done with Little Fox and Half Moon.

"You used the noisemaker," Little Fox said with a grin as they sat by their fire.

"Yes, just as with the Chelaquens, and I will need you to use it for me when the time comes," Sun Dog replied. "Blow into it and squeeze its guts."

"Give it to me."

Sun Dog passed the bladder with its three pipes to Little Fox and told him how to inflate it with the blowing tube. Half Moon's eyes widened as the bag swelled to three times its size.

"Now squeeze it."

Little Fox placed the bladder between his right arm and his ribs and eased into it, producing a long fart that wheezed away as the bag emptied.

Half Moon gave a hearty laugh and begged for a chance to try it. When another round of hilarity was done, Sun Dog unveiled his plan.

"The Seneca have gathered shamans from many tribes, but all have been useless," he said. "We will appear among them with a promise to rid them of the demon, asking only that they accept us, not as slaves, but as members of their families."

"But brother, father, know this. If anyone reveals that I am the *Hanishé* then it is the death of us all. Tell no one! A whisper to your wife may be heard by a child, and then to another, and then to our deaths. Tell no one! No one!"

Little Fox and Half Moon swore on the graves of their fathers and mothers that not a word would cross their lips. Sun Dog gazed into their eyes, knowing that divulging the secret of any magician was a risk, but he had taken so many risks before. What was one more?

"No one," he whispered.

"We have faith in your plan," old Half Moon spoke. "What other plan can there be? We have traveled two moons from our homeland, over the mountains and across many rivers with the wild men always at our backs. You have defeated the Chelaquens and have driven the Great Snake back to the underworld. We are in your hands now. For good or bad, we will follow your plan."

"Then it is good, father," Sun Dog replied. "And if we fail, we will meet again in the spirit land and journey on from there."

"There can be no failing," Little Fox said with his face growing dark, "though we will need more than your noisemaker to sway them."

Sun Dog chuckled and slapped him on the back. "Ah we will have it," he said. "We will shake them to their bones!"

"So you say."

"Wait and see brother. I will make you a believer."

Little Fox gave him a wary look, and Sun Dog realized that he was only half convinced. He was bursting to tell the warrior the full details of his plan, but that would never do, for everyone, even his own people, must be shaken to their bones by the ceremonies to come.

Nor could they know of his dream of becoming the Exalted One among the Seneca—no one knew but the spirit of the master, lurking behind his eyes.

Two days later, Sun Dog led his people to the palisade of Ga-ogwah Kanotaye, dressed in the white robe and headdress of the Exalted One that he had taken from the pyramid in Coosa. The robe was woven from the inner bark of the mulberry tree, and no one among the Seneca had ever seen the likes of it. Nor had anyone ever seen the power of his mask to catch the light of the sun.

Sun Dog had sewn these things and other relics from the master within a bundle of deer hide greased with the fat of a bear to make it waterproof. The bundle had been carried north by the people of Tali with the admonition that any attempt to open it would release a cloud of demons that would feed on the transgressor's soul. No one dared touch it as it was borne on a pole between two boys.

How easy it is to lead others with a few simple tricks, he thought as he took what he needed from the bundle. The rest of the master's relics would remain stowed away for now.

Sun Dog thought of the Exalted One, the frog-faced man with the big belly and eyes, swimming with horror who had disappeared soon after the white men had arrived. Bringer of the Rain, Son of the Sun, Guardian of the Maize ... he too had been a magician to deceive so many people for so long. Now, the master stirred within his thoughts. *You too ... can be ... exalted ... Do it, do it...*

He had risked everything when he'd been shot with the arrow of Stone Eagle before a crowd of hundreds but had counted on the archer to strike him exactly where he'd painted a cross in red above his heart on the white robe. He had worn the cotton jerkin of the conquistador's squire beneath the robe along with a bladder filled with the blood of a rabbit and a tea of red sumac. It was the same bladder that the master had used so long ago to make him jump at the sight of his stuffed monkey.

Sun Dog knew that the squire's jerkin served as a form of armor, but as an added precaution, he had worn a slab of pine over his heart. He reasoned that the bladder, pine and jerkin would be all that he needed to stop an arrow.

Even so, he was well aware that the finest archer of the Seneca could just as well fire an arrow through one of his eyes if he chose to do so. He had breathed a prayer to the sun, hoping that Stone Eagle would find the cross over his heart irresistible.

Sun Dog knew a great deal of magic. The master and those who came before him had taught him everything that they knew, but he knew nothing at all of bow-craft or how easily an arrow might be diverted from its course. A puff of wind, the flap of a passing bird's wing, a twitch in a bowman's arm, an arrow with the slightest bend or a point that was too heavy or too light—all of these things might easily spell his death.

When he faced Stone Eagle, all of these things dawned on him, and then, just before he took his place, Little Fox had warned him that the archer would need to give a full draw of his powerful bow if he was to hit his mark. "Think on this, brother, it is not too late to walk away," he had said. "His arrow will pass through your body as if you are no more than a spider web."

But it *was* too late. Sun Dog was surrounded by a crowd of hundreds, all waiting to see the magic of a man who could not be killed. He looked across the way to where Stone Eagle stood, nocking his arrow. Now, thirty paces seemed a very long way, and the red hand on his robe seemed very small.

Before Sun Dog had time to think on it further, Stone Eagle raised his bow and fired, not appearing to even take aim.

The crowd had gasped as the arrow flew a hand's breadth from Sun Dog's right ear. He heard the whirr of the shaft as it flew by him and felt its hiss on his cheek. What had happened? He looked around, gazed at his chest, then up to the grim-faced archer.

Stone Eagle walked up to him and whispered in his ear. "That was a warning shot, brother. Are you sure you wish to do this?"

No, Sun Dog had not wished to continue, but the master roiled within him, telling him it must be so. *Prove yourself or all is lost.*

He looked then into Stone Eagle's eyes and nodded. "Do it."

And it was just as the master had taught him. *Tell people what they will see and then show them ...* Stone Eagle had taken care to fire his bolt straight at the red hand on Sun Dog's chest. The bladder had exploded on impact, and the pine plank was shriven in two, but those had expended the arrow's power, and the cotton armor of the squire's jerkin had saved Sun Dog from what would surely have been his death.

All of it had been rehearsed in his mind, from the cry, "Ah! You have killed me!" to his burial in the pyre of dry corn stalks. Sun Dog had whipped off his robe within its smoke-filled confines, knowing that the bladder, pine plank, and jerkin would be consumed by the fire. He had waited until the flames were singeing his hair, and he could hold his breath no longer before bursting from the engulfed hut to proclaim that no man could kill him.

Oh, how he had reveled in the screams and cries of adulation as he stood naked with his body painted red—the color of life—before the eyes of hundreds gathered around the flaming pyre! Every face was alive with wonder, and their voices were louder in his ears than even the crackling fire.

But not all. Staring at him impassively were an old man with lank gray hair reaching his shoulders and a tall, younger man with a club foot. Neither looked to be from among the people of the Seneca. Behind them stood the blind sachem, Walking Turtle, whose ears were being filled with the outcome of the ordeal by one of her sister-cousins.

The two strangers gave him a hard look and turned away, melting into the cheering crowd.

CHAPTER 29

LONG TONGUE

Even the villagers of Tali had been awestruck with horror and disbelief at Sun Dog's death and rebirth in the fire, keeping a respectful distance among the murmuring crowd. No one could believe their eyes, and a hum of voices buzzed in Sun Dog's ears as his feat was recounted and pondered over and over again. The first to congratulate Sun Dog was the back-climbing warrior, Long Tongue.

Long Tongue rushed to Sun Dog's side and leapt before his eyes like an excited puppy. *What fool is this?* Sun Dog wondered as he donned a leather breechclout to cover his nakedness.

"Great one, you have filled our eyes with a dream!" Long Tongue babbled, continuing on with a stream of little-talk. "What? How?"

"I have walked with the dead many times," Sun Dog replied in a sepulchral tone, turning away as the warrior, Stone Eagle, approached him.

Stone Eagle bowed his head and said, "Forgive me, brother. I only did as you wished." Sun Dog could see that his hands, which had been so steady at his bow, were shaking now.

"You shot well, brother," Sun Dog replied with a grave look. "I thank you for your skill. Let us be friends."

"Eh … I would have it so," the archer muttered before slinking away.

Long Tongue had gazed back and forth at them with the look of a dog trying to understand. "He's the best of our bowmen, you know."

"Yes, he was called for." Had this idiot not understood? He was like a buzzing fly that Sun Dog was anxious to be rid of.

But then Long Tongue revealed that he was the son of the Seneca war chief, Blackbird. "It was I who led the raid against the *Hanishé* on the night that our people swept from our gate," he said.

"Yes?" Sun Dog took a sudden interest.

"Yes, and we would have killed the demon if only my father had listened," Long Tongue went on. "I called for torches, but he would have none of it."

Long Tongue had a greasy way of letting on that he was a big man among the people of Ga-ogwah Kanotaye. "When my father goes to the land of the spirits I will take his place as war chief of the Seneca," he vouched without being prodded. "Perhaps even before that! Then we will sweep over our enemies among the Erie and take their women and children and..."

He rambled on, boasting of his small feats as a hunter and deeds as a camp-tender among the warriors on some long-ago raid, failing to ask Sun Dog a single question about himself or the people of Tali.

"...It was I who traveled far to the north among the Ojibwe and Odawa to seek their shamans," he went on. "Oh, they could have killed us, but I think they were afraid..."

Gradually, Sun Dog deduced that Long Tongue had been the emissary who had brought a great shaman, Wabeno-iniini and his underling, Animi-Ma'liingan, to the Seneca in the hope of defeating the *Hanishé*. Man of the Dawn Sky and He Who Outruns the Wolves were held to be powerful men among the people to the far north, but like the other shamans who had been called upon, they had been confounded by Sun Dog's magic.

"Were they the men standing by Walking Turtle during the ceremony?" he asked.

"What? Yes, they are often by her side," Long Tongue replied, confiding, "I think the old man fancies her—an old, blind hag!"

"You think little of her."

"And why not? A blind woman cannot lead our people," Long Tongue said scornfully. "We should do away with her."

"Perhaps you could replace her," Sun Dog said.

"I would, if I had the parts of a woman."

"A woman?"

"Yes, a council of women guide the Seneca and other tribes among the Haudenosaunee," Long Tongue explained. "But they are often overruled by the chieftains who guide the warriors."

Sun Dog mulled this over. He had no wish to be a sachem among the Seneca, nor a war chief. He planned to be something far greater.

Around the lodge fires at night, he had been told the story of Tododaho, the evil sorcerer of the Onondagas, who wove snakes in his hair and struck fear into the hearts of all who saw him. Surely, Tododaho had been a magician, just the same as Sun Dog and the master. No, Sun Dog would have none of the make-work of a sachem or a war chief. Rather, he would be exalted among the Seneca—worshipped. And when the time came, he would pass his name on to a youngling who was worthy. In that way, the master would live on forever, feasting on one life after another, just as he had done since the time of the Old Ones. *Eya,* he had walked the earth even long before that—he was as old as the stars. To the spirits, the master was known as the Soul Eater, and even they feared to speak his name.

All that he needed were helpmates like the fool, Long Tongue, who never ceased with his chatter and preening.

Long Tongue said that Wabeno had given Walking Turtle a small stone that she wore on a leather thong around her neck, while the Sun Dog's own gift of a beaded necklace had been passed on to the young woman who attended her.

"Is this true?"

"It is true! Wabeno's gift is no different than a gray pebble from the lake while your gift is the delight of every woman who lays eyes on it. If I had such treasures, I would have women laying before me like logs on a raft, but that is a small thing because many women fancy me. More than I can count on my fingers and toes," he bragged. "There are many desirable women who would like to test my stones and have my children."

"Your stones? I do not understand." Sun Dog had enjoyed the favors of many women himself, but no man among the Coosa would dream of boasting of such a thing. Did the Seneca have no shame, or was it only this big-talker?

Long Tongue scooped at the scrotum beneath his breech clout and gave it a tug. "Stones," he leered.

"Ah yes, your man parts," Sun Dog replied, stifling a grimace. "I'm sure there are many maidens in your path, brother. You are finely made."

"Yes," Long Tongue replied with a wavering look and a lack of conviction. "But I am better known as a warrior, and someday I will lead our men when my father steps aside."

"Yes, so you have told me."

Sun Dog rewarded Long Tongue with a placid smile, but his thoughts were filled with cunning delight. Here was a fool who could be swayed with sly words and flattery as easily as the wind bowed the rushes. A puppet.

"Come, you must eat with my people and smoke by our fire," Sun Dog said with his eyes twinkling. "You will meet our own war chief, Little Fox, and tell him of your deeds. It will be an honor to have you among us."

Beaming under Sun Dog's gaze, Long Tongue could hardly believe his ears. He was to share a pipe with this powerful shaman who had cheated death? But wasn't that his due as a big man among his people? He had enlisted Wabeno of the Ojibwe and now had risen even further in the eyes of this great sorcerer of the south.

"You do me honor, father!" he cried. "I will see that a turkey is prepared for the feast!"

CHAPTER 30

LITTLE BY LITTLE

Sun Dog waited seven days before his next ceremony, allowing time to gather converts from among the people of Ga-ogwah Kanotaye. Each night, he performed feats of magic in the town square, pausing only when the howls and squawks of the *Hanishé* sounded far off in the distance.

"It won't be long, my brothers and sisters. Not long!" he addressed the crowds. "I am speaking with the spirits of my *own* land, and they are coming to do battle with your demon though me. They are warriors of the dead—no demon can stand against them! They will suck on the *Hanishé*'s bones and drink its blood."

News of Sun Dog's army of spirits was soon on the lips of everyone in town, and as if in a prophecy, one night the lights of the Great Spirit flickered in a curtain of blue, red, purple, and green on the northern horizon.

No one could know that it was Little Fox sounding the noisemaker far beyond the fields, choking with laughter as he howled and pumped the squealing bladder.

"What do you think?" Wolf asked Wabeno as they sat through their third evening of Sun Dog's magic.

The old man shifted and squinted in Sun Dog's direction, who was busy pulling flowers from a maiden's ears.

"A great power lives within him, dwelling like a shadow," Wabeno replied.

"What? How?"

"I see a darkness within him. Can you see it? A shadow at the center of his chest, dark red like a coal that is almost dead. His magic is nothing but dust in our eyes, but there is something deeper. Something very old and malignant."

"A demon?"

"Who knows what a demon is?" Wabeno replied with a shrug. "I have not seen one lately. He says he will kill the *Hanishé*, and that could be just one demon killing another. Perhaps we've found one."

"We'll see."

"Yes."

Wolf strained his eyes at Sun Dog but saw nothing except other maidens flocking to his side and begging to repeat the flower trick. Sun Dog leaned toward a young woman's ear and pulled a toad from her hair, sending the maidens screaming with delight.

"Eh," he snorted, "and his death, was that a trick too?"

"Surely," Wabeno said, nodding. "But he was a fool to risk such a thing."

"Or a sorcerer."

"Yes."

If anyone knew a sorcerer, it was Wabeno, but he had known only three over the course of many lifetimes. They had all gone to their graves and were likely conversing with the shades of the Old Ones by now. But this man was somehow different.

Across the square, Sun Dog looked their way and nodded. Wabeno gave a grave nod in return. "I must speak with Walking Turtle," he said, leaving Wolf behind.

Sun Dog was still exulting over the cheers of the crowd when Wolf sidled up to him. The young people of the town had begun following him like puppies, and though the older folk were wary of his trick with the arrow and the fire, still, they gave him a respectful nod and greetings when he walked by. None had accused him of being a witch. None dared.

Turning, he was surprised to find the Ojibwe with the club foot at his side.

"You have the love of the people," Wolf said mildly.

"Soon they will love me even more," Sun Dog said before catching himself. "I mean, if the gods are willing, I hope to earn their love."

"Gods?"

"Yes. Among my people they are big spirits, living in the sky and beneath the earth."

"Ah, gods," Wolf mused. "Are they with you now?"

"Yes, brother, they are everywhere."

"*Ehn,* like our *manitos,* they are felt but not seen."

"It is just so, brother. Just so," Sun Dog said stiffly.

"I would like to hear more of your gods," Wolf went on. "Perhaps we could share what we know. We too have powerful spirits, though they may be only children compared to those of your land."

This time Sun Dog merely nodded. He sensed that Wolf was playing the fool to get close to him. His boyhood as a trader's son had sharpened his ears to anything that rang false.

Sun Dog was a tall man, lean and strongly built. He had an aquiline nose and sharp eyes that seemed too close together. His long hair fell in two loose braids which were drawn back and bound together at the nape of his neck. A copper disc was draped on a necklace of pearls falling to his chest—like the disc on his staff, it was a symbol of the sun. He cultivated a regal bearing but felt himself shrinking under Wolf's gaze.

Now, the master appraised Wolf through Sun Dog's eyes with a sense of foreboding. Wolf and the old man Wabeno had an inner glow that was the opposite of his own shade. It was a kind of silver fire that only the master could see.

"What do you want of me?" Sun Dog said with a hard stare.

"What do I want?" Wolf protested with a look of surprise. "Nothing, brother. I only wish to share what we know to rid this place of its troubles."

Wolf gave him a beseeching look and Sun Dog collected himself. A crowd was gathering, and no good would come of giving them something to gossip about.

"I only ask because I have heard of your deeds," Sun Dog said smoothly. "The other shamans have all failed and fled, yet you remain."

"Yes," Wolf said. "My great father, Wabeno-iniini, craves to witness your ceremony with the *Hanishé*."

Something passed over Sun Dog's eyes, and for a moment, Wolf thought that he was going to turn and flee. It occurred to him that perhaps the sorcerer had something to fear from Wabeno, who had yet to reveal his powers.

As a *giimaabi*, Wolf was skilled at putting others at ease. His life had depended upon it in far-off lands while serving as the eyes and ears of the Ojibwe shamans. Now, he strove to soothe the fidgeting sorcerer with idle talk.

"How does the wind blow in your land, brother?" he asked.

"What?"

"The heat, the sun. Is it too much to bear?"

Wolf asked Sun Dog if it ever snowed in his land, how the maize grew there, the size of the fish in the southern rivers, and other prattle. Gradually, Sun Dog relaxed and suppressed a yawn, eager to be rid of this buzzing fly who seemed as big a fool as Long Tongue. He began thinking of one of the women in the crowd who had gazed upon him with lustful eyes when Wolf caught him off guard.

"Your people have many scars on their bodies, with some even taking their eyes," Wolf said. "How is this so?"

It was a fair question asked by others, and Sun Dog had decided that truth would serve better than deception. Some of it, at least.

"We had a *Hanishé* in my own land," he replied. "A white demon and his warriors who spread a plague among us."

"I have seen these demons myself," Wolf said quietly. "They ride a creature we call the *sunktanka*."

"I know nothing of that," Sun Dog replied. "I drove the *Hanishé* from our land and will do the same here."

"But why did you come? The sachem did not call for you as she did the others."

"It was the spirits who called us, and we obeyed."

Ah, the spirits. They would have an answer for anything, Wolf thought. He pressed on, but Sun Dog refused to say anything more.

"You are digging at me, brother," he said at last, pointing a long finger at Wolf's chest, "but these are things I cannot answer." He whipped himself for saying too much already. It would not do to cast himself and his people as desperate run-aways from their own land.

"You are digging at me, brother," he said at last, pointing a long finger at Wolf's chest, "but these are things I cannot answer."

"Ah, forgive me, I have been rude," Wolf said, looking down and shuffling his feet. "Wabeno and I are leaving soon. Come and smoke with us. Let us part as friends."

Wolf doubted that Sun Dog would accept his invitation—it was simply bait in the hope that the sorcerer would invite him to his own lodge for more talk. He knew that Long Tongue had been invited to eat and smoke with Sun Dog's people. His loose lips had spread the news throughout the town, talking up Sun Dog as a great man who had taken him under his wing. Now, Long Tongue was a confidant to the destroyer of demons, tamer of wild men, and master of a great snake of the underworld—if he could sit with them, Wolf hoped to glean what he could from the Sun Dog's people. He was a gifted storyteller, used to regaling other people with his tales, but always careful to listen to their own in return.

But it was not to be.

"I would like that brother," Sun Dog said, "but only after I have driven the *Hanishé* from this land. Then we will smoke and dance and be one with these people. But until then, be careful not to tread where you don't belong. The spirits would frown on it."

"Yes, the spirits," Wolf replied, lifting his strange gray eyes to meet those of Sun Dog. "One must be ever watchful with them."

Two lanes over, Wabeno sat smoking with Walking Turtle before the longhouse she shared with nine families.

"Your people have taken to Sun Dog as if he were the sun itself," he said, exhaling a long plume of smoke.

"I fear that is so," Walking Turtle replied as he handed her the pipe. "He is a big man now."

"So soon."

"Yes, and he will grow even bigger if he kills the *Hanishé*. I know you do not believe it is a demon, but if he brings us proof, what can be said?"

"The wounds I saw on your dead were those of a weapon," Wabeno reminded her.

"Yes, but a demon can use a weapon, just as a man, and he has vowed to bring us the thing's body."

"Ah?"

"Yes," she nodded, "in two days' time."

Wabeno reflected on his. A sort of frenzy had gripped the people of the town since the Sun Dog's brush with death, especially among the young, and they included the warriors who were most easily led. Some of the townsfolk had reservations, and some even thought that Sun Dog was a witch, yet none dared to say so.

"He is taking my people from me," Walking Turtle said somberly. "What can I do? I'm old and blind, and the last of the clan mothers who led our town. If he kills the demon, he will step into my footprints as easily as a fish parts the water."

"Do you think he would desire such a thing?" Wabeno asked.

"I can feel it," she said. "Though I have lost my eyes, their loss has sharpened me in other ways."

"If it is not rude, I would ask you how you lost your sight," Wabeno said quietly.

"Oh, there's not much to tell," she replied, rubbing her hands. "There was a raid by the Erie when I was just a babe. My mother was working in the fields while I was wrapped in my cradle board and propped against a tree. I was less than two summers old but can still remember them sneaking up on her from behind. I cried out, but who listens to a wailing babe? I remember one of them raising a club and then nothing more. Long after, my sister-cousins told me that the board that bound me had fallen over and that my head struck a rock.

"But I don't think that is what made me lose my sight," she went on. "It was knowing that my mother was going to die. I closed my eyes on it and never opened them again. I was raised by my grandmother, who was head of all the Deer Clan, and it was through her that I came to be a clan mother here."

Wabeno said nothing to this, and they sat for a time, quietly passing the pipe back and forth. His pipe was finely carved. It was a gift from Wolf, who had fetched it from the place far to the west where the Dakota people dug for the red pipestone. He was about to compliment Walking Turtle on the quality of the Seneca's tobacco when she spoke again.

"This stone you gave me," she said, fingering the pebble strung on a cord around her neck. "It has a power."

"Yes."

"I … I have begun to see shadows."

"Mmm." Wabeno nodded. "Speak of them."

"They are my people, they are only shadows, but I see them."

"Can you see me?"

Walking Turtle turned and placed the pipe on the ground between them.

"You know I can," she said. "You and your man, Wolf. I see you as a soft light, glimmering like the stars I remember when I was just a babe."

Wabeno gave a gentle laugh, and his eyes flickered with something resembling lightning. "That is my gift to you," he said. "You will never see all that there is, but in time the shadows will grow clearer, and those you love will grow clearer still. If you look close enough, you will see their faces."

"But all this from a pebble?" she cried. "What magic is this? How can it be?"

"It springs from within you," Wabeno said, placing his hand on her knee. "It spoke to you when another woman might have scorned my gift as being unworthy. You kept it, and for that you have been rewarded. You are the *orenda*, only you."

CHAPTER 31

THE DEATH OF THE *HANISHÉ*

Brothers, sisters, what came next was told around the lodge fires for many years thereafter. The story changed in small ways with each retelling, but the facts remained. A great sorcerer of the south grasped a demon that had plagued the Seneca by the throat and cast it into the fire before the eyes of hundreds looking on.

As is often the way of such things, it started with the sacrifice of a virgin.

Sun Dog had promised that he would kill the *Hanishé*, whose roaring and squeals continued deep in the night. Many in the town were roused from their sleep with disturbing dreams as the call of the demon crept into their ears. Sometimes watchers from the palisade saw the creature moving at the far edge of the fields surrounding the town. It moved dim in the moonlight, twice as tall as the maize. The boys who watched over the fields from their towers had long since been pulled back into the town, but Sun Dog's lodge remained outside the entrance of Ga-ogwah Kanotaye, and each morning he emerged, refreshed and unharmed.

"The man has no fear," went the word around the town. "The *Hanishé* does not dare approach him."

The futile efforts of the shamans who came before him were forgotten or scorned as suspense built in advance of Sun Dog's ceremony. Led by Long Tongue, the townsfolk followed him everywhere, hanging on every word and gesture as Sun Dog pulled flowers from the ears of maidens or beads of many colors from their hair. A murmur of approval followed him that rose and fell, cresting like the waves of the sea as the converts of the town trailed in his wake with bright eyes and expectations.

It seemed that even the maize had bowed to him, for on the evening of his arrival with the people of Tali, it had rained all night after a long dry spell, and nothing was surer than a life-giving rain to signify the approval of the spirits.

As for Sun Dog, he was dazzled almost blind with ecstasy as the townsfolk swirled at his heels. Who could imagine that such simple tricks of magic could so easily sway hundreds to his bidding? It no longer disturbed him that the master had devoured almost every vestige of Wren. He no longer remembered or cared—he was the master now, and when the *Hanishé* was defeated, he would bid his followers to raise a great mound at the center of Ga-ogwah Kanotaye and take his place high above them.

There was a dance in the square outside the Great Lodge early in the evening of Sun Dog's ceremony. The war chief, Blackbird, looked on with a mixture of disgust and pride as Long Tongue led the throng of hundreds who lifted their hands to the sky, singing and twirling as they circled the square to the sound of drums.

The words had reached Blackbird's ears of his son's plan to usurp him as war chief. Long Tongue presumed too much—the agreement of every chieftain and headman was needed to rise to such standing, yet his son claimed that he needed the approval of Sun Dog alone. To Blackbird's dismay, many agreed, even among the chieftains below him. He meant to speak with Walking Turtle on the matter but held back. It was undignified, and Blackbird knew that Walking Turtle had concerns of her own. Her standing as *sachem* of the town was eroding beneath her feet like a patch of sand flowing from a stream. Everywhere, the talk on every tongue was Sun Dog, Sun Dog, *Sun Dog!*

After the dance, a virgin was brought forth—a girl of less than twelve winters captured from the Eries who had not yet been defiled by the boys of the town. Two warriors held her wrists, dragging her limp body to the Great Lodge.

"She has been drugged," Wabeno said as he and Wolf looked on. "She would be screaming and twisting if she knew what awaits."

"*Ehn,* and she would have lain with any man who would have had her, even you grandfather," Wolf replied.

"Do not mock me."

Wolf eyed the girl as she disappeared into the gloom of the Great Lodge. "I was not jesting," he said.

They entered at the head of the crowd and took their place around the fire ring at the center of the lodge. Hundreds of townsfolk filed in behind them—all who dared enter, at least—until the lodge was packed to its walls.

Sun Dog had fashioned an altar of sorts and stood before it dressed in his dark cloak of raven feathers, backed by twenty warriors from Tali. Wolf recognized Little Fox among them. He had become a companion of Long Tongue, and the two were often seen together. He also recognized a man with a ravaged face named Scalded One, who was said to have come from a people who lived beyond the mountains to the east. Wolf had approached both men, attempting to pry talk of Sun Dog's plans from their lips, but these had remained sewn shut.

The girl of the Eries lay naked on the altar with her eyes swimming in a daze as Sun Dog stood before her. He held a knife of an unknown metal that was as long as his forearm. One side of the blade had a wicked, jagged edge.

Now the magic begins, the master said within Sun Dog's thoughts. *One monster kills another, a demon dies at his own hand...*

The fire had been settled into red coals before the altar with Sun Dog standing behind it, almost invisible in Half Moon's cloak of dark feathers. A silence filled the lodge as he began an invocation to *Eh-noq-waa,* devourer of virgins. He resisted a smile, thinking of how the pyramid guards of Coosa had threatened him with the same fate. Perhaps *Eh-noq-waa* had devoured their own souls by now for lack of more innocent fare.

It was nearly full-dark in the Great Lodge as hundreds crowded together in breathless suspense. Sun Dog droned on hypnotically in the unknown language of Coosa as his warriors began slowly swaying behind him. Wabeno and Wolf sat in a place of honor on the other side of the fire with Walking Turtle, Blackbird and Long Tongue.

"Can you see any of this?" Wabeno whispered to Walking Turtle.

"Something … dark," she replied.

Now, Sun Dog held the long knife before him with its blade glowing red in the light of the dying embers. The crowd gasped as they awaited the fatal blow.

But no one could have dreamt of what came next. A flute sounded from behind Sun Dog's back and then the sonorous tones of a conch shell. Slowly from the rafters, a thing as big as a man's outstretched hand descended on a cord no bigger than a thread. Every eye strained to see it as it passed the tip of Sun Dog's blade and settled on the stomach of the dozing girl.

There was a flash of light as the fire flared almost to the ceiling of the lodge revealing the hideous form of a giant spider on the girl's belly. Screams filled the air as she awakened and saw the thing on her belly. She leapt from the altar like a frog on a hot stone and ran screaming to the entrance of the lodge. The spider hopped on its thread, once, twice, and then dashed into the fire.

Almost as shocking, Sun Dog had disappeared, with only a pile of black feathers marking where he had stood.

Now the Great Lodge convulsed as if it were a living thing with people pushing toward the entrance in a panic, trampling on those in their path and crushing others against the far wall. It would have been far worse, but for a voice that sounded from behind the crowd at the far end of the lodge.

"Brothers, sisters, I am here!"

A torch was lit and there was Sun Dog, standing naked except for a skirt of white swan feathers around his waist and a disc of copper draped in a necklace over his chest. A young woman standing alongside him swooned and fell into her sister-cousin's arms as piercing cries filled the longhouse. Dipping the torch to the level of his knees, Sun Dog looked godlike in its light, casting a giant shadow on the wall of the lodge.

"Did you think that I would leave you?" he said, striding toward the altar. "Did you think I would harm the girl? No, I have traded her life for that of the *Hanishé*. The spider has brought the demon under my power."

Across the way, Wabeno groaned and rolled his eyes, but if Sun Dog noticed, he paid no mind.

Now, Sun Dog lifted a box and opened its lid, freeing a white bird from within that fluttered up, disappearing into the rafters.

"Your *Hanishé* lives in torment tonight and will cry bitter tears, tearing at his breast," Sun Dog called out. "I will shrivel him, brothers. Sisters, I will place him in this box, and tomorrow I will cast him into the fire."

"But how?" Wabeno called from across the way. His voice was dry, disbelieving. "How will you shrivel him?"

Sun Dog gazed back with glittering eyes. "You know the answer as well as I, grandfather," he said. "The spider has woven its web for him."

"These were only tricks that any shaman knows," Wabeno grumbled as he and Wolf sat before their fire that night.

"But what of the spider?" Wolf said.

"A toy, something sewn together by one of the Tali women."

"*Gaawiin,* no, it was not toy. I saw its cousin when you sent me on the mission to the far south. They live in the deserts there. They are hairy and they bite."

"I imagine that is true."

"But it was dead," Wolf went on. "A puppet."

"Is the *Hanishé* the same?" A sour look swept over Wabeno's face as he cast another stick on the fire.

"You know better than me, old one. Perhaps only the spirits know."

"I have asked them many times now," Wabeno said slowly. "They tell me only that we must watch our backs."

As Sun Dog had promised, the *Hanishé* howled and squealed as never before that night with its anguished honks and squawks echoing from the haunted tower of limestone. Few slept as a blanket of dread settled on the town. The girl of the Eries had sped barefoot straight through the entrance of Ga-ogwah Kanotaye, never to be seen again.

There was much talk of the hideous spider that had been called forth, most likely from the land of devils. Only a few had had a good look at it, but as the story passed from one set of lips to another, the spider grew from the size of a squirrel to that of a dog and then a man. Many swore that they had heard it doing battle with the *Hanishé* that night. The demon's screams were proof of it.

But to Sun Dog's disappointment, far fewer dared to enter the Great Lodge on the night of his final performance. He had done his work too well, with the dusty spider terrifying all who heard of it. A refrain was heard throughout the town: "What if the *Hanishé* appears as we are sitting there?" Sun Dog had promised it would be so.

Thus, the Great Lodge was only half full the next evening, and as he expected, the old shaman Wabeno and his partner, Wolf, sat stone-faced before the fire once again. The master smiled within Sun Dog's thoughts, knowing that Wabeno had spoken with the spirits of him, yet had learned nothing. How could the Ojibwe know that the spirits feared the vile thing that was the master and had fled before it as if they were tendrils of smoke in a wind? Now he would show Wabeno something that would confound even the great sorcerer of the north.

Once again, Sun Dog invoked *Eh-noq-waa,* the demon god who was no more than a child's story to the master. Once again, he lifted the cedar box before the fire, opening it for all to see. There was no dove this time—the box was black and empty.

Carefully, Sun Dog closed the lid and laid the box on the altar before the fire. He turned his back on the crowd and lifted his arms toward the ceiling of the lodge as if he were summoning a demon.

"Come to your doom, foul one. *Eh-noq-waa* demands it!"

Then, turning back, the crowd gasped as Sun Dog's face appeared as if it had been set ablaze by the fire. He had donned the mica mask passed down from his father to the master in thanks for saving his life. Now, it gave him the appearance of a sorcerer who was on fire with all his powers.

"He has come," he said in a low voice with his hands beckoning to the empty box. Cries of terror filled the darkness of the hall as many scrambled for the entrance. The tumult stirred a colony of bats roosting in the eaves that added to the horror as they fluttered among the onlookers.

But those who stayed witnessed a sight beyond their imagination.

Carefully, Sun Dog opened the box and pulled a struggling figure from its depths. It had the appearance of a tiny man, the size of a large squirrel. The thing was naked, with long, dangling arms and legs along with a large round head, bulging eyes, and the ugliest face that anyone had ever seen. It was clearly a man—a tiny man—yet not a man. It could only be a demon. Its beady green eyes flared in the firelight as Sun Dog swept it before the gaping crowd.

Sun Dog slipped his middle finger into a slot behind the monkey's head, using his other fingers to waggle its arms in a crazed herky-jerky dance. Little Demon opened its mouth and screamed as it looked right and left around the hall.

Screams rent the air of the Great Lodge as Sun Dog lifted the hideous creature aloft, wriggling its arms and legs. The onlookers surged back, crushing those behind them as they scrambled for safety. To those watching, it appeared to be alive.

"Death to you now foul one! Death to you in the name of Eh-noq-waa!" Sun Dog cried, casting the shaved monkey of the master into the flames.

A tower of sparks flared to the ceiling as the creature hit the flames, illuminating the horrified faces of those gathered in the darkness. Then, with a hideous shriek and a wavering howl, Sun Dog clutched at his chest and collapsed into the arms of his followers.

BOOK THREE

LAKE HURON – LATE SUMMER, 1541

CHAPTER 32

THE WARRIOR

It had been a full day of paddling and then a night and another long day before the warrior chose to take his rest. There, up ahead on the northern shore of Tima Gami, he saw an in-between woman fishing, and drawing closer, he thought to ask her if she had something for him to eat that night.

But as he drew his canoe to the shore, she looked up and their eyes met, and with a single glance he felt an arrow driven straight through his heart.

Found by the River was no beauty, but she had the slim eyes of a fox and was judged fair enough to win a man's heart. Yet there was no accounting for how she took the greatest warrior of the Ojibwe captive without lifting a finger.

She did not like being stared at—too often that had been her fate among the tongue-waggers of the village, and now, this fool was gaping at her as if she had laid an egg.

"What?" she asked crossly as he sat floating offshore, gazing at her with his mouth open. "You are rude."

"Uh!" he shot up, flustered. "My journey has made me dizzy. It is only hunger. Do you…?"

"Would you like a fish?"

"What?" He was confused, for what else was there?

"Fish," she said, mocking him as she dragged her net to shore. "It lives beneath your canoe."

"*Ehn,*" he said, as if he had never heard of such a thing. In his dazzle, he had forgotten himself. There was something about this woman that had struck him like a thunderbolt. But how? Why?

"Yes, I know of fish," he stammered.

"Then you can eat," she replied. "You see? Two fish. A fat one for you and one for me. Come, be a hero and fan the coals."

He laughed, showing a broad smile, and she snickered in return. Pulling his canoe from the water, he overturned it and followed her down the beach to a tiny village, following as shy as a small boy in her footsteps. She led him to a lodge where an older woman sat outside, smoking a pipe beside the cook fire. She was curiously dark, with eyes that were as green as Kitchi Gami and curling hair that fell in ringlets.

"We have a guest," Found by the River called out.

"I see," Willow said, thinking that he was a handsome one at that and brawny to an extreme. "Does he have tobacco?"

The stranger's name was Mitig Bwaa Waagin, Tree That Does Not Bend. He struck Willow as something of an oaf, but he was likable enough and she saw him making shy glances at River as they ate, holding on to her every word. The two women shared a fish, while the big man wolfed his down and then reached for a handful of roasted grasshoppers.

"Sisters, you are too kind," he said. "I was ready to eat a frog."

"They are not so bad," Willow said, "the legs…"

"Raw," he said, "you have saved me!"

"And the frog," River said with a soft laugh. Suddenly it occurred to her that she had been quite unlike herself in her bold words with the stranger. Had she been flirting? Her face flushed a deep red at the thought.

"Why have you come here?" Willow asked as they sat smoking after their meal.

"Wabeno, the Man of the Dawn Sky has called me."

"Old man Wabeno? I know him well, but he has gone far south with my own man, Wolf."

"I know of your man too," he nodded. "I met him once far to the west."

"Then you follow them to the Seneca? How?"

"Birds and dreams, birds and dreams," he said, offering no other explanation. "Wabeno has called me and so I come. Look."

He reached into a leather pouch at his side and unrolled a length of birch bark, upon which were a number of markings. "The shamans of Boweting gave me this to show the way. You see? Here is this lake—it is very long—then a river, then a smaller lake, another river, then another big lake, another river, and the waterfall of many legends. The Seneca live not far beyond it."

"That seems a long way," Willow said, quailing at the thought of Wolf being at such a distance.

"My canoe is swift, and my arms are strong," he said, rolling the scroll and tucking it away.

Found by the River looked up as if she had seen him for the first time, and something akin to hope lit in her eyes. Forgetting herself, she said, "If you say so, then it must be true."

The warrior looked back with an easy smile. To his surprise, the dazzling girl was blushing.

"Yes, it is true," he said solemnly.

Normally, a man would not sit talking into the evening with two women, this being unseemly, but Willow often broke the rules of the band with her headstrong ways and could see no harm in their visitor. If anything, she was glad to have a man's company, for the mood of the village had grown darker with each day that Wolf had been gone. One Toe and Crow's Meat had been as tireless as beavers, spreading stories and condemning both herself and Found by the River as witches. They had dreamt it, so it must be true, and their lies and innuendos had taken root.

Last night, she had been awakened by a rustling at the back wall of their lodge. She had crept from the lodge with Wolf's club in her hand, swinging hard at a shape in the darkness. There was a howl and then the clatter of a clay pot filled with coals as the intruder hobbled away. That day, Willow noticed that One Toe's right leg was badly bruised where her club had struck home.

"Did you trip on a rock, brother?" she said lightly. "You must be careful. The next time it could be your head."

He had glared back before turning away with Crow's Meat hissing in her direction. Now things would get more serious, Willow thought. The next time there might be torches and more villagers than she and the girl could overcome. But she promised that she would bash One Toe's head in before they took her.

Tree That Does Not Bend had meant to creep beneath his canoe as was usual, but Willow had told him something of their troubles and so he spread his sleeping robe before the entrance to their lodge. Willow had turned in first, leaving the two alone.

Sitting by the fire, Found by the River shared her story, confessing all, including the shaking fits that Willow said was an illness and not the work of a demon. At this, the hair rose on the back of Tree's neck, but he was mesmerized by her tale and the accusations of witchcraft, thinking that few would be so forthright.

"Do you think that I am a witch?" she asked at last with a petulant look on her face.

"What?" He barely knew what to say as he looked into her eyes. They were pleading now, drawing him into their depths.

"I have never met a witch before," he said in his solemn way. "But you do not look like a witch to me, and forgive me sister, but if you are, I do not fear you. I have heard that witches can turn themselves into foxes and bats, but I have no fear of these either. Can you do this? Can you fly?"

"What! Silly man!" she laughed, giving his knee an easy shove. "You mock me!"

A thrill ran through him as he realized that he had said just the right thing, rather than the miserable words he usually jabbered upon meeting a woman. How easy it seemed to talk with her. If she was a witch, then what was the harm?

"Would you like me to slay them?" he asked before they turned in.

"Who?" Found by the River asked.

"Those who trouble you. The people of this village."

"All of them?"

"Yes, if you wish."

She gaped in disbelief. "What? No!"

But in the spreading darkness, she saw a small smile on his face and a twinkle in his eye. "You mock me again," she said.

"Do I?" It was the closest he had ever come to flirting with a woman and now, he too blushed. His face grew warm in the dusk as his manhood swelled and stiffened as hard as oak.

But River was looking at his eyes, and not his groin. "You are kind to offer," she said, smiling, "and if you asked Willow, she might say yes, but I do not wish it."

With that she turned in and slept like a she-bear in its winter den, while Tree That Does Not Bend tossed like a muskrat in a waterfall, barely sleeping at all. What witchcraft had possessed him? he wondered.

He had never been close to a woman. The champion of countless races, wrestling matches, games of skill, and feats of strength in the festivals of the Ojibwe, he had been taught that a woman's touch would sap his power and dilute his medicine as a warrior and a hunter. His father had told him that all women were witches, and so there seemed nothing unusual about Found by the River's story, except that the people of her village were unkind to her.

But more than that, he was shy, having been born into a family of five brothers. Maidens giggled to find him blushing in their presence, and the more they tempted and teased, the more he flustered under their eyes. He was a man's man, living in the company of his hunter friends, who preferred to keep to the forests in search of game, rather than the easier way of fishing for their meals. They were a jolly bunch, and the best of his friends nicknamed him Tree That Weeps Much Sap or Tree With Bats in its Branches and the like. But most called him simply Tree.

Not even the wisest shamans of the Mide-wi-win could explain the mystery of love—not even Wabeno, the Man of the Dawn Sky, who was the wisest of them all.

How was it that the murmur of a woman with a trace of husk to her voice could throw a man to ruin for years on end? How was it that the sideways glance of a woman's eyes could transfix a man as if he were a rabbit in a snare? How was it that the tilt of a woman's hips could live in a man's memory forever, making him desire no one else but her? Her wiggle, her smile, her voice. What exalted her above all others? No one knew—so it was that the great warrior-hunter, Tree That Does Not Bend, had no idea as to how Found by the River had plucked the strings of his heart with nothing more than a smoldering look and the toss of her head.

He rose at sunrise the next morning, planning to be well on his way before the day grew warm. But he longed to see how Found by the River would appear in the morning light and was not disappointed when she crept from her lodge with sleep still crusting her eyes.

"Good morning hero," she said, yawning.

"Now it is you who mocks me," he replied.

"Perhaps you need mocking," she said with a wan smile. "You are leaving before I even know you."

Tree had his tongue tied in a knot at this, which seemed a declaration, and yet, who could tell? What did the woman mean, if anything?

"You would know more of me?" he said cautiously.

"Would you know more of me?" she answered, gazing up at him with hopeful eyes.

Again, he did not know what to say, for though bold words and straight talk were the way of things with his friends among the hunters, he had never had such a conversation with a woman. Never even dreamed of it!

He flushed and would have turned and fled like a fawn sprung from its day bed if Willow had not appeared at the entrance of the lodge with a bundle in her arms.

"We're going with you," she said.

"What?"

"This place sickens me, as do its people. We will help you paddle and cook your meals. Come," she said to River, "gather your things."

Willow had heard the warrior's jest of killing everyone in the village the night before and had considered asking him to dispose of One Toe and his wife but dismissed the thought as soon as it arose. What she really wanted was to be free of this wretched place and follow Wolf to whatever fate might await them.

Tree found his head reeling. "This is not possible," he protested. "The way is long, and there are water serpents and bad men all along the way. Your man will never forgive me if you are lost!"

"Hah!" Willow answered. "I have been down this lake with Wolf for ten seasons of the falling leaves and know it as well as anyone. We live with the Tionontati in the winter, and they will guide us further on."

"But…"

"We have nothing to fear of serpents," she continued, "and if there are bad men, then you can show us your skill at chasing them away."

Found by the River looked on with wide eyes, first at Willow, then at Tree. He looked back at her with a twinge in his chest, feeling the pang of desire, but still, taking her along was unthinkable.

"I forbid it," he said with great effort, shrinking even as the words left his lips. Something that was so easily forbidden in the company of men seemed far more difficult when demanded by a woman.

"Then we will follow you in our own canoe, and it will be on your head if anything happens to us," Willow said primly.

Tree had crushed a head or two in his time when called upon to defend his village, but now he felt crushed himself. The woman had made him his fool, and even now was walking down to the lakeside where his canoe lay waiting.

"Come!" she called over her shoulder, and before Tree could say anything further, Found by the River scrambled past him bearing her sleeping robe and the sack of her belongings. "You are good to take us!" her voice tinkled in his ears.

And so it was done. That morning, One Toe strolled down to the lake for his daily shit, and squatting on the beach, looked up to see a strange sight. An unknown warrior who seemed almost a giant was bearing away to the south in a canoe with the two witches who had vexed him so. Where could they be bound, he wondered, and what deviltry was the she-dog, Willow, planning?

CHAPTER 33

THE LOVERS

Men were as unknown to River as women were to Tree, and now as their canoe set south, she felt that she had been too bold in addressing the tall warrior who paddled behind her. She could feel his eyes on her back, or imagined it was so.

As a child who had no clan, she had been teased by the other children of the village. She and her adoptive mother, Woman Walks Tall, lived in a lodge in the forest beyond the ragged fence. There had been friends among the girls of the village, but not many lasted, for their mothers were given to saying unkind things about her, and their children took heed.

But though she had an occasional friend among the girls, River had barely ever spoken to the boys of the village, who were seldom inclined to speak to girls at all until they were of the rutting age.

And then they too were frightened away.

So now, paddling south, she felt that she had been too bold with Tree. She did not know how the flirting words had come to her lips, and she flushed at the memory. How did she dare to speak to him, as free and thoughtless as a chattering gull, sitting all alone together in the darkness? What would any decent man think of her? Besides, he was handsome, and clearly as strong as three men. He must have women sighing for him in every village he visited. He couldn't possibly find her worthy. She was too skinny, too frail, watery, and worthless, or so she had been told. All of these thoughts and more tormented her as they paddled south, and she resolved to speak to Tree as little as possible so as not to embarrass herself any further or tempt him to rebuke her. His scorn would be more than she could bear.

This of course made Tree That Does Not Bend crave her even more. That evening they pulled ashore on a sandy island and grilled some fish that River had caught by trolling her net that day. Filled with ardor and aching to speak with her again, Tree was dumbfounded that River had nothing to say to him. Instead, she muttered a polite goodnight and snuggled in her sleeping robe alongside Willow.

Willow had given him a puzzled glance over the light of their campfire and seemed just as mystified by River's silence. Perhaps it was her time of the moon, she decided.

But two days went by, and nothing changed as the girl maintained a steady silence, barely answering when Tree called out over his shoulder as they paddled further south. He made an attempt to sound jolly, but his voice was strained. It was hard talking to a woman at the best of times, and now he felt as if an arrow had gone straight through his head. Why had she turned so cold? What had he done? Had he been too bold? Had he not treated her with respect? He thought of the night they had spent talking outside Willow's lodge—it had been as nothing he had ever imagined, and he had wrestled all night with thoughts of her, even daring to imagine that she would be his woman. Yet now, all seemed lost.

Willow confronted her on the third morning of their journey after they had made their ablutions on the beach.

"Don't you like him, daughter?" she asked mildly.

Found by the River wavered as her eyes welled up. "Yes, of course I like him. But what could I be to him? I am nothing."

"*Gaawiin,* no! He aches for you, and yet you play him like a fish!"

"I do not mean to, it's just…"

"Don't let the fish get away," Willow warned her. "He has chosen you because *you* have chosen him."

"Do you think?"

"Even a man who wrestles panthers can find it hard to talk with a woman," Willow said. "Give him a crumb at least."

Found by the River was sweeter that day, allowing herself to laugh when Tree made a lame joke. Gradually, she realized that he was just as shy as herself and the panther within her warmed.

That night, she was sweeter still around their fire, listening to his stories and purring when it seemed appropriate. Tree looked at her several times with hopeful eyes as he babbled on with tales of battling the Dakota or balancing on the antlers of a moose. She gazed back with a shy smile, marveling at his features and wondering what it would be like to be encompassed in his arms. His legs and thighs were tight with hard muscle, and she wondered how it would feel to have them thrusting at her. She began to imagine her life with such a man and being welcomed into his clan. Then there would be kinfolk—the brothers and sisters, aunts and uncles she had never known—perhaps even a child.

This went on for another night until Willow thought they would never stop babbling as she tried to sleep beneath the overturned canoe. But on the night after that, she was awakened by heavy breathing and rustling beyond the fire. At first, she thought it was a bear or a raccoon come to eat the scraps of their dinner but then came a lilting cry and a deep moan from the darkness. Willow settled back with a smile on her face, certain that her nights would be just as noisy from then on.

The days slipped by and with it the coast as they made their way along the southern shore of the Lake of the Eries. There was no need to conceal their passage, for Willow was well-known among the Tionontati who lived at the western end of the lake. An escort of warriors paddled along with them both in front and behind, though they often begged for Tree That Does Not Bend to ease the pace. He laughed in reply, stilling his rhythm for a bit until he forgot himself and pummeled on again. Willow marveled at his strength, thinking that only Wolf could paddle as fast.

The great waterfall came and went as the Tionontati gave their farewells. Soon, they came upon people gaping from the shore along with the dugouts of fishermen who waved greetings, and then the sight of

Ga-ogwah Kanotaye itself, with its broad palisade crowning a hilltop surrounded by fields of maize, sunflowers and beans.

As it happened, He Who Outruns the Wolves was preparing to go fishing just as their canoe touched the shore. Fishing was the thing he loved best in all the world, and he had fashioned a barbed spear tied to a long cord of hemp in the hope of snagging a lake trout. He was about to push off in one of the dugouts lining the shore when a strange sensation came over him, a tingling that sent the blood rushing from his head.

He looked to the left where a giant of a man had landed with two women. One of them had a familiar look, but how could it be?

"Wolf?" she called out.

"Willow?" It was her. It was ... Wolf felt his knees melt under him as his vision swirled, and darkness swept his eyes. It was...

Moments later he was lying on the shore, cradled in her lap as she smoothed his face. "You are no warrior!" she laughed with her face streaming with tears.

"I have never been a warrior," he croaked. "But what? How are you here?"

Over her shoulder, the giant peered down alongside Willow's troublesome friend, Found by the River, both of them beaming. Wolf knew the man. They had fished together once, and his feats of strength and prowess as a warrior were legendary among the Ojibwe.

"You!" he said, sitting up and brushing the sand from his arms. "How are you here? You could not know of the summons. It was issued only half a moon ago. Word would not have reached Kitchi Gami yet."

"Summons? I know nothing of it," Tree replied. "Wabeno asked me to fetch you home even before you left. I waited a full moon before leaving, just as he asked."

"And you," Wolf turned to Willow. "My heart has burned for you, but why are you here?"

"We had to flee the devils of the village. But more than that, I could not wait for you," Willow replied, caressing his face.

"Mmm," Wolf murmured. Somehow, he was not surprised to find Willow there. Another man might have been angry at his wife for making such a long and dangerous journey, but Willow had always been a woman who did as she pleased, and Wolf knew enough not to scold her. Instead, he was content to listen.

Willow told of her confrontation with One Toe and Crow's Meat and then the gathering threat of the villagers. "It was then that Tree made land to make camp and…" She was about to say was smitten by the maiden, Found by the River, but thought better of it. "…he heard of our trouble and offered to kill everyone in the village."

She chuckled in remembrance. "But that would not do, so we came with him.

"But what of your demon? The *Hanishé*?" she went on. "Did Wabeno kill it?"

Wolf shook his head. "The *Hanishé* is dead, or else gone back to its place in the underworld. We lingered here to witness the maize festival of the Seneca. I wanted to leave, but old man Wabeno wished to see it."

"Then Wabeno had power over it," Willow said, nodding. "I knew he could do it."

"Oh, woman, if only that were true," Wolf replied. "But even Wabeno is mystified, for it was a great shaman of the south that killed the demon. A sorcerer named Sun Dog."

CHAPTER 34

THE GREEN CORN FESTIVAL

Ten days had gone by since Sun Dog's ceremony in the Great Lodge, and the *Hanishé* had not been heard of since. Wolf had been anxious to head for home as soon as the demon had been declared dead, but Wabeno begged to stay for the Green Corn Festival of the Seneca.

The ragged palisade and hulking longhouses of Ga-ogwah Kanotaye were dreary in Wolf's eyes. The town was too crowded for his liking, and he missed the neat lodges of the Odawa, which were half the size of those of the Seneca at most. Twice he had sullied the fine moccasins that Willow had made him by stepping in the dog shit that lay everywhere, attended by swarms of flies. When it rained, Ga-ogwah Kanotaye was a lake of mud, prompting him to go barefoot. Nor did he care for the hordes of dogs and mobs of children sniffing at his heels wherever he walked, along with the hubbub of pushing through lanes crowded with farmers. All this, and it was a long walk to the beach each morning where hundreds made their dumps.

"This place is crowded, and it stinks of shit," he protested. "How can people live like this?"

"*Ehn*, you speak wisdom, Wolf," Wabeno agreed. "My nose is offended too. But just a little longer. Just a little."

Held in late summer when the maize was fresh and sweet, the Green Corn Festival honored the Great Mother of the Haudenosaunee and her daughter, the Good Twin, who had brought the gift of maize to the people of the earth. It was a joyous celebration because, as all know, by late summer the farmers of every land had depleted their stores of crops from the previous year, yet nothing had yet ripened. Green corn eased the pang of starvation.

Thus, there was feasting along with sacrifices of tobacco and thankful prayers. Wolf and Wabeno witnessed days of dancing, drumming, speeches and songs as the Seneca exulted over the coming harvest.

Through it all Wabeno continued to grouse that the Sun Dog's ceremony had been a sham. "It was only a squirrel," he said of the creature that Sun Dog had cast into the fire. "He plucked its fur to make it appear as if it was a demon."

But Wolf did not think so.

"Perhaps your eyes were dimmed by the smoke," he said. "The thing had arms and legs much longer than a squirrel, and its ears were set on either side of its head just as with a man. I saw it clearly. It was a tiny man."

"With stones for eyes," Wabeno shot back.

"Yes, the eyes were like the beads that Sun Dog showers on the women," Wolf agreed. "But still, it had the look of a demon."

Wolf shuddered in remembrance of the creature's flat nose, wide mouth, and broad forehead. In all his travels, he had never seen such a thing.

"Remember too that Sun Dog called it through the air to his box," he added. "We all saw that the box was empty before he cast his spell."

"There was a magic in that," Wabeno agreed, "But I tell you this, I have never seen a demon made whole. They dwell only in the spirit land."

"Yes grandfather, but somehow one escaped," Wolf said. "We heard it ourselves, and if Sun Dog is to be believed, we saw it as well. Admit it—the thing is gone."

But Wabeno was not to be settled, and each night, he brought up his suspicions once again until Wolf began to think he was merely jealous of Sun Dog's magic. Even Walking Turtle said that the *orenda* of the town had strengthened as her own grip as sachem slipped away. Sun Dog had become a living legend to the dull farmers of the town who scratched at the earth each day with little amusement. He was a Big Man now—as tall as the palisade in the opinion of all.

All except Wabeno. "He is just something for these simple folk to talk about," he fumed.

The master could not have been happier as he gazed through Sun Dog's eyes. Even the powerful sorcerer of the Ojibwe had been fooled by his simple tricks, or so he thought.

He had staged it all as a play. First came the dried and withered tarantula, brought north to Coosa by traders nearly a lifetime ago. Little Fox had lowered it on a thin string as Sun Dog went through the charade of casting a spell. Obscured in the black cloak of raven feathers borrowed from Half Moon, he had fled to the far side of the lodge when the girl screamed at the sight of the spider. A clay pot of oil from the cave had produced the flare that blinded the onlookers, allowing him to vanish. Early on, Sun Dog had deduced that the black ooze in his cave was flammable.

As for the arrival of Little Demon on the following night, that had been a simple matter of hiding the stuffed monkey in the false bottom of the box the master had fashioned long ago as part of his magical ceremonies. The priests of Coosa knew of monkeys, of course, for the trade networks of that great land extended many moons' journey to the south where other traders from much further on offered parrot feathers, chocolate, and exotic creatures. The master had stumbled across the monkey at a market in Coosa long before his pupil, Wren, had been born, recognizing its worth as a magic-maker. It had been alive then, traded with a band of Aztec gold around its neck, and the master had stuffed and shaved it upon its death. Now the horrid thing was gone, having served its purpose, yet in a way the master missed it. But not so much that he didn't revel in his new role as Sun Dog and the slayer of the *Hanishé*.

His scream and the pantomime of near-death at Little Demon's demise had come to him as an afterthought and had affected the onlookers as if they had been struck by lightning. The great Sun Dog had survived death once again!

He had been carried on the shoulders of a cheering crowd all around the town after the *Hanishé*'s death, and the speeches and dances given in his honor during the Green Corn Festival outshone all others. He had moved into town, evicting Walking Turtle, from her quarters in a sly test of his power, humbling her before her people, who seemed more than willing to ignore the insult and bask in his light. In a matter of little more than a cycle of the moon, he had become the Exalted One among the townsfolk in all but name.

There was more. It was Long Tongue who led the warriors now, entranced by his talk of smashing their enemies among the Eries and the Hurons with the aid of Sun Dog's sorcery.

His father, Blackbird, was war chief in name only now as Long Tongue turned the excitable young warriors against him with scornful words and boasts of his place in Sun Dog's eyes. Long Tongue's followers were all young men who wore their hair in a tall band down the center of their skulls, roached with bear grease to stand stiffly up and dyed red with sumac berries as if for war. They strutted around the town, proclaiming that Sun Dog had made them invincible with his magic. No one dared speak against them—even Blackbird could not protest. He kept to his lodge in his shame, leading only a few old warriors among his friends.

The master was content to let Long Tongue babble on with talk of conquest and vengeance. He had no particular interest in such, but who knew? Once the current vessel of Sun Dog was aged and spent, a new disciple would carry on his name. It would take time—a generation, perhaps—but once his pyramid had risen over Ga-ogwah Kanotaye, he would cast his eyes in the direction of the Eries and then the Wendats. Perhaps he would even extend his power as far north as the Ojibwe. The master had all the time in the world.

Only one thing troubled Sun Dog and the creature within him. Well before the ceremony in the Great Lodge, the sachem, Walking Turtle, had sent out a call for the greatest warriors of every tribe to do battle with the *Hanishé*. Sun Dog knew that it had been at the bidding of the meddlesome sorcerer, Wabeno, who had yet to show his own feeble powers. Now, the warriors had begun to arrive at the height of the Green Corn Festival, including Wabeno's own man, a giant of the Ojibwe named Mitig Bwaa Waagin, Tree That Does Not Bend. All were dismayed that the *Hanishé* had been destroyed before they had a chance to challenge it. Some had traveled as far as the O-y-o river to the south, the Misi Sipi to the west, and the Great Salt Water to the east. As a consolation, Sun Dog himself had proposed a series of games to coincide with the end of the festival. The winner would receive Sun Dog's splendid crown of feathers.

By now, Wolf and Wabeno had made themselves comfortable in their quarters near the entrance of the Great Lodge, and with the arrival of Willow, River, and Tree, they set about constructing screens of reeds gathered by the lakeshore to enable a touch of privacy. The ghosts of the lodge had receded, and their voices were barely heard now, but Wabeno was irritated at times to find his sleep disturbed by rustlings and moans from the newly twined lovers.

"They go at it like rabbits in heat," he complained to Wolf, who flushed, thinking of his own tumblings with Willow at night.

"Would you have me speak with them?" Wolf asked innocently.

"No, no, it would not do," Wabeno brushed the suggestion aside, "but this Tree must save his strength if he does not wish to be shamed in the coming games."

"Ah, but perhaps he will have something to strive for."

"Hmph, what could that be?"

"The favor of his woman."

CHAPTER 35

SEVEN CHALLENGES

Wabeno need not have feared that Tree had grown soft, for if anything, paddling from the far north of Kitchi Gami had hardened the muscles of his arms, back, and chest to the temper of green oak.

Seven champions from seven lands had been invited to compete in seven challenges in honor of the seven elders who had died on the first night of the *Hanishé*'s rampage.

All had their strengths and weaknesses. Even Tree That Does Not Bend with his legendary skill as a hunter fell short in the archery contest against the Seneca bowman, Stone Eagle. A captive of the Erie had been forced to stand sideways with a cob of corn in his mouth as each contestant took aim. Tree was loathe to aim too close to the unfortunate man's face and just nipped the cob at its silken end, while Stone Eagle's winning arrow sliced it neatly in two, just shy of the Erie's mouth. To their credit, none of the archers struck the man himself, except for a lone arrow that creased the top of his head, parting his hair and bathing his shoulders in blood. The trembling Erie was praised as a hero for enduring his ordeal and sent back to his people. Like the virgin before him, he ran through the gate of Ga-ogwah Kanotaye as if his breechclout was on fire.

Next came a swimming contest to an island that was almost out of sight in the Lake of the Mohawks. Several quailed at the sight, including a warrior from the Chaiena, whose people lived far to the west along the Misi Sipi where the woodlands met the prairies. At best, he had done some splashing in the shallow lakes and ponds of his homeland.

A wild man of the Chelaquens begged off, saying that he had never learned to swim, but the rest were game to try, and they lined up naked on the beach with every member of the town cheering behind them. At the signal, they dove into the waves, flailing toward the distant island.

Love-struck oaf that he was, Tree had tarried by the shore, hoping to catch the eye of Found by the River before swimming. It was that moment's hesitation that saved the man of the Chaiena, who disappeared beneath the waves as soon as they covered his head. Tree dragged him coughing to shore and darted back into the water, only to find Stone Eagle in the same fix.

"You owe me an arrow," he said, grinning as he dropped the heaving Seneca back on the shoreline.

"Done!"

By now, the remaining swimmers were three long bowshots out into the lake, but Tree was not concerned. The Ojibwe lived along the shores of Kitchi Gami and were as welcome in the water as in the forest. With his long arms and sleek build, he knifed through the water as if he were an otter, soon overtaking the four remaining swimmers. The water was a green murk below them and more terrifying with each stroke away from the shore. One, a man of the land-locked Susquehannocks, panicked soon thereafter and wisely clawed his way back to the beach, facing the hoots and derision of the crowd.

But Tree swam on, and sensing the lake currents flowing from the east, began edging to the northeast as the remaining swimmers kept on straight toward the island. They were strong swimmers, including a man of the Mohawks and one of the Mahicans, but no man could fight the currents of the lake and soon to their surprise they found themselves flailing a long way to the west. Far below, the ghosts of drowned fishermen gazed up from their dreary haunts at the bottom of the lake and placed bets. It was the Mahican who joined them.

But as for Tree That Does Not Bend, in time he was aided by the current and filled a sack on his belt with a handful of the island's pebbles. It was half a day before he made it back to the mainland, learning that a canoe had been dispatched to retrieve the surviving Mohawk.

Now there were six remaining with Tree and Stone Eagle each notching a win. A stone-chucking contest followed, with each man instructed to find a stone the size of his own head.

"Our man is sure to win this one," Wolf beamed. "He's strong enough to knock down the Seneca's fence."

But it was not to be, for though Tree was the tallest among the contestants and likely the strongest, his stone slipped from his hand just as he whirled to cast it and fell with a thud at his feet. He looked up, hoping for a second chance, but none was forthcoming. Instead, the assembled crowd convulsed with laughter, some rolling on the ground in the throes of hilarity. Tree skulked from the square with his head down along with jeers at his back. It was the man of the Chaiena whose life he had saved that won the match.

Now the crowd was in a frenzy. Three of the remaining six had won a match, including their own man among the Seneca, and there were four challenges left. Bets were made all around, pledging their clothing, pipes, weapons, even their wives and daughters, or as it were, their husbands, on the outcome. Some even bet their little fingers, gambling that their favorite would win. Wolf could not resist, betting their sleek canoe of birch bark against a fine belt of purple quahog shells, wagering that Tree would come out the victor.

"But how will we get home if he loses?" Willow cried.

"He will win. Wabeno has foretold it," Wolf assured her.

"Ha! You'll be begging for one of their leaky dugouts if he's wrong."

"Think instead of the fine shells you will soon be wearing. You'll be the envy of every woman in Boweting."

"Shells!" she scoffed. "You could at least have wagered for pearls."

Wolf gazed back with a bemused smile. Who could know what a woman might desire?

Tree was in a fury that night over the disgrace of the stone slipping from his hand. He fumed, unable to sleep, no matter how Found by the River tried to soothe him.

"It was only a slip," she said as they lay in their quarters. "You saved the lives of two brave men. Think of that instead."

"If I lose, it will be the disgrace of all our people," he moaned, staring at the ceiling of the Great Lodge. "I will never show my face there again."

"Now you are being a child," she chided. "Would you leave me too?"

He turned to face her, and their eyes met in the moonlight filtering through the smoke hole above the lodge. "No, but…"

"Then shush, and do better tomorrow."

But would he? All knew that it was unseemly to sleep alongside a woman when it was the custom for men to sleep on one side of a lodge and women along the other. Wabeno had warned him that sleeping with River would drain him of his war medicine when he needed it most. Was that why the rock had slipped from his hands? Had he angered the spirits?

What a foolish thought, and yet, he could not help himself. He knew that River's mother, Woman Walks Tall, had been suspected as a witch, and despite himself, there were times when Tree wondered if River was the same. She had clouded his mind, bewitching him with a yearning that was beyond explanation. The love spells of witches were well known, even to the men of the deep woods.

He thought of his hunting partners—the rough men he had grown up with since the age of six, living like animals in the forest with barely any contact with women. His own mother had been traded away by his father when Tree was able to walk on his own. His father had been a hard man who wanted his son to be even harder. He was a woman-hater, but Tree, thank the spirits, had known so little of women and girls that he had never been infected by his father's rage.

Now, he would give anything for the woman who lay softly breathing beside him in her slumber: he would give his limbs, his heart torn from his body, even his head. He vowed that he would win every remaining challenge even if it meant his death. He would win for her.

Sun Dog did not sleep well that night either. *Treacherous people, how quickly their attention was drawn from him with their childish games and champions.* In his many lifetimes, the master had dwelled within one host after another, yet always living alone like a spider at the center of its web, devouring the soul of his prey. Yet now, he had tasted fame for the first time and found that he enjoyed it. He no longer felt so dead inside, and yet to his anguish, it seemed that adulation was a fleeting thing. He hungered now for the worship of others, and it was with jealous eyes that he looked upon the maidens and young men cheering on their favorites among the competitors, ignoring him. He was already taken for granted! Only the fool, Long Tongue, buzzed at his side like a gnat. He ached to crush his skull and would have if he was not so useful.

The next day came the first of two footraces, a sprint. This, Tree was sure to win. His father had thighs as thick as the backs of twin sturgeons, and he had been blessed with the same. *Eya,* he would pass the same powerful legs on to his yet-unborn son. On his raids against the Dakota to the west, Tree had often been obliged to run for days at a time to escape his pursuers.

Yet to his surprise, the Mohawk outran him in a sprint three times around the town's palisade. Tree ran in a mad rush, heaving his lungs until he thought they would burst. He ran pace-to-pace with the Chelaquen, managing to gain a stride ahead just as the finish line came into view. Yet just as victory seemed only steps away, the Mohawk flashed past both of them as swift as a diving osprey. The man had been running in their shadow the entire time, saving himself for the final sprint. What else could he do but offer his praise and think of the longer race to come?

Now there were four winners among the six—Tree, the Mohawk, the Chaienan, and Stone Eagle. Of the challengers in the long run, the man of the Chaiena was the most formidable. While he was no swimmer, he and his people were accustomed to pursuing buffalo across the prairies of their land straddling the Misi Sipi. Like Tree, he too had run from sunrise to sunset on occasion.

The race was to be to a distant village and back, a walk of three days for most. At midday, after bets had been settled and made anew around the town, the challengers were given the signal to run.

Over the hills and through the forest on a broad track, they ran, first in a tightly knit line, but gradually fanning out as the stronger runners pushed ahead.

Tree's legs were still burning from the sprint, so he started at a slower pace, knowing that many runners pushed themselves beyond their limit in a race and ended up gasping as they faded away. He planned to let the others wear themselves out, creeping up on them as his legs, heart and lungs warmed to the pace.

But the man of the Chaiena was of much the same mind, and Tree was surprised to find the two of them loping along together as Stone Eagle, the Mohawk, Chelaquen, and Susquehannock racers forged ahead.

"You run well, brother," the Chaienan said as they ran shoulder-to-shoulder.

"As do you," Tree replied, dismayed that the man was running as if he'd barely taken a breath.

"Ah, but I am not even trying yet. Soon I will make you my turtle."

"Then I will make you my snail, brother," Tree said, upping the pace.

It wasn't long before they overtook the Mohawk, who, as Tree had predicted, was gasping for breath and staggering alongside the trail, clutching a side-stitch in pain. They reeled in the Chelaquen and Susquehannock runners soon after, passing without saying a word. Then, thinking it was time to leave the Chaienan behind, Tree lengthened his stride.

But his adversary matched him pace-for-pace, and soon they passed Stone Eagle who was vomiting from over-exertion. "You are halfway to the village, brothers," he croaked as they sped past. "Take the fork to the left up ahead and run strong!"

As Stone Eagle had predicted, the trail forked in two directions. Tree and the Chaienan warrior veered left and pounded on. Slowly, the man of the Chaiena pushed ahead as Tree struggled behind and then slowed to a walk.

He waited until the Chaienan had vanished from sight and turned back.

The Chaienan was more a man of the prairies than of the woodlands and had not noticed that the more beaten path ran to the right at the fork in the trail. With his long experience as a hunter, Tree had noticed that the thin path to the left had more in common with a game trail than what might lead to a village. At best, it might lead to a hunters' camp. He made his way back to the fork in the trail and ran down the more traveled pathway.

As he suspected, Stone Eagle was loping along the trail as if he had all the time in the world. "A good trick," Tree shouted as he ran past, "but not good enough."

He gave the Seneca a good-natured shove, tumbling him into the tall grass alongside the trail.

Tree settled into a steady rhythm as the trail ran alongside a river that raged against the stones lining its bed and then through a series of hills and a dark forest. The path twisted and snaked far down into the gloom of valleys which never saw the sun beneath the shade of their trees.

At last, the trail grew broader as he passed a number of huts and smaller pathways leading in other directions. The village hove into view with its people cheering his arrival. As had been arranged, Tree accepted a red feather of a cardinal's tail from the village headman and stuck it in his hair. Turning, he began the long run back to Ga-ogwah Kanotaye.

But he had gone only a short way back when he saw the grim-faced man of the Chaiena pounding his way.

"You're a dead man, brother!" the Chaienan called to him as he streamed past. But he flashed a smile as he spoke and, once again, looked as if he was barely taken a breath as he strode on.

Tree knew that soon the Chaienan would be pounding at his heels. He pushed himself to a lather of sweat, ignoring the rocks and roots beneath his feet as he hammered on. Twice he lost his moccasins in his haste, finding that his feet were bleeding and bruised when he retrieved them. He had scoffed at Wabeno's claim that he was draining himself of his war medicine by laying with Found by the River, but now he appealed to every good spirit that he could think of, and the bad ones too, in the hope that they would come to his aid.

Then he thought only of his woman, and what she meant to him. He would not fail her. He could not! His legs burned, his lungs felt as if they were bleeding, and his eyes blurred as if they would melt from their sockets, but still he ran on.

He had reached the base of the hill beneath Ga-ogwah Kanotaye when the man of the Chaiena overtook him. In a mad dash, they ran uphill between a cheering throng on either side of the path. Tree was only two paces ahead when he burst through an arbor at the finish line and fell gasping to the ground.

"You did well, brother," the Chaienan said with his own lungs heaving as he handed his feather to Walking Turtle's outstretched hand, "but where is your feather?"

Tree's eyes widened in horror as he clutched at his scalp. *The feather!* He could not win without it.

It wasn't until the next morning that Stone Eagle limped into town with a torn tendon, bearing the red feather that he'd found by the side of the trail.

CHAPTER 36

THE TOWER OF THE DEAD

"He can still win," Wolf said, but there was a kernel of doubt in his voice as he and Wabeno sat smoking before the Great Lodge that night. Inside, Found by the River and Willow were tending to Tree's battered feet. The great warrior-hunter of the Ojibwe had never known tears before, but now his face was wet with them as he sobbed over his misfortune.

"It is hard for a man who has never known defeat," Wabeno replied as they listened to the groans from within the lodge. "I would tell him to swallow his fate like a man, but I don't care to lose my head."

"Grandfather, it would not do for him to hear you," Wolf cautioned in a low voice. "There are still two challenges. He can still win."

"Yes, but he will have to win both of them and so far, the spirits have not been kind." This time it was Wabeno who sounded doubtful as he took a long draw on his pipe. He coughed hard, exhaling a lungful of smoke. "Too much!" he wheezed, passing the pipe to Wolf.

Indeed, it seemed as if the spirits had turned against Tree with the rock slipping from his hand, and then the feather falling by the wayside during the race. Privately, Wabeno gave thanks that they had not taken him to the bottom of the lake during the swimming match.

Now it was the Chaienan with two wins and one each for Stone Eagle, the Mohawk, and Tree. The next day's challenge was climbing the Tower of the Dead.

The tower was the same limestone karst where Sun Dog had lingered in his cave, squeezing the noisemaker that filled the people of Ga-ogwah Kanotaye with dread. It served as a gravestone for a battlefield in its shadow.

Well before the Seneca began building their town, they had pushed into the frontier of the Erie people, who had been their enemies for longer than anyone could remember. The Eries had not taken it well. They had slaughtered the advance party of Seneca men who'd been dispatched to clear the hill of its timber. Then they had joined forces with the Wendats to the north, pledging that the Seneca would never take another step within the hunting grounds that they considered their own.

In response, the Seneca had appealed to their brothers among the Cayuga and Onondagas in what was to be a thunderbolt of a raid on the Eries' homeland. How were they to know that the Eries had planned to do just the same?

Thousands of warriors had blundered upon one-another in the shadow of the limestone tower, and though less than two hundred died beneath the grim face of its cliffs in the melee that followed, it was enough to mark the place as a haunted graveyard where no man dared to tread. The arrival of the *Hanishé* had only confirmed what all knew to be true.

When Stone Eagle heard of the challenge, he flatly refused to take it on. His father had died in the battle, and he could not bear to tread on sacred ground. That left four—the Chaienan, the Mohawk, the Susquehannock, and Tree. Without a single win to his name, the wild man of the Chelaque had left for home, wishing them luck.

"I would know your name, brothers," Tree said, walking into their camp on the evening before the challenge.

It was rude to ask a man's name, and the three looked at him warily. Tree shrugged. "I am Mitig Bwaa Waagin," he said. "I only wish to remember you when you are beaten and crying bitter tears with your women."

This produced a chuckle all around.

"I am the cave, and he is the wind," the man of the Chaiena said. This was considered a great jest among his people with the implication of a farting man, but it flew over the others' heads.

"What is this?"

"Eh," the Chaienan said, waving his stab at humor aside. "I am Hotoa'e Ta'emeohe, Buffalo Runs Long."

"Ah, my tongue twists at your name," Tree said with a grimace. "With your permission I will call you only Buffalo."

"As you wish, brother," the Chaienan said. "Your name does not come easy to me either."

"Brother, then call me Tree."

There was an awkward moment and then the Mohawk said, "I am Ganyohso-t-a, Sitting Owl."

"You may call me No Name," smirked the Susquehannock when it came his turn.

They spent a companionable evening together, each taking the measure of the others.

"I know now why you are called Buffalo Runs Long," Tree said wryly to the Chaienan.

"Yes, and it will be a long run home from here unless the Seneca lend me a canoe," he replied.

"I'll paddle you home myself if you will let me win," Sitting Owl said. This produced a laugh, but only a small one.

"Do you fear the ghosts?" Tree asked.

"What man doesn't?" Sitting Owl replied. "But they only rise at night. The Seneca is a fool to fear them."

"It is because of his father," Tree reminded.

"*Faugh!*" Sitting Owl waved it away. "Among the tribes of the Haudenosaunee, the dead journey on to their rest in the sky, but part of them remains here as ghosts, yearning to stay on with the living."

"Here? In their own homes?" No Name asked.

"Yes. That is why you cannot eat food that is left overnight," Sitting Owl said. "It is food meant only for the dead and woe to those who swallow even a bite of it."

"Even the bite of a mouse?" Tree asked casually.

"Not even that."

"Yet I have seen them gorging upon what is left over."

This had the Mohawk stumped for a moment. "Their spirits will pay when their time comes," he said at last.

"The mice?"

"Yes brothers, even the mice have spirits."

Late in the evening, Tree bid his companions a good rest, but not so much that they would be fresh in the morning. Walking back to his pallet in the Great Lodge, he passed the hut where Sun Dog slept. The sorcerer had decided to abandon the quarters he had taken from Walking Turtle and had asked the women of the town to fashion a lodge in which he alone could dwell. They had obeyed, but all thought it strange that any man would wish to sleep apart from his fellows. There was safety in numbers, after all. But Sun Dog had protested that he had no fear of demons creeping in the night and that the spirits who watched over him were bothered by crying babies.

"I would not have your children harmed by the spirits," he said by way of explanation. The women were more than happy to oblige, gathering elk bark to sheath a dome of willow branches erected by their men.

The sorcerer was sitting in the moonlight outside his lodge when Tree passed by. Tree nodded, and Sun Dog nodded in return but said nothing. Yet, he watched Tree as he pushed on down the lane. *Such a big man, brave and strong. And yet one with a terrible weakness,* he thought.

That morning, the people of Ga-ogwah Kanotaye gathered in a meadow as close as they dared to the Tower of the Dead. Over the next hill was the haunted valley where the ghosts of fallen warriors could still be heard on a moonless night. The place was shunned even by daylight. But from the meadow, there was a clear view of the tower, and though the competitors would appear as ants on its face, still, it would be possible to follow their progress.

All four men had been painted with care that morning, choosing whatever signs and symbols they thought would help them the most with the guardian spirit of the tower. With Wabeno's advice, Tree had opted for red paint covering his entire body, emblazoned with jagged white lightning bolts.

"Oh, you are too handsome now," Found by the River cried, upon surveying her work. To her irritation, other women of the town agreed as she accompanied Tree to the meadow. Murmurs and titters arose in their wake as the women of the town—both young and old—took Tree's measure. Gleaming red with paint and oil, his muscular body inflamed their lust, and once River turned and hissed at a burly woman who vowed to lay with him when the challenge was done.

If it had been a contest for paint alone, Tree would have won handily, for the women who painted the other three were not nearly as skillful in their designs. At this, Found by the River took some small comfort, but her heart quailed when they reached the meadow, and the tower came into full view.

"You must not do this!" she cried.

There was a densely wooded slope at the tower's base, but beyond the trees lay a debris field of boulders and scree and then sheer cliffs that looked as slick as an obsidian blade rising to a level peak. Two eagles circled above the peak, as if they were cousins of the clouds.

"It is too much!" she begged Tree. "What do we care of Sun Dog's crown? I need you more than his feathers!"

"Listen to your woman, Tree," Willow said. "If you fall there will be no saving you."

The two women hectored Tree to relent, while nearby the four other challengers shuffled their feet and gazed up somberly at the eminence that might easily mark their graves.

"I know now why the Seneca chose not to climb the tower," Wolf said to Wabeno. "It wasn't the ghost of Stone Eagle's father who held him back."

"But that was a good excuse," Wabeno replied.

"Bring us some ghosts now, grandfather, so that they can end this thing."

"There never was a ghost that came by daylight and never will be," Wabeno replied. "But I would do it if I could."

Sun Dog had suggested the challenge of the tower against the advice of the Seneca, and now, he sidled up to where River and Willow were begging Tree not to climb.

"Does it frighten you brother?" he asked smoothly, gesturing to the tower. "Will you turn away?"

Tree That Does Not Bend was too proud ever to admit such a thing, even to himself. Nor did he have much use for sorcerers, and now this strutting gobbler with his close-set eyes and crown of feathers dared to imply that he was a coward.

"This is an anthill to me," he said evenly as their eyes met with open hostility. "Will you join me in climbing it, brother?"

Sun Dog gave him a hard look in reply. Nodding, he turned away with his black cloak of raven feathers fluttering in the sun.

"The man grows more ridiculous with each breath," Willow said as Sun Dog trailed off.

"Yes, but you would think otherwise if you had witnessed his ceremony," Wolf said.

"Perhaps, but I think he is too clever for his own good, and for that of the Seneca," she replied. "Do you believe in his magic?"

"My eyes fell upon it," Wolf said. "He produced a demon from an empty box and cast it into the fire."

"A doll, or a squirrel as Wabeno claims. A puppet."

"If you saw it, you would think otherwise."

"He has made these men his puppets with this foolish challenge, even Tree," she said bitterly.

"*Ehn,* I agree that we must keep him from climbing, even if we lose our bets. He will push himself too hard. He is too proud. He has no fear of death."

Wolf raised his voice with that of Willow and River, but Tree would have none of it.

"I would not dream of quitting now," he said haughtily. "What would our people think?"

"They would think you are no fool!" Wolf said. "We will speak for you."

Only Wabeno held his tongue as Tree turned his back in a huff and joined the others. All were barefoot and dressed only in their breech clouts. He winced as River sobbed his name from behind his back but didn't turn around.

Wabeno placed his hand on River's shoulder. "He can do it," he said in a quiet voice. "The tower sees him as a brother."

Sun Dog gave the signal, raising his staff crowned by the sun, and the four men dashed forward to the cheers of the crowd. Down the hill from the meadow, they ran and through the haunted valley where the dead gazed up in wonder from their graves, unable to rise in the sunlight.

All four gained the tree line at the base of the tower, but it was a half-hearted effort for Sitting Owl of the Mohawks and No Name of the Susquehannocks. Neither had any intention of attempting to climb the cliffs.

Once again, Tree That Does Not Bend and Buffalo Runs Long found themselves evenly matched as their powerful legs hammered up the slope. "You have the legs of a bear, brother," Tree muttered in between breaths.

"Nay, my father was a buffalo," the Chaienan gasped, "a bull."

"But a buffalo cannot climb a tree," Tree replied, thinking this a great jest.

"Ah, but my mother was an eagle," Buffalo shot back.

Near the top of the tree line, they crossed a faint trail that was almost too slight to notice. With the sharp eyes of a hunter, Tree glanced down, thinking it was only the track of a deer, but to his surprise, there was the indent of a moccasin in the dried mud. Out of instinct, he glanced up in time to see a man's head darting back from behind a ledge. It was no ghost, he was sure of that, but there was no time to stop and look.

Then came the debris field, covered with boulders. Tree and Buffalo wove their way around them, reaching the cliff face at the same time.

"Now you will need your mother's wings," Tree grunted as they paused to catch their breath. The Mohawk and Susquehannock were nowhere to be seen.

"Our brothers have turned back," said Buffalo Runs Long.

"They are wiser than us."

"Agreed."

"Turn back, brother. You are a man of the prairies and cannot climb this," Tree said. "There is no shame."

Buffalo scoffed. "This is no more than an ant hill to me," he said. "Return to your sewing, brother. Return to your sewing."

"Ah, we are both fools then. But watch yourself; I would not care to see you fall."

Tree was happy to see that the cliff face was not as sheer as it looked from a distance. It was pitted with handholds, and there were many fissures and cracks to ease the way up. The challenge for any climber was simply that of overcoming a fear of heights. Tree had raided the nests of eagles and had climbed the painted cliffs on the south shore of Kitchi Gami as well as those of the Sleeping Giant, Manabozho, to the north. He had no fear of falling and started up.

But being a man of the prairies, Buffalo Runs Long was far weaker in thought and practice. He didn't lack for courage. Indeed, he had fought a grizzly bear on the prairie of his homeland with only a spear. But he was no climber, and it wasn't long before a handhold slipped in his grasp, and he fell to the stony ground below.

But Tree never heard his cry as he pushed on, and far in the distance the crowd shouted in awe as they saw him splayed on the side of the cliff, appearing as a red ant under the sun. Sun Dog stood grim-faced among the cheering crowd as those who'd placed bets on Tree exulted over his progress. With all his heart he willed Tree to lose his grip and fall, but that was not the kind of magic that Sun Dog was capable of.

Instead, as Wabeno had predicted, the spirit of the tower smiled on Tree's progress, clutching him to her bosom.

At last, Tree gained the summit, and though he was only a speck to those gathered in the far-off meadow, he raised his arms in victory, hoping that he might be seen. Then, as required, he sought out the eagles' nest and gathered a handful of down lining its branches. This time he took care to place the feathers in a rawhide sack suspended by a cord around his neck.

Late that afternoon, Tree That Does Not Bend appeared back at the meadow with the right arm of Buffalo Runs Long draped over his shoulder. The Chaienan had sprained his ankle in his fall and was badly bruised and scraped along the right side of his body yet was otherwise unharmed as he limped along.

The crowd jigged to the sound of pounding drums and the bugling of conch shells as the challengers returned, and Stone Eagle, No Name, and Sitting Owl came forward to offer their praise. Sun Dog scowled inwardly at Tree's victory while pretending to be pleased. The people had ignored him in favor of these idiots, and he was anxious for the games to be over so that they would be on their way. There was only one challenge remaining.

CHAPTER 37

THE MATCH

Tree was scratched and bleeding in many places from his climb up the tower and though he was grateful to Found by the River for tending to his wounds, he begged to continue wearing the paint that she had so carefully applied the day before.

"You brought me good luck, and Wabeno's designs pleased the spirit of the tower," he said. "I will be a red eagle tomorrow."

"A red weasel," she scoffed. But River mixed more vermilion that night, mixing it with duck fat to repair Tree's paint the next morning.

The final challenge was to be a wrestling match. With two wins each so far, either Tree or Buffalo Runs Long would be declared the overall champion if they alone could win a match. But if No Name, Sitting Owl, or Stone Eagle won, there would need to be another match.

It was to be a day-long event in the square before the Great Lodge, again to be witnessed by people of the entire town with only a few slaves dispatched to scare away the crows and varmints raiding the precious maize in the fields.

Again, the challengers appeared, barefoot and wearing only their breechclouts and paint as they paraded into the square with each cheered by hundreds of voices. Bets were made all around, with many wagering what they had won in the days before, and just as likely to lose as much today. Once again, the drums sounded from all sides, accompanied by the ululations of women and an orchestra of conch shells, flutes, and rattles. The people of the town danced in place as the champions entered the square.

"We haven't had this much celebration since the town was born," Stone Eagle said as the five of them lined up before the cheering crowd.

"It has been good vying with you brothers, but I will celebrate leaving," Sitting Owl replied. "Risking my soul here has made me think more of my woman and children. I will be happy to return to them."

All agreed on this except Tree That Does Not Bend, who felt curiously disturbed, knowing that he had no woman or children to return to. He had only the rough company of his fellow hunters, who were scattered to the winds by now.

Although there was something implied between himself and Found by the River, neither of them had spoken of what they would do once they made their way home. He had not made a formal bid for her as an honorable man, and now to his surprise, the thought of asking her to marry him was more frightening than all the challenges he had faced so far. *What if she said no?* Troubled thoughts washed over him.

So troubled, in fact, that he nearly lost his first match against Sitting Owl. The Mohawk was much smaller but much faster and sharper on the attack, while Tree was still bound by the web of his thoughts. Unexpectedly, he found himself on the verge of being pinned, and just shy of his shoulder touching the earth, he gave a tremendous heave and flopped the Mohawk onto his back. Off to the side, he saw Found by the River beaming with love in her eyes. Could there be any doubt? The greatest hunter-warrior of the Ojibwe stood and roared in triumph.

One by one, the challengers were eliminated as they grappled with one another in the dust of the great square amid thunderous cheers at a win or groans at a loss. It was a hot day, and soon every challenger was wringing with sweat as paint ran in rivulets from their bodies. Tree was nearly blinded by the oily vermillion streaming from his forehead, and twice he begged River for a handful of cattails down to clear his eyes. That, and gourds of water to staunch his thirst.

Despite his sprained ankle, Buffalo Runs Long put up a good fight, defeating Stone Eagle. Now he too had three wins. Yet there would be no match against Tree to decide the overall champion because he was easily defeated by No Name of the Susquehanna.

Unknown to the others, No Name's greatest strength was as a wrestler. The Susquehannocks were a mighty people living south of the Seneca, and the grappler was legendary among them. He was nearly as tall as Tree That Does Not Bend but much burlier, and his arms were even longer. He had never been beaten.

At last, there were only two of them, and with Buffalo Runs Long having been beaten, the final match would either result in Tree's triumph as overall champion or produce a tie that would require another contest.

"What do you think, old one?" Wolf asked as he and Wabeno looked on from a place of honor at the side of the circle drawn in the earth. Any wrestler who was pinned or else thrown beyond the circle would lose the match.

"I think the sun will rise again tomorrow no matter who wins," Wabeno replied. "I think that somewhere, a moose will slip and fall in the mud today."

"True enough, but I would not care to lose our canoe," Wolf replied, thinking of their wager.

"You have more to fear from your wife," Wabeno chuckled. "She told you not to gamble."

"She gambled when she chose me."

"Then she was lucky. Let's hope our man is the same."

Tree That Does Not Bend had noted the Susquehannock's skill in defeating Buffalo Runs Long and gazed upon him with a sense of unease as they crouched before one another in the final match.

"Your defeat will make me champion," he called across the way.

"Brother, preen yourself now, but tonight you will cry like a blue jay," No Name replied. "I have never lost a match."

"Then this will be good for you," Tree said in a low voice. "You need humbling, brother. It will do you much good."

"I would rather eat shit."

"As you wish. I will serve it to you."

No Name glared back, showing his teeth.

Tree reached down and dusted his hands with sand to give himself a better grip. Across the way, Wolf and Wabeno gave him signs of approval, while Willow and River shared a laugh. A bitter taste lodged in Tree's throat as he gulped hard, thinking of what losing the match would mean. They would try to soothe him with kind words, saying it didn't matter, but he would never be able to face them again without feeling diminished, shrunken, and less of a man. And what would River say? It was too much to bear. He looked up and saw confidence drawn on No Name's face as if it were carved in stone.

It was Sun Dog who presided over the match, dressed in a dazzling multi-colored cloak of songbird feathers and his tall crown of macaw plumes. He stood before the crouching men, each of whom was covered in dust and bleeding through small cuts from the nails of their opponents.

"Brothers, the sun looks down upon you, reflecting his glory from my staff," he said, hoping that his words would not be lost on the crowd. But only Long Tongue replied with a yip from the sidelines as the crowd craned their necks in anticipation of the match. In exasperation, Sun Dog dropped a feather and said, "Let the best man win."

The feather touched the ground, and Tree and No Name charged each other as if they were male black bears, slamming against each others' chests with a force that would have killed a lesser man. In a lucky break, Tree caught the Susquehannock around the middle and slammed him to earth, intending to fall on him with a victorious pin.

But No Name leapt up as if his legs were that of a bull frog and stood grinning before him. "The earth only makes me stronger, Ojibwe," he jeered. "I am the son of Grandmother Earth."

Tree gave him a ghastly smile with his teeth bathed in blood where they'd been elbowed by the Mohawk. "Then your grandmother will have a spanking today," he said, spitting off to the side.

Once again, the two giants slammed together, grappling now for some handhold that might send the other eating dirt. This time it was Tree who was slammed hard to ground, twisting away just as No Name fell like a stone upon him. Once again, No Name shot up as if fired from a bow as Tree struggled to regain his feet.

Tree was a great hunter, a warrior of renown, and even a fair musician at the flute, but except for tumbling with a few friends as a child, he had little experience with wrestling and now he realized that there was something more to it than brute strength. Several times he had felt No Name striving for a grip that would land him on his back, and only his strength had saved him, but just barely. Before the match, Wabeno had reminded him that even a tree that does not bend can be torn out by its roots. Now, he did everything he could to stay upright.

But there was little chance of that against the champion of the Susquehannocks.

"You cannot win. You are a child against me!" No Name taunted as he rushed Tree once again, twisting around to his back to wring a final thrust. But instead of struggling against him, Tree hooked a foot behind his opponent's ankle and fell backward in a somersault, pushing No Name off balance as the two slammed a third time to the earth.

This time Tree heard a rib crack, but whether it was his own or that of No Name, he could not say. He struggled to turn over and pin the Susquehannock, but the man slipped away from under him as easily as an eel and leapt to his feet.

If No Name was injured, he did not show it. "You see, child, I am not even winded," he called as they crouched at one another once again. "I will sit on your back and have you eating dirt from my hand."

"Brave words from a big talker, but I see you fading, brother," Tree replied, flashing his bloody teeth again. "The crows will eat my liver before I bow to you."

Even so, it occurred to Tree that No Name's boast of being a grandson of the earth might be true. The man had indeed seemed stronger each time that he'd been hammered to the ground, leaping to his feet with a power that seemed beyond human. He was not fading. There was only one way to win.

It was true that No Name had broken a rib in their last clash, but he seemed not to notice. The two circled one another, searching for a weakness as they feinted back and forth. Several times No Name rushed, seeking a grip with his long arms, only to have Tree slip away to the roars of the crowd.

"He's running! Go for him!" a follower of the Susquehanna called out. A chorus of voices joined him as Tree skipped away, appearing fearful of losing. Buoyed by the crowd, No Name lifted his arms aloft as if he was already the victor and turned in a circle as Tree backed away amid hoots and hisses from the crowd.

"What is he doing?" Wolf muttered to Wabeno from beyond the circle.

"He is making him his pet," the old man replied. "Just as a raccoon may be tempted with a scrap of meat before it is clubbed for the spit."

And so it was. Overwhelmed by hubris and the cheers of the crowd, No Name charged as Tree stumbled backward. He ducked just as the Susquehannock reached out for him, sending the man flying overhead and sprawling on the ground. Reaching down, he seized No Name's ankle.

Now, the son of Grandmother Earth twisted and writhed like a snake as he tried to whip his body back upright. But Tree held onto his ankle with both hands as if it were gripped by the roots of an oak tree. Slowly, inexorably, he dragged the writhing man to the edge of the circle; then, releasing his ankle, Tree dropped to the earth and kicked him in the back with both legs as hard as he could.

It was enough. No Name had another two broken ribs and groaned in pain as he lay defeated beyond the circle drawn in the earth. Tree sat up and looked dumbly at his defeated opponent. A sound filled his ears like that of the distant waves by the shore. Gradually it grew louder and then to a roar as the crowd screamed their approval. Tree That Does Not Bend was champion overall.

That would have been the end of it, if not for the master's fury behind the Sun Dog's eyes. He had no intention of giving up the feathered crown of the Exalted One, nor the adulation of his people to this rustic oaf from the wilds of the north woods. A daring thought had taken shape in his thoughts as he watched the painted warriors wrestling that day, and what had once been wisdom and a surfeit of caution, was now carried away by the poison of pride as the master considered that all things were possible. As with No Name, the master had never been beaten, and now, in the vain imagination of an ancient being that was blinded by his own light, he would prove himself the Exalted One in the eyes of the Seneca through the vessel of Sun Dog and his magic.

Sun Dog raised his staff with the copper disc flashing in the sun. “I would give you one more challenge before the crown is bestowed,” he shouted, turning for all to hear. “Tomorrow, you will wrestle with me!”

CHAPTER 38

BLACK MAGIC

It was not true that Wabeno-iniini had been powerless against the *Hanishé*. The Man of the Dawn Sky had not even bothered. Instead, he had put all of his powers of sorcery into the pebble worn around Walking Turtle's neck.

He had deduced that the woman's blindness was due to the lightning stroke of fear that she had suffered as an infant when her mother had been slain. And though his gift of the stone had nothing magical to it at all, he reasoned that the simple belief in it might clear Walking Turtle's eyes. He had left the sly suggestion of it in his gift-giving, and now to his satisfaction, his medicine was working.

Now, little by little, the shadows were growing clearer to her, and though he warned that she might never fully see again, she had begun to sense the light within others and even the outline of faces.

"Do you think he should wrestle Sun Dog?" she asked as they passed a pipe that evening.

"He is a man. He can do as he wishes," Wabeno replied.

"But if Sun Dog killed a demon, what hope can a simple man have?"

"Tree That Does Not Bend is not a simple man. That is why I called him here."

"Yes, the greatest warrior and hunter of all your people," she said, scoffing gently, "and yet he is no sorcerer."

There came a long pause and then, “Neither is Sun Dog,” Wabeno said. “He is just a man overtaken by a bad thing. A bad spirit.”

Walking Turtle digested this in silence. “That may be so, but he had taken hold of my people. They worship him now and he means to humble your champion so that they will worship him even more. He is up there with the sun.”

“I do not believe in gods, only spirits,” Wabeno said. “Son of the sun? What foolishness. Pardon me, sister, but if there truly was such a god, he would have killed the *Hanishé*, and yet the sun does nothing more than rise and fall each day.”

“Perhaps tomorrow.”

“Yes, but Sun Dog will taste dirt at the hands of a warrior, not the sun. He is a fool to even try.”

“But you must agree that he has a powerful magic,” she reminded. “He will use it on your man.”

“Tricks, only tricks,” Wabeno said dryly. “They vanish when you know their secrets.”

“I hope that will be true, but how is Tree to know?” she said gruffly. “He has no more sense of magic than a chipmunk. He will not see his doom coming.”

Wabeno scowled at this, knowing it was true. “The spirits will aid him,” he said lamely.

But the spirits had been of little use to Walking Turtle. She thought of the many among the Seneca who had turned away from her and the clan mothers who had been appointed as the new council of the town. Increasingly, they had been overruled, not by the council of warriors as was tradition, but by Sun Dog himself who held her people in his hand. He had evicted her from her own lodge as if he were a dog kicking its excrement with its hind legs and then had demanded that the women make a new lodge for him alone. It was an intolerable insult, yet what could she do? Sun Dog had made it clear that he and his people intended to stay for good, and now he had the slavish support of the impudent fool, Long Tongue, who had led the warriors away from his father’s will.

She should have had Sun Dog killed on the day he arrived, she thought bitterly. The *Hanishé* was of little concern by comparison.

Sun Dog slept easy that night, comforted by the master's voice as it whispered in his dreams. He chuckled in his sleep, the last shred of Wren had been devoured, only the ancient one remained in his stead. He had magic on his side—a black magic that would humble the warrior of the Ojibwe in the eyes of everyone, securing his role as the Exalted One.

And then he would find a new soul to feed upon.

Already, emissaries from the other tribes of the Haudenosaunee had arrived from the Mohawks, Cayuga, Oneida, and Onondagas, eager to learn more of Sun Dog. They had stayed on for the games, planning to report back to the great Council in the town of the Onondagas. Perhaps he would go with them; already, he was a giant in their eyes. He was *THE* Sun Dog now, a demigod in the eyes of many.

The emissaries stirred Sun Dog's thoughts on the future. Why should he limit himself to this single town of the Senecas when tens of thousands lived across the lands of the Haudenosaunee? Coosa would rise again, yet this time in the north. They would smite the Eries, the Wendats, and the wild men of the south and then turn their eyes to the west.

"We should flee," Found by the River begged as she sat with Tree outside the Great Lodge that night. "We should gather our things and go—tonight!"

"He is a big man, but he is a mere priest, not a warrior," Tree replied. "Am I to fear a shaman?"

"He is much more than a shaman. Wolf warned you to stay away from him. He would not have challenged you unless he was sure of winning."

"Ha! The Susquehannock was also sure of winning and now he lies sobbing in his lodge, nursing his ribs."

Tree reared back and farted, grinning at River, who looked back in disgust.

"Yes, but…"

"But I will win you the Sun Dog's feathers, and you will be the talk of women everywhere," Tree said with an assured smile.

"His headdress is cursed. I do not want it."

Tree shrugged. "Then I'll give it to Wabeno or someone else who is deserving. No Name, perhaps. He fought well."

"That would only humble Sun Dog, and he will cast an evil spell on you. Please, let us go. Let us go now! I know that something bad will happen if we stay. Please."

Her eyes welled up by the fire as she pleaded, yet Tree looked straight ahead, stone-faced.

"And have tales told around the fires for six lifetimes that I was a coward?" Anger flared in Tree's eyes as his voice rose to a shout. "Understand me, woman, I have won! I am champion and will not be denied by this jester. He will eat dirt tomorrow, no different than the last!"

For the first time, Found by the River saw the rage within her lover that made him a great warrior. All this time, she had considered him a strong but gentle man. But a warrior is not a gentle man. He is hard and cruel when he is called upon. She knew that, but she had chosen not to see. Yet now she was afraid, both for herself and for Tree.

Once again, she wondered what he saw in her. His chest was as wide and firm as a slab of basalt with rippling muscles carving his abdomen. He towered over her; she was only a slip of a child in his mighty arms. A sob welled up in her as Tree walked away, for she knew that if he lost to Sun Dog on the morrow, she would never see him again. In his shame, he would banish himself to the forest; in her heart, she knew that she was nothing to him, nothing, nothing, nothing…

The next morning brought two parades as the challengers were carried on the backs of their supporters around the square to the thunderous sound of drums, war cries, and ululations. Sun Dog was cheered to see that there were four times as many townsfolk in his parade as that of Tree That Does Not Bend. But soon there would be only one as his foe lay prostrate in the dirt, perhaps dead.

That morning, he had instructed Long Tongue and his warriors to tamp down the earth in the combat circle and dampen it so that no dust would foil his plan. The two would fight at midday when the sun was at its peak. Thus, the winner could claim that the Sun God had smiled on him. Sun Dog had already rehearsed what he would say.

Tree wore the same red paint emblazoned with jagged white lightning bolts, yet Sun Dog wore no paint at all as he was paraded around the square. It was only when he alighted that Long Tongue came forward with a large gourd, and several women hastened to paint him a deep, dark black.

It was the same strange fluid that Sun Dog had found seeping in the floor of his cave. It stank, almost like the stink of death, but this was of no consequence to Sun Dog as the women sponged his body from neck to toe with the black ooze. Only his head and hands remained free of it.

"Even my cock," he muttered, "even my cock."

The women hesitated, but obeyed, finding him stiff there.

Now Sun Dog stood, looking as ghastly as a ghoul under the full glare of the sun. Though he was painted black, the ooze of it shone almost as bright as a mirror. *Now would be a good time for my mask to add to the horror,* he thought, knowing that the mica mask would only hamper him in the ring.

Tree looked impassively from the far side of the circle, betraying no emotion. Yet he was troubled. Found by the River had been silent since his outburst the night before and had grown distant, retreating within herself. Running away had been impossible, but far worse would be losing her. She had called him a child once before, and it was true! Wabeno had told him that each man and woman had a frightened child living within themselves, and now, he was sobbing inside. He had not meant to hurt River. What did she see of him? He was no more than a low beast of the forest, and she was everything! He was nothing, nothing at all, he did not deserve her ... He had been an arrogant fool, unkind ... a fool! What if she left him? Slowly, his fear turned into blind anger as he glared across the way at Sun Dog. Black demon or sun god, it made no difference to him. He would tear the man apart and stamp on his feathered crown.

Then he would ask Found by the River to marry him.

The moment came, and Walking Turtle dropped the feather between them. Uttering war cries, both men rushed forward, slamming against one another, just as in the match with No Name. Tree clutched at Sun Dog, intending to drop him on his head with an easy win, but his hand slipped away as if he had grasped a snake greased with bear fat. Sun Dog's paint had made him as slippery as an eel.

Yet Sun Dog's hands were free of it, and now he grasped Tree's arms and twisted his foot behind his ankle, sending him tumbling to the ground to the gasps of the onlookers.

"You are not the warrior that you think," he hissed as Tree scrambled to his feet. "I have cast a spell on you, and a snake crawls in your belly. Fear is its poison. Can you feel it? It bites, little one. I see it within you."

Wabeno had warned Tree not to listen to such words. "They are only meant to frighten you," he had said. "They are his only weapon. Close your ears to what he says."

Now, Tree took heed, and finding no clever words to utter in response, he growled and barreled into Sun Dog instead, this time grasping his right arm with both hands. But again, the ooze of Sun Dog's paint allowed him to wriggle free, and Tree's own hands were soaked with it. Sly words could not hurt him, but without the use of his hands, he was defenseless.

Once again, Sun Dog managed to throw him down, this time to cheers from the crowd who smelled victory. Children jigged at the edge of the circle, and a ring of women chanted as their men shouted approval. Those who had bet on Sun Dog began savoring their wins, mocking those who had wagered on Tree. The crowd of hundreds swayed and shook like the wind-blown maize in their fields as the fight went on. Only the knot of Tree's companions sat silent and grim-faced at the edge of the ring.

Sun Dog was lean and slender, yet as tall as Tree. Although he was not half as brawny, the magic of the black ooze was working just as he had expected. Now he would toy with the Ojibwe for the benefit of the crowd, enough to show that his magic was beyond reproach. He pointed straight up to the sun, and all eyes rose to follow his finger while at the same moment he pulled a snake from its pouch at the rear of his breechclout with his other hand.

It was as if the snake had appeared out of the air itself to those who gazed back at him and now Sun Dog held it aloft and shouted an ancient invocation to *Eh-noq-waa,* Drinker of Blood and Devourer of Virgins. No one but Sun Dog and the people of Tali knew what the words meant in their language, but the chant and the snake had its effect on the crowd, who raised a deafening cry. Finishing, Sun Dog flung the snake at Tree who batted it away and roared.

Perhaps there really was a Sun God gazing down, who frowned on the invocation to *Eh-noq-waa,* or perhaps it was *Aireskoi,* the Haudenosaunee god of war, who saw Tree That Does Not Bend as one of his own, but just as Sun Dog finished his invocation a small cloud passed over the sun and remained there, darkening the town with its shadow.

"It is time," Wabeno said. "Stand ready to collect your bet."

"How can you tell?" Wolf replied as Found by the River gave a hopeful glance their way.

"It is time."

And so it was, for now Sun Dog charged with an answering roar and grasped Tree by his arms, yanking him forward as he strove to trip him up. It worked. No matter how he tried, Tree's hands remained covered with the black ooze, and Sun Dog remained drenched in it. Tree fell as heavily as a tall pine in the forest as Sun Dog bore down on his shoulder, pushing with all his strength.

Yet even though he had one shoulder down and the full weight of Sun Dog bearing down on him, Tree That Does Not Bend had been aptly named. Just as Sun Dog cried out in triumph, Tree reared back his fist and struck a terrific hammer blow to the middle of his chest, just between his lungs.

As any fighter knows, a strong blow to the center of the chest ends a battle with a single punch. Truly, it is often a death blow. Sun Dog's body flew straight up into the air as he flipped over on his back, unable to breathe. Both of his shoulders were pinned to the earth.

Tree gazed down upon him. He had won, but he needed the words.

"If I sit on you now, you will die," he spoke in Sun Dog's ear. "You will not breathe, and none of your followers will save you. Nor will the sun. Only you can save yourself now, brother. Say it. Say that I have won."

Sun Dog was panting now, still unable to breathe with his vision going black. Above him, even the sun seemed black. He raised an arm in defeat and croaked, "He … wins…"

Silence had gripped the crowd when Sun Dog fell, but now, as Tree rose, the watchers found their voices again, roaring both their approval and dismay. Tree strode over to where Long Tongue held the Sun Dog's feathered crown and snatched it from his hands. "Go to your master, slave, and drag him away," he growled. "Let him recover in his lodge away from mocking eyes."

Then, striding back across the circle, Tree placed the feathered crown atop Found by the River's head. It was far too big for her, and fell lopsided over her head, with her right eye peering out from beneath its headband of pearls. The egret wings on either side of the headdress fluttered as if they meant to fly away. Despite herself, she smiled.

"You look ridiculous," Willow said, smiling as she jostled alongside her.

"Yes, and I will not have it," River said. Standing, she embraced Tree in full view of the crowd to the shock of everyone gathered there. Truly, it was a time of wonders when a woman was so bold as to embarrass a warrior of such renown before the eyes of others!

Then, lifting the crown of macaw feathers from her brow, Found by the River placed it atop the head of Buffalo Runs Long, the man of the Chaiena who had almost bested Tree.

"Keep this for me, brother, so that you and my man will be friends forever," she said.

Four men carried Sun Dog to his lodge as he gasped like a dying animal before hundreds of onlookers.

"There is a witch among us," he gasped as Long Tongue and his fellows laid him on his bearskin pallet. His breath had returned in hiccoughing stabs as his fright ebbed. He had come close to dying from the Ojibwe's blow, and now his thoughts were a hornets' nest of rage.

"Witches, all of them!" he cried. "He could not win without their help. I know it!"

A knowing smile crossed Long Tongue's face as Sun Dog raged on. "Oh, great one, it is so," he said.

Sun Dog's eyes narrowed, and he sat up, stinking and greasy in his paint.

"Tell me."

"When I was returning from the north with Wabeno and his man, we stopped on a small island, and there I met a man named One Toe," Long Tongue said. "He spoke of an *otgo* who bedeviled his people. She had a snake within her."

Sun Dog prepared himself for another one of Long Tongue's rambling tales, full of lies and boasting. "What does this mean to me?" he said irritably.

"The witch is among us," Long Tongue said with his eyes sparkling at the revelation. "The *otgo* is the woman of the Ojibwe."

CHAPTER 39

PRISONERS

It was quiet in town the next day. Most of the townsfolk had gone to the fields, gathering the ripening maize. As is the way of things, there had been much talk around the lodge fires of Sun Dog's defeat the night before, but now it was time to harvest the crops that the people had worked so hard for over the spring and summer.

Willow and River joined them. The maize was plentiful and free to all who cared to pick it. They set about plucking the ripest cobs for the evening meal.

"I feel eyes on my back," River said as they picked a few beans to go with their maize.

"I too," Willow replied. She had seen both men and women among the farmers scowling at them. "There are bad birds speaking of us."

"But what? We have done nothing."

"Your man humbled their hero and took his feathers," Willow reasoned. "Sun Dog is a smaller man now and they resent it."

"Why must women suffer for the deeds of men?" River muttered.

"Many of them wagered everything on Sun Dog and now they are licking their wounds," Willow said. "We are targets of their wrath."

They did their best to ignore the spiteful looks, but as they were leaving the fields Willow froze at the sound of a hiss at her back and the word that every woman feared.

"Witch!"

Sun Dog had spent the day in the gloom of his lodge being scrubbed by four women, who labored, mostly in vain, to cleanse the black ooze from his skin. They scrubbed until his skin was raw, and when he could stand it no more, they left him, still tinged a faint gray. He reasoned that in time he'd come clean, but for now he'd wear a cape to cover his limbs. It would not do to look filthy.

Yet, his own dirty work had been done the night before by Long Tongue, who babbled like a river to the warriors who followed him, and they in turn to their women, while Little Fox had been dispatched to the far-off cave with careful instructions. In a town filled with gossips, where a chieftain's fart might be reported from one end to the other in a twinkling, the rumor was quickly on the lips of all.

All through the day, Sun Dog sat stewing with rage. The Ojibwe had cheated him with the blow that emptied his lungs, humbling him before the people of Ga-ogwah Kanotaye and the emissaries of the Haudenosaunee.

He vowed that he would have his revenge along with regaining his standing among the Seneca. The rule of the Exalted One was still within his reach. He would twist blood and tears from the Ojibwe's heart to have it.

That evening, the *Hanishé* came again.

First, a slave boy of the Wendats was torn from his watchtower overlooking the fields and sliced along the left side of his body by the monster's claws. The warriors who guarded the town gate had rushed to his aid, saving him from bleeding to death.

No sooner had they carried him screaming into the town than the creature's eerie cry was heard across the fields from the direction of the graveyard. Late that night, it came again from the far-off Tower of the Dead—a sound that was half human and half bird-like in its honks and squeals.

“I know this thing,” Willow said to Wolf as they sat listening in the darkness of the Great Lodge. “I have heard it before.”

“You had such a demon in your land?”

“Not in my land, but from somewhere,” she whispered. “I know its voice, but it is no demon. I have heard it, but it is different than I remember.”

Willow only knew that the squealing thing was not of this land.

“It will come to you in your sleep,” Wolf said. “That is the way of memories.”

The town was in an uproar that morning. The men who stood watch atop the palisade had seen something moving in the fields that night, rustling in the corn. A crowd gathered before the Great Lodge where Walking Turtle and the newly appointed clan mothers of Ga-ogwah Kanotaye sat waiting.

“What do you make of this?” Walking Turtle asked Wabeno as they waited.

“A madman,” he replied dryly. “It is no bear, nor a demon.”

“But the people think it is so, and many saw Sun Dog destroy it.”

“Yet it comes again.”

“Yes.”

“Then he will have an answer.”

Indeed he did, for soon thereafter Sun Dog strolled into the square in his cloak of black feathers with a line of young warriors trailing behind him.

“This does not look good,” Wolf murmured to Wabeno as they sat off to the side with the clan mothers. As yet, the women had not appointed a new sachem to lead the town. Now, they fidgeted uncomfortably as they sat on the ground in a half circle, waiting for Walking Turtle’s guidance.

Sun Dog walked up to the women and turned his back on them, facing the crowd.

“The *Hanishé* has returned!” he cried. “It is angry!”

The townsfolk rustled and murmured assent as Sun Dog’s sharp eyes looked directly at Tree That Does Not Bend. He was sitting across the way with Wolf and Wabeno while Found by the River and Willow sat just behind them. They were a small island in a swamp of hostile faces.

"Witches," Sun Dog went on. "Witches have done this. Witches have raised him from the dead!"

Now the crowd rippled like a twisting snake, for no one feared the power of witches more than the five tribes of the Haudenosaunee. When an infant died of the coughing sickness, it was the work of a witch. When a hunter broke a leg or fell through the ice of a lake, it was because a witch had cursed him. When warriors were killed in battle, it was because a witch had fouled their war medicine. When a woman suffered a miscarriage or stillbirth, it was due to the spell of a witch. Bad food, illness, drought, or killing cold—all were the work of witches who must be rooted out and sent to the fire. A witch could weave her spell from far away or might simply dwell in the next lodge over. A witch might even dwell in one's own lodge, only a few steps away, conjuring evil while one slept.

The word of witches at work had sped through town like a wildfire and now there was only the naming to be done.

"Who is the *otgo*?" Sun Dog shouted. "Who has brought evil among us?"

"It is her!" Long Tongue burst from line of warriors and ran to where Found by the River was sitting. "It is her! Her own people denounced her!"

Sun Dog feigned surprise. "What!?"

"Yes," Long Tongue hurried on. "When I brought the Ojibwes from the north, I met a great chieftain whose people lived in terror of her! She is the daughter of a witch! She has a snake inside her! She is the reason you lost the match!"

Willow and Found by the River leapt to their feet as the crowd froze, weighing Long Tongue's words. All eyes turned to Sun Dog as he stepped forward and raised his staff.

"The *Hanishé* cannot die as long as she lives!" he cried.

"Burn her!" came a cry from the crowd. "*Burn her!*"

Then, to Willow's horror, Found by the River crumpled in her embrace and fell twisting to the ground with her face as white as death and her eyes rolling in their sockets. Those standing nearby fell back in terror as she writhed and moaned with a bubbling foam on her lips.

She would have been seized right then and bludgeoned to death were it not for Tree That Does Not Bend.

Tree was a seasoned warrior who was well aware of every move that an enemy might attempt. Thus, he had carried his war club with him that day in the event that Sun Dog's followers dared to attack him. It was a fearsome thing, as long as his arm and carved of oak, topped by a wicked edge of obsidian. He had taken it from a Dakota warrior when he was only seventeen winters of age.

Now, he swept the club in a wide circle before the surging crowd as Wolf lifted Found by the River in his arms and backed toward the refuge of the Great Lodge. Her writhing had dwindled to spasms, but she was barely conscious and draped in his arms as limp as a fish. Across the way, Sun Dog's eyes glittered as the crowd ranted for her death. *How easy it is to bend them,* he thought. With bulging eyes, he stuck out his tongue and waggled it at Tree as the warrior edged backward, sweeping his club toward anyone who dared approach. Tree paused long enough to point at Sun Dog's chest, making the death sign, but the sorcerer only smiled in return. Counting all eight hundred of the Seneca as well as his own people, he had nearly a thousand followers, including all of the warriors. There was no way that the emissaries of the Ojibwe could escape. He would see that they all burned. First the witches and then their champion.

That afternoon, Walking Turtle came to the Great Lodge accompanied by Buffalo Runs Long. "I am with you brother," he said to Tree as he entered the lodge.

Tree nodded his thanks. "You are a good man, but there is no need to risk your hair helping us," he said.

Buffalo Runs Long grinned at this. "Ah, you forget, you promised to help me get home. I am with you to the end.

"Besides," he added darkly. "I was beaten by Long Tongue's men who came to take back Sun Dog's headdress, and I plan to beat it from his head."

"If the spirits are willing," Tree replied gravely.

Wabeno rose to his feet and joined hands with Walking Turtle as she stood silhouetted in the entryway. “What news do you bring?” he asked.

“You are all free to come and go, but your woman must stay here,” she said, gazing into the darkness where Found by the River sat with Willow. “I am sorry, daughter, but your fate will be decided tomorrow.”

All knew what River’s fate would be.

“I have asked the clan mothers to grant you an easy death, but they may be overruled by Sun Dog,” she added quietly. “He will make the rest of you bear witness.”

“What does this mean?” Tree asked with his eyes darting in the gloom of the lodge.

“They will make a spectacle of her,” Wabeno said. “They will take their time.”

“We won’t sit by as our sister is tortured,” Willow cried. But to this, Walking Turtle spread her hands in defeat.

“I have no say in this,” she said.

“I will take Sun Dog’s head tonight then,” Tree said. “The words will never leave his lips.”

“Oh, I wish that could be so, for he has taken my own people from me!” Walking Turtle cried. “I would kill him myself if I could, but now he walks everywhere with Long Tongue’s warriors both ahead and behind. A ring of them stood guard around his lodge last night.

“But even so,” she went on, “Sun Dog’s death will mean nothing if the *Hanishé* lives on.”

Walking Turtle left, warning Willow not to leave the Great Lodge, lest she be seized as a witch as well. “As for you,” she spoke to Tree, “watch your back. It will fill with arrows if you leave these walls.”

Each was lost in their own thoughts as the afternoon turned to evening. Tree sat alongside River, caressing her hair as she lay as still as a fawn in its day bed. He could see no evil in her and had renounced any notion that she might be a witch. Willow had explained her illness and had been seconded by Wabeno. Witches! A man would be a fool to fear such a thing, and yet he and River were trapped in a town that was full of fools.

Across the way, Wabeno and Wolf considered various means of escape. A diversion might do, but what then? They would be pursued and perhaps even captured before they made it to the dugouts on the lakeshore.

The five of them shared a cold meal that evening, finishing the last of the dried venison that they'd brought from the north. Too disheartened to share stories around their fire, they went to their sleeping pallets early.

But as they lay together with their limbs entwined, Tree whispered in River's ear. Gazing back under the thin light of the moon, her eyes filled with tears as she whispered, "Yes."

Late that night, Willow was roused by a gentle tug at her shoulder.

"What?" she whispered, seeing Found by the River bent over her by the light of the moon shining through the smoke hole above.

"It's Tree, he's gone!"

"What? Where?"

"It's that thing—the demon. He heard it calling and said he would kill it. He said he knew where it lived."

"The *Hanishé*? When did he leave?"

"Just now. I am going with him."

"What? Where?" Willow said again. By now, she was fully awake, and to her surprise, it was only herself and River lying in the darkness of the Great Lodge. Wolf and Wabeno had left to spy on the Sun Dog's lodge, leaving Buffalo Runs Long to guard the entryway. He was gazing steadily ahead at the guard of Long Tongue's warriors, unaware of their whispering.

"You can't do this," Willow said. "You'll never get past them."

"I can't let Tree go alone. I've got to try! He has more courage than wisdom," River said with her whisper growing to a wail.

"Then you are a mated pair. You're blinded by your feelings for him, a child. You'll get yourself killed."

"Better now than tomorrow. You know what awaits me."

Willow couldn't argue with the sense of this. If River attempted to creep past the guards, she would likely be clubbed. Even if she succeeded, there were more guards at Ga-ogwah Kanotaye's entrance.

"Do you really mean to do this?" Her eyes met those of River's in the moonlight. "Your man will be far off by now."

"I'm going and nothing will stop me," River replied. "He has gone to the place they call the Tower of the Dead. It's not hard to find by moonlight."

"Then you really are a witch," Willow said wearily. "Wait, I know a way out."

Wolf had told her of the loose sheathing of bark at the rear of the Great Lodge and of the hinged trees in the palisade. These were the ways by which he and Wabeno thought that the *Hanishé* had entered the lodge. Quietly, Willow led River to the dark end of the lodge, finding the loose elm bark there, just as Wolf had described it. They crept outside and hugged the shadow of the lodge.

Voices carried from down the lane between the longhouses, and several dogs ran up to them, sniffing at their feet before moving on. Two walkers came their way—a man and the woman he lusted after—but they took no notice of the two women as they pushed on in search of a place for their coupling.

"Let's go," Willow said, searching for the thin pines in the palisade that Wolf had described. They were only a few steps away.

Then, she and Found by the River were beyond the palisade, running through the tall stalks of maize. There was a shout from the walkway atop the wall and the twang of an arrow, but they were hidden by the corn with nothing to fear as they pushed on. Far in the distance, they heard the howl of the *Hanishé*, sounding from the Tower of the Dead.

CHAPTER 40

THREE WITCHES

Tree That Does Not Bend had not forgotten the footprint he had seen on the pathway, nor the face that he had glimpsed peering over a ledge when he had climbed the limestone tower in the sixth challenge. Now, with his war club in hand and an obsidian knife sheathed at his side, he ran toward the tower under the moonlight, determined to do battle with the thing that the Seneca called a demon.

That, after all, was why he had come to this miserable town in the first place.

Tree did not fear the *Hanishé* any more than he feared a squirrel or a jay. Demon, man, it was all the same to him. He hoped that he would find Sun Dog lurking on the ledge in the moonlight, but Wolf had told him that the sorcerer was sitting outside his lodge in the company of Long Tongue's warriors, all chuckling and japing over the coming sacrifice to the Sun God. Although he did not know it, they had laid bets on how long Found by the River would last under the caress of their firebrands.

But he suspected as much, and now, his eyes were ablaze with fury as he pounded on toward the karst, glowing white in the moonlight. It looked almost like a long finger, pointing to the moon. Drawing near, he saw the faint glow of a fire near the top of the tree line where the cliffs began.

Far above, Little Fox sat by the fire and set the noisemaker aside. He had roared along with it until his throat felt as if it was bleeding. Now, he gazed into the darkness beyond the fire, fearful of the ghosts far below.

Sun Dog had assured him that the ghosts were no threat, and by the light of day, this seemed reasonable. But sitting alone at the mouth of the dreary cave in the dark was quite another thing, and like any man, Little Fox shivered at the thought of being alone with the dead. Sun Dog had told him that the noisemaker would frighten them away. But was it so? He had agreed to come alone to this lonely place because Sun Dog said that no one else must know of his deception, not even his own people among the Tali.

He heard a rustling on the path below. A raccoon or porcupine, perhaps. Yet on it came, edging closer up the trail to the base of the ledge. Something big was moving in the brush, scrambling his way. Sun Dog would have called out a greeting, he thought; that was what they had agreed to. He heard a grunt below, and then a deep voice that was thick with menace.

"*Hanishé*, I come for you."

It was no ghost. Cautiously, Little Fox backed away from the ledge and fled into the recess of the cave, careful to pick his way around the slippery pool of black ooze that served as Sun Dog's paint. Below was a chamber off to the side where he was sure that no one could find him.

But Tree That Does Not Bend had clawed his way up to the ledge just as he heard the patter of feet running down the cave's mouth and caught a glimpse of Little Fox's back by the firelight. Without thinking he lunged forward, hoping to seize whatever the *Hanishé* was and strangle it. He had taken three long strides into the cave when his feet flew up from under him, and he came crashing down on the limestone floor.

That would have been the end of the great warrior-hunter, Tree That Does Not Bend, if Little Fox had turned around. But between his fear of ghosts and the unknown intruder, he had fled as deeply into the cave as he dared, searching for the side chamber in the utter darkness. Rounding a corner, he crouched there with his heart beating like a rabbit under the gaze of a wolf, not daring to move.

Yet above there was no sound at all.

Time dragged on and still Little Fox did not move. He knew enough of warcraft to know that an enemy might wait as long as two days in ambush, and now, he reasoned that was exactly the sort of trap that had been laid for him. He shivered in the dampness of the cave, maddened by the steady drip of water at his back. Gradually, he heard the sound of voices murmuring up above. Women!

"Tree!" Found by the River cried as she knelt before her fallen lover. As with Sun Dog's first visit to the cave, Tree had slipped on the pool of greasy fluid oozing from pores in the limestone and was just coming around when River and Willow arrived with their eyes as large as owls.

"What are you…?" He tried sitting up and collapsed down again. Turning, he vomited. "My head."

"You slipped," Willow said, picking up his club. "There is someone else here, or something down in the cave. We must leave before it returns."

She tried hefting the club, but it was far too heavy, and with Tree knocked senseless, they'd be helpless if the *Hanishé* appeared. But looking off to the side, her eyes grew wide in recognition. It was the Sun Dog's noisemaker, lying crumpled by the fire.

Down from the depths of the cave, they heard a rustling, and then the ghostly figure of a man appeared. Little Fox crept from his hiding place to find Willow and Found by the River kneeling over the Ojibwe champion. With life or death poised on the edge of his war club, he chose life.

"You have unmasked us," he said to Willow as he helped Tree to his feet. "I cannot play at this any longer."

They sat by the fire at the mouth of the cave as Little Fox told the story of Tali and his people's hope of finding a new home in the north.

"We never meant any harm, we only hoped to be accepted by the Seneca," he said. "It was Sun Dog who led us over a cliff when we arrived. Even my people do not know that he is the demon who plagues the town. How it came about, I do not know."

Little Fox offered a shoulder to Tree That Does Not Bend and, together with the women, helped carry him down the hill.

They were met by Wolf as they made it halfway back to town. He appeared as a ghost under the moonlight on the trail ahead.

"What have you done, woman?" he asked wearily. "I knew I'd find you here."

"Tree went to do battle with the *Hanishé* and was defeated by the thing's shit," she said.

"What?"

"He slipped. Help us carry him, and I'll tell you all."

They parted with Little Fox at the town's palisade. "Thank you, brother," Willow said to him. "Tomorrow I will shame the sorcerer."

"I cannot speak against him," Little Fox replied. "It will harm my people if the Seneca think that I helped to trick them."

Willow gazed back under the moonlight and gave a small laugh. "Have no fear, I have all that we need," she said.

So it was that Willow emerged from the Great Lodge the next morning, squeezing the bladder of the Sun Dog's noisemaker as she paraded around the square before the eyes of hundreds.

It was a thing called a *gaita de barquin,* a bagpipe of the Spanish peasants that she had heard many years ago on her passage across the Great Ocean Sea.

She had shared her plan with the others before leaving the lodge.

"It's a squalling thing that sounds like a goose having its tail feathers pulled," she said, "but it is a sort of flute to those who use it."

"For music?" Wabeno said with his eyebrows lifting. "I think not."

"Even so," Willow replied, "Sun Dog raised his voice along with it to make it sound like a demon."

"It does that," Wabeno agreed.

Wabeno and the others followed Willow as she exited the Great Lodge, pushing their way through the guards at the entrance. Although she did not know the secret of making music with the finger holes on the thing's pipes, she knew enough to blow into it to produce a sound that could be heard across the town.

Soon, almost everyone in Ga-ogwah Kanotaye lined the square as she made her way along its perimeter. At times she howled like a she-wolf, mingling her voice with that of the pipes.

"Here is your *Hanishé*!" she said, flinging the bagpipe at the feet of Walking Turtle, who stood before the council of clan mothers. "We found it at the Tower of the Dead. It is the thing that Sun Dog used to trick you. There is no demon. There is no witch. There is only him!"

But if Sun Dog felt unmasked, he didn't show it. He stood off to the side in the company of Long Tongue's warriors with a sneer on his face. All eyes were upon him as he stepped from the crowd and walked to where Willow was standing.

He prodded the *gaita* with his foot, prompting a soft wheeze.

"More witchcraft," he said in a voice loud enough for all to hear. "I do not know this thing! It is the work of a demon, created by a witch!"

Sun Dog had dressed in his splendid cloak of raven feathers, and now, they dappled silver and black in the morning sun as he raised a hand and pointed at Willow.

"She is the witch that made this thing!" he cried. "She and her sister. They are both witches!"

With that, Willow lashed out at him with her hands curled in claws, but she was a small woman, and Sun Dog easily stepped away, swirling in a circle with his feathered cloak fluttering in the morning sun.

Wolf rushed forward meaning to throttle Sun Dog by his throat, only to be seized by Long Tongue's warriors. If Tree had been able to rouse from his pallet, there would have been bloodshed, but he was still nursing the blow to his head. As it was, there was a melee joined by Willow as she and Wolf struggled in vain to get past the warriors.

"Enough!" Walking Turtle cried from across the way. "Let them go!"

Walking Turtle had had enough of Sun Dog, who had upset the *orenda* of Ga-ogwah Kanotaye, stepping on her guidance of the town and that of the clan mothers. Now she saw the town's affairs balanced on a knife's edge that could only fall one way if talk of witchcraft continued. Her eyes had not healed completely under Wabeno's medicine, but she had a half-sight now, along with the ability to see the light within others for good or bad. What she saw in Sun Dog disturbed her.

"Enough of witches. Enough of demons," she spoke to the crowd. "The Ojibwe are our guests, and we have no reason to believe that these two mean us any harm.

"But I see a jealous man whose pride was injured in his humbling," she went on, staring to where Sun Dog stood. "I could not see his tricks when he cast the *Hanishé* into the fire, but I see him clear enough now and would have him gone."

It was a startling accusation, and one that Walking Turtle had spoken in anger without thinking, for by now, Sun Dog had seduced the town and made its people love him.

The crowd stirred. "He spoke of witches and now there are two," someone cried.

"Two!" cried another. "Burn them!"

A murmur ran through the crowd that rose to a sound like a swarm of bees. Willow realized that her play on the bagpipe had done little to convince them; it was beyond their imagination to think that such a thing could be the fearsome *Hanishé*.

"It is easier for them to believe in witches than the lies of this trickster," she breathed in Wolf's ear.

"We have a friend in Walking Turtle, and that will be enough," he replied. But looking at the frowning crowd, he was not so sure.

But there was little hope for Walking Turtle, for now Sun Dog turned upon her.

If there had been anything left of Wren, then he never would have accused Walking Turtle. She was the only woman among all of the Seneca who had treated his mother kindly during her captivity. Indeed, she had allowed his mother to escape.

But the last vestige of Wren had been devoured by the age-old master, and now, he saw his chance to seize the town and bury his enemies with nothing more than a few sly words.

"Grandmother, you have accused me, but what of yourself?" he cried for all to hear. "How is it that only *you* were spared on the night that the elders of Ga-ogwah Kanotaye died under the claws of the *Hanishé*? How is it that you alone invited the witches from the north to perch among us like ravens on the body of a fawn? How is it that you called seven warriors to humble our own brave men among the Haudenosaunee, casting a spell upon me when I was sure of victory?"

Raising his arms and turning in a circle, Sun Dog addressed the crowd as if he could not believe his ears. "And now, grandmother, you stand in our way? It is *you* who summoned this evil. *Otgo!* Confess! Confess what you are!"

No one needed to be told anything more. *The people believed him!* The light of ecstasy flared behind Sun Dog's eyes. He had swayed everyone, and if there were a few doubters left among them, they would not dare to raise their voices against him. He had become the Exalted One, and tomorrow three witches would burn.

CHAPTER 41

THE DUEL

As Willow had said, it was easier for the townsfolk to believe in witches than to cast aside their worship of Sun Dog, whose magic had been the wonder of all. Sun Dog had shriveled the *Hanishé* to a small thing and had burned it before the eyes of hundreds. The demon had reappeared only when the great man was humbled by the spell of a witch. Everything he said was as clear as the sky that morning.

Off to the side, Half Moon and Little Fox of the Tali frowned and muttered to one another, but catching the warning glare in Sun Dog's eyes, they did not dare to speak. The fate of their own desperate people depended on their going along with the sorcerer's schemes.

Sun Dog was on the verge of ordering Long Tongue to seize Walking Turtle and Willow when he heard a small voice at his side.

"I challenge you."

Turning, he saw the frail girl with the drawn face who had writhed in the square only the day before. She was a nearly grown woman now of fifteen summers, betrothed to the warrior of the Ojibwe.

"What is this?" he said to Long Tongue. "Take her away."

But she said it again, "I challenge you," and this time her words were passed from one to another in the crowd.

"You challenge me to do what, child?" Sun Dog said with his eyes hooded in disdain.

"My life for yours," River said, wavering before him as if there was a strong wind blowing, and she was only a stalk of corn. "I will kill you tomorrow. I will kill you before the eyes of everyone."

Now it was Sun Dog who recoiled in disbelief.

"You have gone mad," he said.

But Found by the River stood beneath his chin and pushed him in the chest.

"Coward."

"What?" He looked to where Willow was standing. "Take this fool away."

It was then that Found by the River gave him a hard slap across his face. *"I challenge you!"*

"You cannot kill him!" Long Tongue cried. "No man can kill him!"

"I am not a man," River replied. "He has called me a witch, and yet I see the witch in him. He has condemned me to the fire and has nothing to lose.

"But now," she turned and addressed the crowd with a rising voice. "I tell you that he will lose! If you desire a witch, I will give you one. But it will be Sun Dog and not me!"

Ah, who could resist?

"No!" Willow cried, but the crowd did not agree, for here was a spectacle in the making that would enliven the dull days of Ga-ogwah Kanotaye's farmers. Here was the seed of a story that would be told around the lodge fires for many lifetimes. Bets were made even before Sun Dog agreed to the match with a look of cold contempt, but not many; for who would be foolish enough to bet on the slight in-between woman who had no more substance than water? It was obvious that she only hoped to spare herself from the fire by accepting a blow from Sun Dog's club instead.

"Your wits are addled," Willow spoke as she led her away. "You cannot win."

"Have faith, sister," River replied. "Last night I dreamt of his death."

A dream? Willow looked sideways at the grim look on River's face. She was about to speak again, but the girl turned to her with a cold glare in her eyes that froze the words on her lips.

"I will kill him," she said.

Tree That Does Not Bend groaned at the news and said he would forbid it. "I will fight for you," he said.

"Shush, you are still injured, and it is I who has challenged him, not you," River said. "There is no going back."

"Then you go to your death," he said with a stern voice, but there were tears in his eyes. He vowed that he would kill Sun Dog as soon as he was able, but that would not come easy. He had cracked a bone in his right arm, and though Wabeno said that it would heal in time, it was useless for now.

Only Wabeno thought that River had a chance against the sorcerer. How, he did not know, but there seemed a lightness in the air about her and to his surprise, a warrior spirit. But he kept his thoughts to himself, knowing that a few careless words might spoil her magic.

"How can you do this?" Willow asked as they sat smoking by the fire that night. "You are a woman more of water than fire."

"All my life I have been tormented as the daughter of a witch," River replied. "There were whispers at my footsteps all through my days as a child. And who could say otherwise of a child who had been found by a river as a baby? Perhaps I am a witch."

"You would know it if you were."

"Yes, I think so too. I am no hag, but when everyone says otherwise you start to believe their evil words. I tell you I am sick of it. He is the witch, and everyone knows it, yet no one will raise their hand against him. It is Sun Dog who is casting spells, not us. See how he has us in his web."

"But he is far stronger than you. He almost defeated Tree. You are as a mouse compared to a panther."

"Yes, there is that."

"How then?"

Found by the River hesitated a moment and then met Willow's eyes.

"Only the spirits know," she said.

There was a tumult in town the next day as once again the harvest was forsaken so that everyone in Ga-ogwah Kanotaye could gather for the duel between Sun Dog and River.

The captives had argued among themselves the night before, yet every scheme seemed useless. Found by the River and Willow were condemned to die as witches, and now it seemed likely that Walking Turtle would share the same fate. There were those in town who sneered and spat in her path now that Sun Dog had accused her.

Wabeno had called upon the spirits, begging for lightning to strike the town, or perhaps a wind strong enough to blow down its walls, but all in vain. Ancient spells, full of power, dropped from his lips like dead birds falling from the sky. For once he seemed powerless in the land of the Haudenosaunees. Still, he pounded on his drum and chanted on until it was time to go, beseeching any spirit that might listen. He looked to the sky in search of a sign yet found nothing.

"Willow, if I fail then you must challenge him too," River said as they left the Great Lodge that morning.

"Sister, I will be in your footsteps," Willow replied, "but with a knife at least."

To Willow's surprise, River had refused any weapon.

"What will you do then?" she said in exasperation. "You can't fight him with only your hands!"

River looked at her as if in a trance. "I will kill him," she said.

Long Tongue and his warriors had gathered a pile of pine branches that rose higher than a man's head at the center of the square in preparation for the burning. Sun Dog had said that he would cast River's lifeless body on the pyre to be fully rid of her once he had bludgeoned her to death.

But then it occurred to him that a finer spectacle would be to merely wound the girl so that she might be burned alive before the crowd. "Set it ablaze as soon as the ceremony begins," he told Long Tongue. "I will toy with her as the flames grow."

Tree had offered River his war club that morning, but she would not accept it. "I cannot lift it, and its *manito* belongs only to you," she said.

Tree accepted this with a nod, but a strange look passed over his face as they exchanged words, promising to meet again in the spirit land if it came to that.

"You are brave," he said.

"I take it from you," she replied. "Will you watch me?"

"I cannot."

River gazed back in reproach.

"With your eyes upon me, I will win," she said.

Tree gazed back at the unwavering eyes of his woman, so brave and certain. "So be it."

But Tree had no intention of watching River die at Sun Dog's hands. Splitting head and wounded arm or no, he planned to creep up from within the crowd and rush the sorcerer before he could strike a fatal blow. Then, he would go down swinging, if only with his left arm.

That was the plan, but it was not to be.

Sun Dog planned to make a great ceremony of the killing that day. It wouldn't do to simply dispatch a thin and trembling girl with the sweep of his mace. There was no magic in that and he craved to look the part of a witch-killer. The emissaries of the Onondaga, Cayuga, Oneida, and Mohawks were still in town, as were dignitaries from many Seneca towns and villages. Above all, they must be impressed. They must come away feeling that he had strengthened the *orenda* of Ga-ogwah Kanotaye far beyond what was called for.

So it was that he emerged from his lodge on the Great Square that day bearing the mace he had taken from the Spanish knight along with the staff of the Exalted One with the carved snakes rippling along its shaft, topped by the disc of the sun.

Once again, he had his women paint him black with the ooze of the cave, leaving his hands and head free. Now, he simmered black under the sun like a nightmare come to life, but there was more to come. He called out for his crown, and a slave brought forth the macaw headdress of the Exalted One with its white-feathered egret wings adorning either side. Then he called for the box containing his mask.

The sun struck its thousand crystals as soon as the lid was opened. It was a joy to behold, sparkling as if the stars had fallen to earth and were gathered like the Path of the Gods across its silvered face. Carefully, he attached the mask to his own face, tightening the drawstring behind his head.

Coming toward him across the square was the frail girl of the Ojibwe, dressed in her dirty deerskin tunic with her hair in twin braids. Her face was set grim in a way that Sun Dog had never noticed before. She seemed smaller and frailer than ever, no bigger than a fawn, yet there was a dark cloud of sorts swelling around her.

He brushed the vision aside, thinking it was only the darkness of his mask and its narrow eye slits. Raising the staff of the Exalted One, a drumbeat began on cue.

Drenched in black with the feathers of his headdress bobbing, Sun Dog strutted before the Great Lodge with his arms upraised and cried, "Witches are for burning. Is it not so?"

There was a deafening cry of approval from the crowd, and off to the side, Walking Turtle could see that all was lost with her people. Though none but her could see, the *orenda* of Ga-ogwah Kanotaye was broken.

Found by the River looked on as Sun Dog preened before her, pandering to the crowd. Then, stepping forward, she whispered, "I will kill you," and picked up her weapon.

It was a dry stalk of corn that had been trampled into the dust of the square.

The story was told for many years after that by those who survived. How a woman-girl of only fifteen years defeated a great sorcerer of the far south who could not be killed by any man.

It was the enchanted mask that did Sun Dog in, for he could see only straight ahead through its narrow slits. He did not notice that Long Tongue had set the bonfire ablaze as he had requested, nor did he see Found by the River as she swept her cornstalk through the flames, and then across the black ooze covering his body.

Sun Dog raised his mace for the killing blow, not yet realizing that he was engulfed from his neck to his toes in a flame that could not be quenched. With a scream, he dropped the mace and fell rolling on the ground before the gaping mouths and frightened eyes of those who'd come to savor his victory.

But the flames would not die. No matter how Sun Dog writhed in the dust, they only sprang forth once again as the black ooze reignited. Alongside him, the bonfire meant for the three witches grew in a towering blaze that crackled and roared like a beast. With a final scream, Sun Dog rose to his feet, a flaming human torch, and disappeared within the entrance of the Great Lodge.

Left behind, lying beside the roaring fire was the body of Found by the River. She had fainted as soon as her blazing stalk of maize swept over Sun Dog's body.

Only Wabeno had seen what came next. While everyone was watching Sun Dog's fiery dance of death, he had seen the shadow of an old woman leaning over Found by the River. The shadow was dim against the flames, but Wabeno could see it well enough. She turned and looked into his eyes.

My daughter is no witch, but I am. I have always been and ever will be, she said, mouthing the words. Then, turning, she drifted slowly across the square as nothing more than tendrils of dark smoke, following Sun Dog into the Great Lodge.

That was the end of Ga-ogwah Kanotaye. That night beneath the glittering Pathway of the Kitchi Manito, Wolf dipped a paddle at the stern of a long dugout of the Seneca and shoved off from shore. With him were Walking Turtle, Wabeno, Buffalo Runs Long, Tree, and River, who lay cradled in Willow's lap. On the hilltop behind them, the longhouses of the town blazed like a volcano as its horrified people gathered in the fields below. Sun Dog's flaming body had been the seed of its destruction.

"How did you know?" Willow asked as she stroked River's hair.

"I ... I did not know," the dazed girl replied.

The Lake of the Mohawks was at peace as they paddled on with Buffalo Runs Long at the prow of the dugout. Wolf and Tree had promised him that they would guide him home, but first he would visit the land of the Ojibwe, and in this slow dugout, it would take more than the cycle of a moon to reach it.

"It was her mother who knew," Wabeno said at last, calling over his shoulder. He'd been thinking of Walking Turtle and what his wife would think of having another woman in their lodge. Perhaps they'd be friends, but he doubted it.

"It was her mother," he said again.

"Her mother? Woman Walks Tall?" Willow called out. "It can't be. She died a year ago."

"Yes, and yet she lived on through her daughter, never leaving her side as long as she was in danger."

"Then where is she now?"

Visiting One Toe and Crow's Meat, Wabeno thought, but that is not what he answered as their dugout sped on under the waning moon.

"Oh, I imagine she is a tadpole by now," he said, "and someday she will be found by a river."

THE END

AFTERWORD

Although it is now largely forgotten, the realm of Coosa extended for nearly four hundred miles from central Tennessee deep into Alabama, holding sway over 50,000-100,000 people at the time that Hernando de Soto and his army of six hundred conquistadors arrived in 1540.

Coosa was a chiefdom, meaning a theocracy or autocracy ruled by nobles, priests, and warriors with a supreme ruler up top. Its capital, also named Coosa, was located in northern Georgia, and its power was such that it ruled over fifteen other chiefdoms and tribes in what is now the southeastern United States.

There's evidence that diseases spread by De Soto's men devastated Coosa, along with many chiefdoms across the South. When another Spanish expedition under Tristan de Luna arrived ten years later, they found the capital and outlying towns in ruins with survivors of this developing civilization living in the forest "like animals." Many refugees fled to neighboring tribes, especially that of the Muskogee Creeks.

One account written by a conquistador claimed that, in its heyday, Coosa was as large as Mexico City, which was then one of the largest cities on earth. This is unlikely, but the capital surely had a sense of grandeur. Its earthen mounds, squares, palisades, and pyramids awed the archeologists of the 19th century, who dubbed its ruins "Little Egypt." Today, its ruins are believed to lie beneath Carters Lake in Georgia.

The story of Coosa's downfall is largely repeated here from the journals of three Spanish eyewitnesses, including the meeting between De Soto and the ruler of Coosa. That said, certain characters such as Black Serpent and *Eh-noq-waa,* the "Devourer of Virgins," are invented.

It's no great stretch to imagine that a group of Coosa's survivors could have trekked from the area around Knoxville, Tennessee to the shores of Lake Ontario. French voyageurs writing in the 18th century said that Indian warriors thought nothing of making trips of up to one thousand miles on raiding expeditions. This, and when the Tuscarora were driven out of North Carolina by the British in the early 1700s, they traveled nearly seven hundred miles north to become the sixth tribe of the Iroquois Confederacy—roughly the same distance as the Tali people in the novel. The Indians, in general, were highly mobile, pulling up stakes and moving whenever the need arose.

ABOUT THE AUTHOR

A journalist of more than 30 years, **Robert Downes** is the author of nine books, including a nonfiction history of the Indians of the Midwest. An ardent traveler, touring cyclist and musician, he and his wife Jeannette live in Traverse City, Michigan when they're not on the road.